PERIHELION

Stories of the years of Halley's Comet

Byron Grush

Copyright © 2021 Byron Grush
All rights reserved.

This book is a work of history and fiction. All characters, names, places, and businesses are the result of the author's imagination or are used fictitiously, except when they are not. An effort has been made to portray historical events, stories and myths of the time periods as accurately as possible; however, any resemblance to actual events or persons, living or dead, is purely coincidental, except when it is not. No part of this book may be reproduced or transmitted through any means, electronic or mechanical, or stored in a retrieval system.

Cover illustration: "Rosa," from *Kometenbuch* (The Comet Book) by unknown artist, published in 1587, and is in the public domain. Electronic publishing by Universitätsbibliothek Kassel, Landesbibliothek und Murhardsche Bibliothek der Stadt Kassel. All illustrations inside are in the public domain.

Published in the United States by Broadhorn Publishing, Delavan, WI
ISBN: 978-0-9985454-6-2

Contents

2020 AD: The Ghost of Novels Past
2020 AD: The Custodian of Yerkes
4268 BC: The Dark Star
467 BC: The Greeks Had a Word for It
164 BC: Light One Candle
12 BC: Snaking and Dark, like Hairy Eyes
530/536 AD: The Worst Year in History
1066 AD: Where Steel on Steel was Ringing
1222 AD: Angel or Devil
1301 AD: Black and White and Red All Over
1456 AD: The Angelus Rings at Noon
1531 AD: Miracle of the Flowers
1607 AD: The Gift of God
1682 AD: Riding Over an Arm of the Sea on a Cow
1758 AD: A String of a Thousand Grains of Wampum
1835 AD: Return of the Wayfaring Stranger
1910 AD: Fire and Ice
1986 AD: The Astronomer's Lament
2061 AD: The Fifth Horseman

The Ghost of Novels Past

It was a particularly sultry night in mid-July of 2020, almost tropical with humidity although this was southeastern Wisconsin. I was tossing and turning, throwing off sheets damp with sweat, mostly tormented with worries: there was a pandemic racing through the world that nobody seemed able (and some unwilling) to stop. But there was more that was keeping me awake.

The fear of the virus had kept us from visiting our favorite restaurants, carry-out was not quite up to our standards, and I was getting bored with my usual repertoire of chile, pulled pork, and the obligatory bratwursts. I had decided to do something atypical, perhaps exotic. Asian fare, East Indian cuisine, Ethiopian dishes, all required ingredients I was unlikely to find at our Piggly Wiggly store, however.

I settled on Welsh Rarebit for no reason other than that I had been perusing some books from my library that reprinted old comic strips and had come across a series of Windsor McCay's "Dream of the Rarebit Fiend" from the early twentieth century. McCay's protagonist had dreams in which his bed would fly away with him after having eaten the dish just before bedtime. The inference was that Welsh Rarebit had hallucinatory characteristics, but I was only thinking of the rich, flavorful melted cheese on toast that could be comforting, even on a torrid summer day.

Following an ancient recipe I found online, I blended a good Wisconsin cheddar and some brown mustard into a sort of béchamel sauce, added a pinch of paprika and a splash of Worcestershire sauce, and slowly melted this concoction over a low heat. I dipped pieces of bread in Scotch Ale (New Glarus "Winter Warmer" Ale which I did find at the Piggly Wiggly) and started them toasting under the broiler. Lastly, I poured the cheese sauce over the bread and cooked it until it was golden brown and resembled a road-killed Welsh *rabbit*. I had indulged in a second helping late that evening, not heeding the lessons of the Rarebit Fiend.

Byron Grush

Although it was a moonless night there was a soft, sparkling glow in the room as if the air were made of milk glass illuminated by a thousand fireflies. I had the window open because our air conditioner was on the blink. The pseudo lace curtains fluttered in the slight breeze—a breeze that seemed like the hot breath of some malignant spirit or goblin, intent on adding to my discomfort. I considered closing the window but as I gazed at the undulating cloth the glow intensified and took to the curtains like melting butter. The shape of these curtains changed, solidified into a complex lump. The lump took on human form, a specter or apparition that stood, now translucent and shimmering.

"A ghost!" I blurted out in my half-sleep. "But I don't believe in ghosts."

"Certainly you must, if only in your unconscious. Else I would not be here," said the apparition.

The features of the thing were taking shape, becoming clearer. Its countenance had a familiar look. An old man, wizened face with furrows of unmistakable character, bushy eyebrows overhanging deep-set dark eyes, full mustache in which numerous small creatures might possibly be hiding, a head of wild white hair like windblown excelsior, a costume harking from a by-gone time: white suit and vest, wide lapels, and sharply tied ascot (also white) secured by an oval pin of gold metal. His smile was intoxicating, reassuring, intriguing.

"Are you the writer of our most famous book, the *Adventures of Huckleberry Finn?*" I asked.

"People still remember me for that trifle?" he replied. "I have written better. *The Prince and the Pauper* was pretty good, and my best writing, I think, was *Personal Recollections of Joan of Arc*. I worked on that one for a long time, seeking perfection. Maybe I achieved it with that one."

"I have not read it," I admitted, "but I will look up a copy."

"Do so, you will not be disappointed."

"May I ask, why are you appearing before me? I am afraid I've caught the virus and I'm dying…you're here to take me to the afterlife, like this is some bizarre 1940s movie. Tell me, will it be Heaven or Hell?"

"Go to Heaven for the climate, Hell for the company. Well, I don't like to commit myself about heaven and hell…you see, I have

Perihelion

friends in both places. No, this is just a friendly visit. You see, you have mentioned me in several of your novels."

"I find you to be a fascinating character."

"You use me to fill in gaps in your narratives when you run out of ideas. I know. But that is all right. Truth is stranger than fiction, but that is because fiction is obliged to stick to possibilities. Truth isn't."

There was a pause in our conversation. The author, famous for his wit, was insightful, conjuring realizations in my meandering mind. Gaps. Running out of ideas. Me. So I said:

"I am at an impasse. I want to start a new novel, but my imagination is all dried up, a bottomless pit of empty air."

"That might be a mixed metaphor. Anyway, have you no memories? When I was younger I could remember anything…whether it happened or not."

"Your books have been pure genius. Inspirations for the writers who came after you. And nice targets for school boards intent on censorship."

"In the first place, God made idiots. That was for practice. Then he made school boards. Anyway, thousands of geniuses live and die undiscovered…either by themselves or by others. My books are like water; those of the great geniuses are wine. Fortunately, everybody drinks water."

"Well," I said, "I would sure appreciate any old idea you might suggest. Something you discarded, perhaps."

"I tell you what. You know my most famous quote? Nearly any invented quotation, played with confidence, stands a good chance to deceive, but this one I actually said. I came in with Halley's Comet in 1835. When I heard it was coming again in 1910 I said, 'It will be the greatest disappointment of my life if I don't go out with Halley's Comet. The Almighty has said, no doubt, now here are these two unaccountable freaks; they came in together, they must go out together.' And I did."

"Halley's Comet? How is that a story?" I asked, anticipating that the answer would involve a biography of this man even though so much had already been written about him."

"Think about the comet as heralding important events. It comes, what, every 75 years or so? Look to history. Look to those years of the comet for stories. But be a bit careful, the very ink with which history is written is merely fluid prejudice."

I thought about this. A very good idea indeed. Of course, if I were to write a story for every year the comet came to hang in the sky over our Earth, it would be very long book."

"Tell me something, Mr. Twain…"

"Sam."

"Sam. Are you working on a new book now that you have an eternity of time on your hands?"

"They don't have any typewriters where I am now. Only a bunch of old quill pens. I tend to get ink on my fingers…quite annoying. Also, they don't let me smoke or drink! I used never smoke to excess…that is, I smoked in moderation, only one cigar at a time."

"I think the world would very much appreciate one more book from you…even if it has to be read posthumously."

"I must go now, my boy. Remember, get your facts first, then you can distort them as you please."

"Boy? I am older than you were when you died. Even if the reports of your death have been greatly exaggerated."

"Age is an issue of mind over matter. If you don't mind, it doesn't matter. Goodbye, stay safe, wear your mask, wash your hands, and don't touch your face."

Upon which the apparition dissolved, the air in my chamber darkened, and I felt extraordinarily drowsy. I must finally have fallen asleep for when I woke it was morning. The cooing of mourning doves came through my window. The smell of bacon and coffee came from downstairs. I determined to charge up my laptop and begin googling Halley's Comet. If that big ball of ice had stories to tell, I would make an attempt to tell them.

The Custodian of Yerkes

In setting out to write histories of the years of Halley's Comet I needed to learn something about the celestial wanderer itself. Exactly what was a comet? Why did it appear every 75 years or so? Did it cause momentous events? I googled a lot of information about the various sightings, the structure of comets, and so forth. But I wanted to talk to someone who had actually seen Halley's Comet. The last visit of the comet was in 1986. I hadn't been aware of it at that time (there were other things happening in the sky that year, as we shall see later in these pages). But there must have been scientists, astronomers, glued to their telescopes that year. Luckily, I lived close to an observatory, the Yerkes Observatory in Williams Bay, Wisconsin. I would go there and see what I could find out.

I learned from an article, "Yerkes Observatory: Home of Largest Refracting Telescope." by Steve Fentress on space.com, that Yerkes houses the largest refracting telescope ever built for astronomical research. It has a main lens 40 inches in diameter and a main tube 60 feet long. Fentress says "The dome housing the big telescope is 90 feet (27m) in diameter, according to a pamphlet published by the observatory in 1920. The wooden floor surrounding the pier that supports the telescope is 75 feet (23 m) across and can be raised or lowered by an electric elevator so that astronomers can reach the eyepiece end of the telescope whether it is pointed high or low in the sky." The observatory opened in 1897 as the home of the University of Chicago's astronomy and astrophysics department.

What I did not know, however, was that Yerkes had closed to all activities in 2018. When I arrived at the access road I found a gate with a sign reading "Facilities Closed To The Public." I went in anyway...perhaps there would be someone around who could direct me to one of the scientists that worked there. A custodian, at least. I walked across the lawn and marveled at the imposing, castle-like building which was the observatory.

It is characterized as "Romanesque" or possibly as "Beux Arts," a mix of styles created by architect Henry Ives Cobb. A large dome dominates one end of a long rectangular building with two smaller domed turrets flanking the other end. There are a series of sculptures representing some of the movers and shakers responsible for its funding and construction, as well as a few well-placed gargoyles (more properly grotesques, as they do not function to drain water) shaped as winged lions. The landscaping was designed by the firm of Frederick Law Olmstead who did New York's Central Park; there are 77 acres of grounds here. I could not identify the number of trees I saw but I later read they included white fir, yellowwood tree, golden rain tree, European beech, fern leaf beech, Japanese pagoda tree, little leaf linden, Kentucky coffee tree, ginkgo, cut-leaf beeches, and chestnut trees.

Although the observatory does not front on the lake, you could possibly find your way through the trees to the shore. There you would be on the grounds of George Williams College. Geneva Lake is one of Wisconsin's largest, pristine fresh-water lakes, a destination during the Gilded Age for the wealthy of Chicago who built mansions along its shores. It is a premiere tourist attraction, bringing people to its three towns, Lake Geneva, Fontana, and Williams Bay, every summer. Even Covid-19 does not keep them away. But it was not the lake that drew me on this day. It was the sighting of a man in a garden around back of the observatory.

He was tending to some rose bushes, sprinkling white powder on them from a cardboard container. Gardener? Custodian? A loosely woven straw hat freckled his brow with specks of sunlight—a brow too smooth to betray his actual age. He wore an open short-sleeved shirt of Hawaiian design over a tee-shirt which displaced the logo of the Sierra Club and a lone tall pine, both faded white on dark green. Blue jeans and soiled Keds completed his costume. I approached.

I introduced myself as a writer, intent on telling the stories of those years in which Halley's Comet had appeared and had been documented. I wanted to know, I asked, could he tell me where I could find a scientist who could tell me more about comets?

Perihelion

"A scientist?" he laughed. Now I saw he was probably close to my own age, approaching the silver and the gold only allocated to codgers. "So, you want to know about comets, do you? Well, that's a pretty broad subject."

"I'm sorry," I said, "I didn't realize..."

"My name is Frederick Valarian. I am of the scientific persuasion, although these last few years I have adopted an attitude of detachment...some people call it retirement. I used to scan the heavens with the big lens here back in the day. I come here now to nurture these blooms...isn't this one lovely? It is called Rosa Ingrid Bergman, after the Swedish actress. Damn aphids, though. Hard to keep ahead of them." Upon which he sprinkled another shower of white chemical dust unto the dark green foliage of the bush of brilliant crimson tea flowers.

"I wondered if you were here in 1986 when Halley's Comet was last seen. What was that like?" I asked.

"That was a disappointment for naked eye comet scholars. Better ask about the comet of 1910. Yerkes played an important role in recording that occurrence of 1P/Halley. There was a Professor Burman here at Yerkes back then...before my time, of course...who was the first person to actually sight it visually. Ed Barnard photographed it. That was through the big lens in 1909. We've had many notables doing research here over the years. Edwin Hubble did his graduate work here. Gerard Kuiper who they named the Kuiper Belt after did observations at Yerkes. Carl Sagan worked here...him I did get to meet."

"Mr. Valarian, I don't want to interrupt your gardening. Can I buy you lunch, though? I brought my notebook, and I'd really like to learn more about comets in general, and Halley's in particular."

"I'm just about done here. Lunch would be appreciated. Somewhere informal though. I'm not exactly dressed for it."

We carried his gardening tools and supplies to a shed not far from the building. Curiously, it also sported a small domed roof. He cleaned up and we were off on a short drive up the road to a local restaurant called Daddy Maxwell's Diner. Curiouser and curiouser, Daddy Maxwell's was also a dome-shaped building—some called it an igloo. It was famous for its breakfasts, but as this was a Friday, we both opted for the fish fry: batter-dipped haddock, tartar sauce, coleslaw, and homemade grated potato pancakes.

Because of the pandemic, the restaurant was observing social distancing and mask-wearing for the servers. We had waited for a table for what, in the past, would have been a crowded, noisy, aroma-filled room. The usual bustling was subdued, but the kitchen smells were delightful. Valarian began his lecture; I scrambled to take notes.

"A comet is basically a big ball of frozen water vapor and cosmic dust. We think comets like Halley's originated either from the Kuiper Belt. It is a ring of bodies of ice and rock outside of Neptune's orbit where the dwarf planet Pluto resides. Anyway, the icy bodies are leftover matter from the formation of our Solar System billions of years ago and occasionally they are pulled into the Sun's gravitational field and become comets."

"They aren't balls of fire, then? What about the fiery-looking tail?"

"The ion tail is known as a coma, which means a small atmosphere. It consists of volatiles such as water, methane, ammonia, and carbon dioxide. There is a secondary tail of dust particles. As the comet nears the sun these stream off in a direction pointed away from the sun. They encounter the solar wind of ultraviolet photons and become ionized. They reflect the sun's energy as light. The body of the comet is actually dark."

"And why do we see Halley's comet only every 75 years or so? If it is orbiting the sun like the planets, shouldn't it always be in sight?"

"Its orbit, like our planets, is elliptical. It has so much larger an orbit than that of our Earth that it only comes close to the sun once a rotation…at its perihelion…and therefore close to our own orbit. We see it coming and going, so to speak. The farthest point it is at from the sun is called its aphelion. We can't usually detect it that far away because it is no longer ionized. Incidentally, it has a retrograde orbit, that is, it rotates in the opposite direction that we do. It is also tilted with respect to Earth's orbit, about 18 degrees."

"How big is it?"

"We estimate it to be about 9 miles long and about 5 miles wide. The coma, however, can stretch out for 6 million miles."

"What was it like, seeing it in 1986? You said it was disappointing?"

"That is a story I do not wish to tell. Maybe at another time. It was disappointing for others because of the cloud cover and light

Perihelion

pollution from street and house lights. For me...well, there were circumstances that are personal."

There was a quality of remorse I sensed in his voice. I decided not to pursue it further. But I said, "May we get together again some other time? I am a good listener."

"We shall see. What are you going to start with in your book?"

"The earliest recorded sighting, I guess."

"Why not start at the beginning, in prehistory? Then you can let me know when you get to 1986."

"I will. Desert?"

Byron Grush

The Dark Star

AT the beginning the world was a waste of water called Nu. and it was the abode of the Great Father. He was Nu, for he was the deep, and he gave being unto the sun god who hath said: "Lo! I am Khepera at dawn, Ra at high noon, and Tum at eventide." The god of brightness first appeared as a shining egg which floated upon the water's breast, and the spirits of the deep, who were the Fathers and the Mothers, were with him there, as he was with Nu, for they were the companions of Nu.

Ra spake at the beginning of Creation, and bade the earth and the heavens to rise out of the waste of water. In the brightness of his majesty they appeared, and Shu, the uplifter, raised Nut upon high. She formed the vault, which is arched over Seb, the god of earth, who lies prostrate beneath her from where, at the eastern horizon, she is poised upon her toes to where, at the western horizon, bending down with outstretched arms, she rests upon her finger tips. In the darkness are beheld the stars which sparkle upon her body and over her great unwearied limbs....

Nut took the form of the Celestial Cow, and Shu lifted Ra upon her back. Then darkness came on. Men issued forth from their hiding places in great fear, and when they beheld Ra departing from them they sorrowed because of the rebellious words which had been spoken against his majesty. Indeed they cried unto Ra, beseeching him to slay those of his enemies who remained. But Ra was borne through the darkness, and men followed him until he appeared again and shed light upon the earth....

In millions they came to praise and glorify Ra. Unto Shu, the god of atmosphere, whose consort is Nut, was given the keeping of the multitude of beings that shine in thick darkness. Shu raised his arms, uplifting over his head the Celestial Cow and the millions and millions of stars....

The sun god is reborn in the twelfth hour-division. He enters the tail of the mighty serpent, which is named "Divine Life", and issues from its mouth in the form of Khepera, which is a beetle. Those who are with the god are reborn also.

Byron Grush

The last door of all is guarded by Isis, wife of Osiris, and Nepthys, wife of Set, in the form of serpents. They enter the sun bark with Ra.
                    ——Creation Legend of Sun Worshippers[1]

Four and one-half Billion years ago, when our solar system formed from particles of dust and interstellar gases, there remained some bits and pieces that had not coalesced into planets. In an orbit around our sun at a distance nearly of 50 AU (AU = the distance our Earth is from our sun) is a region of such matter, a flattened donut of small, icy bodies of cosmic dust and frozen water vapor and gases, called the Kuiper Belt. Besides the sun's gravitational pull, the main influence upon the belt is the large planet Neptune which is about 30 AU from it. The dwarf planets Pluto, Haumea, and Makemake also reside there.

In the main part of the belt Neptune's gravity field keeps things steady. But at the outer fringe, a distance from the sun of 100 AU, things can be more chaotic. This area is known as the "Scattered Disk." Neptune can act upon objects in the Scattered Disk, sending them outward, into stable or unstable orbits. Some of these scattered objects in unstable orbits enter the solar system as small planetoids called Centaurs. Some become comets. One such comet, the one we know as 1P/Halley, may have been born in this manner.

Halley's Comet orbits our sun as an ellipse with a period of between 74 and 79 years. Its point nearest the sun, between the orbits of Mercury and Venus about 0.6 AU distant, is called its Perihelion. Its point farthest from the sun, about 35 AU, is called its Aphelion. Like other scattered bodies, it is composed of dust, frozen water vapor, and gases such as carbon monoxide, carbon dioxide, and methane. As Halley approaches the sun, it expels jets of the more volatile gases and particles of dust. These absorb solar light and re-radiate it, resulting in a long "tail" which makes the otherwise dark body visible. The tail, propelled by solar wind, always points away from the sun.

4268 BC,[2] the Nubian Desert of present-day Egypt. Some 700 miles south of where the Great Pyramid of Giza will one day rise, in a basin of sandstone and limestone, is the Nabta Playa. Low sand dunes interrupted by scarps and wadis stretch through the plains

Perihelion

where vegetation is seasonal due to typical drought and the lack of protection for standing water. But during the rainy season the wildlife thrives; gazelle, hare, and ostrich seek out temporary lakes in flooded wadis. Domestic animals are here when cattle, sheep, and goats arrive with the nomadic Ru'at El Baquar people.

The Ru'at El Baquar have dug wells dipping into the sparse water table. When the dry season begins they will migrate to an oasis to the north or to the eastern Nile Valley. But for now there is sufficient grass and water for the animals and it is time for hunting and gathering and, of course, the ritual sacrifice of a young calf once the stars are in agreement.

Ekua and Amara have a thatched hut under an Acacia tree whose umbrella-like leaves provide shade for a small herb garden and the single goat that is their property and gives them status in the community. Ekua once owned three goats, an inheritance from his mother's clan, but traded two of them for Amara. He is hopeful she will provide him with children before the dry season forces them to migrate.

Amara wears a necklace of polished ostrich shell beads. Her dark skin glistens with the dewiness of her perspiration. With a sharpened flint tool she is scraping an animal skin which she will stretch and tan with sap from the Acacia tree. Some leg meat from a recent hunt, the couple's meager allocation, waits on the hearth; it is a luxury since hunting has been dismal these past few moonrises. She is worried that the sacrifice of the calf will not bring more game to the area; the practice has proved fruitless before. Not far from her hut is the place of death, where many sacrifices are buried (future archeologists will call this the Valley of Sacrifices[3]), sacrifices that did not always bring about the abundance of game or the advent of monsoon.

The religious leader of the Ru'at El Baquar is named Tapiwa. He is an ancient being who has seen at least 30 seasons and has an indisputable knowledge of the celestial beings and their desires. Tonight he will be at the Star Circle to view Sopdet who will rise to be the most brilliant and fortuitous of the heavenly entities. [Sopdet, the Nile Star, corresponds to our Sirius, the Dog Star in the constellation of Alpha Canis Majoris; it is the brightest star in the sky. The ancient Egyptians identified Sopdet with Isis.] The north-pointing steles are aligned toward the doorway to the afterlife which Sopdet will open. Long ago was the Star Circle constructed. The two pathways, rows of stone megaliths representing the ancient ancestors, are sightlines which Tapiwa will use to communicate with the eternal gods and goddesses.[4]

Ekua is on the grassy plain helping tend the herd. He does not believe that sacrificing one of the cattle will accomplish anything except to reduce the tribe's source of milk. Cattle are not used for food. This will be a waste—especially since a young calf will be selected. He is alone in this radical belief. The others follow the traditions of the Old Ones like Tapiwa. Ekua turns to Onkwa, one of the other herders, a youth of his own age, and broaches the subject.

"Onkwa," he asks, "why do we not select the oldest cow that is not giving sufficient milk anymore? Surely this would be more practical."

"The gods would be displeased that we did not sacrifice our best," replies Onkwa. "Next, would you suggest we give a bull, as it does not provide even milk?"

"But it provides more calves, so no, I would not wish to see a bull sacrificed."

"You should be careful that the elders do not hear these strange ideas that you talk so freely about. I would not like to see you take the place of the calf! So do be cautious!"

Ekua moves closer to the herd. The youngest calf stands next to its mother. It has not yet been weaned and nuzzles her utter. Ekua is moved by the scene. What if…he wonders…what if the calf should disappear before the sacrifice? What if someone were to take it away?

Dusk. The clouds, heavy with rain, have moved away now; the heavens are clear, open for the appearance of the constellations, those figures drawn in points of light like sparkling gemstones, figures of the gods who move with the seasons, gods who are guides for the people, guides for the nomadic lives of the people, guides to the afterlife. Kauket, serpent-headed Bringer-in-of-the-Darkness, sister of Ket, Bringer-in-of-the-Light, has guided the sun barge of Ra into the underworld. Ma'at, goddess of Truth, is setting the stars in their places including the five Stars-That-Know-No-Rest: Sebegu [the planet Mercury], God of the Morning [Venus], Horus the Red [Mars], Horus Who Limits the Two Lands [Jupiter], and Horus Bull of the Heavens [Saturn].

Perihelion

Tapiwa is at the Star Circle. The heavens fall into deep blue-blackness revealing the constellation of Orion (which Tapiwa sees as Sah, the consort of Sopdet the Nile Star—together they are the astral forms of Osiris and Isis). It is Sopdet that appears first, her brightness a beacon for the other stars. Tapiwa feels the presence of the Ogdoad, the primal creation gods: the gods of life-giving water, of infinity and darkness, of obscurity and of place. The gods that give balance and harmony to the universe. He stands at the end of the pathway of stone megaliths. Sopdet is rising, centered exactly at the other end of the pathway. Soon the River Nile will flood bringing fertility to the land.

But what is this? A brighter star appears. It stretches like a fiery serpent across the night sky. Is it Apep, the celestial serpent that assaults the sun barge of Ra as it moves toward the dawn? But night has just fallen. Even Iah the moon god has not yet presented himself. Where is Seth the Destroyer, the red beast with cloven hooves and forked tail whose job it is to kill Apep? Suddenly Tapiwa is frightened. This is a bad omen. It is time to kill the sacrificial calf…and possibly a human.

Ekua and Amara leave during the night, leading the goat who is carrying the few belongings they have been able to bring wrapped in a gazelle skin and tied to its back. They head to the pasture to get the young calf but the calf will not leave its mother. Ekua ties a rope around the mother cow's neck and leads it away. The calf follows. This is an awkward entourage. Their progress will be slow and they will surely be followed. If they can put a great enough distance between themselves and the community before the discovery of the stolen calf…

The desert is dark and cold. In the night sky above, like a beacon, the comet appears. Amara is startled by the sight of the hairy star. But Ekua uses it to navigate; he is headed northeast toward the bank of the sacred river to where they might find refuge in one of the villages farther up the Nile.

Ekua has heard of a community called Nekhen,[5] the City of the Hawk. There are many people there who do not wander but who live permanently in houses of stone plastered with mud. They farm and raise cattle and sheep and sail in ships made of papyrus to fish and to travel for trade. They make vessels of clay and string beads of a reddish-yellow metal. They worship Horus, the son of Osiris and Isis. But Nekhen is many miles distant. They will not see the great plaza or the temple of Nekhen in the coming days, but there are other villages they may reach with settled people—people who do not sacrifice calves.

In the morning the theft of the cow and calf is discovered. Tapiwa is furious. He summons Onkwa and another man named Adamou. These young men are skilled trackers. Tapiwa orders them to find the cow and calf and bring back the thief. There will be a double sacrifice. They start on their way. Onkwa thinks he knows who the thief is—it must be Ekua! He had warned his friend not to anger the old ones, or the gods for that matter. Ekua had not listened. Now he will pay a terrible price for his foolishness. Onkwa does not mention his assumption to Adamou, however. Maybe there is a way out of this dilemma.

This afternoon Ekua and Amara have reached a small settlement near the west bank of the Nile. Here the people live in huts partially dug into the ground but rising on wooden poles supporting roofs thatched with river reed. They appear to be primarily a culture of farmers, utilizing the rich land near the river periodically inundated by flood waters. They have simple boats of papyrus which they used to fish. There is a corral in which a few cattle are contained.

The fugitives are exhausted and try to rest but the villagers surround them, exited to see the livestock they have brought. Will they trade? They are offered pottery of red clay with painted black tops that seem useful but much too heavy for the nomads to carry, especially if they trade away their goat. They are offered jewelry of ivory, quartz, and copper, wonderous to see but of questionable value to Ekua and Amara in their present predicament. Tools of flint with edges so sharp they would surely speed the process of skinning and scraping the animal hides of gazelles, if such animals were brought to them by hunters—again, an unlikely prospect.

Then, the inevitable happens: Onkwa and Adamou have tracked them for most of the morning and now they have found them. Adamou brandishes a hunting mace. He threatens Ekua, telling him he must come back with them to the Nabta Playa where the ceremony sacrificing the calf is to take place. He does not mention that Ekua will be part of that ceremony, but it is obvious. Ekua is steadfast. He tells Adamou that the people here are his friends.

Perihelion

Would you fight them all, he asks?' Onkwa takes Adamou aside. "Let me negotiate," he says.

By now several of the villagers, curious as to the confrontation that is taking place and still desirous of trading for the livestock, approach Onkwa and Adamou. They do not possess friendly attitudes, and this shows on their faces. Onkwa (perhaps in another lifetime, in another era, could become a skilled politician) sees an opportunity.

"We only want the calf," he tells the villagers. "We will leave the man and woman for you to deal with as you wish if you give us the calf. Otherwise, there are many warriors in our tribe who will come." (This is a lie, but it is a strong point for the side of the Ru'at El Baquar trackers.)

There is much discussion. Finally, it is decided. Onkwa may take the calf and leave. The one with the mace must go as well. The young couple are free to stay as long as they wish. But the cow and the goat...? Adamou, as he and Onkwa lead the calf away, turns to give Ekua a menacing look. He will be back, the look clearly says. He will bring his mace. The calf is crying and must be dragged. Ekua is shocked; saving the calf, even at the cost of leaving his home has been his sole concern. Now what? It will not be safe to stay in this village.

"I will trade," he tells the villagers. "I will give you the cow and the goat. Give me in return one of your boats."

Boats are easily constructed; this is an offer they cannot refuse. It is settled. Through all of this Amara has said nothing. She has deferred to her husband, not only out of loyalty, but because she must follow and obey him for another reason. She has not told Ekua, but he will become a father soon after the rainy season has come and gone. Now she will go with him on a journey over the sacred river. A journey into the unknown. In the sky above, the comet hangs like a sentinel. It is on a journey of its own.

The journey along the Nile in the little boat had not been uneventful. Sightings of river crocodiles slipping from the bank into the water as they passed were frightening, although the large reptiles, longer even than the boat, had not attacked them. More unnerving had been the hippos. These huge beasts occasionally approached the boat with open mouths displaying tusks as big as a hand. Ekua learned to avoid the boiling up of the water which indicated the surfacing of a hippo.

Then there were the snakes. Banded cobra, red spitting cobra, black mamba, and several other poisonous vipers patrolled the riverbanks while water snakes could be seen in the shallows chasing after the smaller fish. There was a fierce-looking fish with sharp, fang-like teeth called a Tiger Fish (for obvious reasons) which was best to avoid. But the river provided: soft-shelled turtles, giant perch, a monitor lizard that could be trapped and eaten or its eggs collected, waterfowl (although difficult to catch), and varieties of edible vegetation lining the banks. They also saw the stately ibis strutting on long legs and fishing with curved beak. Sacred, it would not be bothered, after all, it was the embodiment of Thoth.

At the beginning of their journey the comet could be seen even in daylight. At night it seemed to have set the rippling Nile on fire with its reflections It no longer felt like a bad omen; it was familiar like an old friend showing the way through the dark unknown with candle or torch. By the time they reached Nekhen it was gone. Amara had given birth at the City of the Hawk: twins in fact. A boy and a girl. It was this fact that had kept them from becoming slaves. The children were considered gifts of the gods. Even Horus, who was called Nekheny here, had a twin. Ekua and Amara were assimilated into the culture of Nekhen without incident. To Ekua's dismay, however, animal sacrifice was practiced here.

Now it has been four years since they had left the Nadta Playa. The children, the girl named Nebet, the boy named Pepi, are playing in the courtyard, a long oval of hardened clay surrounded by a reed fence plastered with mud. At one end of the courtyard stands a tall pole of cypress wood topped with a carved figure of a hawk or a falcon: Nekheny, god of the sky, symbol of power. Near this is a large pile of sand. This represents the primordial earth emerging from the waters of Nu at the beginning of time and is used for ceremonial purposes—although Nebet and Pepi would dearly love to climb on it, dig in it, throw handfuls into the air.

At the other end of the courtyard is a dome-shaped enclosure serving to protect carved images of the gods: Bat the cow goddess of fertility, Hathor the daughter of Ra and the mother of Horus, Serket the scorpion goddess and the protector of children, Wadjet represented as a rearing cobra, and Horus of Nekhen. Here is a raised platform of slate where King Seka[6] sits to watch the ceremonies performed within the courtyard.

Ekua has risen in importance in the few years of his residence here. The king has assigned Ekua the task of assembling a menagerie, a living collection of animals from all parts of the kingdom, the world's first zoo.[7] Among other animals, he has gathered a baboon, a leopard, a jackal, and a lion cub. Ekua and his crew have endured difficulties and hazards in the collecting and often have had to injure the animals to capture them. These are not food animals but are revered for their spiritual values. They will be ritually sacrificed. This does not please Ekua and he considers leaving Nekhen. But Amara and the twins are happy here. So he will continue in his duty without complaint.

The most difficult acquisition had been the elephant. Ekua and his crew had to journey down river to First Cataract and the Island of Abu.[8] There on the border with Nubia the ivory trade was centered. From there they set out to hunt the large beasts. Ekua found that they were within a half day's walk from Nadta Playa but he wished to avoid that place; no doubt there were still hostile enemies in the region— Adamou, for one.

It was a small herd, one bull and several females, one with a young calf. The pachyderms were wary of humans, having been hunted for their ivory tusks for years, almost to extinction. The herd took off at a run but the bull turned and charged Ekua and his men. A man named Chimwem went down under the elephant's feet before spears thrust against its underside discouraged it enough that it too ran away. They buried Chimwem where he had fallen covering him with a cairn of rocks and set to tracking the herd.

The female with the calf had lagged behind the herd. They caught up with her and she turned on them more furiously even than had the bull. Spears brought her down; the young calf trumpeted a mournful sound that Ekua would remember for years to come. They lassoed the calf to pull it away from the mother, probing it with their spears when it refused to move. It was a long journey back to Nekhan, but somehow they managed it.

King Seka honored Ekua for the capture of the elephant, giving him the title of Master of Animals.[10] From that day on he was charged with the allocation of food and milk animals to the rest of the settlement. When Ekua died at age 36 (a ripe old age, as they say) the current ruler of Nekhen, Seka's son King Ho-wem, adopted Ekua's children Nebet and Pepi.

Predynastic Egypt belongs to the period of prehistory of which there is little if any written record. What we know or assume comes from archeological findings. The appearance of Halley's Comet at the time of this story is undocumented, but it certainly happened within a few years of 4268 BC. We now jump ahead in time about 825 years to when Halley's Comet may have come back: 3443 BC. Again we visit Nekhen which the Greeks called Hierakonpolis. Again there is a lack of written documentation, but we have two sources of visual record upon which to draw our conclusions: the Gebel el-Arak Knife,[11] and Tomb 100 at Nekhan,[12] the oldest known tomb with a mural painted on its plaster walls.

The narrative presented on the mural may show a battle, perhaps referencing the king or significant person buried in the tomb. One interesting theory is that it shows an attack by Sumerians for a raid upon the Nekhens' cattle.[13] Another theory is that the fighting shown illustrates one of the conflicts between Nekhen and a Nile city to the north, Abydos,[14] both powerful ruling centers during this time. The ruler of Abydos was named Ka, while in Nekhen the king was Selk called King Scorpion.[9,14] After many battles among the early Egyptian city/states, Ka's successor, Narmer, rose to become the first king of a unified Egypt (although this has been debated by historians).

In this year of the comet Nekhen has changed. The old temple has been abandoned and a new one built within the town walls. The sacred sand mound has a mud-brick dome over it now. There are several new cemetery sites, some devoted to sacrificial animals, some to humans, or both. A falcon of malachite tops the pole in the courtyard, surveying the ceremonies which reinforce the reign of the Scorpion King. Different sections of town are dedicated to kilns for pottery, workshops for fabricating flint tools, storage silos for grain, great vats for producing porridge or the large quantities of beer that rival the output even of Abydos.[15] Nekhen is now one of the largest communities in Upper Egypt and a political center.

The cemeteries for the most important figures contain elaborate tombs lined with brick, often protected by pillared enclosures, and surrounded by lesser graves often laid out in geometric grids.[16] Selk the Scorpion King is overseeing the construction of his own tomb;

Perihelion

he has commissioned a mural for its walls which will tell something of his history and the history of Nekhen. There will be scenes of hunting, using the throwing stick to capture gazelles or antelopes, and scenes of sheep and goats in corrals. Does Selk have the slightest inkling that one day, far into the future, all these premises will be looted by bandits, and then by archeologists?

He stands on the rise where the tomb is being dug. He is unaware at this moment of the approach of the boats from Abydos. He looks skyward to watch the comet shining unheeded by cloud—the rains are far off, it is the season of drought. His astrologers have warned this comet is a bad omen, but Selk is not concerned. There is grain in the silos and beer in the vats. His wives have given him many children. There are animals in the menagerie enough for the ceremonies the gods require. What can go wrong?

There six boats in all, each with a raised standard of a palm frond carved from cedar and painted bright green. Each has one or two cabins in which warriors are huddled. Each has the pointed bow and stern that give them the shape of crescent moons, moons afloat in a liquid universe over which the comet flies and may be beckoning them on. The warriors leap from the boats in a surprise attack. At first they are intent only upon capturing the animals in the corrals and leading them back to the boats. This occurs on the outskirts of town so they are unopposed. But soon fighting breaks out between the men from Abydos and the townspeople of Nekhen. It has happened before, and it will happen again.

The mural from Tomb 100, or at least the copy of it made by F. W. Green in 1899, illustrates the following: men carrying staves with a forked base; men kneeling on the ground, tied with rope; a man swings a club against the head of another man; a ruined village hut; a figure wearing a leopard skin and carrying a heka scepter and a mace; a warrior standing before a noble who may be the Scorpion King; he is captured and bends his knees and bows; he is placed in a neck stock but he escapes and kills his captor. There is also an image of a man standing between two lions: the Master of Animals (see footnote 10).

There has been a raid and Selk has barely escaped capture. He rallies his soldiers and the invaders are driven off; only a few animals have been taken, but there are the dead to be buried. Perhaps the astrologers were correct: the comet *was* a bad omen. The raid and the victory of the Nekhens will be immortalized on the mural Selk has commissioned.

Scholars, archeologists, historians, scientists, novelists, and artists—all interpret data from various sources (often incomplete, mostly debated, sometimes selectively picked over, sometimes faulty or misrepresented, sometimes even irrefutably accurate) to bring to us the story of humankind and the world. History of the world according to Halley? As Mark Twain said, the very ink with which history is written is merely fluid prejudice. But we do the best we can with what we've got. In this volume I have found it necessary to fill in blanks, interpret or interpolate much conflicting documentation, inject a little fiction for entertainment purposes, and come up with a best guess when needed. So, reader beware as we follow the comet through history: My loyalty always is to *story*.

---

1   "Creation Legend of Sun Worshippers," *Egyptian Myth and Legend*, by Donald Mackenzie, [1907], at sacred-texts.com.

2   My rationale for the appearance of Halley's Comet in the African skies at this date is based on description and analysis of the astronomical site, the so-called "calendar circle," at Nabta Playa by several sources, and the carbon dating of its construction for stellar alignment to 4280 +/- 130 BC. The nomadic inhabitants of the area may have seen a comet and adjusted the arrangement of the megaliths accordingly. Donald T. Haynie suggests:

"Aligned megaliths radiate outward from a central complex, apparently having targeted the brightest heavenly bodies, based on comparisons of megalith coordinates and star positions. ...but the southernmost alignment to the northeast did not point at a notable star.... The unified design hypothesis is consistent with a combination of celestial and terrestrial targeting. Here, a consensus megalithic alignment date is shown to coincide with a computed apparition of a great comet. Ritualistic activities at Nabta Playa may have sought to align key 'inhabitants' heavenly and earthly realms.... The unassigned northeastern alignment will have pointed at a celestial or a terrestrial target. Possibilities include a supernova, a comet,

Perihelion

3   "Along the western rocky bank of a wadi entering Nabta Playa from the north, which we have called the Valley of Sacrifices, there are about ten identifiable tumuli. Built of broken sandstone blocks, the tumuli contained offerings of parts of butchered cattle, goats and sheep. The largest and perhaps the oldest tumulus contained an entire young cow, the most precious offering that a pastoralist can make."

——Malville, John McKim. "Astronomy of Nabta Playa, Proceedings of the African Astronomical History Symposium held in Cape Town on 8 & 9 November 2005." African Skies No. 11 ISSN 10278389 July 2007.

4

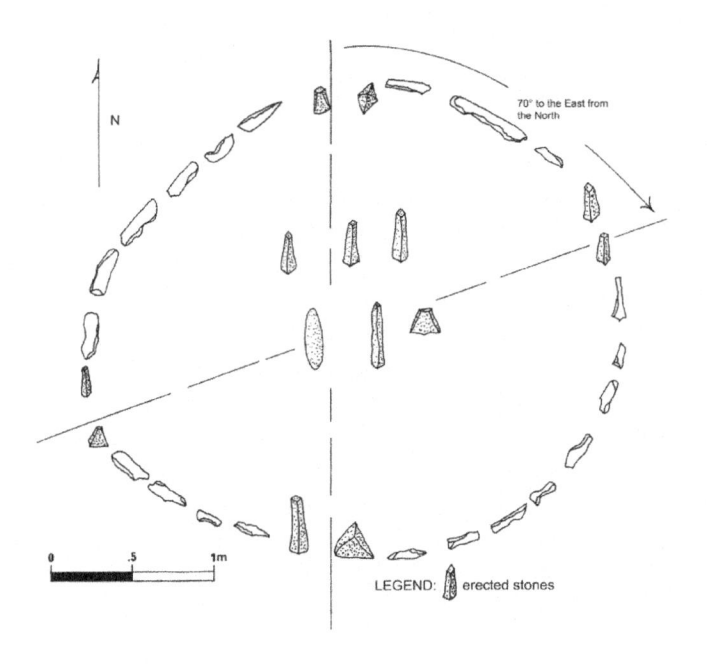

"The stone circle consists of pairs of narrow upright slabs, two lines of sights, one north to south, which parallels the line of the tumuli to the north and megalithic alignments to the south, and one of which points approximately to the place where the sun rose at the summer solstice at the start of the rainy season some 6000 years ago…. Several of the stones remained upright, 8 out of the presumed

14, and many more were flat, forming what appeared to be a circle. An additional six uprights were initially identified aligned east to west, and consisting of two parallel lines of three.... All the alignments were built of quartzitic sandstone, which could be sourced at a maximum of 1km away. Stones were either roughly shaped or unshaped, and many were fractured, some naturally but others apparently as the result of deliberate destruction.... Alignment Group A...orients it to the rising position of circumpolar star Dubhe, the largest star of the Big Dipper.... Alignment C...was aligned towards Sirius...."
——Byrne, Andie. "Case Study 1: Nabta Ru'at el-Baqar" from "Modelling Early Food Production in the Mid Holocene of the Eastern Sahara." https://polstudy.files.wordpress.com. 2019.

5   Nekhen in Ancient Egyptian; in Ancient Greek: Hierakonpolis "Hawk City"...was the religious and political capital of Upper Egypt at the end of prehistoric Egypt. ...Nekhen was the center of the cult of a hawk deity, Horus of Nekhen, which raised one of the most ancient Egyptian temples in this city. ...The first settlement at Nekhen dates from either the predynastic Amratian culture (c. 4400 BC) or, perhaps, during the late Badari culture (c. 5000 BC). At its height, from c. 3400 BC, Nekhen had at least 5,000 and possibly, as many as 10,000 inhabitants.
——https://en.wikipedia.org/wiki/Nekhen.

6   Hsekiu, alternatively Seka, is mentioned in the Palermo Stone as a Predynastic Egyptian pharaoh (king) who ruled in Lower Egypt. As there is no other evidence of such a ruler, he may be a mythical king preserved through oral tradition, or may even be completely fictitious.
——https://en.wikipedia.org/wiki/List_of_ancient_Egyptians.

7   "It has long been known that the ancient Egyptians buried such animals as dogs, baboons and cattle, sometimes in human tombs and sometimes in separate graves of their own. Now excavation in a cemetery associated with the large settlement of Hierakonpolis has led to the unexpected discovery of a 5700-year-old elephant burial."

Perihelion

——Adams, B., 1998. Discovery of a predynastic elephant burial at Hierakonpolis, Egypt. Archaeology International, 2, pp.46–50. DOI: http://doi.org/10.5334/ai.0214.

"Buried alongside the elite members of society, archaeologists dug up the bones of a baboon, an elephant covered in cosmetics (accompanied by an amethyst bead and an ivory bracelet), numerous cats and dogs, a leopard, two crocodiles, aurochs (an extinct species of wild ox), hippos, gazelles, and other animals. The variety and abundance of species make Hierankopolis distinct from all other Egyptian sites. It seems animals played a variety of roles in the City of the Falcon. They could be pets or objects of affection. Or they could be sacrificial offerings hunted and captured for their spiritual power."
——Boissoneault, Lorraine. "Leopards, Hippos, and Cats, Oh My! The World's First Zoo" Jstor Daily Newsletter, November 12, 2015.
https://daily.jstor.org/leopards-hippos-cats-oh-worlds-first-zoo/.

8 "Other authors have presumed from the depictions known on artefacts that the elephant was still living in Egypt during the Naqada I period, but had been hunted to extinction by c. 3500 BC, in early Naqada II times, an interpretation that fits well with the disappearance of elephants from the rock drawings by c. 3600 BC.
...The objects made of elephant ivory that were found in the famous Main Deposit in the temple of Nekhen at Hierakonpolis are presumed to have been imported through the town of Elephantine (present-day Aswan) from farther south in Africa during the protodynastic period."
——Adams, B., 1998. Ibid.

"Long before the use of the animal for war, Nubia was the key supplier of ivory in Africa. This material was very popular from the earliest period of Antiquity for the manufacture of prestigious objects, the animal itself disappearing from the Egyptian fauna in the historic period and onwards. Recent analysis shows that the tooth of hippopotamus was very often substituted for the ivory of an elephant in Egyptian production.

...However, these elephants had marked the imagination of ancient Egyptians as a border settlement on an island downstream from the First Cataract, established at the end of the 4th millennium to control trade between Nubia and the heart of Africa (such as the trade of ivory), was named after the animal itself: 'Abu', the toponym that Greeks simply translated, much later, into 'Elephantine'."
——http://www.unesco.org/culture/museum-for-dialogue/item/en/81/elephant-statuette.

9 Ka, also (alternatively) Sekhen, was a Predynastic pharaoh of Upper Egypt belonging to Dynasty 0. He probably reigned during the first half of the 32nd century BC. The length of his reign is unknown.
——https://en.wikipedia.org/wiki/List_of_ancient_Egyptians
.

Master of Animals on the Gebel el-Arak handle

10 The Master of Animals or Lord of Animals is a motif in ancient art showing a human between and grasping two confronted animals. It is very widespread in the art of the Ancient Near East and Egypt. The figure is normally male, but not always, the animals may be realistic or fantastical, and the figure may have animal elements such as horns, or an animal upper body. Unless he is shown with specific divine attributes, he is typically described as a hero, although what the motif represented to the cultures which created the works probably varies greatly. ...The motif also takes pride of place at the top of the famous Gebel el-Arak Knife in the Louvre, an ivory and

Perihelion

flint knife dating from the Naqada II d period of Egyptian prehistory, which began c. 3450 BC. Here a figure in Mesopotamian dress, often taken to be a god, grapples with two lions.

——https://en.wikipedia.org/wiki/Master_of_Animals.

11   "The knife handle preserving a scene of combat is known as the Gebel el-Arak handle after its presumed find-spot, though it was bought on the art market. Its scene of fighting is one of the best-known images of violence from Predynastic Egypt; the imagery on the handle has also received much attention because of its apparent iconographic relationship to the Ancient Near East.

…the fight side of the Gebel el-Arak knife handle combines a mode of visual representation that is similar to but not yet the same as pharaonic artistic conventions with a particular motif—hand-to-hand fighting—that has only scant precedent and that never achieved the prominence of, say, the smiting scene. The only extant fight scene before this was in Hierakonpolis Tomb 100 which also focused on combats between individuals rather than ranks."

——Bestock, Laurel (2017). *Violence and Power in Ancient Egypt: Image and Ideology before the New Kingdom.* Routledge. p. 94. ISBN 978-1-134-85626-8.

"This so-called Gebel el-Arak knife-handle is evidently an important example of the aggressive imagery dating from the crucial formative phase of Egyptian civilization. The knife (now in the Louvre) was not found through legitimate excavation but acquired on the antiquities market by the French Egyptologist Georges Benedite in 1914. Its original archaeological context is therefore uncertain: it has been suggested that it may actually derive from Abydos, but at least one scholar has argued that it is so unique that it may be a forgery."

——Shaw, Ian (2019). *Ancient Egyptian Warfare: Tactics, Weaponry and Ideology of the Pharaohs.* Open Road Media. p. 22. ISBN 978-1-5040-6059-2.

12   "This Late Chalcolithic building known as the 'Painted Tomb'" (or Tomb 100) was excavated by Green in 1898-9. It most likely dates to the Gerzean period (Naqada II), but an exact date is elusive as many of the objects excavated in the area were mixed up

during transportation to London, and the tomb itself has been lost. It is generally agreed that the building was a tomb (although Brunton suggested it may be a shrine) which housed the burial of a local leader.

...Red, black, and white paint was applied to the plastered mudbrick walls of the tomb. It depicts a series of boats travelling on the river accompanied by a number of smaller scenes of women dancing, men fighting, and people interacting with animals.

...A particularly important scene involves one man using a mace to subdue another three men, his arm raised above his head in a pose clearly reminiscent of the smiting pose adopted by the pharaoh in countless art works.

Tomb 100 detail

...There is also an image of a man restraining two large animals, most likely lions, which echoes the images on the Gebel el Arak knife and the Narmer Pallette. This is thought to represent the supernatural power of the ruler and his ability to tame the forces of nature which was one of the key elements in legitimizing his right to rule.

...A possible interpretation of the totality of the scenes was proposed by Case and Payne. The decoration charts the progression of relations with an Asiatic peoples. First the Asiatics invade and confront the ruler; the native ruler resists and is victorious adopting a familiar heroic pose; the ruler claims mastery over foreign and native peoples (represented by the red and black lions) and forges a harmonious peace

(represented by the red and back antelopes). This is, of course, speculative, but interesting nonetheless."

———Hill, J. (2016). "Tomb 100 Heirakponpolis" Ancient Egypt Online. https://ancientegyptonline.co.uk/tomb100/.

"It is presumed that the mural shows religious scenes and images. It includes figures featured in Egyptian culture for three thousand years—a funerary procession of barques, presumably a goddess standing between two upright lionesses, a wheel of various horned quadrupeds, several examples of a staff that became associated with the deity of the earliest cattle culture and one being held up by a heavy-breasted goddess. Animals depicted include onagers or zebras, ibexes, ostriches, lionesses, impalas, gazelles, and cattle.

Several interpretations of the themes and designs visible in the Nekhen frescoe have been associated with a distinctly foreign artifact found in Egypt, the Gebel el-Arak Knife (c. 3500-3200 BCE), with a Mesopotamian scene described as the Master of animals, showing a presumed figure between two lions, presumed fighting scenes, or the boats."

———https://en.wikipedia.org › wiki › Nekhen

"One of the most intriguing discoveries, which has been dated to Predynastic Egypt, is Tomb 100. It is the only Predynastic painted tomb that has so far been found. The grave was a rectangular brick-lined and plastered tomb with painted walls and a brick partition (cross-wall).

…Red, black and white paint was applied to the plastered mud brick walls of the tomb, depicting a series of boats travelling on the river accompanied by a number of small scenes. Dated by its material, it most probably belonged to a powerful member of the Hierakonpolitan elite, although it has also been suggested that it was the tomb of one of the legendary kings of Upper Egypt.

…The whole of the mud brickwork, including the floor, had been plastered over with a layer of mud mortar approximately of 5mm thickness. This was then covered with a coat of yellow ochre or whitewash. Generally, the figures were first painted in red, some of which were then overpainted in black.

...The exact technique used to create the painting is not known, although it is thought that the decoration was applied on mud-plaster which was covered with a yellow ochre wash. The paintings themselves were then executed in yellow, white, red, green, blue and black pigments.

...The paintings were removed from the tomb and transported to the Cairo Museum where only faded fragments now remain. Green's full-sized copy of the paintings are housed at the Griffith Institute, Oxford."

——Leeman, Diane (2019). "Tomb 100 -The Painted Tomb of Hierakonpolis"

https://www.academia.edu/40813076/Tomb_100_The_Painted_Tomb_of_Hierakonpolis.

13   "The narrative begins with a Sumerian attack. They arrive in a flotilla of ships, seemingly from out of nowhere. This is a surprise attack, like the one shown on the Gebel el-Arak knife.

...This picture indicates that the Sumerians came to Egypt as 'cattle raiders' and not as conquerors. They would not run off the livestock if they intended to settle in the region.

...The story of the Master of Animals controlling the lions is truly extraordinary. It is an original work of fiction that infuses a dark magic into the events of a local cattle raid, making it into a mythic battle of epic proportions.

...On the Gebel el-Arak knife, the Master of Animals is a Sumerian king. I don't believe this is the case on the Hierakonpolis mural. Neither do I believe that the Master of Animals is the Sumerian commander of the invasion.

...To attack Hierakonpolis, the Sumerians would have to travel the entire length of the Nile, past every major town in Egypt, paddling upstream the entire time, while being attacked by the Egyptians on both sides of the river.

...The battle scenes on both the knife and the mural are 'hypothetical'. They show what would happen if the Sumerians attacked Egypt."

——Jerald Jack Starr, from "The Events Portrayed on the Mural of Tomb 100 in Hierakonpolis." Summerian Shakespeare.

http://sumerianshakespeare.com/748301/855901.html.

14   The Egyptian name was Abdu, "the hill of the symbol or reliquary," in which the sacred head of Osiris was preserved. Thence the Greeks named it Abydos, like the city on the Hellespont; the modern Arabic name is Arabet el Madfuneh.
    ——https://en.wikisource.org/wiki/1911_Encyclop%C3%A6dia_Britannica/Abydos_(Egypt).

"From the various readings we've done, it seems like the identities of Narmer's predecessors are fairly fuzzy. Hornung talks about Narmer being preceded by "Scorpion" and Irihor, with no mention of the name Ka. Hamblin, on the other hand, presents Ka as a king of Abydos who faces off and wins against Scorpion of Hierakonpolis, and is later succeeded by Narmer. How much of either of these narratives is based in evidence, and how much is simply imagination?"
    ——Andrew Mathis. "Pre-dynastic and Old Kingdom warfare, Fighting Pharaohs: Ancient Egyptian Warfare." Joukowsky Institute for Archaeology & the Ancient World, Brown University. 2010. https://www.brown.edu/Departments/Joukowsky_Institute/courses/fightingpharaohs10/10007.html.

[Narmer was an ancient Egyptian pharaoh of the Early Dynastic Period. He was the successor to the Protodynastic king Ka. Many scholars consider him the unifier of Egypt and founder of the First Dynasty, and in turn the first king of a unified Egypt. -Wikipedia.]

15   Friedman, Renee. "Hierakonpolis" in *Before the Pyramids, the Origins of Egyptian Civilization*. Ed. Emily Teer. Oriental Institute, Chicago. 2011.

16   Friedman. Ibid.

Byron Grush

The Greeks Had a Word for It

It was the Year of the Consulship of Mamercus and Vibulanus, 287 Ab urbe condita. By modern reckoning, it was the Gregorian calendar year 467 BC. It was the year commonly thought of as the first historical sighting of Halley's Comet.[1] It was the year that Aeschylus' play, *The Persians*, was given a second performance, unusual during the lifetime of the poet, in Sicily.

In Sicily's capital, Syracuse, the newly constructed Greek Theater sat majestically on the southern slopes of the Temenite Hill, overlooking the city. Only ruins remain today but there are traces that suggest the large amphitheater had 67 rows in nine sections divided by broad aisles. It would have accommodated a large audience. The city itself, founded by the Corinthians and Teneans, rivaled Athens in size and importance in the Fifth Century BC. Although soon it would become a democracy, it was ruled by a tyrant, Hiero I, the brother of his predecessor, Gelo, who nonetheless supported the arts and entertained renowned poets at his court.

Aeschylus moved from Athens, where the original production of *The Persians* took place, after he lost a competition to a younger playwright named Sophocles.[2] His anger and resentment at not being allowed to compose the official elegy for those Athenians who died at the battle of Marathon, in which Aeschylus himself had fought and at which his brother Cynegeirus had died, would keep him in Sicily for the remainder of his life. As a boy, Aeschylus woke from a dream or vision in which Dionysus, the Greek god of, among other things, theater, told him to devote his life to writing. He did. He would die in the city of Gela, Sicily, about 456 BC (legend has it that Aeschylus was killed by a tortoise dropped from the sky by an eagle or a vulture, mistaking his head for a rock upon which to crack open the turtle's shell[3]).

Byron Grush

Now he was presenting *The Persians* in Syracuse with a few revisions from the original. The play concerns a tyrannical dictator who angers the gods and gets a come-up-ins by losing a strategic battle. Not wishing to anger Hiero I, Aeschylus had made the tyrant a little less despicable, giving him a soliloquy about how sorry he was for his foolishness in attacking Greece. Aeschylus has had bad experiences in Athens by not pleasing his audience: he was accused of revealing secrets of the Eleusinian Mysteries, an ancient cult of Demeter he had joined, an act punishable by death; although acquitted, the poet was chased by an angry mob and stoned.[4]

The play is probably the only historical work Aeschylus will write. The tyrant is Xerxes I of Persia, King of Kings, King of Persia, King of Babylon, Pharaoh of Egypt, King of Countries. The play takes place just after the Battle of Salamis and the Battle of Plataea in 479 BC, battles in which Aeschylus fought against the Persians and at which the invasion of Greece was thwarted. The main character is Xerxes' mother, Atossa, who has just been informed of her son's defeat at Salamis. She visits the tomb of her husband, Darius, where his ghost is summoned to lament the folly of Xerxes and explain why he was defeated.

Above the Greek theater as the play was being presented to a great crowd, Halley's Comet could be seen in the western sky. It was a distraction for the Greeks who considered comets to be omens, portents of significant good or evil. An omen such as when, next year, a large meteor will fall on Greece and shooting stars will be seen in the sky—possibly the result of Halley's debris field. Some of those in the audience called for the play to be stopped, but Aeschylus continued with his direction. The scene was the tomb of Darius where his ghost had appeared:

> GHOST OF DARIUS
> *With what a winged course the oracles*
> *Haste their completion! With the lightning's speed*
> *Jove on my son hath hurled his threaten'd vengeance:*
> *Yet I implored the gods that it might fall*
> *In time's late process: but when rashness drives*
> *Impetuous on, the scourge of Heaven upraised*
> *Lashes the Fury forward; hence these ills*
> *Pour headlong on my friends. Not weighing this,*
> *My son, with all the fiery pride of youth,*

Perihelion

Hath quickened their arrival, while he hoped
To bind the sacred Hellespont, to hold
The raging Bosphorus, like a slave, in chains,
And dared the advent'rous passage, bridging firm
With links of solid iron his wondrous way,
To lead his numerous host; and swell'd with thoughts
Presumptuous, deem'd, vain mortal! that his power
Should rise above the gods, and Neptune's might.
And was riot this the phrensy of the soul?
But much I fear lest all my treasured wealth
Fall to some daring hand an easy prey.[5]

In the play, Darius tells his wife that Xerxes' defeat has been caused because he bridged the Hellespont to bring his troops against Greece, thereby angering the gods. This war against Greece was begun by Darius around 486 BC, apparently to punish them for disobedience to his rule. He died before he could lead his troops against them. Xerxes took up the task reluctantly. The historian (some say the inventor of history) Herodotus wrote that Xerxes was visited in the night by the vision of "a tall and beautiful man"[6] who, after three visitations, convinced the king to pursue the attack on Greece. To accomplish this, Xerxes built a bridge across the Hellespont River, but it was wrecked by a storm. Herodotus describes his anger:

So when Xerxes heard of it he was full of wrath, and straightway gave orders that the Hellespont should receive three hundred lashes, and that a pair of fetters should be cast into it. Nay, I have even heard it said that he bade the branders take their irons and therewith brand the Hellespont. It is certain that he commanded those who scourged the waters to utter, as they lashed them, these barbarian and wicked words: "Thou bitter water, thy lord lays on thee this punishment because thou hast wronged him without a cause, having suffered no evil at his hands. Verily King Xerxes will cross thee, whether thou wilt or no. Well dost thou deserve that no man should honour thee with sacrifice; for thou art of a truth a treacherous and unsavoury river." While the sea was thus punished by his orders, he likewise commanded that the overseers of the work should lose their heads.[7]

Byron Grush

Xerxes rebuilt the bridge, this time with strong wood reinforced with iron instead of the reeds of his first attempt. Herodotus liked to embellish his histories with humor, but his description of Xerxes' anger to characterize the king was, if not historically correct, then politically correct. Aeschylus' depiction of Xerxes' admonition of guilt and grief ("and in the anguish of my soul I rent my royal robes…disgrace to me, but triumph to the foe"[8]) is probably less than accurate.

Halley's Comet was also seen in the sky that night over Persepolis in Persia. The city was built on top of a square gray limestone terrace, formed from and set into Rahmat Mountain, overlooking the Pulvar River, a tributary of the Kür. The terrace was first constructed by Xerxes' father, Darius I. It was accessed via a symmetrically designed double stairway of shallow risers (possibly to accommodate riders on horseback), which led through the Gate of All Nations, and into the complex. Persepolis was defended by walls and ramparts with tall towers, but by this time, the fifth century BC, it had never been attacked. That would be left to Alexander the Great who would effectively destroy it in 330 BC.

It was not one of the dynasty's main capitals (those were Susa, Babylon, and Ecbatana) but it was a favorite residence of the King of Kings, Xerxes I, who was in the process of completing some of its structures begun by Darius I. Now he was working on the huge throne hall, the Hall of a Hundred Columns, also called the Imperial Army's Hall of Honor. The hall was well over 200 square feet, with eight arched doorways with bull-shaped capitals, and guarded by two colossal relief sculptures of human-headed winged bulls. Other reliefs decorating the walls showed scenes of the king on his throne giving audience, lines of soldiers, and battles with wild beasts and monsters.

Also on the terrace, just recently completed, was an even larger hall, the Apadana Palace. Here were reliefs of Darius I entertaining delegates of the 23 subject nations over which he held sway, including some, like Greece, Egypt, and Babylon, who were in constant revolt. Here 72 columns rose to a height of nearly 80 feet to support the massive ceiling. These were made of stone with wooden capitals in the shapes of bulls or lions. Here Xerxes had decorated the exterior walls of the palace with colorful enameled bricks. Here were the Royal Chambers and here was a throne room where Xerxes was

Perihelion

receiving his chief advisor, the commander of his royal bodyguards, Artabanus.

"Artabanus, my good friend," said Xerxes, "I had a vision last night. I had been to the north-east tower on the ramparts and I was looking up at the sky where a bright star hangs...perhaps you have witnessed this? And I knew it to be an omen...of what I was not certain. Forthwith I retired to my chamber and there, in the midst of a troubled sleep of much tossing, I awoke to see an apparition standing at the foot of my bed."

"A ghost, your most esteemed majesty?" asked Artabanus.

"Just as in my younger days when I was persuaded by a vision to attack the rebellious Greeks, this entity did not identify itself. But somehow, I knew it was indeed a ghost. The ghost of my grandfather, Cyrus the Great!"

"I wonder, was he urging you again to war?"

"He knew much and told much to gain my confidence. He told of my many victories in war. He told of my conquest of the Babylonians, of the capture of the golden statue of their god, Marduc, which I melted down for its precious metal. He told of my victory in Greece at the battle of Thermopylae, of my burning of the city of Athens."

"And of the defeat at Salamis?" Xerxes ignored Artabanus' ill-considered and ill-timed comment and continued:

"He then began a long discourse on my life and other deeds. He knew that my brother Artabazanes had, by nature of his being firstborn, petitioned my father Darius that he be regent, but was passed over because his mother was of low birth. And mine was a daughter of this same ghost, Cyrus. Thus I was chosen and I called my brother 'Second after the King,' and this seemed to please him. He was obedient and died in battle, still loyal to me and the dynasty that came down from Cyrus the Great."

"Was this of significance, oh Great One?"

"It was but a prelude to a scolding and a warning. For now the ghost related to me that which is known only by some, the story of another brother, my younger sibling, Masistes."

"Oh, that," said Artabanus. "I know this. It is the story of the Royal Robe that Cyrus received from King Astyages of Mede upon marrying his daughter. The same robe that Artaynte, the daughter of Maistes and wife of your son Darius, coveted for herself."

"Ah no, my friend, it was the robe Amestris, my first wife and the mother of my son Darius II, a devoted but jealous woman, wove for me. I had given Artayne the robe in return for her favors…she was my son's wife, but a rare beauty who I could not resist. And Amestris saw Artayne wearing the robe and was inflamed with rage."

"But you punished her mother, not she."

"Amestris knew of my having lain with Maistes' wife. She insisted on being given the woman. She blamed her for her daughter's transgression in wearing the fine robe she had made, and she knew of all my affairs. She came to me at the royal feast of my birthday when she knew I could not refuse her. She took the woman and punished her in the manner that traitors must endure." [9]

"It was, perhaps, well deserved," said Artabanus, "but what of Maistes? Why was this a concern of the ghost of Cyrus the Great?"

"Because I had him killed before he could bring his army to confront me. But, Artabanus, why should this be considered a sin against me? Maistes would have disrupted the peace and order of the empire."

"This is so, Majesty. You have no reason to feel guilty. Always you follow the three-fold path of Asha. Always you have good thoughts, good words, and good deeds."[10]

Xerxes rose from his throne. The sudden movement startled an errant bird that had found its way into the palace and was roosting within the carved bull of one of the columns' capitals. It flew around in circles. Xerxes took notice. Anther omen?

"The ghost seemed to suggest that I should fear an internal revolt. Something threatening my reign or me personally," Xerxes told Artabanus.

"Oh Great King, you have me by your side. Nothing of the sort shall happen. You have my word."

"Leave me now, I wish to consider all this. I shall walk along the ramparts. I need the air."

Artabanus left King Xerxes, bowing. He had reassured the king of his safety, as long as he, Artabanus, was in charge of the bodyguards. But was this true? Could there be a secret plot against Xerxes? All these ghosts and apparitions, could they know of such a plot if it did exist? Could they know who was behind the plot? Someone very close to the king, perhaps? Artabanus hurried back to

Perihelion

the guard station. It was time to make sure that no one under his command, no one who knew the truth, had been telling tales.

Two days after the performance of *The Persians*, Aeschylus was called to the court of Hiero I. Halley's Comet was still overhead. This was one of its longest visits to the orbit of Earth. Perhaps the celestial wanderer was so interested in the affairs of humans that it lingered awhile. Aeschylus had brought his son Euphorion with him to the Palace of Nine Towers to meet the tyrant, perhaps to benefit the young man, himself an aspiring poet, in his future endeavors by appealing to the tyrant's affinity for flattery. Present at this interview was Hiero's brother, Thrasybulus, and the philosopher, Xenophanes. As Aeschylus entered the room, Hiero and Xenophanes were discussing the upcoming Olympian games and in particular, the chariot races.

"Of your victory at Delphi, driving the four-horse chariot, odes have been written, Sire," Xenophanes said, not failing to praise the tyrant who contributed to his well-being financially and remembering the prestige which rained upon him from being often at court.

"I have also read Pindar's *Pythian Ode*,"[11] Aeschylus was quick to add. "A remarkable telling of a remarkable feat!"

"Will you be racing once more, Sire?" asked Euphorion. "Another great victory no doubt."

"Alas, I suffer from the stone these days. My gut complains against my heart's desire. I go to Aetna in a fortnight, at any rate. I'll take the waters there and breath the sea air. I leave my brother Thrasybulus in charge to guard that no enemies are at bay."

"You are well staffed in that regard," said Thrasybulus, referring to the King's private army of bodyguards, the world's first secret police. This assurance was ironic however since, unbeknownst to Hiero, Thrasybulus was plotting to overthrow him and had even been leading Hiero's nephew, the rightful heir, into "a life of sensual pleasure"[12] in an effort to dissuade him from assuming the throne. Thrasybulus adhered to the tactic "to lop off the tallest ears of corn"[13] to eliminate those outstanding citizens who might oppose his aspirations.

"Now you, Aeschylus," said Hiero, "you wrote for me the play you called *The Women of Aetna* when first you came to my court. I remember it well. It was the bittersweet story of a Sicilian nymph named Thaleia, daughter of Hephaestus, made pregnant by Zeus and then swallowed up by the earth at the command of jealous Hera."

"An allegory, your Grace," replied Asechylus. "A favorable omen for those in that city of Aetna which you founded after so many struggles with the peoples of Catania, as it was previously called. And for you in recognition of your great victory at the Battle of Cumae when you saved we Greeks from the Etruscans."

"Yes, but this recent play about Xerxes…you honor him as well? This is no allegory."

"It is not. It is but a history. I do not honor the Persians or their brutal king. I show his faults, his guilt, and the suffering of the people under his sway. In this I honor the Greeks who fought against the Persians."

"Yes, I suppose that is correct and proper. And now what next will you write for my pleasure?"

Aeschylus thought for a moment. In fact, he was not writing anything for Hiero, but to admit this would be imprudent. His latest play, *Seven Against Thebes*, was set to compete at the Dionysia festival where it would certainly win first prize. It was the third play in a trilogy about Oedipus. "I may be traveling to Athens," he replied, "but when I return, I shall endeavor to produce something worthy of your attention."

At home after the audience with Hiero, Euphorion asked Aeschylus, "Father, will we stay long in Athens? I want to work on a play of my own." Euphorion and his brother, Euæon, will go on to become playwrights, and although not as renowned as their father, some say that it was Euphorion and not Aeschylus who wrote *Prometheus Bound*.

"Not long. I am presenting *Seven Against Thebes* at Dionysia. We'll see what that rascal Sophocles has to offer. When we return we will move from Syracuse to Gela on the southern coast. I am getting older and like Hiero, I require the sea air."

"I would not mind getting away from the court. That Thrasybulus seems too ambitious for peace to remain long in this kingdom."

"Your insights are always astute, my son, Indeed, there is trouble brewing."

A Digression

Perihelion

We learn about historical figures like Aeschylus and Xerxes through the writings of ancient historians, Herodotus, Aristotle, Diodorus Siculus, Ctesias, and others. Often we find conflicting accounts and, more often than not, colorful, but somewhat absurd claims (Ctesias' *History of India*, for instance, in which he describes many fanciful animals[14]). Embellishments can be entertaining, but inaccuracies are sometimes appropriated for religious, philosophical, and political justifications. So with a proverbial grain of salt (perhaps a pillar of salt), we now turn to the story, related in the various versions of the *Book of Esther*, of more naughtiness, possibly concerning Xerxes and his friends and family.

The name Esther, according to the *Jewish Encyclopedia* (1906 edition by Emil G. Hirsch, John Dyneley Prince, and Solomon Schechter, JewishEncyclopedia.com), may derive from the Persian word "Stara," meaning star, or from the name of the Babylonian goddess, Ishtar. She is represented in the story as a Jewess of the Exile Period, the orphaned daughter of an uncle of the biblical figure, Mordecai. She has come to the court of the Persian King, Ahasuerus, probably as part of the harem.

King Ahasuerus, during a days-long feast, has ordered his wife, Queen Vashi, to parade naked in front of the assembled revelers. She refuses, displeasing the king who promptly deposes her and seeks a new wife from among the girls of the harem. He is captivated by Esther and marries her, not knowing that she is Jewish. Enter Haman and Mordecai.

There are many more lavish banquets and as many intrigues, one involving an assassination attempt on the king which is foiled by Mordecai. Haman, an Agagite (a descendant of Agag and therefore the enemy of Israel) has been made the king's chief advisor. Mordecai understandably refuses to kowtow to him so Haman, being the heavy in this story, goes to King Ahasuerus and pays him 10,000 silver talents for the right to exterminate all the Jews in the kingdom, Mordecai being the principal Jew he wants to eliminate. Haman casts lots to determine the day for the mass genocide and comes up with the thirteenth day of the month of Adar. Re-enter Esther.

Mordecai has learned of Haman's plan and tells Esther. Esther goes to the king and reveals to him that she is Jewish. The plot is thwarted, Ahasuerus hangs Haman on the gallows he had built for

Mordecai and allows the Jews in his kingdom to kill their enemies on the day Haman had picked, the thirteenth of Adar. Esther asks for a second and then a third of slaughter and Haman's family goes to the gallows. Mordecai and Esther create a yearly feast for the fourteenth and fifteenth of Adar: Purim, which is still celebrated by Jews today.

So why is this intriguing story interjected here? And is there any truth to it? As "Sportin' Life" sings in Gershwin's opera, *Porgy and Bess*, "The things that you're liable to read in the Bible, it ain't necessarily so." It is assumed by many that King Ahasuerus is a stand-in for King Xerxes. That could mean Queen Vashi was Xerxes' wife, Queen Amestris, or possibly Esther herself was Amestris, usurping the spot of some former wife. It seems to make sense until you examine the drawbacks to this theory. Amestris was the daughter of a Persian general and not Jewish. It was unlikely that Jews were that prevalent in Persia in Xerxes' time. The biblical figure of Mordecai by other accounts would have been 129 years old during the twelfth year of Xerxes' reign when the story takes place. An article which appeared on the British Library's Asian and African studies blog points out that the Book of Esther was written in the middle of the 4th century BCE during the reign of Artaxerxes III. It was not found among any of the Dead Sea Scrolls nor do any references to Purim appear in Jewish literature before the 1st century CE.

We don't find any references to Esther in Herodotus or Aristotle or Ctesias who lived closer to that time period. So was it just a nice, albeit a bloody story designed to explain the origin of Purim? First-century Romano-Jewish historian Titus Flavius Josephus suggests that King Ahasuerus was in fact Artaxerxes I, Xerxes' son who succeeded him.[15] Whether it is a true story or not, Purim remains a long established celebration of the ability of an exiled people to survive and persevere, and Esther has become a feminist icon.

Halley's Comet was wanning, finishing its perihelium and beginning the return trip toward its farthest point from the sun. It was barely visible now during the day, but still could be seen in the night sky if you knew where to look. Looking up over the roof of the Pantheon on top of the Acropolis in Athens, you might see it as a bright star just a little past Orion's belt.

Perihelion

It was the first day of the festival of City Dionysia. Already the procession was winding its way up the southern slope of the Acropolis toward the Theater of Dionysus. At the head of the entourage was an honor guard carrying the wooden statue of Dionysus, the Greek god who, for millenniums, had ruled over the grape harvest, the making of wine (and the imbibing of it), of religious ecstasy and ritual madness, and of theater. Next came a large phallus of shining bronze followed by another, too large to carry, transported by ox cart. Baskets of food and casks of wine were carried by the next group of revelers, who walked behind a large bull which was being driven up to the theater where it would be sacrificed to assure the success of the festival.

Nobles were dressed in fine robes, the men crowned with laurel and the women draped in garlands of dried flowers. The Pompe would continue for two days before the plays were presented in competition for the prize. There would be a feast after the bull sacrifice, music, poetry, and even a comedian or two. A bacchanal would spread throughout the city streets. Once the population sobered up sufficiently, the serious celebration of the art of theater would begin.

Aeschylus was standing in front of the ruins of the Temple of Athena Polias where it had stood between the Erechtheion and the Parthenon. The temple had been burned by the invading Persian forces of Xerxes in 480 BC. The Parthenon had also been burned and looted but was being rebuilt. Aeschylus hung his head in sadness as he gazed upon the destruction. In the distance, from the other side of the Acropolis, he could hear a lone flute player playing a mournful lament. Tomorrow he would begin preparations for the scenery and effects that would accompany his production of *Seven Against Thebes*. As he stood, contemplating the propensity of mankind to wage war and reap desolation, his son, Euphorion, approached.

"Father, there is news from Sicily," Euphorion said. "The tyrant Hiero is dead!"

The flute was drowned out by a shout coming from the theater below; the bull had just been sacrificed. Aeschylus noted this and said, "One bull down and another follows. Natural causes?"

"They say it was the ailment he had…the stone. But one never knows for sure."

"Will the son now be sovereign at Syracuse?"

"The son is a drunken fool. He has been warned off by Hiero's brother, Thrasybulus. That man has rallied the army of bodyguards and spies that kept Hiero in power. The family was behind him taking the throne, but it is said there is some unrest about a King Thrasybulus."

"Life's tragedies," said Aeschylus, "are more compelling than fiction could ever be."

Aeschylus won first prize with *Seven Against Thebes*. He returned to Gela, Sicily, and died there in 455 BC, possibly when part of a stage collapsed during a performance. Thrasybulus ruled for eleven months: a new tyrant following in his brother's tyrannical footsteps. The family Deinomenes, having given rise now to two dictators, overthrew him but, as Aristotle tells us in *The Politics*, "The family got together a conspiracy with the aim of bringing about the fall of Thrasybulus, not of the tyranny as a whole. But their supporters in the conspiracy, seizing their chance, threw out the lot of them."[16] After the removal of Thrasybulus, reform slowly came to Syracuse, bringing about the first beginnings of true democracy in Sicily. The country began an expansion which pitted them against Athens in war, soon involving Sparta. After existing under the influence of Greece, Rome, Islam, Normandy, and Spain, she became part of Italy in 1860.

In 465 BC Halley's comet was nowhere to be seen. It was the spring equinox and Nowruz, the Persian New Year, was being celebrated. In Susa, the Persian capital built by Darius I, Xerxes' father, a five-day feast was winding down. Goblets wrought from gold lay empty on carpets of wool, the inebriated guests lay on pillows of silk. King Xerxes summoned his trusted eunuch, Mithridates, to help him stagger toward the royal chambers. They passed by reliefs carved into the enameled bricks of the walls. They passed by inscriptions placed there by Darius I, expounding upon his skill in the design of the palace:

Darius the King says: This palace which I built at Susa, from afar its ornamentation was brought.... The gold was brought from Lydia and from Bactria, which here was wrought. The precious stone lapis lazuli and carnelian which was wrought here, this was brought from Sogdiana. The precious stone turquoise, this was brought from Chorasmia, which was wrought here. The silver and the ebony were brought from Egypt. The ornamentation with which the wall

Perihelion

was adorned, that from Yaunâ was brought. The ivory which was wrought here, was brought from Ethiopia and from India and from Arachosia.... At Susa a very excellent work was ordered, a very excellent work was brought to completion.[17]

The doors to the bed chamber were copper-covered wood and swung open on cleverly designed hinges. They were secured by a hidden latch which was known only to the King's closest servants such as the eunuch Mithridates. The interior was luxurious, as would be expected, complete with incense censors hung on silver chains and tapestries of royal scenes painted on silk. Mithridates eased Xerxes onto his bed and waited patiently until the monarch was snoring. He let himself out but did not secure the latch. Instead, leaving the doors slightly ajar, he went swiftly to an antechamber where the King's bodyguard, Artabanus, was waiting.

"Artabanus," said Mithridates, "I have done as you have asked. Were you not my relative and friend I would not have betrayed the loyalty I have for our sovereign. I only ask, do you this deed swiftly so that there is no suffering."

"You will be well rewarded, Mithridanes," said Artabanus. "The kingdom shall benefit from the removal of this tyrant."

"What of the sons, Artaxerxes, Darius, and Hystaspes?"

"Artaxerxes has always desired to ascend to the throne. He is jealous of Darius, who is next in line. I have Artaxerxes' ear and can easily influence him. Hystaspes, being satrap of Bactria, is away. It will be over well before he can return."

"You will help to make Artaxerxes king then?"

"That is what it will seem…to him. But we shall see. He knows not of this plot. And he will be useful."

Artabanus went to the royal bedchamber. Hanging from his belt was his favorite akinakes, a short sword with a double-edged iron blade honed to an exacting sharpness, perfect for a thrust or a swipe in close hand-to-hand battle. As he approached Xerxes, the King awoke. Seeing his bodyguard standing at his bedside, he was confused.

"What is it, Artabanus?" he asked. "What new devilment has arisen that you wake me so abruptly?"

"Only this, Sire," said Artabanus, drawing the akinakes and thrusting the blade expertly through the ribcage and into the heart of the King of Kings.

The following morning Artabanus went to see Artaxerxes to tell him of the tragic death of his father. He said: "The eunuch Mithridanes discovered the murder in the morning when Xerxes failed to emerge from his bedchamber as was his custom. Mithridanes had been sleeping outside of the royal bedchambers as usual. He tells that in the night, perhaps almost at dawn, he saw someone come from the room and hurry down the corridor. As he watched he became aware of the identity of this person, who we may now assume was the murderer."

"Tell me, Artabanus, who was this person? He shall suffer at my own hands."

"That is wise, my Lord, for it was none other than your brother, Darius. You know of his desire to assume the throne. You know also, I think, that he will not stop at just murdering your father when other members of the royal family are still alive and active."

"This I know."

"It is you who should be king. Shall I summon Darius, not revealing the purpose which you may have in mind?"

"Do so, Artabanus. And my thanks to you for your loyalty."

There are several versions of the story of the death of Xerxes and the subsequent transition of power in the kingdom of Persia. According to Aristotle, "Artapanes killed Xerxes fearing the charge about Darius, because he had hanged him when Xerxes had ordered him not to but he had thought that he would forgive him because he would forget, as he had been at dinner."[18] In other words, Artapanes, or Artabanus as we call him, first killed Darius and then killed Xerxes.

In a recent dissertation on the fragments that exist of Cletias' *Persika*, Andrew Nichols writes that "According to Ctesias' version of events, Artapanos [sic] and the eunuch Aspamitres, both of whom were very influential with the king, conspired to kill him and install Artaxerxes on the throne. After assassinating the king, the two men convince Artaxerxes that his brother Darius was to blame and the latter was put to death. Several traditions of the assassination of

Perihelion

Xerxes survive in the Greek sources all of which shift the blame to Artapanos and remove all culpability from Artaxerxes."[19]

The Byzantine scholar and writer Photius (ca. 820-891) concurs with Ctesias (and is probably drawing his history from him) adding that "Megabyzus revealed the plot, the guilty conduct of Artapanus [sic] came to light, and he met the death which he had intended for Artoxerxes [sic]. Aspamitres, who had taken part in the murders of Xerxes and Dariaeus [sic] was cruelly put to death, being exposed in the trough. After the death of Artapanus there was a battle between his fellow-conspirators and the other Persians, in which the three sons of Artapanus were killed and Megabyzus severely wounded."[20]

All this considered and the various spellings put aside, our own narrative of events will proceed based on the account found in Diodorus.[21]

Artabanus brought Darius to Artaxerxes, telling him nothing of the murder but only that Artaxerxes wished an audience with his brother on a matter that deeply troubled him.

"Darius, my brother, I wish to know…can you account for your actions last night?" said Artaxerxes.

"I left the feast quite earlier if you must know. The wine did not agree with me, nor did the company. I joined my wife, Artaynte in our bedchamber where, if you must know, our relationship has begun to heal since the death of her mother."

"A death for which, no doubt, you blame our father."

"And his vicious wife."

"But you remain loyal to father?"

"I…"

"You were seen coming from his bedchamber in the early mornings."

"I did not visit him there."

"You lie! You have slain him most unmercifully! For that you shall die. Draw your blade!"

Darius hesitated, but then his hand went to the hilt of his sword, a ceremonial sword plated with gold and encrusted with gems and which, unfortunately for Darius, was less suited for fighting than for show. Artaxerxes drew first and thrust, not waiting for a parry or any other defense upon the part of his brother. It was over quickly.

Artabanus watched events unfolding according to plan and smiled. Three of his sons waited just outside the door. He beckoned for them to enter and now, having the numbers on his side, he proceeded to finish his plan by finishing off Artaxerxes. His sword came into play as he leaped toward Artaxerxes. His swing of the blade was wild and only grazed Artaxerxes. Artaxerxes was stunned that his father's faithful bodyguard would so attack him.

"You!" Artaxerxes cried. "Why?"

"I claim the throne, that is why. I have killed Xerxes and you have killed Darius. Now I will kill you!"

But Artaxerxes was not so easily killed. Bleeding and still in shock for having been duped, yet he could move fast enough to dodge the next thrust. Now he attacked and struck the bodyguard with a fatal blow. Artabanus fell to his knees, then collapsed, his life blood pooling onto the floor. Artaxerxes looked next to the sons of Artabanus, expecting a rush but they turned and fled from the room. Their complicity would soon be dealt with as would that of Mithridanes the eunuch.

Artaxerxes reigned for the next forty years. His brother, Hystaspes, the satrap of Bactris, revolted against him but was unsuccessful in removing him from power. Artaxerxes also had to deal with a rebellion in Egypt which the Athenians helped to instigate. He finished the Hall of Thrones his father had begun in Persepolis. He was known to be tolerant to Jews in his kingdom, possibly leading to the theory that he was the model for the king in the Story of Esther. He appears in the Bible in the Book of Ezra and Nehemiah.

---

1   Elsa-Brita Titchenell, "Worlds Aborning," *Sunrise magazine*, January 1974, Theosophical University Press.

2   David Smith, "The Reception of Aeschylus in Sicily," from R.F. Kennedy (ed.), *Brill's Companion to the Reception of Aeschylus*, 2017.

3   Valerius Maximus, *Factorum ac dictorum memorabilium libri IX*.

4   Aristotle, *Nicomachean Ethics* 1111a8–10.

Perihelion

5   Aeschylus, *The Persians*, translated by Robert Potter, http://classics.mit.edu/Aeschylus/persians.html.

6   Herodotus, *The Histories of Herodotus Book 7*, translated by George Rawlinson, p. 8.

7   Ibid, p. 15.

8   Potter/Aeschylus, *The Persians*.

9   from Herodotus, *The Histories of Herodotus Book 9*, 112-114, A. D. Godley, ed, we have the following story:

Nevertheless, since Amestris was insistent and the law compelled him (for at this royal banquet in Persia every request must of necessity be granted), he unwillingly consented, and delivered the woman to Amestris. Then, bidding her do what she wanted, he sent for his brother and spoke as follows: "Masistes, you are Darius' son and my brother, and a good man; hear me then. You must no longer live with her who is now your wife. I give you my daughter in her place. Take her for your own, but do away with the wife that you have, for it is not my will that you should have her."

"Sire," he said, "…No, rather, do not force me to consent to such a desire. You will find another husband for your daughter as good as I, but permit me to keep my own wife." This was Masistes' response, but Xerxes was very angry and said: "You have come to this pass, Masistes. I will give you no daughter of mine as a wife, nor will you any longer live with her whom you now have. In this way you will learn to accept that which is offered you." Hearing that, Masistes said "No, sire, you have not destroyed me yet!" and so departed.

In the meantime, while Xerxes talked with his brother, Amestris sent for Xerxes' guards and treated Masistes' wife very cruelly; she cut off the woman's breasts and threw them to dogs, and her nose and ears and lips also, and cut out her tongue. Then she sent her home after she had undergone this dreadful ordeal.

Knowing nothing of this as yet, but fearing evil, Masistes ran home. Seeing what had been done to his wife, he immediately took counsel with his children and set out for Bactra with his own sons (and others too), intending to raise the province of Bactra in revolt and do the king the greatest of harm. This he would have done, to my thinking, had he escaped to the country of the Bactrians and Sacae. They were fond of him, and he was viceroy over the Bactrians. But it was of no use, for Xerxes learned what he intended and sent against him an army which killed him on his way, and his sons and his army. Such is the story of Xerxes' love and Masistes' death.

10   Persians during the Achaemenid era (648 to 330 BCE) generally followed Zoroastrianism, a religion stemming from the prophet Zoroaster. They believed in a single supreme creator deity, Ahura Mazda, whose spiritual force, Asha, was the epitome of cosmic order, the opposite of chaos. Good and evil were the only dualities, existing in both mind and body, and following the path of either was up to the free will of the individual. Sacred texts, written with gold ink on parchment and stored in the royal library in Persepolis were probably destroyed by Alexander the Great.

11   *"Great city of Syracuse! Sacred precinct of Ares, plunged deep in war! Divine nurse of men and horses who rejoice in steel! For you I come from splendid Thebes bringing this song, a message of the earth-shaking four-horse race in which Hieron with his fine chariot won the victory, and so crowned Ortygia with far-shining garlands—Ortygia, home of Artemis the river-goddess: not without her help did Hieron master with his gentle hands the horses with embroidered reins. For the virgin goddess who showers arrows and Hermes the god of contests present the gleaming reins to him with both hands when he yokes the strength of his horses to the polished car, to the chariot that obeys the bit, and calls on the wide-ruling god who wields the trident."*
    ——Pindar, *Pythian 2.115, For Hieron of Syracuse Chariot Race*, translated at www.perseus.tutts.edu.

12   Aristotle's *Politics* 5.1311b, trans. Sinclair, T. A. (Thomas Alan), 1899-1961, Harmondsworth, England; New York, N.Y. Penguin Books, 1981.

13   Ibid, 5.1311a8.

14   According to the Encyclopedia Britannica, Ctesias, born in the late 5th century, was a Greek physician and historian who resided at the Persian court under Darius II and Artaxerxes II. His work, *Indica*, a "history" of India exists only in fragments and in references by other historians. Here we quote from the translation by J. H. Freese of *Volume 1, Translations of Christian Literature*. The Library of Photius. London, New York, 1920:

Perihelion

The martikhora is an animal found in this country. It has a face like a man's, a skin red as cinnabar, and is as large as a lion. It has three rows of teeth, ears and light-blue eyes like those of a man; its tail is like that of a land scorpion, containing a sting more than a cubit long at the end. It has other stings on each side of its tail and one on the top of its head, like the scorpion, with which it inflicts a wound that is always fatal. If it is attacked from a distance, it sets up its tail in front and discharges its stings as if from a bow; if attacked from behind, it straightens it out and launches its stings in a direct line to the distance of a hundred feet. The wound inflicted is fatal to all animals except the elephant. The stings are about a foot long and about as thick as a small rush.

He also speaks of elephants which knock down walls, of little apes with tails four cubits long, and of cocks of very large size; of the parrot about as large as a hawk, which has a human tongue and voice, a dark-red beak, a black, beard, and blue feathers up to the neck, which is red like cinnabar. It speaks Indian like a native, and if taught Greek, speaks Greek.

He next mentions a fountain which is filled every year with liquid gold, from which a hundred pitcherfuls are drawn. These pitchers have to be made of earth, since the gold when drawn off becomes solid, and it is necessary to break the vessel in order to get it out.

15   *The Genuine Works of Flavius Josephus the Jewish Historian*, Book XI, "From the First of Cyrus to the Death of Alexander the Great," trans. William Whiston, M.A., University of Cambridge, London, 1737:

After the death of Xerxes, the Kingdom came to be transferred to his son Cyrus; whom the Greeks called Artaxerxes. When this man had obtained the government over the Persians, the whole nation of the Jews, with their wives and children, were in danger of perishing; the occasion whereof we shall declare in a little time. For it is proper in the first place to explain somewhat relating to this King; and how he came to marry a Jewish wife; who was her self of the royal family also: and who is related to have saved our nation.... And when Esther had come to him, he was pleased with her, and fell in love with the damsel, and married her; and made her his lawful wife, and kept a wedding feast for her on the twelfth month, of the seventh year of his reign; which was called Adar.

16   Sinclair, Aristotle's *Politics*, 5.1311a8.

17   Jona Lendering, "Susa, Capital of Elam," *History of Iran*, Iran Chamber Society. www.iranchamber.com.

18   Sinclair, Aristotle's *Politics*, 5.1311b.

19   Andrew Nichols, *The Complete Fragments of Ctesius of Cnidus*, Dissertation, University of Florida, 2008.

20   J. H. Freese of *Volume 1, Translations of Christian Literature.* The Library of Photius. London, New York, 1920.

21   Diod. 11.69 (Diodorus Siculus). *Diodorus of Sicily in Twelve Volumes,* Translation by C. H. Oldfather, Cambridge, Mass.: Harvard University Press; London: William Heinemann, Ltd. 1989.

Perihelion

Light One Candle

23:1 And from there I departed and went to another place in the direction of the west until the extreme ends of the earth.

23:2 And I saw a burning fire which was running without rest; and it did not diminish its speed night and day.

23:3 And I asked, saying, "What is this thing which has no rest?" At that moment, Raguel, one of the kodesh malakim, who was with me, answered me and said to me, "This thing which you saw is the course of the fire and this, the fire which is burning in the direction of the west, is the luminaries of heaven".

44:1 And I saw another thing regarding lightning: how some stars arise and become lightning and cannot dwell with the rest."

55:2 And YAHWEH swore by HIS own great NAME that from thenceforth HE would not do as HE had done to all who live upon the earth. And HE said, "I shall put up a sign in the heavens, and it shall become a symbol of faith between ME and them forever, as long as heaven is above the earth, which is in accordance with MY command."
——Enoch Book 2, The Book of the Similitude's[1]

75:8 I also saw chariots in heaven running in the universe above those opening so in which the stars that do not set revolve.

75:9 One circuit is larger than the rest of them all, and it circles the entire cosmos at the extreme ends of the earth.
——Enoch Book 3, The Book of Heavenly Luminaries[1]

An old clay table, a Babylonian astrological record from 164 BC, sat unnoticed, gathering dust in the British Museum until in 1985, anticipating the return of Halley's Comet, the museum published *Halley's Comet in History*, giving a translation of the tablet documenting a sighting of the comet.[2] 164 BC was the year of the Jewish revolt

Perihelion

against the Seleucid Empire in Judaea. It may also have been the year of authorship of the *Book of Enoch*[3] which, allegedly written before the Biblical Great Flood, appears to prophesize the Battle of Beth Zur, now associated with the origins of Hanukkah.

The trials and tribulations of the Jews before, during, and after this year of the comet are told in many sources, among them, Books 1 and 2 of the Maccabees, *The Wars of the Jews or History of the Destruction of Jerusalem* by Titus Flavius Josephus, *The Scroll of Antiochus*, The Book of David, and in animal allegory in The Book of Enoch. My favorite version remains the mystifying Book of Enoch, Book IV 83 – 90, "The Dream Visions". We read:

90:6 Then, behold lambs were born from those snow-white sheep; and they began to open their eyes and see, and cried aloud to the sheep.

90:7 But as for the sheep, they the lambs cried aloud to them, yet they the sheep did not listen to what they the lambs were telling them but became exceedingly deafened, and their eyes became exceedingly dim-sighted.

90:8 Then I saw in a vision ravens flying above those lambs, and they seized one of those lambs; and then smashing the sheep, they ate them.

90:9 I kept seeing till those lambs grew horns; but the ravens crushed their horns. Then I kept seeing till one great horn sprouted on one of those sheep, and he opened their eyes; and they had vision in them; and their eyes were opened.

90:10 He cried aloud to the sheep, and all the rams saw him and ran unto him.

90:11 In spite of this, all those eagles, vultures, ravens, and kites until now continue to rip the sheep, swooping down upon them and eating them. As for the sheep, they remain silent; but the rams are lamenting and crying aloud.

90:12 Those ravens gather and battle with him the horned ram and seek to remove his horn, but without any success.

90:13 I saw thereafter the shepherds coming; and those vultures and kites cried aloud to the ravens so that they should smash the horn of that ram. But he battled with them, and they fought each other; and he cried aloud, while battling with them, so that YAHWEH's help should come.[4]

A theory put forth by Robert Henry Charles,[5] a translator of the Book of Enoch, says the ravens are the Seleucids, the lambs are the Faithful Jews, the eagles are the Macedonians, and kites are the Ptolemies. The one with the great horn is he who has fought the Macedonians, Seleucids, and Ptolemies: Judas Maccabeus. Why the allegory? Enoch, or Henoch, is mentioned in Genesis as being the seventh generation from Adam and Eve. His father, Jared, lived to be 962 years old and begat Enoch at age 162. When Enoch was 65 he begat Methuselah who lived to be 969 years old and who was the grandfather of Noah. We don't know how old Enoch lived to be, but he apparently gave his writings to Noah who saved them on the ark. So Enoch had to be portrayed as a prophet by the writer(s) of his book. Prophets like to be a little obscure, hence the animal allegory.

Our version of the story, at least the part that takes place during 164 BC, the year of our comet, begins, as do many things in history, in Egypt. Ptolemy VI Philometor, Greek for "Loving His Mother," was born around 186 BC to Ptolemy V Epiphanes and Cleopatra I. He came to the throne in 180 BC at the age of 6 and ruled with his mother as regent. He married his sister, Cleopatra II[6] in 173 BC. He was in constant conflict with the Seleucid empire over Syria, and with his younger brother, Ptolemy VIII, over control of the throne of Egypt.

Antiochus IV Epiphanes, Greek for "God Manifest" and also called Antiochus Epimanes "the Mad" was the brother of Cleopatra I and therefore the uncle of Ptolemy VI. He was born in 215 BC. Antiochus had ruled Egypt as Ptolemy V's guardian until the Alexandrians opted for Ptolemy VI and Rome pressured him to leave Egypt. His father, Antiochus III, had conquered Syria, Palestine, and Phoenicia. So Antiochus IV became the Seleucid king of the Hellenistic kingdom of Syria in 175 BC, proclaiming himself co-regent with another son of Seleucus, an infant also named Antiochus whom he then murdered in 170 BC. He will become the king of the ravens of Enoch's story. He is the chief villain during the Jewish revolt.

Meanwhile in Judea, the Jews were divided into two opposing parties: the orthodox Hasideans and a reform party that favored Hellenism. As Josephus puts it, "…a great sedition fell among the men of power in Judea, and they had a contention about obtaining the government; while each of those that were of dignity could not endure to be subject to their equals."[7] There were some shenanigans taking place. Simon the Benjamite, a captain of the Temple and a Hellenizer, informed the king of a Temple treasury and suggested robbing it. The attempt did not succeed but it put the high priest,

Perihelion

Onias, in a bad light. Onias was a traditionalist and found himself ousted from his position by Antiochus IV. Onias fled to Egypt seeking aid from Ptolemy VI. This he got and was able to establish a Jewish settlement complete with temple in Alexandria. The irony of Jews returning to the land of their former Exodus does not escape us.

Sometime between 175 and 168 BC Antiochus "came upon the Jews with a great army, and took their city by force, and slew a great multitude of those that favored Ptolemy, and sent out his soldiers to plunder them without mercy."[8] Chaos reigned in Jerusalem as those with ties to Antiochus pursued a relentless campaign against the traditionalists. Antiochus outlawed the worship of Yahweh and all Jewish rites, and in the Temple, erected an altar to Zeus Olympias, requiring sacrifices to be made at the feet of the idol.[9] The Books of the Maccabees give vivid accounts of atrocities against the Jewish peoples.[10]

Now we come to 164 BC, the year of our comet. Ptolemy VIII has expelled Ptolemy VI and Cleopatra II from power. Ptolemy VI flees to Rome and eventually achieves enough support there to return to Egypt and reign with his brother as co-regent. Antiochus is off fighting King Mithridates I of Parthia and has left his campaign of persecution of the Jews to his captain, a man named Lysias. While on a ship off the coast he is suddenly stricken with an illness and dies. There are two versions of his death. *The Scroll of Antiochus* says he drowned himself in the sea, distraught over the defeat of his troops in Judea (we will get to that in a bit) and because all the people he encountered called him "The Fugitive."

According to the Second Book of the Maccabees "...the all-seeing Lord, the God of Israel, struck him with an incurable and invisible blow. As soon as he stopped speaking he was seized with a pain in his bowels, for which there was no relief, and with sharp internal tortures...and that very justly, for he had tortured the bowels of others with many and strange inflictions. ...And so the ungodly man's body swarmed with worms, and while he was still living in anguish and pain, his flesh rotted away, and because of the stench the whole army felt revulsion at his decay."[11]

Three years earlier, Mattathias the Hasmonean,[12] a Jewish priest from the village of Modin near Jerusalem, refusing to accept the decrees forbidding the worship of Yahweh, had organized a revolt against Antiochus IV Epiphanes. He and his sons Judas, Eleazar,

Simon, John, and Jonathan, and his followers relied on a kind of guerrilla warfare to achieve minor, but decisive victories against the oppressors. In 166 BC, Mattathias died. Judas took over leadership of the revolt, assuming the name of Maccabee which in Hebrew means "hammer."[13]

Enter Lysias, governor of Syria, appointed guardian of the son of Antiochus IV Epiphanes, and now leader of the Seleucid army tasked with subduing the Jewish rebellion. Antiochus, according to Josephus, instructed Lysias "to conquer Judea, enslave its inhabitants, utterly destroy Jerusalem and abolish the whole nation."[14] He had sent two divisions under his captains, Nicanor and Gorgias, to root out the rebels. Maccabees 2 tells that Nicanor came with "twenty thousand armed men of different nations"[15] and that Judas Maccabeus had gathered together only seven thousand. Yet Judas stood before his troops and said:

"They trust in their weapons, and in their boldness: but we trust in the Almighty Lord, who at a beck can utterly destroy both them that come against us, and the whole world."[16]

And the Maccabeans defeated them severely near Emmaus. Nicanor returned to Antioch, a beaten man (although the *Scroll of Antiochus* presents a scenario in which Nicanor is slain in the temple[17]). This is about the time that Antiochus jumped into the sea and died. Lysias was now more determined than ever to annihilate the Jews. Josephus tells us the Seleucid army consisted of fifty thousand footmen, and five thousand horsemen, and fourscore elephants. The scene is set for the Battle of Beth Zur.

"Elephants!" says Jonathan, the brother of Judas Maccabeus. "Elephants cannot be defeated in battle. We shall not prevail!"

"Remember, Jonathan," says Judas, "the story of Daniel. How he slew great Goliath."

"Shall I bring my sling and a few large rocks?"

"We will fight for our lives and our laws," answers Judas. "And the Lord himself will overthrow them. As for you, fear them not."

Lysias' forces have arrayed the elephants each within a legion of one thousand foot soldiers dressed in mail and helmets of shining brass and another five hundred upon horseback. Each elephant has a sturdy wooden tower on its back in which thirty-two archers ride and an elephant driver from India sits upon its neck.[18] Lysias' army is

Perihelion

formable, but he has distributed them in wings which are spread throughout the mountainous terrain; this is an advantage for the Maccabeans.

Judas attacks a flank, felling hundreds of the enemy. His soldiers are motivated and believe God is on their side; the Seleucids are mercenaries and have not expected the Jews to be so ferocious. Nor are they familiar with the territory. Still, there are those elephants to consider. Another of Judas' brothers, Eleazar, remembering Jonathan's remark about the invincibility of the pachyderms, makes a decision: he will prove they can be defeated. He sees one of the elephants harnessed with what seems to be the king's emblem—surely Lysias is mounted upon it! He fights his way toward the elephant, swinging his sword right and left and bringing down several of the enemy who now lie bleeding out their lives on the battle ground. At last he is to the elephant; he jumps under it between its legs. He thrusts his sword up and into the belly of the beast with a great shout of triumph. He has struck its heart and the elephant dies instantly, collapsing downward, pinning Eleazar against the hard dirt; Eleazar is crushed and dies.[19]

Lysias' chariots and his elephant legions turn out to be somewhat useless in the mountains. Judas' guerrilla warfare pushes him back from the citadel of Beth Zur. It is a victory for the Jews. Now Judas turns his attention to the recapture of Jerusalem. (The Second Book of the Maccabees places the time of the purification of the Temple before the battle of Beth Zur, telling that Judas moved from Beth Zur to a camp at Bethzacharam. There was another battle there at which Judas was defeated. Other sources give conflicting versions.[20] In our story he next goes to Mount Zion, drives out the gentiles, and begins to cleanse and rebuild the Temple.)

There is a comet is the sky above Jerusalem. It is December, 164 BC. Lysias has returned to Antioch to assemble a greater force; he has not given up on his campaign to destroy the Jews. Judas and his followers have entered the Temple. They find "the sanctuary desolate, and the altar profaned, and the gates burnt, and shrubs growing up in the courts as in a forest, or on the mountains, and the chambers joining to the temple thrown down."[21] There are stragglers in the Temple who have not fled at the approach of the Maccabees. Judas assigns some soldiers to root them out. They smash the alter of

Zeus and throw the broken stones away. They clean the pig's blood from the sanctuary. They build walls all around the mound of Zion.

At last the evil that occupied the Holy place has been purged. Judas decrees that a feast should take place. A celebration. A renewal of the keeping of the tradition of the Feast of Tabernacles. A dedication of a new altar to be celebrated for eight days amid sacrifices and songs.

And I saw that a white bull was born, with large horns and all the beasts of the field and all the birds of the air feared him and made petition to him all the time. And I saw till all their generations were transformed, and they all became white bulls; and the first among them became a lamb, and that lamb became a great animal and had great black horns on its head; and the Lord of the sheep rejoiced over it and over all the oxen.[22]

It is the twenty-fifth of Casleu, the traditional celebration of the winter solstice. It is also the anniversary of the miracle of the relighting of the altar-fire by Nehemiah after the rebuilding of the Second Temple in the fifth century BC.[23] And it was on this day three years ago that Antiochus Epiphanes, at his pagan altar here in the Temple made burnt offerings and sacrifices. They have torn down the old altar which had been defiled and built up a new one from clean whole stones and set upon it new holy vessels and the Holy Candlestick.

But the lamps of the Holy Candlestick are empty of oil. A search is made for oil but most of what is found is spoiled. One bottle of olive oil is found with the seal of the Kohen Gadol intact. But this will not be sufficient to last for the eight days of the Feast of the Tabernacle. Judas orders it to be lit anyway.

"And they arose before the morning on the five and twentieth day of the ninth month (which is the month of Casleu) in the hundred and forty-eighth year. [December 25, 164 BC] And they offered sacrifice according to the law upon the new altar of holocausts which they had made. According to the time, and according to the day wherein the heathens had defiled it, in the same was it dedicated anew with canticles, and harps, and lutes, and cymbals. And all the people fell upon their faces, and adored, and blessed up to heaven, him that had prospered them. And they kept

Perihelion

the dedication of the altar eight days, and they offered holocausts with joy, and sacrifices of salvation, and of praise."[24]

And the oil in the lamp lasted for the whole eight days. And the people deemed it a miracle. And so Judas degreed that the day of the dedication of the altar should become a yearly celebration. And they celebrate it even to today—it is called the Festival of Lights, Ḥanukkah.

There is a story in the Babylonian Talmud about two Rabbis who are on a voyage at sea: Rabbi Gamliel and Rabbi Yehoshua. They both had brought a quantity of bread but they had exhausted their supplies in the middle of the voyage. Rabbi Yehoshua had also carried a supplementary amount of flour and this reserve supply the two Rabbis now used.

"Did you know that this trip would last longer than usual, when you decided to carry this flour reserve?" Rabbi Gamliel asked Rabbi Yehoshua.

"There is a star that appears every 70 years and induces navigational errors. I thought it might appear and cause us to go astray," answered Rabbi Yehoshua.

This has been interpreted as being a reference to the sighting of Halley's Comet in the year 66 AD.[25] If we jump ahead a few perihelions to that date, we find that the Roman emperor is Nero Claudius Caesar Augustus Germanicus, the same Nero who fiddled while Rome burned. Nero has appointed Titus Flavius Vespasian legate of the army of Judea. The First Jewish–Roman War, also known as the Great Jewish Revolt, now begins.[26]

Jewish Zealots lay siege to Jerusalem and annihilate the Roman garrison. King Herod Agrippa II, together with Roman officials, flees Jerusalem. Cestius Gallus, the legate of Syria, brings the Syrian army reinforced by 30,000 Roman troops to quell the revolt. By November Gallus abandons the siege of Jerusalem and withdraws west to winter quarters; there he is ambushed and defeated by Judean rebels. This is the Battle of Beth Horon and 6,000 Romans are killed. Nero is not happy. Nero sends General Vespasian to crush the rebellion in 67 BC. Vespasian wages a bloody war against the Zealots, taking many Jewish strongholds. Nero commits suicide in 68 AD. Vespasian is called to Rome and appointed as Emperor in 69 AD; his son Titus continues to besiege Jerusalem. In 79 AD the walls are breached and the Temple is destroyed. The rebellion has been put down.

The comet will be back.

---

1   The Book of Enoch is an ancient Hebrew apocalyptic religious text, ascribed by tradition to Enoch, the great-grandfather of Noah. Enoch contains unique material on the origins of demons and Nephilim, why some angels fell from heaven, an explanation of why the Genesis flood was morally necessary, and prophetic exposition of the thousand-year reign of the Messiah.
——Wikipedia.

"The return of the long lost Book of Enoch to the modern western world is credited to the famous explorer James Bruce, who in 1773 returned from six years in Abyssinia with three Ethiopic copies of the lost book. In 1821 Richard Laurence published the first English translation. The famous R.H. Charles edition was published in 1912. In the following years several portions of the Greek text surfaced. Then with the discovery of cave 4 of the Dead Sea Scrolls, seven fragmentary copies of the Aramaic text were discovered."
——from the introduction to *Book of Enoch with YAHWEH's Name Restored.* https://pdf4pro.com/view/the-book-of-enoch-with-yahweh-s-name-restored-564d5f.html.

"The theme of the Book of Enoch dealing with the nature and deeds of the fallen angels so infuriated the later Church fathers that one, Filastrius, actually condemned it openly as heresy (Filastrius, Liber de Haeresibus, no. 108). Nor did the rabbis deign to give credence to the book's teaching about angels. Rabbi Simeon ben Jochai in the second century A.D. pronounced a curse upon those who believed it."
——Fortner, Michael D. *The Book of Enoch the Prophet with Commentary* (Introduction).
https://esoterictexts.tripod.com/BookEnoch.Commentary.htm.

2   "The return of Halley's comet in the fall of 1985 was celebrated by modern historians and astronomers with a series of studies that examined records of previous visitations of the comet in

Perihelion

the premodern world. Foremost among these was the British Museum publication *Halley's Comet in History*, in which a team of scholars joined together to study visitations of Halley's Comet from 240 BC until its return in AD 1682, when it was identified by Edmund Halley, whose name it now bears. In *Halley's Comet in History*, the cuneiformists published two Babylonian astronomical diary tablets for the second half of the year 148 of the Seleucid Fra (164/163 BC) recording observations of Halley's Comet in the sky over Babylonia in the autumn of 164 BC. As a comet visible over Babylonia would have been visible over Judaea at the same time, this means that Halley's Comet shone in the sky over Jerusalem during the autumn of 164 BC, when Judaea was in revolt against the Seleucid Empire and its king Antiochus IV Epiphanes.

New evidence which was not available to Wolters now demonstrates that a comet (not Halley's Comet, of course) was visible in the sky over the ancient Near East in 163 BC, the year after the return of Halley's Comet in 164 BC. This evidence, from the British Museum's exemplar, BM 33850, of a Babylonian astronomical diary for the year 149 of the Seleucid Era (163/162 BC), shows that this comet was visible over Babylon during the summer months.

Thus, the Judaean victory over the Seleucids was marked not only by the appearance of Halley's Comet in 164 BC but also by the appearance of a second comet the very next year. This extraordinary set of circumstances strengthens Wolters's argument that the appearance of the comet(s) became part of the background of the Jewish Hanukkah Festival, a festival which celebrated Judaean freedom."

——Horowitz, Wayne. "Halley's Comet and Judaean Revolts Revisited." The Catholic Biblical Quarterly Vol. 58, No. 3 (July 1996), pp. 456-459 (4 pages). Published by: Catholic Biblical Association.

——Referencing: H. Hunger. R R Stephenson. C, B R Walker, and K K C, Yau. *Halley's Comet in History* (London; British Museum Publications, 1985).

3   "The following work, chapters 83-90 in Sefer Ḥanokh (Book of Enoch), dates from the period of the Maccabean struggle, circa 165-161 BCE. It is a remarkable chronicle presenting world history as a predatory conflict. All created beings, from angels to humans, are demoted, one step as it were, to human beings and animals. (The

demotions are not static; in the narrative we can read references to the angelification of figures like Noaḥ and Mosheh.) The people of Israel are presented as domesticated creatures — sheep — and her enemies as predators."

——Aharon N. Varady (transcription), Isaac Gantwerk Mayer (naqdanut) and Robert Henry Charles (translation).
https://opensiddur.org/readings-and-sourcetexts/mekorot/non-canonical/exoteric/second-temple-period/the-animal-apocalypse-with-aramaic-fragments-and-translations-in-geez-and-english/.

"Like the book of Daniel, the 'Animal Apocalypse' [Dream Visions, 1 Enoch 83–90] alludes directly to the Maccabean Revolt. First Enoch 90:9 mentions a sheep who sprouts a horn—a reference to Judas Maccabeus, the leader of the Judean uprising that began during the reign of the Seleucid king Antiochus IV Epiphanes (175–164 B.C.E.). This suggests that the 'Animal Apocalypse' was written around 165 B.C.E., or at least that an older version of the book was updated at this time, when the final version of Daniel was written."
——The "Dream Visions" (1 Enoch 83–90). The Oxford Encyclopedia of the Books of the Bible.
http://www.oxfordbiblicalstudies.com/article/opr/t280/e94.

4   Book IV 83 - 90 The Dream Visions, *Book of Enoch with YAHWEH's Name Restored*. https://pdf4pro.com/view/the-book-of-enoch-with-yahweh-s-name-restored-564d5f.html.

5   Charles, Robert Henry (1911). "Enoch, Book of". In Chisholm, Hugh (ed.). Encyclopædia Britannica. 9 (11th ed.). Cambridge University Press. pp. 650–652.

6   Cleopatra II (c.185-116 BC), a queen of Egypt, daughter of Cleopatra I, became regent for her son Ptolemy VII in 145 BC on her husband's death and married her other brother, Ptolemy VIII. In 144 BC, he slew Ptolemy VII and made himself king. In 142 BC he took her younger daughter, his niece, Cleopatra III, as wife without divorcing his sister and made his new wife joint ruler. Cleopatra II led a rebellion against Ptolemy VIII in 131 BC and drove him and Cleopatra III out of Egypt. Ptolemy VIII had a son by Cleopatra II,

Perihelion

Ptolemy Memphites, who he then had dismembered, and had his head sent back to Alexandria to Cleopatra II as a birthday present. A public reconciliation of Cleopatra II and Ptolemy VIII was declared in 124 BC. After this she ruled jointly with her brother and daughter until June 116 BC when Ptolemy died. Ptolemy VIII left the kingdom to be ruled by Cleopatra III and one of their sons. At the wishes of the Alexandrians, Cleopatra III chose Ptolemy Lathyros, her elder son, as her co-ruler. Cleopatra II disappeared from historical records sometime around October 116 BC. She is believed to have died in about 116 or 115 BC.

——Wikipedia.

7	Titus Flavius Josephus. *The Wars of the Jews or History of the Destruction of Jerusalem.* William Whiston, translator. Project Guggenheim, EBook #2850, 2013.

8	Ibid.

9	Hans Volkmann: "Antiochus IV Epiphanes Seleucid king." https://www.britannica.com/biography/Antiochus-IV-Epiphanes.

10	from The Second Book of the Maccabees:

Chapter 5

11 Now when these things were done, the king suspected that the Jews would forsake the alliance: whereupon departing out of Egypt with a furious mind, he took the city by force of arms.

12 And commanded the soldiers to kill, and not to spare any that came in their way, and to go up into the houses to slay.

13 Thus there was a slaughter of young and old, a destruction of women children, and killing of virgins and infants.

14 And there were slain in the space of three whole days fourscore thousand, forty thousand were made prisoners, and as many sold.

15   But this was not enough; he presumed also to enter into the temple, the most holy in all the world, Menelaus, that traitor to the laws, and to his country, being his guide.

16   And taking in his wicked hands the holy vessels, which were given by other kings and cities, for the ornament and the glory of the place, he unworthily handled and profaned them.

17   Thus Antiochus going astray in mind, did not consider that God was angry for a while, because of the sins of the habitants of the city: and therefore contempt had happened to the place:

18   Otherwise had they not been involved in many sins, as Heliodorus, who was sent by king Seleucus to rob treasury, so this man also, as soon as had come, had been forthwith scourged, and put back from his presumption.

19   But God did not choose the people for the place's sake, but the place for the people's sake.

20   And therefore the place also itself was made partaker of the evils of the people: but afterward shall communicate in the good things thereof, and as it was forsaken in the wrath of almighty God, shall be exalted again with great glory, when the great Lord shall be reconciled.

Chapter 6

1   But not long after the king sent a certain old man of Antioch, to compel the Jews to depart from the laws of their fathers and of God:

2   And to defile the temple that was in Jerusalem, and to call it the temple of Jupiter Olympius: and that in Gazarim of Jupiter Hospitalis, according as they were that inhabited the place.

3   And very bad was this invasion of evils and grievous to all.

4   For the temple was full of the riot and revellings of the Gentiles: and of men lying with lewd women. And women thrust themselves of their accord into the holy places, and brought in things that were not lawful.

5 The altar also was filled with unlawful things, which were forbidden by the laws.

6 And neither were the sabbaths kept, nor the solemn days of the fathers observed, neither did any man plainly profess himself to be a Jew.

7 But they were led by bitter constraint on the king's birthday to the sacrifices: and when the feast of Bacchus was kept, they were compelled to go about crowned with ivy in honour of Bacchus.

8 And there went out a decree into the neighbouring cities of the Gentiles, by the suggestion of the Ptolemeans, that they also should act in like manner against the Jews, to oblige them to sacrifice:

9 And whosoever would not conform themselves to the ways of the Gentiles, should be put to death: then was misery to be seen.

10 For two women were accused to have circumcised their children: whom, when they had openly led about through the city with the infants hanging at their breasts, they threw down headlong from the walls.

11 And others that had met together in caves that were near, and were keeping the sabbath day privately, being discovered by Philip, were burnt with fire, because they made a conscience to help themselves with their hands, by reason of the religious observance of the day.
    ——The Second Book of the Maccabees.
The Deuterocanon Old Testament - Holy Bible.
https://st-takla.org/pub_Deuterocanon/Deuterocanon-Apocrypha_El-Asfar_El-Kanoneya_El-Tanya__9-Second-of-Maccabees.html.

11   Ibid.

12   "Mattathias was already old when the religious persecution under Antiochus Epiphanes broke out. The king's soldiers under Apelles, who is mentioned by Josephus but not in the Book of Maccabees, came to Modin, a small city in Judea. They set up an altar to the heathen god, and ordered Mattathias, as the most influential citizen, whose example would be followed, to sacrifice in accordance

with the king's command. But Mattathias said: 'Though all the nations that are under the king's dominion obey him, …yet will I, and my sons, and my brethren, walk in the covenant of our fathers.'

…From his hiding-place he [Mattathias] scoured the neighboring districts of Judea, drove out small bands of the king's troops, punished the renegade Jews, destroyed the heathen temples and altars, and brought children, who through fear had not been circumcised, into the covenant of Abraham."

———Richard Gottheil, Samuel Krauss. "Mattahias Maccabeus."
The Jewish Encyclopedia.
https://www.jewishencyclopedia.com/articles/10482-mattathias-maccabeus.

13   "One suggestion is that the name derives from the Aramaic maqqaba ('makebet' in modern Hebrew), 'hammer' or 'sledgehammer' (cf. the cognomen of Charles Martel, the 8th century Frankish leader), in recognition of his ferocity in battle. It is also possible that the name Maccabee is an acronym for the Torah verse Mi kamokha ba'elim Adonai, 'Who among the gods is like you, O Adonai?', his battle-cry to motivate troops."

———https://military.wikia.org/wiki/Judas_Maccabeus

14   Titus Flavius Josephus. *The Wars of the Jews or History of the Destruction of Jerusalem.*

15   The Second Book of the Maccabees. The Deuterocanon
Old Testament - Holy Bible.

16   Ibid.

17   "At that time Antiochus arose and sent Nikanor his commander, with a huge army and many people. He came to the city of Yehuda - to Yerushalayim. He slaughtered a huge number of people and built an altar in the Beis Ha Alikdash in the place where the God of Israel had said to His servants the prophets 'There I will rest My Presence forever.' In that place they slaughtered a pig and brought its blood into the holy sanctuary.

Perihelion

It happened when Yochanan ben Matisyahu the Kohein Gadols [priest] heard that such a deed had been done, he was filled with fury and anger and his face changed color. He took advice within himself as to what could be done about this. Then Yochanan ben Matisyahu made himself a sword with a double blade. It was two zeres long and one zeres wide and he concealed it under his clothing.

Then Yochanan was brought before Nikanor. Nikanor said to Yochanan, 'You are one of the rebels who rebelled against the king and who doesn't want peace in the kingdom'. Yochanan replied to Nikanor and said, 'My master, I am he, now I have come before you. Whatever you wish I shall do.' Nikanor answered and said to Yochanan, 'If you will do what I wish, take a pig and slaughter it on the altar. Then you may wear royal robes and ride on the king's horse and be as one of the king's close friends.'

Then Yochanan ben Matisyahu cast his eyes to the Lord of Heaven and prayed before His G-d. He said, 'Lord, and Lord of my fathers Avraham, Yitzchak and Yaakov. Please don't allow me to fall into the hand of this non-Jew, for if he kills me he will go and offer praise in the Temple of Dagon his god, and will say 'My god gave him into my hand.' At that moment he took three strides forward and stabbed the sword into Nikanor's heart, and threw his corpse in the holy sanctuary before the Lord of Heaven."

——Megillat Antiochus. *The Scroll of Antiochus.* Translated by Rabbi David Sedley. TorahLab. Monsey – Jerusalem. 2007.

18   The First Book of the Maccabees. Coptic Orthodox Church Heritage. https://st-takla.org/ pub_Deuterocanon/ Deuterocanon-Apocrypha_El-Asfar_El-Kanoneya_El-Tanya__8-First-of-Maccabees.html

19   Ibid.

20   "During Judas Maccabaeus's leadership there were eight major military confrontations with regular Seleucid forces: four before the purification of the Temple (the battles against Apollonins and Seron, the campaign at Ammaus, and the clash at Beth Zur) and four in the period 162-160 B.C. (the encounter with Lysias near Beth Zacharia, the battles against Nicanor at Kafar Salama and Adasa, and Judas' final battle against Batch ides near Elasa)."

———A. S. van der Woude in a review of *Judas Maccabaeus. The Jewish Struggle Against the Seleucids* by Bezalel Bar-Kochva (Cambridge University Press, Cambridge, New York, New Rochelle. Melbourne, Sydney 1989). Journal for the Study of Judaism in the Persian, Hellenistic, and Roman Period.
https://www.jstor.org/stable/24658389.

"A Judean priest, he assumed command of Judean resistance to Greek forces after his father's death (165 BCE). His defeat of the Greek governor of Samaria led to even more stunning victories over larger Greek armies at Beth-horon & Emmaus. After this, Judas captured Mt. Zion, purged the temple of Hellenistic cult paraphernalia, reconstructed the sanctuary according to Torah prescriptions & reconsecrated it to the worship of YHWH (Dec. 164 BCE). The festival of cHannukah was later instituted to commemorate this triumph. Judas was repelled, however, in his attempt to drive the Syrian garrison from the rest of Jerusalem & was defeated near the village of Beth Zechariah, southwest of Jerusalem (162 BCE). He died in the battle of Elasa [north of Jerusalem].
———https://virtualreligion.net/iho/Judas_mac.html

21   The First Book of the Maccabees. Coptic Orthodox Church Heritage.

22   The Book of Enoch

23   "...for when our ancestors were led into [exile], the sacred priests hid some of the fire. ...Many years later Nehemiah sent their descendants to retrieve the hidden fire, but they found only thick muddy water. ...Nehemiah commanded the priests to sprinkle the wood and offerings with this water. ...then the sun shone, which afore was hid in the cloud, there was a great fire kindled, so that every person marveled."
———The First Book of the Maccabees.

24   Ibid.

25   "Rabbi Yehoshua was born in 35 AD and died in 117 AD. Rabbi Gamliel died in 115 AD. The only appearance of Halley's

Perihelion

Comet in the interval 55-155 (when Yehoshua was older than 20), is in 66 AD."

———Ne'eman, Yuval (1983). "Astronomy in Israel: From Og's Circle to the Wise Observatory". Tel-Aviv University. Retrieved 15 March 2007. http://wise-obs.tau.ac.il/judaism/jewish_astro.html.

26   The cause of the outbreak, according to our historian Josephus (Titus Flavius Josephus: *The Wars of the Jews or History of the Destruction of Jerusalem*) was provoked by Greek merchants sacrificing birds in front of a local synagogue. A Jewish Temple clerk, Eleazar ben Hanania, ceased prayers and sacrifices for the Roman Emperor at the Temple. Violence also broke out in protest over unfair taxation as Roman citizens were attacked at random.

Snaking and Dark, like Hairy Eyes

In April of the first year of Yuanyan, Dingyou, Tian Jiaoyan, Yin Yin was like thunder, with a meteor head as big as a fou, more than ten meters long, bright red and white, going southeast from Sunxia. The four sides may be as big as a glen or like a chicken, shining like rain, until faint. All counties and countries say that the stars are falling. The spring and autumn stars fall like rain, and the king loses power. Later, Wang Mang sued the country. The birth of Wang's sprout from Emperor Cheng is a result of a stellar change. Later recklessly usurped the country.

——From Volume 26 of *Hanshu, the Book of the Former Han* (history of the Han Dynasty) by Ban Biao and Ban Gu, approx. 82 AD

If you reckon by the Gregorian calendar, it is 12 BC. By the Julian Calendar it is 742, the Year of the Courtship of Messalla and Quirinus. In Rome, Emperor Augustus has just become Pontifex Maximus and Tiberius Claudius Nero has journeyed to Pannonia to quell a revolt. In India King Azes II has died and a Kushan empire is about to rise. In China it is the eleventh year of Emperor Cheng's reign, the beginning of the Yuanyan era. The Han Dynasty is at its midpoint.

The Dowager Empress Wang Zhengjun, wife of the former Emperor Yuan and mother of the current Emperor Cheng, was in the Yongning Hall, the Hall of Perpetual Tranquility. Through the portals leading to an open courtyard she could see a garden of chrysanthemums and plum trees and willows, and just beyond that, a pond where swans swam in circles as if tracing a figure of the Taijitu, the symbol of the Supreme Ultimate, the swirling forms of Yin and Yang. Here in the East Palace at Chang'an City, The Chánglè Gōng

Perihelion

(Palace of Lasting Joy), tranquility was not immediately forthcoming for the Empress. There was much on her mind.

Born in 71 BC, Wang Zhengjun was the daughter of an official in the Han Dynasty. Her father brought several suitors to the young woman, but each died mysteriously before they could be wed. A soothsayer was consulted, the jade divinity cups were thrown down and the broken pieces interpreted, and Father Wang received the prophecy that Zhengjun was to marry nobility. Apparently, the deaths were ordained by fate. She was then sent to the palace where, after two years, she was paraded along with other ladies-in-waiting before Crown Prince Liu Shi whose favorite consort had just died. It is said that Wang Zhengjun was extremely beautiful and that Liu Shi was captivated by her. Becoming the new favorite consort of the future Emperor, she bore him a son in 51 BC. By 47 BC, Liu Shi became the Emperor Yuan, Zhengjun was made Empress, and her son, Prince Ao, became the Crown Prince. Upon Emperor Yuan's death in 33 BC, Ao became the Emperor Cheng.

The rise to fame and prominence was not easy. Although the Consort Wang was well liked, there was much intrigue and opposition at court. During the end of Emperor Yuan's life he had begun to waver about making Ao the heir to the throne. Yuan had two other consorts, Lady Fu and Lady Feng Yuan and each had given him a son. Yuan was leaning toward making Consort Fu's son, Prince Kang of Dingtao the heir apparent. The first of many struggles now descended upon Lady Wang. Hard fought, Ao remained Crown Prince until Yuan's death.

Wang Zhengjiun had five brothers: Wang Zhang, Wang Feng, Wang Yin, Wang Shang, and Wang Gen. She had a nephew, Wang Mang.[1] The Empress convinced her son to reward these men with positions as marquesses, an act which smacked of nepotism and was contrary to tradition. Each in turn became commander of the armed forces and their power in the government grew rapidly. It would be Wang Mang who would usurp the power of the dynasty following Cheng's death but the Empress had no inkling of this possibility.

She was, however, concerned with Emperor Cheng's lack of an heir. Neither of his two concubines, the Empress Xu nor the Consort Ban had bore him a child. Cheng seemed uninterested in taking more concubines but Dowager Empress Wang insisted. Still without issue, in 19 BC Cheng did finally bring two more women to the harem:

dancing sisters from the household of Princess Yanga named Zhao Feiyan and Zhao Hede. Zhao Feiyan now became the Emperor's favorite. He called her the Flying Swallow and it was said that she was so slender she could dance on the palm of a hand. The sisters would become the catalysts for much turmoil in the years to come.

Much of this was on the Dowager Empress's mind as she gazed out at the garden. A soft wind shook the willows, the slender branches beckoning her as they caressed the pond. She pulled on slippers and tightened the belt of her silk hanfu, deciding that a walk in the garden would calm her nerves. Her hands ran along the silk robe, smoothing it. Silk, as everyone knows, was invented by the goddess, Leizu when a cocoon fell into her teacup. When she pulled it out it unraveled into one long thread. This gave her the idea to plant mulberry trees to raise silkworms and to weave the fine threads into cloth—cloth limited to the aristocracy.

Dowager Empress Wang Zhengjiun took an ivory hair comb from a dragon decorated ceramic vase and a bronze mirror from a lacquerware box. The image in the mirror reassured her of her beauty; age lines on her face were covered with powder and a touch of rouge—she might have been made of porcelain. But there were other beauties at court now. And plots as thick as mud.

As she walked along the path next to the pond a yellow oriole flew from its perch in a plum tree. The flash of its reflection in the silvery pond reminded her of a vision she had had two nights ago at this very spot. She had walked next to the pond that evening and glanced down to view the star-specked sky on its mirror-like surface. She saw a bright shape nearly as large as the moon. It had a tail, like a huge celestial snake. Snaking and dark, like hairy eyes, she thought to herself. That was a line from a poem, perhaps. It seemed appropriate for a prophetic vision...but what did it mean?

Now as she remembered the chilling feeling the vision had brought to her, she had an idea: why not consult an astrologist? Not one from the court, though, it was best to keep such things secret. She would ask her lady-in-waiting Lady Zhong Yeung to find someone for her. There was too much corruption at court to trust an official astrologist. And she had too many questions that would be dangerous if they became widely known.

Perihelion

Across the city, high on a ridge sat the massive Weiyang Palace, known as the "Endless Palace" for being perpetually under construction. It was the seat of government and current residence of the Emperor. The walls surrounding the palace were over 2,000 yards long and the palace sprawled across an area of 16,000 square feet. The Front Hall stretched for nearly 1,200 feet from the northern main entrance and was 500 feet wide. There were 40 main halls; the Empress lived in the Jiaofang Hall, the Emperor met with diplomats in the Qingliang Hall, and with his advisors in the Shaoyang Hall. Today, in the Shaoyang Hall, Emperor Cheng was debating a crucial change in government personnel with two of his trusted advisors, Jianhong Ma and Wei Lim Chou.

"Feng Yewang," said Wei Lim Chou, referring to a government official who was well liked and considered deserving of promotion, "is desirous of becoming a marquess. This has been brought to my attention by Wang Zhang. He has suggested that Feng Yewang should replace Wang Feng."

"Feng Yewang is the brother of my departed father's Consort Feng_Yuan," replied the Emperor. "It is proper that he should advance in rank. But Wang Feng is my mother's brother. She will not stand for such an action! Who is this Wang Zhang? He is not of my mother's family."

"He is a minor official in the treasury. He is ambitious and only has my ear because he voices his opinions loudly."

"I have a solution for this which is very simple. I will order the execution of this Wang Zhang. That will quiet him. Wang Feng will remain Marquess."

"As you desire, Lord," said Wei Lim Chou.

"Jianhong Ma," the Emperor now asked, "have you quizzed our chief astrologers about this new shooting star that has appeared in the heavens?"

Jianhong Ma sighed. He was not looking forward to giving his report. The interpretations he had heard were not favorable to the Emperor. Some editing was called for.

"Well, first of all," he began, "it is not a shooting star. It moves too slowly. It can be measured against the Year Star.[2] It was three feet distant three days ago and has only moved one half of one foot since then. It is what the astronomers call a sky sphere. The astrologist Gan said that this type of star with a sharp end and several feet long is abnormal. Stars do fall and become as stones upon the earth, and monarchs may share their fate…but only foolish monarchs that heed fearful suppositions."

"This Gan refers to me?" demanded the Emperor.

"It is only folk lore, Lord," answered Jianong Ma. "I would disregard warnings from these too zealous prophets. It may be an auspicious sign that there will be success in battle. Perhaps success in the production of an heir."

"This is more to my liking," said Emperor Cheng.

"This sky sphere," interjected Wei Lim Chou, "it reminds me of some news from the west. News and rumors travel fast along the trade routes like a thief on a stolen camel."

"Tell your news then," said the Emperor.

"There is much unrest in those lands where the spices come from. The Romans say their emperor is a god but the people who he subjugates are rising up for they have their own god. They say this sky sphere is a sign that a new king is being born among the peasants. A king who will lead them in a revolution against the Romans."[3]

"The Romans will no doubt crush this new king. That will be the end of it."

"As you say, Lord."

A traveler or a caravan on the Silk Road[4] approached Chang'an by crossing the bridge over the Wei River. Entering the walled city through the Xuanpingmen gate brought one to the Nine Markets, just to the north of Weiyang Palace. This large market was named for the nine regions into which the city had become divided over the centuries. It was the eastern terminus of the Silk Road which linked China to Greece, India, Persia, and Egypt. The Nine Markets featured goods from these exotic locales as well as local fruits, vegetables, leather and fabrics, ceramics, and livestock.

Lady Zhong Yeung wandered among the market stalls where venders shouted out their offerings. "I have pistachio nuts from Persia," yelled a man wearing a turban. "Also dates and cumin and saffron and nutmeg!" Zhong walked on by. Another stall displayed jars of frankincense and myrrh and other colorful sticks of incense. Another showed items made from Indian sandalwood and quilted or beaded fabrics. A table with urns of wormwood and calamus plants reminded her of the coming, in the fifth month, of the Dragon Boat

Perihelion

Festival. That was a bad month and although the festival celebrated the legend of Qu Yuan, who had drowned himself the Miluo River out of shame, it was a chance to eat the red bean rice dumpling called Zongzi and to drink rice wine.

She passed by an array of harnesses suitable, said the proprietor, for Heavenly Horses,[5] but stopped to examine a table of Egyptian glassware. A slender green perfume bottle with a flared opening caught her eye. Perhaps she would come back for that. But she was not shopping for herself; her mistress wished her to seek out an astrologer. An honest one. That would be difficult but not impossible.

Just beyond a series of small corrals containing sheep and goats and cages filled with chickens and geese was an area where people offered services. Red lanterns hung from tall poles and banners were draped across tent roofs with hand-painted characters identifying their owners as experts in healing herbs, spiritual cleansing, letter writing, fortune telling, and other useful activities. Here she found the tent of a man named Xun Kwok. The design on his banner depicting the animals of the zodiac indicated his role in life as an astrologer. But was he honest?

Xun Kwok was a small man, stooped and gray of hair and beard. His hemp robe betrayed his social status: he was not a noble or a person of wealth and means. Inside the tent the walls were hung with paper charts with columns of characters that Lady Zhong recognized as Wu Xing, the Five Elements: wood, fire, earth, metal, and water.

"You are interested in Wu Xing?" asked the little man. "The Seng cycle or mothering cycle is this: wood feeds fire, fire creates earth, earth brings forth metal, metal causes water to run off, and water makes wood grow. The Kè cycle which is also called the weakening cycle is that fire melts metal, metal chops wood, wood breaks through earth, earth swallows water, and water quenches fire. This represents the changes of the states of being. Sometimes we describe the Five Elements as azure dragon, vermilion phoenix, yellow dragon, white tiger, and black tortoise. Poetic, do you not think? How may I be of service?"

Wishing to take the measure of the old astrologer, Lady Zhong asked, "If you made my horoscope and it was not fortuitous but spoke of impending doom, would you tell me?"

"Of course. What use is happy ignorance? Knowledge is a weightless treasure one may carry easily."

"And what if I refused to pay you for an unfavorable fortune?"

"Have much money and you can make the devil push your grindstone…what is the good of that? It is only the man who knows when he has enough who is rich. I need not color the truth for profit."

"I have a mistress who wishes to learn what the stars portend. She is of nobility and wishes to remain anonymous in her search for wisdom. Will you honor her in this?"

"This woman who seeks the truth will have my discretion in all things and wisdom regardless of her tears."

"Then I will return tomorrow to bring you to her abode. She will pay you well, no matter of the outcome of your reading. Thank you for your honest answers to my questions. Goodbye for now."

Lady Zhong Yeung left the tent of Xun Kwok to hurry back to Chánglè Palace to report to the Dowager Empress. Her path took her past the table of Egyptian glassware where she made a purchase before returning to the Empress' residence.

Perihelion

The Flying Swallow, Zhao Feiyan

It was well known that Emperor Cheng indulged in lustful passions. He had built three palaces, the Xiaoyou Palace, the Flying Palace, and the Yunlei Palace where he brought many beautiful women for his own pleasure. His concubines were many. *Hanshu, the Book of the Former Han* tells us of Ban Jieyu, a maid of Ban Jieyu's named Li Ping, Majie Yu and Ma Jieyu who were the Empress' grandfather's sisters, Wang Meiren who was cursed by Empress Xu's sister Xu Ye, the younger sister of Wang Feng's concubine called Zhang Meiren, and others. With all these women and the Emperor's daily visits to his pleasure palaces, one would think he could have produced an heir. As we will see, the lack of an heir was no accident.

When the dancing sisters, Zhao Feiyan and Zhao Hede came to live in the palace they were jealous of the other consorts. They began to accuse Empress Xu and the Consort Ban Jieyu of witchcraft. Emperor Cheng was persuaded to banish Ban Jieyu and to depose Wu Ye. He wished to make Zhao Feiyan his new empress. The Dowager Empress Wang opposed this because of Zhao Feiyan's low social status as a former dancing girl. Cheng elevated Feiyan's father Zhao Lin to Marquess of Chengyang thereby rising Feiyan's status. The Dowager Empress capitulated and Feiyan became Empress.

Character assassination was the least of the sisters' tactics toward assuring no other consort would produce an heir. Forced abortions, poisonings, and assassinations were alleged by early historians. It may have been Hede, the younger of the sisters, who instigated these atrocities. Earlier this year, before the appearance of the comet, a favorite consort of the Emperor named Cao Gong had given birth to a male child. The child was undoubtedly the Emperor's son and a possible future heir to the throne. But it was sickly. Zhao Hede tended to the baby with medicine which failed to effect a cure. The child died. Soon after, Cao Gong was forced to commit suicide. An investigation many years later would link the sisters to the deaths. Now another consort named Xu Meiren, a relative of the former Empress Xu, was pregnant. The sisters went into conference.

Consort Zhao Hede lived in the Zhaoyang Hall of the Weiyang Palace. The threshold was lined with copper covered in gold and the steps leading into the chamber were carved from white jade. The hall was painted a deep red, the color of dried blood, and the bedroom was painted black as a starless night. Everywhere there was gold and jade decoration. Zhao Feiyan and Zhao Hede sat across from each other on raised platforms of elm wood lacquered with sap from the Rhus vernicifera tree, a tree sometimes called poison oak and ironically, highly toxic just like the dancing sisters.

They no longer danced unless you counted the horizontal form of gyration they performed with various lovers, lovers selected for their virility. It wouldn't matter who the father was if they produced an heir. But they had not and so the endless program of elimination of rivals continued. Zhao Feiyan spoke first:

"It should be allowed to come to term, I think. After all, it might be a girl. It is too soon for another death."

"Perhaps you should seduce the father of Lady Xu's blessed circumstance. He at least has proven his potency," said Zhao Hede.

"The Dowager Empress is watching me. She has too much power and influence to ignore."

"You will someday be the Dowager Empress, my dear sister."

"No...you would not..."

Perihelion

"Oh, certainly not. But one never knows what the stars may ordain. That big star in the night sky, for instance. There is some purpose to its just hanging there. Waiting for something to happen. It is said that a crisis is an opportunity riding the dangerous wind."

"It is also said that patience is a bitter plant, but its fruit is sweet," said Zhao Feiyan.

Lady Zhong Yeung arrived at the tent of the astrologer Xun Kwok the next morning with a palanquin and four strong carriers who supported the litter's long wooden poles on their shoulders. It was large enough to accommodate two people seated facing each other and curtains that hung from the roof provided anonymity for its passengers. Xun Kwok was surprised at how ornate the palaquin was with its lacquering and gilded decoration. Clearly, it had been obtained from India and had crossed the Silk Road carrying some person of great wealth. Now the humble servant that was he would be transported in luxury. And the curtains would prevent him from seeing where he was going.

The avenue was divided into two lanes by a strip of plantings of chrysanthemums and, at each intersection, a large domed pagoda tree whose drooping branches were alive with greenish-yellow leaves and bean-shaped pods. Just past Shanglin Park the palanquin veered off onto a narrow street that crossed one of the city's canals on an arched wooden bridge. Here in this district were some of the newer palaces and temples. The Dowager Empress had commandeered the house of the grandparents of one of her ladies-in-waiting for this meeting. Those who knew of it thought the former Empress had simply arranged a tryst with some dignitary who should not be seen at the Chánglè Palace.

Xun Kwok saw nothing unusual about the house he now entered except that it must belong to someone of wealth and importance. That gave him no clue as to the person's identity who had summoned him. In the antechamber a woman sat on a stiff-backed wooden chair (undoubtedly imported, like the palanquin, from India). This was the Dowager Empress Wang Zhengjun but the astrologer did not recognize her. She wore a scarlet hanfu of fine silk, dark brown silk slippers decorated with pearls, and her hair was done up in a mound held by an ivory comb. Her face was hidden by a veil. Lady Zhong

Yeung now bowed and backed out of the room leaving the astrologer alone with this mysterious personage.

The bowing was a clue: this was no ordinary rich lady! Xun Kwok decided he had better bow as well. He did so. "My Lady," he said, "I am at your service."

There was no reply. Xun Kwok said, "A horoscope? I am an expert at the art of Zi Wei Dou Shu…the astrology of the Purple Star. I only need to learn from you the Four Pillars of your destiny. These pillars are the year, which will determine your sign, the month, which will tell us your age, and…"

The Dowager Empress held up her hand. "I do not wish a horoscope," she said.

"Then what…?"

"There is a strange new star in the heavens with a long tail which hangs there ominously like a snake ready to strike. I would know what this portends and how it might affect the country."

Now there was little doubt in Xun Kwok's mind as to the identity of his client. He was wise enough not to let on that he knew for the consequences of that might be dire. He answered the Dowager Empress:

"The star is not common, but its type has been seen before. It is called a comet by the Arabs who have studied this phenomenon in detail. And yes, it may have great impact upon our country's future."

"Tell me how this can be," commanded the Dowager Empress.

"It is said," continued Xun Kwok, "that in the epoch of the 242 years, there were 36 solar eclipses, three comets were seen, the night stars disappeared and fell like rain. Thirty-six princes were killed, fifty-two were subjugated, and there were countless princes unable to protect their communities. When the Tian clan usurped the Qi, the three families were divided into the Warring States and were therefore divided into battles. The military revolution took place. There were several massacres in the city. Zhou Zu was destroyed by Qin. At the time of the First Emperor, comets were seen everywhere in fifteen years."[6]

"This is but history," said Wang Zhengjun. "What does it mean for the future? How can you know?"

"By the Four Pillars of the Emperor we can plot the destiny of the country."

"You have done this?"

Perihelion

"I have. The comet intercedes, however. What should be happiness and tranquility has been disrupted."

"And so?"

"If this comet does not go out by Rooster month it means chaos and suffering. The reading tells us there will be a chaotic king who will break the country and die, and the rest will be endless drought, fierce starvation, and violent illness. Within three years there will be an army under the star, and if the monarch is lost the land will be lost."[7]

"And this king...you mean the Emperor."

"No matter how tall the mountain is, it cannot block the sun. All things change."

The Dowager Empress was silent for a time. Then she waved her hand in a slow arch as if pushing the image of the astrologer away from her vision. "The woman who brought you here will pay you. You have my permission to leave," she said.

After returning to the astrologer's tent, Lady Zhong Yeung turned to Xun Kwok and said, "Before I give you your money I want to know what you told my mistress."

"I'll tell you that if you confirm my feeling that I was just talking with the Dowager Empress."

"I cannot, of course, give you an answer about that."

"I will tell you this," said Xun Kwok, "she asked me about the comet."

"The sky sphere that hangs in the night sky?"

"She wished to learn its import."

"And?" said Lady Zhong Yeung, holding a leather purse just out of reach. "What did you tell her?"

The Lady Zhong Yeung had come to the Imperial city of Chang'an from Guanghan, a small town in the Sichuan province. She had a brother, Zhong Qing, who had followed her some years after her arrival at the palace. Zhong Qing had become a revolutionary of some importance to the factions in the city opposed to the Emperor. This was a fact that Lady Zhong Yeung took pains to conceal from her mistress and anyone else in the court. She was not herself a member of any group, nor did she share any beliefs common to her brother's compatriots, but out of love and regard for her sibling, she often gave him information.

One evening later that week she met her brother at a lantern festival that had just begun in a park near the Nine Markets. Lamps were being erected in elaborate displays by people attempting to outdo each other. One display affected a large wheel hung with silk ribbons which turned, rotating numerous oil lamps. The crowd lifted up cups of a wine made from fermented grains in which flower pedals floated. There was singing and dancing and trained animals performed tricks. Brother and sister sought a quiet place away from the crowd.

Lady Zhong Yeung told her brother what the astrologer had told the Dowager Empress. Zhong Qing realized at once that the prophecy could be used to energize the dissidents with whom he associated. Later in that same month, Zhong Qing and dozens of others attacked a temple, released prisoners from a garrison, robbed the soldiers' treasury, and escaped into the mountains. Zhong Qing would become their leader, styling himself as the Mountain Monarch. By winter, the rebels numbered ten thousand but were scattered throughout several counties. They had little impact on the workings of the government however and could not penetrate the defenses of the palace. Some years later, Zhong Qing was captured and beheaded along with several of his followers.

Lady Zhong Yeung, despite her stealth, was unable to conceal her betrayal of the Dowager Empress for long. The day she was summoned to the Chánglè Palace to account for her sins was the worst day of her life. She stood in front of the Dowager Empress and cried, proclaiming that her love for her mistress was as great as her love for her brother…greater! She was spared the fate of the revolutionary but was banished from the province. She managed to take with her the small collection of jade ornaments and pearls she had accumulated over the years when she returned to Guanghan. She lived there the remainder of her life dejected, shamed, and hovering on the edge of poverty.

In the year following the appearance of the comet (which would be named after the English astronomer Edmund Halley many centuries later), Consort Xu Meiren gave birth to a healthy male child. The Zhao sisters could not let this child become the Crown Prince. Zhao Hede went into action; mother and infant son were murdered. By this time, the Empress Zhao Feiyan was falling from favor with the Emperor. He had turned his affections to her sister,

Perihelion

Hede. Jealousy between the sisters threatened a split and only their program of ruthless malfeasance kept them together. Although both sisters engaged in many trysts they were unable to become pregnant.

By 9 BC the Emperor was still without an heir. Two choices presented themselves: his younger brother Prince Liu Xing of Zhongshan, and his nephew Prince Liu Xin of Dingtao. Lobbying by Wang Gen and Prince Liu Xin's grandmother Consort Fu, and the showering of gifts in various quarters (including upon the Zhao sisters) finally resulting in Xin being named Crown Prince. He would very soon become the Emperor Ai. Emperor Cheng said:

"Virtue can't take care of the world, and the people grumble. Without God's blessing, there are no heirs, and the world has nothing to do with him. Seeing the precepts of the past and recent events, and the adversity of disasters, I say, Tao Wangxin is as a son to me, kind and filial, can inherit the order of heaven, and continue to sacrifice. Qi Lixin is now the crown prince."[8]

Emperor Cheng and Consort Zhao Hede relaxed on silk cushions in the Emperor's bed chamber. The year was 7 BC, the second year of the Suihe era. Zhao busied herself caressing the Emperor in an effort to arouse him but it seemed her efforts were in vain. Now she reached for a bowl in which was a powder made from a stringy black fungus called the Herbal of the Divine Plowman. This was the rare invasive fungus called Cordyceps which grew inside silkworms and which was considered one of the best aphrodisiacs in China. She sprinkled a quantity of the powder into a bowl of wine and offered it to the Emperor.

"This potion will energize you, Lord," she said, adding, "My sister obtained this for me. Was not that thoughtful of her?"

The Emperor drank from the bowl and indeed, within a few minutes, he was ready for sex. The lovemaking would not yield a new heir, much to the disappointment of Consort Hede. The stress of the session and the effects of the Divine Plowman in the wine (which some would later suggest was not devoid of additional ingredients) was too much for Cheng. He collapsed with a stroke. He died shortly thereafter and now sister Zhao Feiyan became the Dowager Empress.

Dowager Empress Wang now became the Grand Dowager Empress. A memory came to her of a prophesy related by an old astrologer many years ago. If the monarch is lost the land will be lost, he had said. She commissioned an investigation of the Zhao sisters and learned of the poisonings they had done. She convinced the Emperor Ai to strip members of the Zhao family of their titles of marquess and to send them into exile. Zhao Hede, from grief or from guilt, committed suicide. Dowager Empress Zhao Feiyan was spared for the moment.

When in 1 BC the Emperor Ai, then only 14 years of age, died suddenly, Grand Dowager Empress Wang moved to take back power over the Empire. She made her nephew Wang Mang regent and the ambitious Mang usurped the title of Emperor, disposing Ai's heir, Emperor Ping. Emperor Wang Mang demoted Dowager Empress Zhao Feiyan from her title and, becoming once again a commoner, she committed suicide. Grand Dowager Empress Wang died in the spring of 13 AD. Wang Mang's new dynasty was…well, that's another story.

---

1   Chinese names have two parts: first is a character which is a generational name, shared by all family members that we would call a surname; second is a character or characters which represents that person's given name. Thus Wang Gen and Wang Mang belong to the same family. Emperors, at least before the Tang dynasty, were known by a posthumous name. For instance, Prince Liu Shi became the Emperor Yuan and Prince Ao became Emperor Cheng.

2   Jupiter

3   Although this appearance of a comet thought to have been Halley's took place in 12 BC, over a decade before the presumed date of the birth of Jesus, some astronomers and theologians suggest this might have been the Star of Bethlehem. There may have been other comets that appeared closer to the historical date of the birth of Jesus, however. The comet was also observed over the city of Rome in that year and supposedly foretold the concurrent death of Marcus Vipsanius Agrippa.

4   China opened the so-called Silk Road during the second century BC. It stretched across Asia to the Mediterranean. The

Perihelion

Greeks called China "Seres" which meant "land of silk" for that unique commodity was China's main export. The term Silk Road, however, was coined by historian Ferdinand von Richthofen in 1877.

5   The soil in China lacked some nutrients essential for breeding strong horses suitable for use in wars. The "Heavenly Horses" came from Dayuan, a Greek kingdom in Central Asia, and these were desired by the Han. This instituted a war known as the War of the Heavenly Horses in which the Han were victorious. They used the Heavenly Horses to great advantage in their war with the nomadic Xiongnu.

6   *Hanshu, the Book of the Former Han* (history of the Han Dynasty) by Ban Biao and Ban Gu, approx. 82 AD, Volume 26

7   Ibib.

8   Ibib; Volume 10. (Qi Lixin refers to Prince Liu Xin of Dingtao.)

Byron Grush

The Worst Year in History

The worst year in the history of the world—2020 AD? Absolutely. The Covid-19 virus caused the deaths of 318,000 people in this country, over 3 million world-wide. At the time of this writing (March 2021) the United States has topped 525,000. I will not begin to get into politics, the cries of "Fake news" from the twice impeached president, the lies and anti-science, the anti-maskers, the national insanity running through the fake president's supporters and his party; these things probably contributed to many more deaths than should have happened. History will tell its own story. But there was another year that has been called "The worst time in history to be alive": 536 AD.

"…the Sun gave forth its light without brightness, like the Moon, during this whole year, and it seemed exceedingly like the Sun in eclipse."[1] (Procopius)
"…the Sun was dark and its darkness lasted for eighteen months; each day it shone for about four hours, and still this light was only a feeble shadow."[2] (Syrien)

In 538, the Roman statesman Cassiodorus wrote that "the light of the sun was weak and that crops had failed." The sixth-century British monastic writer Gildas reported large-scale fires and widespread destruction of the landscape at about that same time.[3] Irish history records tell that a "dust veil" and "running stars" were shining for 20 days.[4] In 536 AD the world was without sun. A mysterious fog blanketed Europe, Asia, and the Middle East. Temperatures dropped severely. Crops failed and people starved. These conditions probably lasted for at least a decade and this period has been cited as the cause of what is called "The Late Antique Little Ice Age"[5] which lasted until 680 AD. What followed in 541 AD was the first breakout of bubonic plague, the Black Death, which killed between one-third and one-half of the population of Europe.

The popular theory for the cause of the mysterious fog and blotting out of the sun was a climatic event such as the eruption of a large volcano or multiple volcanos. Dendrochronologist Michael Baillie (a tree ring expert) first put forth the theory in 1994. The glaciologist Lars Larsen found evidence for a major eruption in multiple ice cores at both poles.[6] More recent studies, however, seem to favor the impact upon Earth of a comet or asteroid.

Two undergraduate students, Emma Rigby and Mel Symonds under the supervision of Dr Derek Ward-Thompson at Cardiff University in the UK, studied the tree ring evidence and other data and concluded that the debris from a giant explosion enveloped the earth in soot and ash, blocking out the sunlight, and this was caused by a comet hitting the earth and exploding in the upper atmosphere.[7]

In a paper in *Astronomy and Geophysic* in 2004, Rigby, Symonds, and Ward-Thompson noted that no evidence was found in the Greenland and Antarctic ice cores for the type of acid layer that would be caused by the eruption of a super-volcano. Since no impact crater could be linked to a 536 event either on land or in the seabed, they deduced the comet, if that had been what it was, had exploded in the atmosphere, spreading comet dust and causing forest fires.[8] As an example, they pointed to Comet SL9 which broke up and collided with Jupiter in 1994:

"The fragments of SL9 that collided with Jupiter ranged in diameter from 300 m to 2 km. The scars created on Jupiter were typically about the size of the Earth or larger. This appears to corroborate our basic premise that a relatively small fragment could have been responsible for the 536 event."[9]

A fragment of a comet. Any comets in the neighborhood in 536 AD? During the sixth century astronomical observations were recorded by Chinese astronomers. A comet later identified as Halley's Comet was seen in 530 AD. Six years earlier. But as F. Richard Stephenson and Kevin K. C. Yau point out in an article on early observations of Halley's Comet, the Chinese calendar was "luni-solar" that is, years were not counted continuously from a common starting point but began from the reign of each successive monarch: "careful consultation of chronological tables is necessary to obtain the correct year BC or AD."[10]

This from Popular Astronomy:

"The return of 530 was the longest period on the record, being nearly seventy-nine and a half years from the last apparition in 451. The observation was clearly described in the Annal of Wei, the North Reigns, it stated as follows: 'In the 3rd year of Yung An, in the 7th month, on the day Chia Wu (August 29, 530), a comet appeared in

Perihelion

the northeast sky near to the east of Ursae Majoris in the morning, its tail was 6 cubits long, its color was perfect white, whence it moved to the northeast again and its tail was pointing to the southwest. On the day Ting Yeou (September 1, 530) the comet appeared in the northwest of Ursae Majoris, then it was in conjunction with the sun in the morning.

On the day Ken Tse (September 4) the comet appeared in the north-west in the evening, its tail was about one cubit long pointing southeast, then it moved gradually to Libra. In the 8th month, on the day Ki Wei (September 23) the comet appeared again and disappeared on the day Koei Hai (September 27).' Hind identified this as Halley's Comet."[11]

So, did a piece of Halley's Comet break off during its return in 530 and orbit the Earth for six years before slamming into the ocean or exploding in the atmosphere? Are the calculations of the Gregorian equivalents of these Chinese years of astrological observation accurate? Or was there a different comet in 536—remember the "running stars" shining for 20 days as observed in Ireland? Or was it an asteroid? Or a super-volcano?

Speaking of Ireland, 1P/530AD/Halley would have been around in 530 AD to have been seen by Brendan of Clonfert Brénainn moccu Alti, one of the early Irish monastic saints and one of the Twelve Apostles of Ireland, on his return from his legendary journey to the Isle of the Blessed. *Nauigatio sancti Brendani abbatis*[12] (the Voyage of St Brendan the Abbot) tells the story of his fantastic journey—reminiscent of *Gulliver's Travels* or perhaps Doctor Doolittle's search for the giant sea snail.

John, Third Marguess of Bute, in a 1911 lecture on Brendan's Fabulous Journey,[13] tells us that "Brendan, the son of Finnlogh O' Alta, was born at Tralee in Kerry, in the year 481 or 482. He had a pedigree which connected him with the rulers of Ireland, and thus perhaps secured for him a social prominence which he would not otherwise have enjoyed. ...He lived to an extreme old age, and was in his 96th year when the end came." He suggests the Abbot, although apparently well-traveled and highly regarded, led a rather "humdrum" life yet "had the ill luck to be selected by some unknown antient Irish novelist as the hero of a romance of the wildest kind." John does not characterize the tale as, in Swift's *Gulliver*, social or political satire, nor does he think it an allegorical romance such as Bunyan's *Pilgrim's Progress*. He does think a voyage really occurred and that Brendan did discover some islands, perhaps in the Canary Archipelago, perhaps Madeira, the Cape de Verde Islands, or even as far as the Azores—but definitely not North America as some suggest. He concludes, "I look upon the Fabulous Voyage as a composition which is really only differentiated by the elements due to the time and place of birth from religious novels such as those which enrich the pages of the *Leisure Hour* or the *Sunday at Home*."[14]

Sometime around 493 AD another priest named Barinthus came to see Brendan one evening and told him of having journeyed to an island called the Isle of the Blessed, a most holy place. Brendan determined to find this island. He gathered fourteen of his monks and said, "I have in my heart resolved to go forth in quest of the Land of Promise of the Saints, about which Father Barinthus discoursed to us." From the *Nauigatio sancti Brendani abbatis*:

"Then St Brendan and his companions, using iron implements, prepared a light vessel, with wicker sides and ribs, such as is usually made in that country, and covered it with cow-hide, tanned in oak-bark, tarring the joints thereof, and put on board provisions for forty days, with butter enough to dress hides for covering the boat and all utensils needed for the use of the crew."[15]

After fasting once every three days for 40 days, the monks and Brendan were joined by three others. They set sail on a voyage which would take them to several islands, perhaps ten or eleven in number, although, as we will see, one of the islands turned out to be a whale. On the first island upon which they landed they encountered a dog who led them to a mansion in which they saw a demon "in the guise of a little black boy, at his work, having in his hands a bridle-bit, and beckoning to the monk."[16]

Landing on another island they found no grass or other vegetation, nor did they find sand on the shore. They built a fire but when "the cauldron began to boil, the island moved about like a wave; whereupon they all rushed towards the boat…they cast their boat loose, to sail away, when the island at once sunk into the ocean."[17] The narrator describes the sinking island as a fish (actually, a whale) that was trying to make its head and tail meet but which was too enormous to so do. Its name, he tells us, was Jasconius.

Perihelion

One of the next islands they came to was covered with grass, flowers, and trees, and one large tree was filled with snow-white birds, obscuring its branches and leaves. Brendan addressed one of the birds asking if it were a messenger from God. It, being a talking bird, replied in length that they, the birds, had dwelled in that place in ruin after the fall of Lucifer and that they been doomed to be there by God. The name of their island, it said was the Paradise of Birds. The bird prophesized that the monks would wander for six more years but at last find the Land of Promise of the Saints which they sought.

More sailing, more islands. On one they drank water which made them sleep for 24 hours. On another they met an old man with snow-white hair and a glass-like countenance. This, he said, was Island of St. Ailbe. As they sailed the sea became curdled. Another period of forty days went by…this seems to have been the average increment separating events in the story.

As they sailed a "fish of enormous size appeared swimming after the boat, spouting foam from its nostrils, and ploughing through the waves in rapid pursuit to devour them."[18] Brendan prayed for salvation and God caused the water to form great waves which rushed toward the monster. Brendan again prayed saying, "Deliver, O Lord, Thy servants, as Thou didst deliver David from the hands of the giant Goliath, and Jonas from the power of the great whale."[19] And another great monster then appeared and attacked the first, cutting it into three pieces, then disappearing back beneath the sea. On the next day they landed on an island and drew their boat up upon the beach. They found that the hind portion of the slain monster fish had washed up on the shore. They had a feast and ate it.

Another island, flat, level, and covered in white and purple flowers. On it they saw three groups of monks; the monks each chanted and sang. There were boys dressed in white robes and young men in violet, and old men in purple. Next an island with trees abundant with grapes larger than they had ever seen before. Suddenly a Gryphon flew toward them. The Brothers were afraid but the Abbot said "Fear not, for God is our helper." And as if sent by God another great bird flew into the sky near them and attacked the Gryphon. The fight was fierce and lasted a long time but at last the Gryphon was vanquished and its lifeless body fell into the sea.

Byron Grush

Always, whether on an island or at sea, the party of monks celebrated mass and holy days such as Easter. They were at sea one day celebrating the festival of St. Peter when the ocean became so clear they could see all the way to its bottom. There they saw monsters of the deep and fish in shoals "like flocks of sheep in the pastures, swimming around, heads to tails."[20] Next they saw a column so far away and it could not be reached in three days. When they approached it the height of it seemed to pierce the sky. It looked like hardened marble colored as silver, yet it was crystal clear.

The column was surrounded by a network of some material, also like silver and harder than marble. They sailed around this, found an opening between four pavilions, and entered. On the fourth day of their exploration there they found a silver chalice like the one used by Christ at the last supper, or so Brendan said. "A great gift to us from our Lord," he said.

They passed an island with inhabitants who were very hairy and hideous; the island was rocky, covered with slag, and filled with fire and smoke: The Island of Blacksmiths. When one man saw them he withdrew into his forge, crying, "Woe! Woe!" Other inhabitants of the island threw burning brands at them. They hurried away. They passed another island with a high mountain and watched smoke issuing from its peak. One of the monks who had joined the group late jumped onto the island saying, "Woe is me father, for I am forcibly torn away from you, and cannot return!" They watched in horror as some demons dragged the hapless monk, who was now on fire, down to Hell. They hurried away once again.

They had revisited the island called Paradise of Birds and the island that was not an island, Jasconius the whale. Seven days later they sailed into a dense cloud. In this was a large rock upon which sat a man "with a veil before him as large as a sack, hanging between two iron prongs; and he was tossed about like a small boat in a storm."[21] Brendan asked him what crime he had committed that he had been placed there. The man replied that he was Judas Iscariot. This place was not one of punishment but of partial reprieve, allowed to him periodically by the Redeemer in honor of his Resurrection. Judas said:

"I have this cooling relief, as it is now the Lord's Day; while I sit here, I seem to myself to be in a paradise of delights, considering the agony of the torments that are in store for me afterwards; for when I am in my torments, I burn like a mass of molten lead, day and night,

Perihelion

in the heart of that mountain you have seen. ...I will tell you of the refreshing coolness I have here every Sunday from the first vespers to the second; from Christmas Day to the Epiphany; from Easter to Pentecost; on the Purification of the Blessed Virgin Mary, and on the festival of her Assumption. On all other days I am in torments with Herod and Pilate, with Annas and Caiphas; and, therefore, I adjure you, through the Redeemer of the world, to intercede for me with the Lord Jesus, that I may remain here until sunrise tomorrow, and that the demons, because of your coming here, may not torment me, nor sooner drag me off to my heritage of pain, which I purchased at an evil price."[22]

They still wandered, passing islands, sometimes landing and celebrating as monks will do. It had been seven years. The great whale swam with them toward the Paradise of Birds. He told them to prepare their boat with water-skins from the fountain and to follow as he would now lead them to the Land of Promise of the Saints. The birds all sang as they left, wishing them a happy voyage.

The land they found was thick with trees laden with fruit and light always shone, even at night. They explored for forty days (of course) and came to a river which they could not cross. Along came a young man of pleasant features who greeted them and said, "This is the land you have sought after for so long a time; but you could nothitherto find it, because Christ our Lord wished, first to display to you His divers mysteries in this immense ocean. Return now to the land of your birth, bearing with you as much of those fruits and of those precious stones, as your boat can carry; for the days of your earthly pilgrimage must draw to a close, when you may rest in peace among your saintly brethren."[23]

And so they returned home to Ireland where Brendan died. Saint Brendan's feast day is celebrated on the 16th of May. The location of Saint Brendan's Island has been one of conjecture. Maps in Christopher Columbus' time placed it in the western Atlantic Ocean. Christopher Columbus may have learned from the *Navigatio* how to navigate west following a southerly route from the Canary Islands. Tim Severin,[24] explorer and filmmaker, in his 1978 documentary *The Brendan Voyage*, demonstrated the plausibility of a leather-clad boat reaching North America from Ireland.

Severin built an Irish currage, a boat as close to the description of Brendan's as possible. The wood and leather boat was christened the

"Brendan". In 1976 he set sail from Brendon Creek on Ireland's Dingle Peninsula following prevailing winds across the north Atlantic. He and his crew encountered friendly whales that followed the boat. Past the Hebrides islands they came to the Danish Faroe Islands. Here they found the Island of Mykines where there were thousands of seabirds, prompting them to think that this was Brendan's Paradise of Birds. When they reached Iceland they wintered and considered that the extinct volcanos there might have been active in Brendan's time. Then there were the icebergs. Brendan's silver, marble-hard columns? They reached the island of Newfoundland on June 26, 1977, proof that Brendan's voyage was possible and giving tempting explanations for some of the wondrous things the monks saw.

There is a theory that an Irish colony existed in South Carolina, predating Columbus' voyages to the New World.[25] An historian, Peter Martyr d'Anghiera, was appointed chronicler for the new Council of the Indies in 1520 by Charles V, ruler of the Holy Roman Empire. His publication of 1526, *De Orbe Novo, The Eight Decades of Peter Martyr D'Anghera,*[26] was a series of letters and reports of the early explorations of Central and South America based on interviews. In it Martyr described the indigenous peoples of the Americas, including the area of what is now Georgia and South Carolina.

The Spanish colonists, he reported, treated the Native American Chicora Indians with brutality. But there was another tribe with whom they were friendly: The Duhare. The Duhare were taller than the Spanish, unlike the other Native Americans with whom they came in contact. They had light tanned skin, red hair and grey eyes and appeared more like European Caucasians than Indians. Enter the People of One Fire.

People of One Fire is an alliance of Creek, Choctaw and Seminole scholars, who since around 2006 have been studying the heritage and languages of the Muskogean peoples, comparing languages across various cultures. They translated the words of all the tribes that had been recorded by the Spanish, these having many things in common, but were unable to translate the language of the Duhare. Dr Joseph Kitchens, Director of the Funk Heritage Museum at Reinhardt University in Georgia, was studying symbols carved into a boulder that was on display at his university; they were identical to those carved into boulders along the west coast of Ireland, dating to thousands of years ago. Prompted by this discovery, the People of Fire compared Duhare words to those in ancient Gaelic dictionaries and found they could then translate them consistent with Duhare culture.[27]

---

1   Procopius; Dewing, Henry Bronson, trans. (1916). Procopius. vol. 2: History of the [Vandalic] Wars, Books III and IV. London, England: William Heinemann. p. 329. ISBN 978-0-674-99054-8.

2   Michel le Syrien; Chabot, J.-B., trans. (1901). Chronique de Michel le Syrien, Patriarche Jacobite d'Antoche [Chronicle of Michael the Syrian, Jacobite Patriarch of Syria] (in French). 2nd vol. Paris, France: Leroux.

Also from the same source:
"However, a little earlier, in the year 848 [according to the Greek calendar; 536/537 AD according to the Christian calendar], there was a sign in the sun. One had never seen it [before] and nowhere is it written that such [an event] had happened [previously] in the world. If it were not [true] that we found it recorded in most proven and credible writings, and confirmed by men worthy of belief, we would not have written it [here]; for it's difficult to conceive. So it is said that the sun was darkened, and that its eclipse lasted a year and a half, that is, eighteen months. Every day it shone for about four hours and yet this light was only a feeble shadow. Everyone declared that it would not return to the state of its original light. Fruits didn't ripen, and wine had the taste of what comes from sour grapes."

3   Emma Rigby, Melissa Symonds, Derek Ward-Thompson Authors: "A comet impact in AD 536?" Astronomy & Geophysics, Volume 45, Issue 1, February 2004, Pages 1.23–1.26. https://doi.org/10.1046/j.1468-4004.2003.45123.x

4   A. A. Mardon, Antarctic Institute of Canada. "The Mystery of the 536 A.D. Dust Veil Event: Was it a Comentary or Meteorite

Impact"
https://www.lpi.usra.edu/meetings/impacts97/pdf/6019.pdf

5   Becky Little. "The Worst Time in History to Be Alive, According to Science." 2018. https://www.history.com/news/536-volcanic-eruption-fog-eclipse-worst-year.

6   Dr. Tim Newfield, Princeton University. "The Global Cooling Event of the Sixth Century. Mystery No Longer?" 2016. https://www.historicalclimatology.com/features/something-cooled-the-world-in-the-sixth-century-what-was-it.

7   "Astronomers Unravel A Mystery Of The Dark Ages: Undergraduates' Work Blames Comet For 6th-century 'Nuclear Winter'." ScienceDaily, 4 February 2004.
www.sciencedaily.com/releases/2004/02/040204000254.htm

8   Emma Rigby, Melissa Symonds, Derek Ward-Thompson, Ibid.

9   Ibid.

10   F. Richard Stephenson and Kevin K. C. Yau. "FAR EASTERN OBSERVATIONS OF HALLEYS COMET: 240 BC to AD 1368". Journal of the British Interplanetary Society, Vol. 38, pp. 195-216, 1985. University of Durham, Durham, England.

11   Tsu, W. S. "The observations of Halley's comet in Chinese history". Popular Astronomy, Vol. 42. p.195. (1934) SAO. Ts ASA Astrophysics Data System (ADS). Bibliographic Code: 1934PA..42..191T.

12   *Nauigatio sancti Brendani abbatis* [the Voyage of St Brendan the Abbot]. Edition by Archbishop P. F. Moran, Translator: Denis O'Donoghue. O'Donoghue, Brendaniana. 1893.

13   John Patrick Crichton Stuart Bute. "Brendan's Fabulous Voyage" [A LECTURE DELIVERED ON JANUARY 19, 1893,

Perihelion

BEFORE THE SCOTTISH SOCIETY OF LITERATURE AND ART.] New Edition, 1911. Project Gutenberg EBook #17343. 2004.

14 Ibid.

15-23 *Nauigatio sancti Brendani abbatis.* Ibid.

24 *The Brendan Voyage*, Tim Severin.
See: https://en.wikipedia.org/wiki/Tim_Severin

25 Pat Kehoe. "Did the Irish reach America before Columbus?" https://ireland-calling.com/lifestyle/could-the-irish-have-reached-america-before-columbus/

26 *De Orben Novo The Eight Decades of Peter Martyr D'Anghera* Translated by Francis Augustus MacNutt. Vol. 2. G. P. Putnam's Sons, New York and London The knickerbocker Press. 1912. https://books.google.com

27 Kehoe. Ibid.

Byron Grush

Where Steel on Steel was Ringing

> Where battle-storm was ringing,
> Where arrow-cloud was singing,
>   Harald stood there,
>   Of armour bare,
> His deadly sword still swinging.
> The foeman feel its bite;
> His Norsemen rush to fight,
>   Danger to share,
>   With Harald there,
> Where steel on steel was ringing.
>   —— Arnor, the earls' skald.[1]

The appearance of Halley's Comet in 1066 was documented as an embroidery of wool yarn on the linen ground of a secular tapestry called the Bayeux Tapestry. The tapestry, a rare survival of Romanesque art, chronicles the events leading up to the Norman conquest of England and the rise of William the Conqueror in that year. It consists of 72 panels stitched together to form a banner 224.3 feet long and 1.6 feet high. Sequential scenes are presented in left to right order prompting modern commentators to describe it as the world's first comic book (or perhaps an elegant storyboard for future cinematic realization). But it is serious stuff. It portrays a significant turning point in the history of Great Britain.

Significant to our interests here is scene number 33. King Harold of England is seated on his throne while a group of men, frightened by the sight of the comet, gesture up at the sky. Halley's Comet is rendered above them.

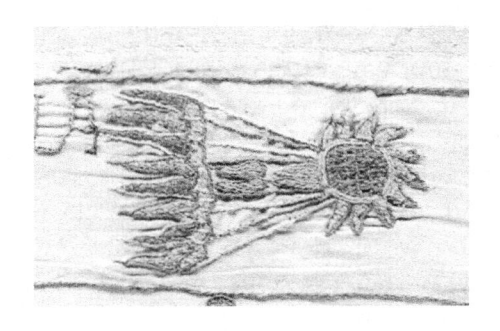

Byron Grush

The first written record of this observation of the comet is a sighting by Chinese astronomers on April 2, 1066. Elsewhere, William of Malmesbury, a medieval chronicler at Malmesbury Abbey, recorded that "...a certain monk of our monastery named Elmer, bowing down with terror at the sight of the brilliant star, wisely exclaimed 'Here art thou again, cause of tears to many mothers. It is a long time since I saw thee last, but I see thee now, more terrible than ever, thou threatenest my country with utter ruin.' "[2] Elmer may have seen the comet of 1009 which heralded the conquest of Britain by Canute. King Harold's advisors, as shown on the tapestry, may have been correct in their fear.

The comet year 1066 is a tale of two Harolds: the Saxon king Harold Godwinson (Harold with an "o"), and the Norwegian king Harald Hardrada (Harald with an "a"). Also part of the tale are Tostig Godwinson, Harold's brother, and William, Duke of Normandy, who will come to be known as William the Conqueror. It is the tale of three battles: The Battle of Gate Fulford, The Battle of Stamford Bridge, and The Battle of Hastings. And it involves a solitary defender who might be called the Last Viking.

The Bayeux Tapestry provides us with a backstory.[3] In the first scene we see the Royal Palace at Westminster in 1040. Edward the Confessor, future King of England, is talking to his brother-in-law Harold Godwinson, Earl of Wessex. Edward, one of the last Anglo-Saxon kings of England and the last of the House of Wessex, will rule England from 1042 to 1066. Next we see Harold, holding a hawk, with his followers and hunting dogs. They go to Harold's family estate at Bosham in Sussex. This must be much later. A feast is held, then Harold sails across the English Channel, possibly to obtain release of family members held hostage since his father, Earl Godwin was sent into exile there in 1051.

Harold's ship is blown off course and lands at Ponthieu where he is captured by Count Guy I of Ponthieu and taken as a hostage to the count's castle at Beaurain. Enter William, Duke of Normandy. William has been a foe of Count Guy. About the time that Edward exiled Harold's father Godwin, William visited England and became a favorite of Edward. Edward promised William he would be his successor. So now word goes to William that Harold has been taken prisoner by Guy. William demands Harold's release.

Perihelion

The Tapestry gives us a scene in which Guy obeys William's order and takes Harold to him. Guy points to Harold. Both men carry hawks. Hawks seem of some importance on the tapestry. There follow scenes in which Harold and William fight Duke Conan of Brittany. Eventually, Harold swears an oath of allegiance to William, supporting him as Edward's successor. He returns to England.

We have arrived at 1066, the year of Halley's Comet. Some more of the players: Tostig Godwinson is the Anglo-Saxon Earl of Northumbria and the brother of King Harold Godwinson. He had been exiled the previous year by King Edward because of his unjust tax practices. He will be supporting the Norwegian king Harald Hardrada's invasion of England. Edith the Fair, also known as Edith Swanneck, is the wife of King Harold Godwinson. She hasn't much to do with the story, but she has the best name. There is another Edith, Edith of Wessex, also known as Gytha or Ealdgyth, who was the daughter of Goodwin, Harold's father and therefore his sister, who married King Edward in 1045.

Turning to the tapestry. There is a new Church, Westminster Abbey, but Edward is ill and cannot attend its consecration. He will, however, be buried there. It is the 5th of January 1066. The panel is divided in two parts: Above, King Edward is in his bed talking to Harold and Queen Edith; below he is shown dead with a priest in attendance. Next, two noblemen offer Harold a crown and an axe, making him King. Apparently, Edward has indicated his wish to hand over the protection of the country to his widow and to Harold. The nobles, the Witenagemot, go along with this.

Harold is crowned King of England on 6th January 1066. Now we come to panel number 33. Here is the description: "The new king sits on a throne with nobles to the left and Archbishop Stigand to the right. At the far side people cheer him. On the far right Halley's comet appears; people think it is an evil omen and are terrified. News of the comet is brought to Harold; beneath him a ghostly fleet of ships appears in the lower border—a hint of the Norman invasion to come."[4]

March 20, Halley's Comet reaches perihelion. It is seen for two months in China. The *Anglo-Saxon Chronicles*, a chronological account of events in Anglo-Saxon and Norman England from the reign of King Alfred (871–899) until 1154, tells us:

Byron Grush

"1066. In this year King Harold came from York to Westminster during Easter, which occurred after the midwinter in which the king had died. This Easter was on the 16th day of the kalends of May. At that time round all of England were seen portents in heaven such as no man had seen before. Some said that what other men called the 'hairy' star was in fact a comet, and it first showed itself on the eve of the Greater Litany, that is the 8th of the kalends of May, and so shone all seven nights."[5]

King Harold II marries Ealdgyth, daughter of Earl Ælfgar of Mercia (his former marriage was considered not sanctioned by the Church, goodbye Edith Swanneck). This leads to an alliance with northern earls but causes his brother, Tostig, to form an alliance with King Harald Hardrada of Norway. Tostig had been unseated as earl of Northumbria by a coup led by Edwin and Morcar of the house of Ælfgar (we will meet them again later). William, Duke of Normandy, learns of King Edward's death and Harold's coronation. Harold had sworn an oath of allegiance to William but has now betrayed him. William believes he should have inherited the throne as Edward had promised. He decides to invade England. So does Tostig.

Harald with an "a", Harald Sigurdsson, son of Sigurd Syr, was born in the year AD 1015. He was called Harald Hardrade, which means severe counsellor, tyrant, ruthless ruler. Exiled from Norway in 1030 during a civil war, he returned in 1046, and became king in 1047. Magnus Magnusson, in his introduction to *King Harald's Saga*, says, "By 1066 he was the most feared warrior in northern Europe, the last of the formidable Viking kings of Scandinavia; and at the age of fifty-one he embarked on the most ambitious enterprise of his relentless career: the conquest of England."[6]

Norse court poets of the age of the Vikings were called skalds. Their poems, those which survive in texts such as *King Harald's Saga*, give us an interpretation of the history as heroic, romantic, and sometimes tragic. Skald Thiodolf describes Harald:

> *Severe alike to friends or foes,*
> *Who dared his royal will oppose;*
> *Severe in discipline to hold*
> *His men-at-arms wild and bold;*
> *Severe the bondes to repress;*

Perihelion

Severe to punish all excess;
Severe was Harald -- but we call
That just which was alike to all.[7]

And King Harald also composed verses. Here he talks about himself:

I have, in all, the death-stroke given
To foes of mine at least eleven;
Two more, perhaps, if I remember,
May yet be added to this number,
I prize myself upon these deeds,
My people such examples needs.
Bright gold itself they would despise,
Or healing leek-herb underprize,
If not still brought before their eyes.[8]

Sigurðarsonar describes him in Harald's Saga: "King Herald was a handsome man, of noble appearance; his hair and beard yellow. He had a short beard, and long mustaches. The one eyebrow was somewhat higher than the other. He had large hands and feet; but these were well made. His height was five ells. He was stern and severe to his enemies, and avenged cruelly all opposition or misdeed."[9]

Tostig Godwinson had petitioned King Svein of Denmark for help in returning to England.
"I wish to return to my estate in England," he told the king. "If you will go there with the Danish army and take the country as Canute, your uncle did, I will support you with all the power I may muster."
"I am not Canute who took England blow by blow. I have difficulty defending my own kingdom against the Norsemen."
"I must seek friendly help from unlikely quarters, then. From one who is less afraid, king, than thou art."
Tostig then went to Norway, to King Harald. Harald had been fighting for the last few years with Svein, army against army, fleet against fleet. King Harald, at that time, had little interest in invading England. Tostig would try to persuade him.

"If you will take England now, I will bring most of the principal men in England to be thy friends and assist thee."

"People say," answered Harald, "that the English are not to be trusted."

"Nothing is wanting to place me at the side of my brother Harold but the king's own desire. If you go, all men will say that there never was such a warrior in the northern lands as Harald Hardrada. It is extraordinary that thou hast been fighting for fifteen years for Denmark, and wilt not take England that lies open to thee!"

And so gradually, King Harald came around to the idea of taking the island of England for himself. On the western coast of Norway, in the group of small islands called the Solunds, he assembled a fleet of 300 war ships. His dragonship was as large and formidable as the *Long Serpent*, built by Harald Fairhair, the first king of Norway in 868, and now a thing of legend.[10] It was long enough to have benches for thirty-five rowers. On the bow the head of a great serpent looked out over the waves while its long tail graced the stern.

> *With lofty bow above the seas,*
> *Which curl and fly before the breeze,*
> *The gallant vessel rides and reels,*
> *And every plunge her cable feels.*
> *The storm that tries the spar and mast*
> *Tries the main-anchor at the last:*
> *The storm above, below the rock,*
> *Chafe the thick cable with each shock.*[11]

Tostig went to Normandy and met with William, the Duke of Normandy, sometimes called William the Bastard having been born to an unmarried father and his mistress. William needed no coaxing to invade England. He began building a fleet of ships at Saint-Valery-sur-Somme. The Bayeux Tapestry shows scenes of ship building, an array of coats of chain mail, helmets, swords and lances. William's wife Matilda (who some believe commissioned the tapestry later in 1070) bought him a ship. It was named the Mora. We see scenes of the many soldiers and a vast fleet upon the ocean, sailing toward England. William, Tostig, and Harald all have claims to the throne; all are headed to the island with their armies. William and Harald will experience some delays; Tostig will arrive first.

Perihelion

Tostig assembled a small army in Flanders and sailed toward England, landing at Wight. He picked up more men there who were loyal to him and opposed to his brother, Harold Goodwinson. He fought his way up the coast and arrived at Sandwich where he paused to await reinforcements by King Harald of Norway. It was September 1066. Harald arrived in England later than Tostig but they were able to rendezvous in the Humber estuary on 18 September. The two armies marched toward York.

Tostig, you may remember, had been unseated as the earl of Northumbria during a coup led by Edwin and Morcar of the house of Ælfgar, then was banished by his brother Harold. At this time, Edwin and Morcar, at the head of an army of their countrymen, marched to do battle with the invading Norsemen. At Gate Fulford, about half a mile from York, the two armies met. There were about 6,000 warriors on each side. But the terrain defied the two earls; along the River Ouse there was marshland that the Norwegians negotiated easily from vast experience of such battlefields.

The English split their troops between the riverbank and the marsh. Harald sent his best troops slashing their way with axe and sword right through the English along a point where the river turned. Edwin and Morcar found their two divisions cut off from each other. With Tostig and his Englishmen flanking for support, Harald then turned against the English led by Morcar on the marsh. It was, as they say, no contest.

Edwin and Morcar, seeing so many men and horses struck down or drowned, abandoned the battle and with what survivors there were, fled toward York. So many dead:

> *Lay in the fen,*
> *By sword down hewed,*
> *So thickly strewed,*
> *That Norsemen say*
> *They paved a way*
> *Across the fen*
> *For the brave Norsemen.*[12]

Byron Grush

September 25th, 1066, Stamford Bridge, Yorkshire. King Harold Godwinson had been readying an army in anticipation of an attack by William, Duke of Normandy. But William had been delayed because of weather. Harold had heard of this, and had also heard of the disastrous defeat of the earls Edwin and Morcar. He had decided there was time to deal with the Viking invasion before William arrived. A mistake? Five days ago, with his brother Gyrth and an assembly of around 15,000 men, King Harold Goodwinson had started hurrying north on an old Roman road toward Yorkshire, a distance of about 185 miles.

King Harald Hardrada and Tostig Goodwinson had negotiated the terms of York's surrender, but instead of occupying the town, had returned to their ships. They were to exchange hostages and receive bounty in the form of cattle and other goods. The Norsemen selected the site of a wooden bridge over the Derwent River at an intersection that crossed the old Roman Road. They were unaware that the English King approached. Snorri Sturluson, in *King Harald's Saga*, suggests that King Harold Goodwinson and twenty of his men approached Hardrada and Tostig at the bridge to attempt to negotiate peace. The exchange, Sturluson says, went something like this:[13]

[King Harold may have been disguised as a herald; Tostig would have recognized him but allowed the deception for some unknown reason.] King Harold addressed his brother Tostig, probably believing his disguise was working:

"Thy brother, King Harold, sends thee salutation, with the message that thou shalt have the whole of Northumberland; and rather than thou shouldst not submit to him, he will give thee the third part of his kingdom to rule over along with himself."

"This is something different from the enmity and scorn he offered last winter," Tostig answered. "And if this had been offered then it would have saved many a man's life who now is dead, and it would have been better for the kingdom of England. But if I accept of this offer, what will he give King Harald Sigurdson [Hardrada] for his trouble?"

Now King Harold Goodwinson reined back his black steed and answered, "He has also spoken of this; and will give him seven feet of English ground, or as much more as he may be taller than other men."

Perihelion

Realizing the implication that the king was referring to the grave he would prepare for Hardrada, Tostig replied, "Then go now and tell King Harold Goodwinson to get ready for battle; for never shall the Northmen say with truth that Earl Tostig left King Harald Sigurdson to join his enemy's troops, when he came to fight west here in England. We shall rather all take the resolution to die with honor, or to gain England by a victory."

King Harold and his men turned and rode away. Dumbfounded at this strange exchange, King Harald Hardrada pressed Tostig for an explanation. "Who was the man who spoke so well?" he asked.

"That was King Harold Godwinson."

"That was by far too long concealed from me; for they had come so near to our army, that this Harold should never have carried back the tidings of our men's slaughter."

"It was certainly imprudent for such chiefs, and it may be as you say; but I saw he was going to offer me peace and a great dominion, and that, on the other hand, I would be his murderer if I betrayed him; and I would rather he should be my murderer than I his, if one of two be to die," said Earl Tostig.

And Harald replied, "That was but a little man, yet he sat firmly in his stirrups."

The weather had been muggy and hot. Marching from their docked ships at Riccall to Stamford Bridge had been long and tiring, so Hardrada had allowed his warriors to not wear armor on the march. They needed only take swords, axes and spears with them, he had said, and nearly all their shields were left behind. They had relaxed, not being aware of the English army just beyond the bridge. Many sunbathed and others went swimming in the river. King Harold Goodwinson waited for the propitious moment, then attacked.

Yet the enemy was on the other side of the river. Only a narrow bridge gave access to the surprised Norwegian horde. King Harold's soldiers could only pass single file across the bridge…except. Except there was a lone warrior standing at the middle of the span wielding a wicked looking axe. This man, let's call him Olaf the Berserker for we do not know his real name, was the Last Viking, if there was to be such a person. The other Norsemen had long ago ceased being

Vikings, the likes of the first king Harald Fairhair and his sailors of the dragonships.

Olaf the Berserker swung his axe with such power that no lance or sword could reach him. The *Anglo-Saxon Chronicles* say that Olaf dispatched over 40 men, holding the English army at bay, unable to cross the bridge. The delay allowed the Norwegian army to form a shieldwall with what few shields they had. Tostig advised a holding action by leaving a rearguard and doing a quick retreat back to Riccall. Harald Hardrada refused but allowed that a runner could be sent back to tell Eystein Orri to come with all the troops that had remained with the ships. Would it be enough?

Olaf the Berserker cut many a man in twain. The bridge ran with their blood and spilled into the Derwent tinting it with crimson rivulets. One of the Englishmen found a half-barrel upstream and turned it into a small boat. In this he floated down and under the Stamford Bridge. With a quick thrust of his lance between the floorboards he skewered Olaf the Berserker like a stuck pig. The Last Viking fell and with his death the way was open for King Harold's attack.

The Norsemen were arrayed in a defensive circle on a small hill called High Catton. The lack of shields and armor and the sudden surprise of the attack left them at a disadvantage. Yet Hardrada called for action. Snorri Sturluson tells that King Harald Hardrada composed these verses at that time to rally his troops:

Advance! advance!
No mail-coats glance,
But hearts are here
That ne'er knew fear.

In battle storm we seek no lee,
With skulking head, and bending knee,
Behind the hollow shield.
With eye and hand we fend the head;
Courage and skill stand in the stead
Of panzer, helm, and shield,
In hild's bloody field.[14]

Perihelion

The Englishmen streamed across the bridge in single file, their horses' hoofs clattering against the bloodstained wooden slats. They circled the Norse shieldwall thrusting long spikes wherever they could find an opening. Slowly the Norsemen were pushed back. Now sword against axe and pike against lance, the carnage was grim on both sides. The valiant Vikings, however, were not to be victorious; hundreds fell, lacking armor and shields and being fatigued from their recent battle at Gate Fulford. Where was Eystein Orri?

King Harald Hardrada wore a coat of mail which was so long that it reached to the middle of his legs; it was impenetrable to sword or arrow. But an arrow found his unprotected throat. He was down. Dismayed, the Norsemen still fought, but perhaps not as enthusiastically now that their king was dead. Then, says Snorri Sturluson, Thiodolf sang these verses:

> *The army stands in hushed dismay;*
> *Stilled is the clamour of the fray.*
> *Harald is dead, and with him goes*
> *The spirit to withstand our foes.*
> *A bloody scat the folk must pay*
> *For their king's folly on this day.*
> *He fell; and now, without disguise,*
> *We say this business was not wise.*[15]

King Harold Godwinson offered his brother, Earl Tostig, peace, and offered quarter to the remaining Norsemen. Tostig was agreeable, but the Norsemen decided to fight on, to die with their beloved king. The battle began again. Eystein Orri now arrived with his men, having marched double time 18 miles in full armor. This, in Norse legend, is celebrated as "Orri's Storm." Although he fought gallantly, by nightfall, the Norsemen were all but annihilated. Orri was dead, Tostig was dead, a truce was signed on the condition the Norsemen leave England forever; only 24 ships from the fleet of over 300 were needed to carry the survivors away.

Bayeux Tapestry, scene 43: William Duke of Normandy and his troops had reached the south coast of England on the 28th of September and landed at Pevensey. They had been unopposed and settled in to build a fort. In this panel we see that a feast is being prepared with skewered chickens and a stew cooked over an open fire. Servants carry food to the banquet on their shields. Bishop Odo says a grace. William speaks words of encouragement to his men. There is a scene in which the Norman soldiers burn a house, a woman flees with her child.

King Harold and his army have not yet recovered from their battle with the Norsemen at Stamford Bridge when a messenger arrives with news that William has landed and is camped near Hastings. Perhaps, Harold thinks, they can surprise the invaders. They begin another march, this time south to engage the enemy. But William has scouts out looking for the English and learns of their approach. William also begins to move.

It is October 14, 1066. The battle takes place near Hastings, East Sussex, England. The English, led by King Harold Godwinson, his brothers Gyrth Godwinson, and Leofwine Godwinson, are on foot. Their strength will be in the skill of their archers. The Normans, led by William of Normandy and Alan the Red, have an infantry as well as a calvary. Men on horseback charge against the shields of the English, breaking their defense. Perhaps if Harold had not stopped on his way to engage the Norsemen... The tapestry depicts the bloody battle:

"As the air fills with arrows and lances, men lie dying. The lower border of the tapestry is filled with dead and injured soldiers. The violence continues as men hack and spear each other to death. Harold's brothers both die fighting. The battle rages on; men and horses crash to the ground, the lower border is strewn with slaughtered troops and animals. Bishop Odo appears in the thick of the fighting waving a club and encouraging his followers."[16]

Duke William falls from his horse, alarming the Normans. He raises his helmet to show he is unharmed. The tapestry shows one of William's men, Count Eustace, carrying a banner given them by Pope Alexander II to show his support for their invasion of England. More scenes of gruesome confrontation; a man's head is cut off and the field is strewn with bodies. There are captions embroidered on the Bayeux Tapestry describing scenes or identifying people. Near the end of the tapestry are two scenes with the title, "Harold." Each shows the death of a warrior, one in which an arrow has found the man's eye, another in which he is being hacked to death. The caption on the second scene says, "he is slain." The Normans are victorious.

Perihelion

Harold's body was found on the battlefield the following morning. Legend has it that Harold's mother, Gytha, offered to pay the weight of her son in gold for his body; William refused and had the body thrown into the sea.[17] Alternately, Harold may have been buried at Waltham Abbey in secret. William continued his conquest of England, raiding and burning from town to town and finally entered London. He was crowned King of England in Westminster Abbey on Christmas Day of 1066.

---

1   Skald Arnor. *Haralds saga Sigurðarsonar* (*Saga of Harald Hardrade*).
https://www.sacred-texts.com/neu/heim/10harald.htm.

2   "…in the archives of the cathedral at Viterbo, Italy: 'In the vear 1066 from the incarnation of the Lord, on April 5th a comet appeared in the East, and shone for fifteen days, i.e. until the 19th, and the same appeared in the West in the evening on the 21th, like the eclipsed Moon, the tail of which streamed like smoke, up to nearly half of the sky.'

…a Korean chronicler reports that '…a star like the moon rose in the northwest. Presently it transformed into a comet…'

The Byzantine record states '…a hairy star was seen at Constantinople following sunset, which at first equalled the full moon in size, then with a tail and diminished…'

In his contemporary History of the Normans, written in 1070, William of Jumicges reported: 'In those days in the part of the circle (ecliptic?) a comet appeared which with three long extended rays illuminated a very great part of the south for the space of fifteen nights.'

The fragmentary Frankish History relates: 'At the same time a comet appeared, for nearly three months, sending out many rays to the south…' "

——Botley, C. M. & White, R. E. "Halley's Comet in 1066". Astronomical Society of the Pacific Leaflets, Vol. 10, No. 452, No. 452, p. 9-16. 1967.

3   The Victorian replica of the Tapestry; The Reading Museum & Town Hall website. http://www.bayeuxtapestry.org.uk/Index.htm.

4   Ibid.

5   *The Anglo-Saxon Chronicles*, quoted by Todd B. Krause and Jonathan Slocum in "Old Norse Online, Lesson 7". http://www.utexas.edu/cola/centers/lrc/eieol/norol-7-X.html.

6   Magnus Magnusson and Herman Palsson, translators. *King Harald's Saga, From Snorri Sturluson's Heimskringla*. (Introduction). Penguin Books. 1980.

7   Thiodolf. *Haralds saga Sigurðarsonar (Saga of Harald Hardrade)*. https://www.sacred-texts.com/neu/heim/10harald.htm.

8   *Saga of Harald Hardrade*.

9   Ibid.

10 Snorri Sturluson, *The Saga of Olaf Tryggvason*, quoted in an article on Norwegian King Olav Tryggvason:
    https://penelope.uchicago.edu/~grout/encyclopaedia_romana/britannia/anglo-saxon/maldon/longserpent.html.

11 Thiodolf. *Haralds saga Sigurðarsonar*.

12 "Harald's Stave." *Saga of Harald Hardrade*.

13 Snorri Sturluson. *Saga of Harald Hardrade*.

14 Ibid.

15 Ibid.

16 The Victorian replica of the Tapestry; The Reading Museum & Town Hall website. http://www.bayeuxtapestry.org.uk/Index.htm.

17   Huscroft, Richard. *The Norman Conquest: A New Introduction.* New York: Longman. 2009.

Angel or Devil

By the Armenian calendar it is the year 671. The Berbers call it 2172. In Byzantium it is between 6730 and 6731, by the Coptic calendar it is between 938 and 939, and for Hebrews it is between 4982 and 4983. The Chinese calendar points to Metal Snake and Water Horse. The Julian calendar (and the Gregorian calendar which won't go into effect until 1582) say it is 1222.

There is a major earthquake of the magnitude of 7 to 7.5 in Cyprus in May. It unleashes a tsunami that reaches Libya and Alexandria. The byzantine fort at Paphos collapses and has to be abandoned. The sea retreats but returns with a vengeance, destroying the town. There is no record of the death toll, which is considerable.

The Crusades have begun fizzling out. In 1219 Papal forces under Pelagio Galvani (1165 – 1230) were in Egypt trying to wrest control of Damiette from al-Kamil. The sultan wanted to negotiate and offered to trade Damiette for Jerusalem but Pelagio rejected this. Pelagio eventually occupied the port but needed reinforcements. The Holy Roman Emperor Frederick II failed to supply the needed troops. Nevertheless, the Crusaders in 1221 began a march on Cairo. Some of the soldiers deserted. Al-Kamil attacked their flanks repeatedly. The Nile River flooded, disease and starvation resulted and there were many deaths. Pelagio was forced to surrender. The Fifth Crusade was a staggering defeat. There were other complications. Pope Innocent had secured the participation of Georgia's powerful army in the crusade. Now in 1222, the Moguls under Genghis Khan are invading Georgia.

This year, Japanese astronomers record the sighting of a star as large as a half moon, whose color is white with red rays. The star is Halley's Comet. In Mongolia, Genghis Khan also takes note of the star. He claims it as his personal star, an omen telling him that the conquest of Europe is his destiny. It is his Angel number 1222[1], an energetic guardian angel assuring him of heaven's help with his ambitions if only he will be governed by intuition and the harmony of nature. Or perhaps, it is his Devil number 1222.

In the Caucasus Region of Central Asia between the Caspian Sea and the Black Sea lies the Kingdom of Georgia. The reigning dynasty,

Perihelion

the Bagrationi or House of Bagrat, is said to have descended from the biblical prophet King David. The present monarch is George IV (also known as Giorgi Lasha), the son of the former regnant, Queen Tamar the Great[2]. King George IV is known as javakht' up'ali, or "Lord of the Javakhans." He has been forced to divorce his wife by the Christian clergy and the nobles in his council because of her status as a commoner. Saddened, he has refused to marry again and prefers the company of ladies loose of morals regardless of their status. He is a bit of a mystic and, although a Christian, has been accused of the study of Islamic Sufism[3].

The capital city of the Kingdom of Georgia is Tbilisi. It sits in the Southern Caucasus Mountains between the Saguramo Range and the plains of Lori and Trialet, straddling both banks of the Mt'k'vai River. Because of its proximity to the Silk Road, Tbilisi is an important center of commerce and industry. This is the height of the Georgian Golden Age. The wealth and cultural heritage of the Kingdom is showcased here in the palace. Mosaics depicting scenes from the Georgian Orthodox Bible rendered in the Byzantine style of two-dimensional representation share wall space with scenes of Georgian military history.

The Lady Rusudan[4] is seated on an embroidered divan in her quarters in the palace. Her costume is that of the royal family, geometric patterns offset by rows of large pearls against a violet velvet background, a silver inlaid belt, sleeves encrusted with precious metals, and a high collar, not unlike that of an Egyptian princess. Indeed, she is a princess, the daughter of Queen Tamar and the sister of King George IV. She closes the book she is reading. It is an epic poem entitled "The Knight in the Panther's Skin" written by Shota Rustaveli and dedicated, although not outwardly, to her mother.

It is a favorite of hers, expressing the ideals of courtly love, friendship, and the celebration of a ruler of strength and character—and beauty and femininity. She loves the story of the two friends, Avtandil and Tariel as they strive to rescue their love, Nestan-Darejan. The poet decries forced marriages, another reason she admires the poem. Like her brother the King, she has resisted pressures from the council (and ironically, the King) to remarry. Her first and only marriage was a disaster[5] lasting the few years to give her a son and a daughter, but no longer. She has other notions; her mother was Queen, why not she? She is next in line for the succession and these turbulent days, anything might happen. Besides, there are plenty of male suitors to satisfy her romantic and sexual needs. If her brother can have concubines, why not she? She will be a Nestan-Darejan to some Avtandil or Tariel when the time suits her.

Rusudan's nephew, David VII Ulu is at her door beckoning to enter. She nods. The boy is seven years of age and quite precocious. Some day he may wish to become king and he may challenge her[5]. It is never too soon to be wary of the young. Rusudan would like to follow in her mother's footsteps and become the second female monarch of Georgia. This boy could present a problem.

"Father wants to see you," says David. "He is going to war. I want to go too but he will not allow it."

"Silly boy," says Rusudan, "there is plenty of time for you be a soldier. There is always a war going on somewhere."

"Aunt Rusudan, could you talk to father?"

"I'll consider it, but David, if your father goes into battle, you must remain here to help me keep the kingdom in good order until his return." It would not do, she thinks to herself, to have the boy killed on the battlefield, now would it?

Beholding the stars
Being one having a pillow of earth[6]

The sentinel guarding the royal yurt of Genghis Khan looks up at the bright star and ponders its purport. The great Khan has said it is a good omen, therefore it must be so. Since 1206 the man named Temüjin Borjigin from the Khentil Mountains has had the title of Genghis Khan, or Chinggis Khaan as it is spelled in Mongolian, which means "universal, oceanic, and firm/strong ruler and lord." The sentinel is serving in an honored position as a night guard. Of all Genghis Khan's soldiers, the nightguards are the most revered. It will be written in the *Secret History* that the great Khan said:

My sincere-hearted nightguards
Which, in the snowstorm which is moving,
In the cold which is making one to shiver,
In the rain which is pouring down.
Standing, not taking their rest.
Round about my tent with a frame of lattice,
Have caused my heart to be at peace

Perihelion

Have thus made me to attain unto the throne of joy.
My trusty nightguards
Which, in the midst of enemies which are making trouble.
Round about my tent with a band of felt
Have, not winking an eye, Stood, staying their assault.[7]

Inside of the yurt Genghis Khan and his first wife Börte Üjin Khatun are relaxing on a fur cushion, enjoying a cup of wine while two of their sons, Jochi and Ögedei, are sitting cross-legged on the floor. Each has a small wooden box in which a giant centipede is raveling and unraveling in furious anger against its imprisonment. The two young men have participated in the military campaigns of their father's in China and Iran and now in Central Asia, and they often compete for his attention. The Khan will not live forever and these siblings have ambitions of grandeur appropriate to the offspring of the world's greatest, and bloodiest, warlord.

They have marked off a circle on the yurt floor and placed the boxes at either side of this, waiting for the moment when their father notices the grim contest which is about to begin. The Khan looks upon the scene and smiles. "Death worms?[8]" he asks. "Be careful not to touch them. Highly poisonous!"

The boxes are opened and the insects scurry out. Börte has witnessed this horrifying game before, but she never delights in it the way her sons do. In fact, she gives a little gasp and stands, preparing to leave the yurt. Her husband grabs her arm and forces her back down upon the cushion. "It is life and death," he tells her. "It is avenging the avengement, requiting the requital. It is fitting you should watch."

The insects run at each other. When they meet their jaws seek a purchase each upon the other's slimy, worm-like body. They are locked together and roll about, emitting sounds like the screams of eagles, impossibly loud for such small creatures. Jochi and Ögedei urge them on. A black fluid which must be centipede blood is spreading on the floor. Suddenly, they are still. One has been victorious and now begins to consume his enemy. Which son has won? It is impossible to tell under the slime and gore. The victor begins to slither away from the circle. Jochi smashes it under his heavy boot.

Byron Grush

"Jochi," says Genghis Khan, "go you to find Subutai and Jebe, those two of my Four Dogs[9], and bring them here. We have much to discuss."

Rusudan has entered the day chamber of King George IV. She finds him arrayed in a short kuartis wildly embroidered with floral elements and wearing the sharply pointed crown usually reserved for formal occasions. Attending to the King is his tutor, a most important advisor and former general of the Georgian army, Ivane Zararian. Although Armenians, Ivane and his brother Zakare had been military commanders under Queen Tamar and had taken the town of Ani and all the surrounding towns, greatly extending the territory of Georgia. Tamar had granted them Ani and the City of Dvin in recognition of their service and from there they ruled Eastern Armenia.

King George IV sees in Zararian a wise and experienced warrior. Rusudan just sees an old man. Yet this old man had been victorious in battle and now the King needs his leadership to protect his country against the Mongol invasions from the south.

"Welcome, Sister," says King George IV. "The news has been dire. These barbarians have devastated the Khwarezmid Empire of Shah Ala ad-Din Muhammad. It was thought that the Shah's vast armies could easily hold the Mongols at bay, but it has not been so."

"Perhaps," comments Zararian, "he had spread his forces too thinly across Persia. And this Genghis Khan has used the Chinese catapult to fling projectiles of exploding powder at their enemy. They are masters at inspiring fear. Did you know that at Urgench, once that city had fallen, the women and children were given to the soldiers as slaves and many of the remaining civilians were massacred. It is said the Khan ordered each of his soldiers to kill 24 men apiece."

"The Khwarazmian Empress Terken Khatun has been taken captive and the Shah himself has fled to India," says King George IV. There have been Mongol attacks in the north of Armenia and our own cities in the south have been looted. These are affronts and bode of the danger of all-out war."

"But why, my brother," asks Rusudan, "do you summon me now? I cannot advise you in matters of war."

Perihelion

"My good friend Ivane Zararian is amassing his troops and with the preparations we made to give aid for the Crusades, our combined forces are considerable. We are preparing to meet these barbarians and once and for all put an end to their aggression. Thus I will lead my army at its forefront. It is meet and right that I should designate a regent to rule in my absence and, if fate should prove ill…"

"You will appoint your son, young David Ulu, no doubt. And, because of his age, you desire that I should oversee his application of this duty."

"He is very young and, I am afraid, a bit hot-headed."

"Our mother, Queen Tamar, once assured me that *I* would become the reigning monarch of Georgia. Yet when the time came she chose you as regent."

"The nobles and the council would not relish another female as king. This was not our mother's choice. And I am first born. Have I not been a good ruler?"

"Yes, my lord and brother, you have been true to our mother's vision. And now you strive to ward off the barbarians."

"This is what I would do. I would make you regent with the stipulation that David would be heir upon your demise. I would have you journey now to the winter palace in Geguti. That is a stronger fortification than this. I would have you take the prince with you and guard him well during the coming conflict."

"Do you fear the outcome of engaging battle with these barbarians?"

"Have you not seen the new star in the heavens? It has a broad aura that trails it like the tail of a falcon. This may be a bad omen. Yes, I have fear, but I have courage and confidence in my soldiers and in Ivane. We shall be victorious."

Rusudan looks at her brother—the King, splendid in his regalia and his crown. Yes, she will go to Geguti Palace and watch over her nephew. It may be that she will not see George IV again. If that is the outcome of his foolish war-waging, what will become of the country? If the campaign against the Mongols is not successful, what use is it to become queen? Queen of a conquered nation, subject to the whims of the barbarian hordes. But she acquiesces.

"I will take young David with me to the winter palace," she says. "It will be safe there. But you must keep yourself safe as well. Do not think to lead from the front when it is wise to lead from some vantage point where arrows cannot find your breast. Let Ivane take the forefront. Heed my wishes in this."

The King sadly nods. But will he take heed?

Mongol General Subutai

"It *is* a good omen," Genghis Khan is saying to his "Dogs," Subutai and Jebe who have come to the yurt by his command. "The bright star with a tail is like a friendly dragon in the heavens. Good luck shines upon us."

"We have been successful in Azerbaijan and in Iran, oh Great Khan," says Subutai. "How may we now serve you?"

"In the year of the hare when we passed by Arai and set forth against the Sarta'ul people and I assigned my son Ögedei to the task and I sent you, Jebe, as vanguard and you, Subutai, as succorer of Jebe, and I said go you to the yonder side of the Sultan and when we arrive, assault him from your side. Do you remember this manner of strategy?"

"This flanking attack is brilliance. It has sprung from your superior wisdom, oh Great Khan."

[Author's note: some of the following dialog, complete with metaphor and allusion, is based on passages from *The Secret History of the Mongols*.[10] I have tried to retain its poetic flavor.]

Perihelion

"And will you, Subutai, and you, Jebe, be sent forth again by me to press the necks of the mighty ones and the buttocks of the strong men, and shatter the stones at the moment I say, and smash the cliffs, breaking the bright stones, cutting asunder the deep waters?"

"This will I do," says Subutai. "I shall rush forward for you so as to cleave the deep water asunder."

"And I also rush forward for you so as to break the bright stones," says Jebe. "And if I am caused to die by the Khan, I shall remain rotting on a piece of ground the size of the palm of a hand."

"Go you then to prepare your troops. Tomorrow we run like a straw-yellow horse with a curved back to encircle the enemy. We ride with four horses apiece against the Georgians! Avenging the avengement. Requiting the requital!"

The two generals are unique among Genghis Khan's commanders. Subutai is not a Mongol but was born into a neighboring tribe called the Uriankhal or Reindeer People in the wilderness along the Onon River around 1175. He came as a 14-year-old boy to work as a servant for Genghis Khan. He rose quickly through the ranks and now is the chief commander and strategist of the Khan's forces. Jebe had been born Jirqo'adal and had come from the Besud clan of the Taichud tribe, one of the warring factions in conflict with Genghis Khan's Mongols. He had wounded Genghis Khan in the neck with an arrow during the Battle of Thirteen Sides in 1201 and was captured. Because he confessed to wounding the Khan and because of his prowess in war, Genghis Khan did not execute him but caused him to serve in the Mongol army, renaming him Jebe. He has been, like Subutai, one of the most important and successful generals for the Mongols.

After Subutai and Jebe have left the tent, Ögedei asks, "Father, will you again send me to lead the cavalry?"

"This I shall do," answers Genghis Khan.

"Am I your heir?" he asks bluntly. "When your body like a great tree falls down, to whom will you bequeath your people like unto stalks of hemp?"

The Great Khan only grumbles and turns away.

"When your body like unto the base of a pillar tumbles down, to whom will you bequeath your people like unto a flock of birds?"

"Go and assemble your war gear, your scimitar and your bow, and cease your bothering," answers Genghis Khan.

Byron Grush

The Royal Palace in Geguti began as a one-room hunting lodge in the eighth century. The room is still a central part of the structure and features a fireplace large enough to simultaneously roast an entire stag and a brace of fowl. The structure, expanded by King George III, has a cruciform shape with massive walls and four round towers at the corners. The fortification, four tiers of brick rising from a stone plinth, lies on an escarpment along the Rioni river just south of Kutaisi. It was here that George III proclaimed his daughter, Tamar, to be his regent, and here that rebellious nobles staged a failed coup against her to crown Prince Yuri Bogolyubsky as presumptive king.

Rusudan enters through the pillared north doorway and walks from the vestibule past a bathhouse and the servant quarters. In the central hall she looks up at the domed ceiling, a cupola over 45 feet in diameter. She then climbs the staircase to the royal quarters. Frescos of hunting scenes adorn the walls. There are windows with glass panes and tapestries woven of fine wool from the Caspian mountains. The furniture is gilded. On a divan in the king's bedroom reclines David Ulu. Rusudan is furious.

"You are to occupy the rooms in the west wing, David," she says, the anger in her voice not disguised. "The king's chambers will be my abode during our sojourn here in Geguti Palace."

"I may be king in due time, what with father at war and in constant danger," replies the boy. "Father wishes you to marry Sultan Melik of Khlat, the ruler of Persia. You will be far from these environs soon."

"This is none of your concern, boy. I will not marry the Persian Sultan. Nor the Shah of Shirvan,[11] nor any of the suitors my brother submits to me. And you would be wise to be more concerned for your father's wellbeing."

The boy smirks, but slowly rises from the divan and walks from the room. His gait is hesitant, like a confused hare retreating from an approaching fox, inching its way through thick brush.

"I'm going to the monastery at Bagarti Catheral this afternoon to visit your Grandmother Tamar's tomb," she calls to the boy as he exits. "You are welcome to come with me. Perhaps some sense of history and tradition would give you a better perspective." There is no reply.

Perihelion

The Kür River, "the river that eats its way through the mountains," flows through a vast lowland south of the Greater Caucasus Mountains as it makes its way to the Caspian Sea. Here near the steppes of the Caucasus are rolling meadows of wildflowers and tall grasses that give way to an arid plain in the Kura-Aras Basin. The conditions here are both familiar and favorable to the armies of Genghis Khan which have reached Ganja in western Azerbaijan and ravaged the town. They are camped along the Berduji River, a tributary of the Kür, and here they are engaged in building catapults from the local trees, a practice which allows them to move swiftly when on the march, not having to drag along heavy engines of war.

To the northwest the Kür skirts the environs of the Georgian capital, Tbilisi. Here King George IV has assembled his knights, armed and armored and ready for battle. Ivane Zararian has brought his Armenian army and together, they number in the tens of thousands, three times the strength of the barbarian hordes. The calvary, seated upon horses armored with chain mail, carry lances and bows and shields emblazoned with the Georgian coat of arms. Foot soldiers carry heavy broadswords like those of the Knights Templar. They are orderly and have been training for over a year in anticipation of joining the Pope's forces in the Fifth Crusade. But the Crusade will have to wait.

The Mongols have pitched tents close to the river. In the center of their encampment are corralled their horses, the mares hobbled to make milking them for the Mongols' food supply easier. Wagons are used to form the corral fence and these are piled high with thousands of arrows and extra quivers, as well as cast iron containers filled with gunpowder called "the heaven-shaking thunder bombs," These will be used during the siege of a city, fused and lit and hurled by catapult over city walls. So too, the longer arrows can be set aflame and shot from heavy crossbows. But the siege engines are less useful when the army encounters an enemy force on a battlefield.

Jebe and Subutai have taken prisoners from the cities they have raided on the outskirts of the Kingdom of Georgia. In case of a battle with an organized force in the open, the prisoners and some defectors will become a kharash for the Mongols, that is, they will be placed as a vanguard in the front lines, taking the brunt of the first arrow barrage and becoming human shields. Very few will survive.

Byron Grush

Now on the outskirts of Tbilisi, King George IV is astride his horse facing the assembled troops. He speaks in a loud voice and his speech will be answered with cheers and the raising of halyards:

"People, my brothers, you have one spirit and one faith! You know how great it is to die for your faith and the Gospel of Christ. We always bless those who follow Christ's steps and die for Him with their perishable bodies. You see how much better it is to die manfully than to linger from a wasting disease, for the good example and your good name will remain forever with us. Knights! The best among us will be the one who strikes the standard-bearer, for destroying him will mean delivering a deadly blow. Now, my winged lions, take lances and pikes and strike those who do not believe in the divinity of the One, who sacrificed himself for our sake!"[12]

Ivane Zararian has sent spies out the night before to determine the Mongol strength. Subutai and Jebe, also having spied on the Georgians, know the enemy's numbers are greater than their own and so they resort to a clever trick: they cause each camp site to light five fires instead of the usual one, thereby making it seem they are a larger force than in reality. But the false estimate returned to the Georgian army by their spies is no deterrent for Ivane and King George IV. They are confident in their own prowess, and after all, God is on their side.

In the sky above, Halley's comet has reached its perihelium; it is bright enough to be seen in the daylight. King George sees that it is shaped like a crescent moon—the comet has two tails. This reminds him of the many Muslim empires Georgia has conquered, especially during the reign of his mother, Queen Tamar. Perhaps it is not an omen of evil after all. It is a sign, however, that will mark the occasion of this, the Battle of the Khunan Plain.

Genghis Khan has not accompanied his troops on this particular invasion of Central Asia, instead he has sent two of his sons, perhaps to learn how each of them will fare during the campaign. Jochi is the eldest and expects to become Khan after his father dies. He will prove to be a disappointment to the Great Khan who will instead, name his third son, Ögedei as his heir. Jochi and Ögedei have also seen the comet in the sky. Their father has told them it is a good luck dragon. Judging by the superior numbers of the approaching Georgian army, they will need that good luck.

Perihelion

"We should retreat," says Jochi. "The Georgians have many knights, many archers. We are out in the open here."

"My dear brother," says Ögedei, "you never fail to amaze me. Of course, the Georgians will expect a retreat. Here is what I propose. I will send Jebe and one third of our force to the north. To the south I will send Subutai with an equal number. They will go just so far that the dust from their horses will not be visible. You will take the kharash and a small number of our best archers and advance toward the Georgians once we see their dust. I shall remain here readying the catapults and the large crossbows."

Jochi frowns at his brother's arrogance in taking command, but he listens. Ögedei continues:

"You will begin to engage the enemy but, and I think you are well suited for this, you will feign a retreat, rushing back to this camp. The Georgians will follow. Once they are within range I will loose the heaven-shaking thunder bombs. This will be a signal for Jebe and Subutai to attack their flanks. We will have at them from three sides. That is my plan. Our father would do the same."

Jochi is not happy, especially with the implication that he is a coward, but he agrees. The strategy is set in motion. There is little time for it, as the Georgians are advancing, slowly, but with resolve. They are disciplined and orderly. The Mongols, though, are used to fighting in small independent groups. Their command structure allows their individual captains to make spur of the moment decisions. And the ruse they are orchestrating has been successful before. Not everything will be up to the good, or bad luck of the comet.

No, Jochi is no coward. He is as clever as his brother, although perhaps more conservative. He retrieves from the spoils of the city of Ganja a large wooden cross they had taken from its monastery. He instructs his flag bearer to carry this symbol of the enemy's religion at the front of the vanguard as they march toward the Georgian army. He knows it will confuse and disorient them just long enough for an advantage, however slight.

The Georgian army also has a cross-bearer. As they march toward the enemy camp they climb a small hill. Once on top the cross-bearer who leads the formation looks down to see the approaching enemy. But what is this? They also carry a large cross. Are they Christians too? He stops, halting the march momentarily.

Byron Grush

Word goes back through the ranks and reaches the commander of the advance guard. This man turns his mount and rides to report to General Zararian. Just as he reaches the general, a barrage of arrows thick as a swarm of hornets, slams into the Georgian's advance guard. The metal armor they wear deflects most of the arrows, yet some find a mark in an exposed neck or a horse's flank.

There is a yell as Jochi's warriors rush the Georgian army. The wooden cross has been dropped. Now, shields up and lances thrusting forward, the Georgians begin to move again. Mongols on swift horses attack the advancing vanguard of Georgians who are on foot. Scimitars swing down with deadly accuracy. The heavy broadswords the knights carry are too unwieldy to be much use against the mounted enemy. The Mongol horsemen use stirrups which allow them to stand while riding and so to shoot arrows with accuracy as the horses' four feet leave the ground.

The Mongol hoard has damaged the enemy vanguard severely, yet the superior numbers of the Georgians take a toll. Jochi makes his decision. A trumpet sounds and the Mongols turn and retreat toward the Mongol camp. A fast rider has been sent ahead to warn Ögedei who is ready with catapults armed with gunpowder bombs and arrows in cocked crossbows which can be set aflame quickly. Ögedei sees that Jochi and his men have nearly reached the camp but waits until they are clear. The mounted knights of the enemy are raising dust within range. Now Ögedei gives the order to send the rain of fire and brimstone down upon them.

Jebe and Subutai have observers on the plain. Seeing the arc of flaming arrows and hearing the explosions of the heaven-shaking thunder bombs, they ride to their generals to give the signal. The Georgian army has reached the Mongol camp and hand to hand fighting has begun. But Ivane's and George's forces are diminished and demoralized, wounded and fatigued. The Mongols fight with a fury that seems superhuman. And now two more Mongol armies are attacking from both sides.

Ögedei brings out another gunpowder weapon acquired from the wars with the Chinese: the flying fire lance. This consists of a long tube of layers of rolled paper stuffed with charcoal, iron fragments and gunpowder. When the fuse is lit it can shoot flames for more than ten feet and it is light enough to be carried by an infantry man. Several of his foot soldiers are outfitted with these, others have battle

Perihelion

axes and lances. The Mongols try not to injure the enemy horses as they will take as many as they can as the spoils of war. The knights are another matter. They do not make good slaves and they tend to fight to the death. The ones that do survive the Battle of Khunan will run away.

King George IV sits high on his battle steed. He shouts words of encouragement to his troops, troops whose numbers are now pathetically small. Suddenly, an arrow strikes him in the neck, the only unprotected area of his body. He slips from the horse. His attendants immediately rush to his aid. Ivane Zararian makes a decision—with the monarch down and possibly dead, it is time to withdraw. The King is laid out in a wagon and as the trumpet sounds the retreat the Georgian army limps away in the only direction left open to them: back to Tbilisi. The Mongols let them go; they will catch up to them later.

Historians will point to the Battle of Khunan as the turning point in the Mongol conquest of Georgia. They will continue raiding Georgian cities and by 1240 Georgia will be under Mongol dominance. King George IV will survive his wound but later this year he will travel to Bagavan in Armenia to negotiate Rusudan's marriage to the Shah of Shirvan where he will fall ill and die. Rusudan will become the second female "king" of Georgia but will never live up to her mother's greatness. Her nephew David VII Ulu will eventually become king but he will have to rule jointly with Rusudan's son, David VI Narin. The Golden Age will be over for Georgia.

Genghis Khan will die in 1227 and his third son, Ögedei, will become Khan. The empire will continue to expand through Asia and into Europe, eventually becoming twice the size of the Roman Empire at its height. Mongol conquests will range from Persia, Armenia, Burma, China, India, Japan, and Korea, to Russia, Poland, Bulgaria, and Serbia. After the death of Kublai Khan in 1294 the empire will begin to disintegrate into competing factions. By 1335 the end will be beginning for the Mongol Empire.

Halley's Comet will return in 1301.

---

1   In the King James version of the Christian Bible, Psams 91 makes reference to the concept of God sending angels to "keep thee

in all ways." Although the Bible only specifies seven angels, a certain school of thought suggests there may be millions. From believers in Tarot and numerology (and possibly people that dance with snakes) comes the idea of Angel number 1222. The number 1 refers to the first book of the Old Testament, Genesis, which stands for creation and beginnings. The number 2, which is repeated three times, symbolizes unity, perhaps since Genesis contains a lot of "begetting." Doreen Virtue, a writer and Angel Therapist Practitioner, claims that guardian angels are alerting you to the path of your destiny when they show you the number 1222. From Psalms 91:

> *11 For he will command his angels concerning you*
> *to guard you in all your ways;*
> *12 they will lift you up in their hands,*
> *so that you will not strike your foot against a stone.*
> *13 You will tread on the lion and the cobra;*
> *you will trample the great lion and the serpent.*

2   Queen Tamar the Great was the daughter of George III. She became the first female ruler of Georgia (called "King Tamar" because there was no term for a ruling queen) and is known for advancing the prestige and power of the country during her reign. She survived a coup orchestrated by her husband Yury Bogolyubsky, the prince of Novgorod. She was married twice, the second marriage producing George IV and his sister, Rusudan. In 1208 the Georgian city of Ani was attacked and 12,000 Christians were killed. Queen Tamar retaliated conquering the Persian cities of Tabriz, Arbabil, Khoy, and Qazvin. Legend has it that she attempted to obtain the relics of the True Cross, once held in a Georgian Monastery in Jerusalem and taken as booty by Saladin, by offering him 200,000 gold pieces, but she failed to regain it. For more information on the most famous "female king" in history, see https://www.wikiwand.com/en/Tamar_of_Georgia.

3   Sufism is a mystical practice within Islam concerned with the purification of the inner self. Also known as Tasawwuf, it is the science of the soul using intuition and emotion for the direct experience of Allah.

Perihelion

4   Rusudan (1194 – 1245) is the daughter of Queen Tamar by David Soslan and the brother of George IV. There are several other Georgian women, some queens, who were named Rusudan and their histories are sometimes confused in various sources. There is the possibly illegitimate daughter of George IV and an unknown mother, and the daughter of David VI of Georgia and his first wife Theodora, and there is the daughter of David VII Ulu (the son of George IV) and one of three possible mothers.

In *The Chronicle of Michael Panaretos*, translated from the Greek by Scott Kennedy aka. Basileos Nestor, this is found: "Theodora Komnene, the first daughter of lord Manuel the Grand Komnenos by Russadan from Iberia." Rusudan of Georgia, Empress of Trebizond was the second Empress consort of Manuel I of Trebizond and according to another source, reigned during the 1240s and 1250s. (*Our* Rusudan was Queen of Georgia following her brother's death from 1223 to 1225.) Trebizond was a client state of Georgia, created by Tamar in 1204 until 1227, and under control of the Mogul empire from 1243 to 1336. It is more likely that this Rusudan was the daughter of George IV and not his sister.

It was apparently common to name children after their parents or grandparents. There was a Rusudan who was the daughter of King Demetrius I and sister of Kings David V and George III, and a Rusudan who was the younger daughter of King George III and sister to Queen Tamar, but these two women are not to be confused with *our* Rusudan. According to Wikipedia, "very little is known about her." The definitive genealogical description!

5   *The Georgian Chronicles* of Kartlis Tskhovreba refer to a certain prince of Seljug, the son of the emir of Erzurum, who was being held as a hostage at the Georgian court. His name was Ghias ad-din and he was 17 years of age when Rusudan first saw him, much younger than she. She took him for a husband after he converted to Christianity. They had a daughter, Tamar, and a son, David VI, who became king after Rusudan;'s death in 1245. The Khwarezind Empire attacked Tbilisi in 1226 causing Queen Rusudan to flee the capitol. Ghias ad-din may have informed for the enemy, and Rusudan consequently repudiated their marriage.

In 1240 Georgia was under Mogul rule. Rusudan, who had become queen by that time, greatly feared David VII Ulu who showed indications of usurping her throne. She had him held prisoner by her son-in-law, Sultan Kaykhusraw II and sent her own son David VI as the official representative of the Georgian dynasty and the heir apparent to the Mongols. She died in 1245 before the return of her son from Mongolia.

6   *The Secret History of the Mongols*, translation by Francis Woodman Cleaves, Harvard University Press, Cambridge, Massachusetts, London, England, 1982, p.111

7   Ibid. p. 168

8   The Mongolian Death Worm is a large creature reportedly living in the Gobi Desert, but probably mythical. In *On the Trail of Ancient Man, A Narrative of the Field Work of the Central Asiatic Expeditions* by Roy Chapman Andrews, the author cites Mongolian Prime Minister Damdinbazar's description of the worm as, "shaped like a sausage about two feet long, has no head nor leg and it is so poisonous that merely to touch it means instant death." Andrews doubted its existence.

9   In *The Secret History of the Mongols*, p. 125, we find Temujin (Genghis Khan) describing his best generals—his "Four Dogs":

"Temujin, hath [learned] to nourish four dogs with the flesh of men and to bind [them], using chains of iron. Those who draw nigh, pursuing those our watchmen, are they. Those four dogs
    Having helmets [which are] copper.
    Having snouts [which are] chisels.
    Having tongues [which are] awls.
    Having hearts [which are] iron.
    Having whips [which are) swords,
march, eating the dew and riding the wind—those.
On the days when [they and the enemy] kill one another They eat the flesh of men—those.
On the days when [they and the enemy] encounter one another, They take the flesh of human beings as their provision— those.
Those four dogs, who are those? Both Jebe and Kublai and both Jelme and Subutai are those four."

Perihelion

10   Cleaves, *The Secret History of the Mongols.* pp. 32, 74, 146, 151, 180, 198.

11   After the war with the Mongols in 1223, King George IV went to Bagavan in Armenia to negotiate Rusudan's marriage to the Shah of Shirvan. He had been wounded during the battle and died there at the age of 31. Rusudan succeeded to the throne.

12   *The Georgian Chronicles* of Kartlis Tskhovreba. pp. 230-231.

Although the King claims the barbarians deny God and Christ, sources say that the Mongols believed in a single god. In fact, in the same history just quoted, a section on Genghis Khan (p. 320) describes the following:

"But the story of how Genghis Khan ascended a high mountain, and how the Lord Jesus Christ appeared before him, the God of all, is also often told. He taught Genghis Khan the law, faith, innocence and truth, unacceptance of lies, and many other things, telling him: 'If you remember these rules, all the lands and tribes will be given to you. Go and take as many of them (the lands), as will be in your power.' After becoming khan, he went to Khat'aeti and entered the church and beholding the image of the Savior Jesus Christ bowed instantly before it saying: 'That is the man I have seen on the Chineti mountain; the same in appearance, and he taught me all those laws.' And Genghis Khan fell in love with Him, blessed Him and observed accurately all the laws given by Him."

But according to Eskildsen, Stephen in *The Teachings and Practices of the Early Quanzhen Taoist Masters.* SUNY Press. p. 17, "Genghis Khan was a Tengrist, but was religiously tolerant and interested in learning philosophical and moral lessons from other religions. He consulted Buddhist monks (including the Zen monk Haiyun), Muslims, Christian missionaries, and the Taoist monk Qiu Chuji."

Byron Grush

Black and White and Red All Over

> *...The noise*
> *Of worldly fame is but a blast of wind,*
> *That blows from divers points, and shifts its name*
> *Shifting the point it blows from.*
> ——Giotto to Dante from Canto 11 of "The Purgatory"

In his *The Lives of the Artists*, Giorgio Vasari described Giotto as a youth tending sheep in the hills between Florence and Vespignano when the Italian painter Cimabue came upon him and observed that he was "sketching one of them in a lifelike way with a slightly pointed rock upon a smooth and polished stone without having learned how to draw it from anyone other than Nature." Cimabue took the boy to his studio in Florence and trained him in the art of painting. He soon eclipsed even his master and "became such an excellent imitator of Nature that he completely banished that crude Greek style and revived the modern and excellent art of painting...." Vasari goes on to say that "Among his drawings which can still be seen today was one in the Chapel of the Palace of the Podesta in Florence of Dante Alighieri, his contemporary and greatest friend, and no less famous a poet during this period than Giotto was a painter."[1]

Also among the most excellent works of Giotto di Bondone is a fresco in the interior of the Scrovegni Chapel in Padua entitled *Adoration of the Magi*. It was one of a cycle of frescoes begun in 1303 and probably executed between 1305 and 1306. The paintings were paid for by Enrico Scrovegni, a merchant who sought to purge his sin of usury by donating to the church. (Dante put him in the seventh circle of hell in the *Inferno*.) In the painting, Giotto depicts the Magi as wealthy foreigners bringing gifts to the newly born Messiah as prophesied by a star. The star appears above the group and resembles none other than Halley's Comet, which Giotto is said to have seen in the year 1301.

Byron Grush

Dante Alighieri

The city-state of Florence, 1301. The Duomo, the Cathedral of Santa Maria del Fiore is still under construction and the building of a new seat of government, the Palazzo della Signoria, has just begun. Public spaces are being profusely decorated by the professional guilds and these endeavors are financed by wealthy patrons as well as by the confraternities, priests, and nuns wishing to enhance the religious experience through spiritual art and architecture. The old style of Italo-Byzantine is being replaced by a new realism championed by artists like Pietro Cavallini, Nicola Pisano, Cimabue, and Giotto. Talented young painter apprentices fill the large workshop of Giotto di Bondone. These include Taddeo Gaddi, Bernardo Daddi, and a young man named Bindo Corda who will be the protagonist of this story.

Today Bindo Corda and Bernardo Daddi have left the workshop and traveled on foot to find a suitable watering hole. They are crossing the Ponte Vecchio over the Arno. The old bridge dates back to 996 but was swept away in the flood of 1117, after which it was rebuilt of quarried stone with three harmonious arches, suggesting its ancient Roman influence. There is a main piazza at its center and shops line each side of the span offering goods of every variety. There are butchers and fishmongers and tanners and jewelers and, more importantly, establishments offering food and drink. Bindo and

Perihelion

Bernado stop at a pub here where wines from the nearby region of Chianti are the feature. They meet some fellows of their familiarity and sit at a long table of much abused wood to debate affairs of the day.

Going round the table as if boxing the compass we see at north, Maffeo Paganaucci, an apprentice at the Compagna del Bardi, a major banking and trading company, and sitting next to him, Lisabetta Medina, Maffeo's best girl and fiancé; at east, Bindo and Bernado have squeezed in next to Rustico Severigi, a veteran of the battle of Campaldino[2] and the oldest among the group of friends; at south on the hard wood bench sit Volta Malfici, the son of a Florentine wool merchant, and Carafina Bambelli, a good friend of Lisabetta's; finally at west we find Grifuccio Bacchini, a budding poet and wanderer, Teramo Dragonetti, who has applied for an apprenticeship at Giotto's workshop through encouragement by Bindo, and lastly, Bona Ambrosini, who is the love of Bindo's life.

Severigi summons the waiter to bring another bottle of Chianti. "These are troubled times," he tells the friends. "Blacks and Whites can't see eye to eye," he says, referring to the two estranged factions of the Guelphs,[3] (the name of the supporters of the Pope who were opposed to the authority of the Holy Roman Empire.) The Neri or Black Guelphs are an extreme papal faction while the Bianchi or White Guelphs are more moderate and have moved away from supporting the current Pope, Boniface VIII. Political struggles between the two factions abound.

Grifuccio Bacchini agrees adding, "Guido Cavalcanti is dead. He was a great poet and a leader among the Guelphs but was exiled to Sarzana last year. He tried to return but caught the malaria. Who is left to maintain peace in Florence?"

"That other poet," answers Teramo Dragonetti, "that Dante who is a prior now. He is a Bianchi."

"Yes," says Bacchini, "but his wife is a Neri.[4] Dante only joined the Bianchi out of friendship for Cavalcanti."

"You poets!" says Maffeo Paganaucci. "Your concern is not for politics but for the 'manly love' of each other." Here Lisabetta giggles in a most unladylike fashion. Responding to the ridicule in his own way, Bacchini recites a stanza from Cavalcanti's well known sonnet, "Voi che per gli occhi mi passaste il core":

Byron Grush

You whose look pierced through my heart,
Waking up my sleeping mind,
behold an anguished life
which love is killing with sighs.

Bindo and Bona look at each other longingly. The talk of love opposed to politics has a special meaning for them. Bindo Corda's family is aligned with the Bianchi, the White Guelphs, while Bona Ambrosini's family is strictly Neri, Black Guelphs. Truly they are star-crossed lovers.

"Not to change the subject," says Carafina Bambelli, "but is anyone...I should say, anyone else...going to the dance at the Piazza di Santa Trinita next Sunday?"

"Oh yes, Maffeo, let us go!" says Lisabetta.

Volta Malfici says to Carafina, "Cara, I did not say for certain I would take you..."

"Yes, you will," she answers.

"Don't pay any attention to the wench," he says.

"Don't call me a wench...you brute."

"Okay...trollop."

"Bastard!"

"Bitch!"

"Please! Friends!" shouts Bindo. "Let us be civil. Carafina, Bona and I will go to the dance and you are welcome to accompany us...with or without Volta. If he is still so hot-headed by Sunday, then we will all be happier if he doesn't come."

"Of course I am coming," says Volta. "I never said I wouldn't."

"Well now that that little merriment is finished," says Rustico Severigi, "let us drink to the secession of strife from our lives...both in politics and in love!"

It is the following morning. Giotto has agreed to review the portfolio of Teramo Dragonetti. Bindo introduces Teramo to the Master and the procedure begins. Teramo has brought a selection of his best drawings rolled into a tube and secured by a piece of twine. He loosens the twine and unrolls a dozen large sheets of paper covered with markings of conté crayon in a dark red hue. These are renderings of the figures of people seen toiling in the fields or sitting at tables at some restaurant or reclining on divans.

"Excellent," says Giotto, smiling. "You are drawing from nature…observing the reality of form and grasping the idea of light and shade which defines our vision. Your hand is not the most capable but that can be trained. Here…see here where you fail to turn an edge, and there where the shape of the chin is off? With practice you may achieve a mastery. It will be hard work and you must devote yourself to the discipline of never stopping short of perfection."

Now the work of the studio commences, focusing on a commission Giotto has received to produce a polyptych for the high alter in the Badia Florentina. Five panels have been prepared with gesso and the cartoon, that is, the outline of the figure, has been traced onto the panel which will contain a portrait of John the Evangelist. Giotto is sketching ideas for the center figure which will be of the Virgin while the apprentices work to add a background around John the Evangelist. Teramo has been instructed to watch and learn.

Through the door comes a man wearing a scarlet robe trimmed in cream and a matching cap. His face is long and accented by a hawk-like nose. Giotto stops what he is doing and goes to greet him. The man is Dante Alighieri. They are old friends and have few differences save that Giotto, needful of commissions, is sensitive to the whims and wishes of Pope Boniface VIII, while Dante holds the pope in great disdain. Dante freely rants:

"We no longer live under the overlordship of the Holy Roman Empire; the Hohenstauten dynasty is gone. The Bianchi hold great influence in the government of Florence. Why then must we tolerate the interference of this meddling pontiff?"

"Boniface holds England and France at bay," answers Giotto, "saving us from taxation we could not afford. If he is a bit heavy-handed…"

"Mark my words, he will invade Florence and establish the Neri as rulers if we are not vigilant. He is ruthless. It is said that he deposed Pope Celestine by yelling into his ear trumpet to make him abdicate. He is said to have tossed ashes in the face of kneeling archbishops who angered him."

"What can you do, my old friend?"

"I go to him with a company to plead his…I cannot bring myself to say, mercy…his tolerance. But I fear this will be in vain. Those of God who should be the brides of holiness, do prostitute for silver and for gold and care not for the individual. I see him after death cast deep into Hell, hanging upside down with burning feet."[5]

"That is a bit extreme."

"His avarice afflicts the world, trampling the good and uplifting the depraved. But I am not here to rage against simoniacs. I come to ask you while I am in Rome that you may look after my wife Gemma and the children, Pietro, Jacopo, Giovanni, and Antonia. If anything should happen…"

"Of course. You see, I take good care of my own offspring, it should be no different to manage yours."

"Yours work for you here toiling on works for the church which I oppose. And I must say, they all resemble you in countenance. How is it you paint such beautiful pictures but produce such ugly children?"

"Ah, my friend, I make my pictures by day and my babies by night."

It is Sunday evening. Bindo, Bona, Carafina, and Volta cross the River Arno via the Ponte Santa Trinita to the triangular square of the Piazza di Santa Trinita. On the western side of the piazza rises the façade of the Basilica di Santa Trinita where the high alter was painted by Cimabue. Already a carola is underway. The circular dance revolves around a small fountain at the center of the piazza; men and women joining hands dance to the music of a lute and the rhythm of a tambourine. This is no country dance. The women are dressed in flowing gowns of silk and lace, the men in tunics of bright colors decorated with emblems of their rank. They dance clockwise, stepping out with the left foot and following it with the right in a sideways fashion. Some hold hands firmly, some only touch their fingers together. The music is augmented by a song:

> *What was the charm I cannot rightly tell*
> *That kindled in me such*
> *A flame of love that rest nor day nor night*
> *I find; for, by some strong unwonted spell,*
> *Hearing and touch*

Perihelion

And seeing each new fires in me did light,
Wherein I burn outright;
Nor other than thyself can soothe my pain
Nor call my senses back, by love o'erborne.

O tell me if and when, then, it shall be
That I shall find thee e'er
Whereas I kissed those eyes that did me slay.
O dear my good, my soul, ah, tell it me,
When thou wilt come back there,
And saying "Quickly," comfort my dismay
Somedele. Short be the stay
Until thou come, and long mayst thou remain![6]

The dancers stop and bow. Bindo and his friends join the circle and then, at the beat of the tambourine, the carola begins again. As they dance Maffeo Paganaucci and Lisabetta Medina come across the bridge and enter the piazza. They do not immediately join the dancers but stand and watch. Lisabetta's gown is sleeveless and has a scoped neck. Maffeo's tunic is richly embroidered and a sheathed ceremonial sword hangs at his side. Maffeo carefully scans the faces of the other watchers. He is a bit nervous. Lisabetta notices this and asks him why he seems so troubled.

"Do you not remember? It was a year ago at this very piazza when men on horseback entered and a fight began between Whites and Blacks.[7] Many were injured. It is crowded venues such as this that invite violence."

"But Maffeo, it is such a peaceful gathering. Surely nothing can happen."

Torchlight illuminates the piazza casting the shadows of the revelers onto the church and the nearby buildings, palaces of the nobility of Florence. The moon has risen although a wisp of cloud crosses its face, giving it the countenance of a disparaging deity; what can be the matter with so jubilant a gathering? Up the Via de' Tornabuoni comes a contingent of horsemen. At the piazza they dismount and approach the crowd of dancers with their hands on the hilts of their swords. The menace expressed in their body language does not go unnoticed. The dancing stops and all turn toward the interlopers.

Byron Grush

A man calls, "You there, Bondo Cordo, come you forth. I would speak with you." He is tall man, wearing the spotted tunic of a soldier, but he is not in uniform, nor is he currently in the army. His sword is military issue, however, and as he draws it partly from its sheath, it glitters in the torchlight.

Bondo cautions Bona to remain with the dancers, then goes to meet this probable antagonist. When he is close enough to recognize the man he stops short. It is Rambaldo Ambrosini, Bona's brother. This is not good. The brother has resented Bondo from the first moment they met as youngsters—this was also the first moment Bondo fell in love with Bona and determined one day they should marry. But the Ambrosinis were affiliated with the Donati family and therefore the Black Guelphs, while the Cordos stood with the Cerchi and the White Guelphs.

Rambaldo taunts Bondo: "You are the son of a pig, a filthy worm-head! I hate you! I challenge you to a duel, you rotten prattler."

"Rambaldo," answers Bondo, "I would not fight you. You are the brother of my love and one day we will be family."

"You're lying in your throat you rotten, traitor. You mouth-stinking bastard. Goat…ribald…cuckold…I'll see you dragged through town you dog-worm! Fight me, you coward!"

By now Bondo is getting a little unnerved. But he holds firm. "I will not fight you, Rambaldo. You see, I have no weapon."

"We shall find you a blade," retorts Rambaldo, "though I sense you know not which end to hold."

Now Maffeo Paganaucci and Volta Malfici come to stand behind Bondo. Four of the horsemen who accompanied Rambaldo close in behind him. An Italian standoff. The crowd of dancers and others who have come into the piazza at the sign of a commotion now form a new circle, this one around the opposing protagonists. Rambaldo, enraged, pulls his sword from its scabbard and points it menacingly at Bondo's throat. Maffeo steps forward.

"Bondo has no weapon," Maffeo says, "but I have a thirsty blade that will find your repulsively thin blood and drink it deeply!" He draws his sword. Everyone backs away, giving the men room to fight, if indeed, a fight will take place. Where are the officials, the arbitrators, the night guards?

Overhead a single hawk is on the wing, slowly circling, a small black speck against the dimly moonlit clouds. From the corner of the

Perihelion

piazza, from between palaces, a stray cat peers. Seeing the throng of humans and sensing impending turmoil, she ducks back among piles of trash discarded there in the alley. The tense anticipation of the crowd is as thick as the ensuing silence.

Then, the flash of blade against blade. Like the tolling of broken bells, the parry and counter-parry rings out. Parry and thrust, parry and thrust. First blood on the wrist of Bambaldo, for, although Maffeo is not the superior swordsman, he is cool-headed and fights not with blind anger like his opponent. But as the battle goes on, Maffeo begins to tire.

The swordplay is a macabre ballet in the torchlight; they dance the dance of death-inevitable. Each contingent of Blacks or of Whites within the lookers-on cheers for their champion. Scuffles break out on the fringes. Some of more cautious spectators make exit, not concerned with the outcome, only with their own safety. Bona, Carafina, and Lisabetta cling to each other, paralyzed with dread.

A final thrust. Maffeo is down, bleeding from a chest wound. A cry of anguish from the Whites breaks the silence but is drowned out by a rave of triumph from the Blacks. Bondo runs to Maffeo's side, cradles him in his arms as his friend's life pours out onto the pavement. Suddenly Maffeo is still, a last gasp issues from his lips, then a death rattle. Standing over this profile of pity, this pieta, is the villain, Bambaldo. He laughs. Incensed, Bondo grabs the fallen sword of his protector and thrusts upward, piercing Bambaldo in the gut. It is a scenario, sadly, that will be all too familiar in the days and weeks to come as Florence explodes in senseless strife.

The court of Pope Boniface VIII, the city of Alagna, in Campagna. Dante Alighieri and his delegation have been waiting for an audience with His Holiness in Rome for weeks now. Boniface keeps them waiting. Instead, the pontiff is conferring with his legate, Cardinal Matteo d'Acquasparta, who has recently returned from Florence, and Charles of Valois, brother of King Charles of France.

The Cardinal paints a discouraging picture of events in Florence. "These Bianchi," he tells the pope, "have taken much of the control of the government. Indeed, many of the Neri who support you as the Bianchi do not, have been expelled. Corso Donati, your avid follower, with his deputies has been banished to the village of Pieve where they wait under the most dire circumstances for the opportunity to return."

Boniface had sent for Charles of Valois primarily regarding aid for the king in his war on Sicily, but also to suggest that he might cause Charles to become Emperor of the Romans or at least an imperial lieutenant for the Church. The old dynasty that opposed the papistry is now gone and a new one, obedient to his Holiness was in order. Now Boniface addresses Charles of Valoris saying:

"You have come here from Lucca with your barons and counts and your 500 horsemen only to be biding your time until spring. Yet I would not have you pass this winter in vain nor see your troops idle. I therefore give you the title of Peacemaker of Florence and bid you go forth to that city, perhaps at the annoyance of the Guelphs who rule there…that is just too bad, and restore peace and prosperity and above all, obedience to Rome."

"Your Holiness," answers Charles, "this I will undertake for you. I will bring to them the goodwill and the desire for peace you express, and I shall do so without striking a blow."

"You will find much support among the Neri. Now as you hasten to your duty, remember the future I have promised for you depends upon the result in Florence."

Pope Boniface VIII returns to Rome after Charles of Valois leaves for Florence. There he does meet with Dante and in delegates, expressing his wish…no, his insistence upon a peaceful union between the warring factions of Guelphs (and secretly desiring the elimination of the Whites). He dismisses the delegates but commands Dante to remain in Rome. It is nearing the end of October. Events await a certain sentinel, a certain celestial wanderer.

Giotto has walked into the courtyard of his palazzo in Florence to enjoy the brisk night; the temperature remains at a pleasing 50 degrees. It is October 30, 1301. He looks to the heavens hoping, perhaps, for some inspiration for his next project. There, just above the western horizon, a flash of light breaks through the clouds. The comet one day to be known as Halley's has returned in its perihelion.

On a balcony at the Villa Medina other eyes glimpse the shining visitor. "It's as if the Star of David has returned," says Lisabetta. "Perhaps this is the second coming."

Perihelion

"One can only hope for such deliverance," says Bona. She and Bondo are in hiding at the villa from the Neri, including some of her own family, who are searching for Bondo. The Medina family has allowed them this sanctuary in deference to Bondo who avenged the murder of Lisabetta's fiancé, however accidental it might have been.

On the ledge of the balcony sits a large woven basket in which have sprouted several sprigs of sweet basil.[8] Lisabetta was watering this when she spotted the comet and called Bona and Bondo to come see the phenomenon. She spends her time with domestic chores these days, still despondent over the death of her lover.

"I've seen him, you know," she says. "His ghost has come to me. He urges me to join him in the darkness of the afterlife. I am afraid…I cannot end my existence thus, yet the pain…"

"It is so," says Bona. "We too have talked of suicide. But we are not Pyramus and Thisbe[9] to fall upon our sword in sorrow or in fear! There is a time and a place for us."

"Perhaps not here in Florence anymore," says Bondo. "There is much danger in the streets."

On All Saints Day. Charles of Valois had entered Florence. He had come unarmed, after some negotiating with city officials, White Guelphs who at first were wary of allowing him in. But he had convinced them of his good intensions and his wishes for peace. They had met him with a procession of their own horsemen carrying standards and riding steeds draped in silk. It was a festive occasion. Now, five days later, at the Church of Santa Maria Novella, the Priors and other officials of Florence are presented with a demand: give over the charge of the city to Charles and grant him absolute authority to make peace among the Guelphs. After some debate they agree.

Corso de' Donati, that banished leader of the Black Guelphs, has been made aware of the coming of the son of the king of France and what it portends. He has left Pieve and come with many men to the gates of Florence. Finding them shut he goes to another location, the postern of Pinti near San Maggiore, and at this gate, beats it down. Once he has gained the piazza the company shouts, "Long live M. Corso! Long live the baron!" He answers, "To the prisons, to the palace of the Podesta. We will release our fellows. We will confront the priors." Five days of wrath will follow. Charles of Valois will do nothing to stop it.

The friends[10] have gathered for a farewell celebration for Bona and Bondo who are leaving the city. One last time they are met at the little pub at the piazza on the Ponte Vecchio. The poet Grifuccio Bacchini proposes a toast to the couple in the form of verse:

> *Within the gentle heart abideth Love,*
> *As doth a bird within green forest glade,*
> *Neither before the gentle heart was Love,*
> *Nor Love ere gentle heart by Nature made.*

Pausing, Bacchini points up at the sky where Halley's Comet still can be seen, then continues:

> *From out the star no glory doth depart*
> *Until made gentle by the sun alone.*
> *When the sun hath drawn forth*
> *By his own strength all that which is not meet,*
> *The star doth prove its worth.*
> *Thus to the heart, by Nature fashioned so*
> *Gentle and pure and sweet,*
> *The love of woman like a star doth go.*

The friends applaud then heft glasses of wine red as blood and drink. Rustico Severigi leans over to Teramo Dragonetti and whispers, "Ha! He stole that from Guido Guinizelli."[11] Carafina Bambelli leans close to Volta Malfici and whispers, "How can she stay with him? He killed her brother." Volta glares back at here. He knows Bindo only acted in the passion of the moment and probably had no choice as the assailant Rambaldo Ambrosini was standing over him with blood dripping from his sword.

These last few days have been turbulent and filled with hatred and revenge. The Neri began by looting stores and advanced to burning houses occupied by Bianchi. Members of the White faction found on the street were attacked and wounded or killed. The Cerchi family fled Florence and again appealed to Pope Boniface for deliverance. The Pope promised to send Cardinal d'Acquasparta back

Perihelion

to sort things out. Meanwhile Charles of Valois reformed the government, electing Black Guelphs as priors. Dante Alighieri, still in Rome, was now exiled, forbidden to return to Florence under penalty of being burned alive at the stake. In later years Dante will people his *Inferno* with many of those who have mistreated and maligned him.

The friends break off their celebration and go their separate ways. Bindo and Bona, having secretly married, leave Florence and travel to Carrara, a newly formed city state aligned with the Ghibelines where White Guelphs were welcome. Bindo works for a time in the marble quarries where he meets the sculptor Giovanni Pisano. Pisano is engaged in carving a marble of the Madonna and Child for the Scrovegni Chapel in Padua. He mentions having met Giotto there who is undertaking many frescoes of the cycle of the Virgin and the Christ. "Giotto has painted the most extraordinary scene," he tells Bindo, "of the Adoration of the Magi, and has depicted the Star of David in the form of that comet of a few years ago."

---

1   Giorgio Vasari. *The Lives of the Artists*. Translators: Julia Conway Bondanella, Peter Bondanella. Ebook, United Kingdom: Oxford University Press, UK. 1998.

2   The battle of Campaldino (1289) was a decisive battle in which factions from Florence supporting the Pope (the Guelphs) prevailed against the factions in Arezzo (the Ghibellines) who supported the Holy Roman Emperor. Dante fought in this conflict and consequently became interested in politics, eventually rising to the position of prior in Florence.

3   The origin of the terms Bianchi and Neri to denote the two factions of the Guelph lies with the conflict within a family named Cancellieri of Pistioa, a small town near Florence. It began with an assault with a snowball, but let Machiavelli tell it:

"Among the first families of Pistoia was the Cancellieri. It happened that Lore, son of Gulielmo, and Geri, son of Bertacca, both of this family, playing together, and coming to words, Geri was slightly wounded by Lore. This displeased Gulielmo; and, designing by a suitable apology to remove all cause of further animosity, he ordered his son to go to the house of the father of the youth whom he had wounded and ask pardon. Lore obeyed his father; but this act of virtue failed to soften the cruel mind of Bertacca, and having caused Lore to be seized, in order to add the greatest indignity to his brutal act, he ordered his servants to chop off the youth's hand upon a block used for cutting meat upon, and then said to him, 'Go to thy father, and tell him that sword wounds are cured with iron and not with words.' The unfeeling barbarity of this act so greatly exasperated Gulielmo that he ordered his people to take arms for his revenge. Bertacca prepared for his defense, and not only that family, but the whole city of Pistoia, became divided. And as the Cancellieri were descended from a Cancelliere who had had two wives, of whom one was called Bianca (white), one party was named by those who were descended from her BIANCA; and the other, by way of greater distinction, was called NERA (black)."

——Machiavelli, Niccolo. *History Of Florence And Of The Affairs Of Italy From The Earliest Times To The Death Of Lorenzo The Magnificent.* Project Gutenberg EBook #2464. 2013.

4   Dante's wife before their marriage, Gemma di Manetto Donati, was the daughter of Manetto Donati, a powerful figure of the Black Guelphs in Florence. Dante had been promised to Gemma at the age of 12, but his true love from the age of 9 was Beatrice Portinari. In the *Paradiso*, the third part of the *Divine Comedy*, Beatrice guides Dante through the celestial spheres of heaven. The head of the Donati family was an aristocratic man named Corso Donati. He led the Black Guelphs against the White Guelphs who, in turn, were headed up by the Florentine banker, Vieri dei Cerchi. We will be hearing more about the Donati/Cerchi feud and how it affected Dante.

5   In the *Inferno*, Dante places Pope Boniface VIII in the Eighth Circle of Hell although the Pope has not died at the time of the writing. He does so by having one of the simoniacs mistake the visiting Dante for Boniface, indicating that it is a sure thing he will join them there where:

Perihelion

Out of the mouth of each one there protruded
The feet of a transgressor, and the legs
Up to the calf, the rest within remained.

In all of them the soles were both on fire;
Wherefore the joints so violently quivered,
They would have snapped asunder withes and bands.

Even as the flame of unctuous things is wont
To move upon the outer surface only,
So likewise was it there from heel to point.

———Dante. *Inferno*, Canto XIX.. Project Gutenberg EBook #1001. 1997 (translation by Henry Wadsworth Longfellow).

6   This song is described by Boccaccio in the tenth story of the seventh day of the *Decameron* as a group "presently fell to dancing about the fair fountain, carolling now to the sound of Tindaro's bagpipe and anon to that of other instruments...." There are few descriptions of Medieval dance and almost no record of the music or songs than accompanied them.
———Giovanni Boccaccio, *Decameron* 1349-1353. Translated by John Payne, Walter J. Black, Inc. New York. Project Gutenberg Ebook # 23700. 2007.

7   The historian Giovanni Villani wrote in 1346 that this incident caused the leaders of the Black and White parties to be banned from Florence to stop the violence between the families of the Donati and the Cerchi:
"On the evening of the first of May, in the year 1300, while they were watching a dance of ladies which was going forward on the piazza of Santa Trinita, one party began to scoff at the other, and to urge their horses one against the other, whence arose a great conflict and confusion, and many were wounded, and, as ill-luck would have it, Ricoverino, son of M. Ricovero of the Cerchi, had his nose cut off his face; and through the said scuffle that evening all the city was moved with apprehension and flew to arms. This was the beginning of the dissensions and divisions in the city of Florence and in the Guelf party, whence many ills and perils followed on afterwards, as in

due time we shall make mention. And for this cause we have narrated thus extensively the origin of this beginning of the accursed White and Black parties, for the great and evil consequences which followed to the Guelf party, and to the Ghibellines, and to all the city of Florence, and also to all Italy."

——*Villani's Chronicle Being Selections from the First Nine Books of the Croniche Fiorentine of Giovanni Villani.* (Archibald Constable & Co. Ltd. London. 1906 Second Edition) Edited by Philip H. Wicksteed, Translated by Rose E. Selfe. Project Gutenberg EBook #33022. 2010.

8   The basket of basil has no real significance in our story save that it allows us to examine yet another of Boccaccio's wonderful stories. Lisabetta's namesake appears as Lisabetta de Messina in the fifth story of the fourth day. Lisabetta's three brothers slay her lover, Lorenzo, with whom she has lain and thus brought shame to the family. Learning of this foul deed and much saddened, she goes to search out the spot where they have buried Lorenzo. Then:

"…she dug whereas her seemed the earth was less hard. She had not dug long before she found the body of her unhappy lover, yet nothing changed nor rotted, and thence knew manifestly that her vision was true, wherefore she was the most distressful of women; yet, knowing that this was no place for lament, she would fain, and she but might have borne away the whole body, to give it fitter burial; but, seeing that this might not be, she with a knife did off the head from the body, as best she could, and wrapping it in a napkin, laid it in her maid's lap. Then, casting back the earth over the trunk, she departed thence, without being seen of any, and returned home, where, shutting herself in her chamber with her lover's head, she bewept it long and bitterly, insomuch that she bathed it all with her tears, and kissed it a thousand times in every part. Then, taking a great and goodly pot, of those wherein they plant marjoram or sweet basil, she set the head therein, folded in a fair linen cloth, and covered it with earth, in which she planted sundry heads of right fair basil of Salerno; nor did she ever water these with other water than that of her tears or rose or orange-flower water. Moreover she took wont to sit still near the pot and to gaze amorously upon it with all her desire, as upon that which held her Lorenzo hid; and after she had a great while looked thereon, she would bend over it and fall to weeping so sore and so long that her tears bathed all the basil, which, by dint of long and assiduous tending, as well as by reason of the fatness of the earth, proceeding from the rotting head that was therein, waxed passing fair and very sweet of savour."

Eventually the brothers discover the pot with the rotting head inside and steal it away from Lisabetta. The story ends with her singing, "Alack! ah, who can the ill Christian be that stole my pot away?"

——Giovanni Boccaccio, *Decameron*.

9   Pyramus and Thisbe are perhaps the original "star-crossed lovers," appearing in Ovid's *Metamorphose* first published in 8 AD. They have been forbidden to wed because of a rivalry between their parents' families and can only communicate through a crack in the wall separating their two houses in the city of Babylon. Pyramus, finding fresh blood under a mulberry tree where the lovers had planned to meet, wrongly believes Thisbe is dead and grieving, kills himself, falling upon his sword. Thisbe arrives latter and finding Pyramus dead, kills herself with the same sword. The story is repeated by Boccaccio in *On Famous Women* and in the *Decameron* in the fifth story of the seventh day. It is widely assumed that Ovid's story inspired the plot of William Shakespeare's *Romeo and Juliet*.

10   A good time for a disclaimer. The friends, Teramo Dragonetti, Grifuccio Bacchini, Volta Malfici, Maffeo Paganaucci, Rustico Severigi, Carafina Bambelli, Lisabetta da Medina, Rambaldo Ambrosini, Bona Ambrosini, and Bindo Corda are all fictitious characters—only the painter Bernardo Daddi is a real person among the friends. The other important characters such as Cardinal Matteo d'Acquasparta, Corso Donati, Vieri dei Cerchi, and Charles of Valois were real as of course were Dante Alighieri, Giotto di Bondone, and Pope Boniface VIII.

11   Indeed, poet Grifuccio Bacchini did steal his verses from the Italian poet Guido Guinizelli di Magnano (1240-1476). Guinizelli was exiled as a Ghibelline in 1274. He has been called the father of "dolce stil nuovo." Dante was greatly influenced by him. These verses are stolen from "Canzone" by Guinizelli.

Byron Grush

———From *An Anthology of Italian Poems 13th-19th Century* selected and translated by Lorna de' Lucchi, Alfred A. Knopf, New York; 1922; pp. 28-32, 348.

The Angelus Rings at Noon

On 7 November of 1455, in the Notre Dame Cathedral in Paris, France, a stooped, weary woman of 78 years stood before a group of robed men whose faces betrayed no telling expressions save that in unison, all were grim. The woman's name was Isabelle Romée. She began to speak:

"I had a daughter born in lawful wedlock who grew up amid the fields and pastures. I had her baptized and confirmed and brought her up in the fear of God. I taught her respect for the traditions of the Church as much as I was able to do given her age and simplicity of her condition. I succeeded so well that she spent much of her time in church and after having gone to confession she received the sacrament of the Eucharist every month. Because the people suffered so much, she had a great compassion for them in her heart and despite her youth she would fast and pray for them with great devotion and fervor. She never thought, spoke or did anything against the faith.

"Certain enemies had her arraigned in a religious trial. Despite her disclaimers and appeals, both tacit and expressed, and without any help given to her defense, she was put through a perfidious, violent, iniquitous and sinful trial. The judges condemned her falsely, damnably and criminally, and put her to death in a cruel manner by fire. For the damnation of their souls and in notorious, infamous and irreparable loss to me, Isabelle, and mine..."

Isabelle Romée and her brothers were putting their case before the Inquisitor of France, Jean Bréhal and a panel of clergy representing Rome. This was not the first attempt at gaining a new trial for her daughter, accused of heresy, but this time it would be extensive and conclusive. It had been condoned by the Holy Father, Pope Callixtus III, who was anxious to see the matter finally settled.

The pope was a Borgia, aged 77, elected only this last April as a compromise candidate and now faced with an impending invasion of Europe by Turks, against whom he was planning a new Crusade. The possibility of this new trial was also on his mind. The Hundred Years War between England and France had ended two years ago and the condemnation of the "Maid of Heaven" (as Romée's daughter was called by some) could now be re-examined without the kind of political consequences (stemming from the collaboration of the woman's own countrymen with her foreign accusers) that existed at the time of the original trial. Or at least that was the idea.

As the new year dawned a new trial began for Jehanne Darc, or Jeanne d'Arc as she is known in modern times. A new star appeared in the sky; Halley's Comet reached its perihelion in early June. At that time the Pope issued a papal bull calling for prayers and the ringing every noon of the angelus bell for the welfare of the crusaders. He saw the comet as an ill omen. Later historians would claim he also called for the comet to be excommunicated.[2]

Meanwhile, Pope Callixtus III had other worries. Sultan Mehmet II of the Ottoman Empire had laid siege to Belgrade. Ladislas Posthumus, the 16-year-old king of Hungary, had fled to the safety of Vienna. Callixtus called Hungary the shield of Christianity and worried greatly it would fall to the Turks. Although Callixtus would send help as best he could, defense of the region lay upon the shoulders of Hungarian general János Hunyadi.

Joan of Arc was born 6 January 1412 to Jacques d'Arc and Isabelle Romée at the village of Domrémy in the Vosges of northeastern France. Isabelle Romée taught her how to spin wool and saw to her Catholic upbringing. At this time the Hundred Years War, begun in 1337, was still raging throughout Western Europe.

The House of Plantagenet and its cadet House of Lancaster, who ruled in the Kingdom of England, were in dispute with the French Royal House of Valois over the right to rule the Kingdom of France. The English launched an invasion in 1415, aware that two factions were quarreling in France: the Armagnacs led by the Duke of Orleans and the Count of Armagnac, and the Burgundians supporters of the Duke of Burgundy. The Armagnac supported the Dauphin who would later ascend to the throne as Charles VII, while the Burgundians would ally themselves with the English. At the siege of Orleans, the Duke was captured by English forces.

Against this backdrop, Joan began to see visions of the Archangel Michael, St Catherine, St. Margaret, and the Archangel Gabriel. These angelic entities ordered her to take part in the conflict, go to war as a soldier, and bring the Dauphin to Reims for coronation. Easier said than done. But she went to Lord Robert de Baudricourt who provided her with an escort through enemy-held territory to the

Perihelion

Royal Court at Chinon where she presented herself to the Dauphin Charles. Charles agreed to allow her to accompany an army to Orleans.

A series of battles followed in which Joan, at the head of her army, took fortress after fortress from the English and eventually her army entered Rheims. The coronation took place the next day, establishing Charles as the presumptive king of France. The English, and those in France who supported them, were not pleased. It was said that they feared Joan of Arc more than a hundred men-at-arms. They claimed that she used sorcery because of the victories that had been won by her.[3]

In one battle, trying unsuccessfully to retake Paris from the English, Joan was wounded by an arrow from a crossbow. In 1430 at the battle of Compiegne she was surrounded and forced to surrender to the Burgundian faction led by Philip III, Duke of Burgundy, who was allied with the English. She spent four months imprisoned in the chateau of Beaurevoir, then was brought to the headquarters of the English army in Rouen where she was put on trial for heresy. She faced a Church court headed by Bishop Pierre Cauchon, a supporter of the English.

There followed, between late February and mid-March of 1431, fifteen separate interrogations in which Joan was examined about everything from her former childhood to the state of her virginity to her act of wearing men's clothing to her belief of having communicated with angels. Efforts were made to entrap her into admitting heresy and the use of witchcraft.

At her trial, which began the day after Palm Sunday, she was read a list of 70 articles of indictment and told that if she refused to answer them it would be a sign of her admission of guilt. On May 24 she was taken to a scaffold in the cemetery next to the Church of Saint-Ouen and told to renounce her visions and to stop wearing men's clothing or be burned alive at the stake. Fearful of dying by incineration, Joan agreed to give up her men's attire (which she wore in battle because it was practical and in prison to avoid being raped[4]) and signed the abjuration document. However, a few days later she recanted and again donned male attire. She was declared relapsed and condemned to death. She was burned at the stake at the Old Marketplace in Rouen on May 30, 1431.

Byron Grush

Charles VII was greatly grieved by Joan's execution but as the English still ruled in Rouen and the Anglo-Burgundian alliance still held sway in Paris, a review of the case had to wait. Finally, in 1450, Charles ordered the theologian Guillaume Bouillé to look into the possible commission of cruel abuse by the judges. The problem was there were many still in France who, although they now switched their allegiance to Charles, had collaborated with the English and some of whom had actively participated in her trial. The only result of the preliminary inquiry was to state that the condemnation of Joan of Arc was a stain against the king's character.

Enter Cardinal Guillaume d'Estouteville. Cardinal d'Estouteville was the papal legate from Pope Nicholas V sent to negotiate an Anglo-French peace in 1451. He had an interest in clearing Joan's name and in removing the stain from Charles' association with the cause. He turned over the inquiry to the Inquisitor of France, Jean Bréhal and by 1452 a new investigation was underway, but it proved not to have gone far enough—there was still the problem of the collaborators and they were not called to testify. Finally in 1455, in response to Isabelle Romée's plea for justice, a new retrial began.

The Principality of Wallachia (modern Romania). Its borders were with Moldavi along the Milcov river, with Dobruja over the Danube River, and over the Carpathian Mountains, with Transylvania. It was from Transylvania that Vlad II, who became Voivode of Wallachia in 1436 had come. Vlad II was called Vlad Dracul for his membership in the Order of the Dragon, which was dedicated to halting the Ottoman advance into Europe. But two of his sons, Vlad III and Radu, were being held as hostages by the Ottoman sultan Mehmed II. Vlad Dracul had to acknowledge the sultan and agree to pay a yearly tribute to him.

When János Hunyadi, the regent-governor of Hungary, invaded Wallachia in 1447, Vlad Dracul and his eldest son, Mircea, were murdered. Hunyadi made Vladislav II, the son of Vlad Dracul's cousin, the ruler of Wallachia. Hunyadi and Vladislav began a military campaign against the Ottoman Empire. Mehmed released Vlad III and Radu and sent them with an armed force against Wallachia. The Ottomans defeated Hunyadi, and Vladislav returned to Wallachia with his remaining army. Vlad III was forced to flee.

Perihelion

Ottoman Sultan Mehmed II now threatened Hungary and had laid siege to Belgrade in Serbia. It was 1456, the year of the comet, the year Pope Callixtus III would send military aid to General János Hunyadi, the year Joan of Arc would get a new trial. The year the angelus would ring at noon. It was the year that Vlad III, now called Vlad III Dracul,[5] returned to Wallachia to avenge the deaths of his father and brother, and to seize the throne.

The capital of Wallachia was then in Târgoviște. Vlad III entered the city crossing the Ialomita River and approached the Curtea Domnească din Târgoviște, the Princely Court, a sprawling compound surrounded by stone walls and a moat. The royal court and residence of the monarch had been situated here since 1431. He entered through the south gate, a great stone arch which cast an ominous shadow onto the courtyard before him. A sentry hailed him, but not recognizing him did not stop his advance. Through the Great Royal Church he walked, glancing up at the frescos of former rulers.

Spies he had sent ahead of him, seeking out the whereabouts of the usurper (as he thought of him), his uncle Vladislav II. Now he entered the watch tower, the Chindier Tower that his father had built in 1440. Slowly he climbed the spiral staircase. From narrow windows placed at intervals he could look out over the fortress. He saw that right on cue his personal guards were surrounding the Princely Court. No alarm had yet been given.

Vladislav stood on top of the tower, his back to the stairwell. He seemed to be watching the guards, not aware that they were not in his own service. But there was something about the way they moved…with caution and stealth…

"Uncle!" shouted Vlad. "Uncle, I have come for your blood."

Vladislav turned, hand on hilt and seeing the pretender to the throne approaching, did not give quarter but stood steadfast, a glare appearing on his countenance that would have stopped an ordinary man short. But Vlad III was no ordinary man. Both men drew their weapons, steel flashed in the sunlight. Both men were able swordsmen having participated in many a battle against Turks or Hungarians or in peasant uprisings. Now Vlad's men had breached the fortress and the palace guards were trying, in vain, to fend them off.

Back and forth around the circular tower platform danced the opponents. Steel rang against steel as heavy blow followed heavy blow. Vlad forced Vladislav up against the parapet, nearly knocking him from the tower. One last lunge by Vladislav failed to find its mark. Vlad swung his sword, already dripping with first blood from a superficial cut, a lucky slice landing on Vladislav's left arm. A blow to the neck! Cleanly, Vladislav's head separated from his body and fell from the height, landing on the pavement of the courtyard below. Vlad III had claimed his birthright fairly and expertly. His vengeance would not stop here. He would now take on another title: Vlad Tepes—Vlad the Impaler.

Vlad the Impaler, so named for his favorite form of execution, impaling people still living on sharp stakes, may have put to death hundreds of thousands of people during his reign between 1456 and 1462.[6] He first rid Wallachi of the boyars who had murdered his father and brother and who opposed his rule. Vlad invaded southern Transylvania and burned villages and poisoned wells and ordered the impalement of all men and women who he captured. His fame as a brutal and blood-thirsty ruler spread, fostering tales which may have been exaggerated, yet were often based on eye-witness accounts. Romanian historians treated him as one of their greatest rulers, having fought for the independence of the Romanian lands. Others had a different opinion.[7]

In December 1476, Vlad was killed in a battle just north of Bucharest. He may have been mistaken by one of his men for a Turk, or he was attacked by Basarab Laiota who succeeded him as voivode. Possibly he was beheaded, and his head given to the Sultan in Constantinople and displayed as a trophy.[8]

July 1456, on the first Sunday thereof, the Turks began their siege of Belgrade. The Italian astronomer Paolo dal Pozzo Toscanelli, who provided Christopher Columbus with a map for his first voyage, observed Halley's Comet a few days later. The comet was measured as sixty degrees long with a golden color like a waving flame.[9]

Pope Callixtus III had sent Franciscan monk John of Capistrano to Belgrade to help assemble a fighting force there. He managed to recruit thousands, mostly peasant stock from the city and surrounding countryside, plus many volunteers came from Poland and Germany. These crusaders numbered about 6,000. Already General János Hunyadi and his brother-in-law Mihaly Szilagyi, commander of the city, had fortified Belgrade with trained

Perihelion

professionals, perhaps 10,000 or more. Hunyadi had gone back to Hungary to raise an even greater force but when he returned he found that the Ottoman army now surrounded the city and their Turkish navy had advanced up the Danube River. The Turks numbered well over 100,000.

On July 14, 1456, Hunyadi's fleet arrived on the Danube just below the Belgrade Fortress. Sultan Mehmed II's army had assembled on the neck of the headland just below the fortress and had started to bombard the city's walls. Hunyadi attacked the Ottoman navy. Surprising the enemy, Hunyadi's cannon took out three large Ottoman galleys. Others fought back but the Sultan had carried most of his cannon to the mainland and so the remaining galleys were easily captured. Now the Turks had only a few small boats; the war on the river was lost for them. Hunyadi navigated up the Sava river along the opposite side of the city from where the siege was strongest and gained access to the fortress.

Belgrade Fortress sat atop a ridge of stone above the confluence of the Danube and Sava Rivers. There were three levels, a lower town, the main fortress where the garrisons were located, and an upper town where the church had been built. Surrounded by thick walls, it was nearly impenetrable. Nearly. Now János Hunyadi's forces were added to the defenders. They were still greatly outnumbered by the Turks.

Next to the King's Gate on the southwest rampart was a deep pit resembling on old Roman well (which it was not—it was a dungeon). In the dungeon were 30 or so Hungarians, traitors, who had conspired to let the Turks into the fortress. Mihaly Szilagyi, the city commander, had them dropped into the dungeon and left them there to starve. He dropped several sharp knives into the pit to allow them to commit suicide as an act of clemency. On the eastern side of the fortress was the Ružica Church on a rise between the Zindan Gate's tower and the Jakšić Tower. In 1403 the remains of Saint Petka[10] were transferred to the Ružica Church. Wherever the caravan with her body stopped along the way to Belgrade, legend had it, a healing spring appeared.

A long-stepped path led up hill to the church from the lower town. János Hunyadi climbed the path in search of John of Capistrano. With him was his eldest son László. They found the monk in the sanctuary, kneeling before a statue of the Virgin. Tall candles illuminating the gloom began to flicker as the two men approached the altar. The odd silence in the sanctuary gave a surreal feeling to being in a city under siege and threatened with destruction, as if this one spot were immune from the danger and death that stalked Belgrade.

"Brother John," said Hunyadi, placing a hand on the monk's shoulder, "I need you to do something for me."

"As you wish, General Hunyadi. I am here to help," he answered.

"Please take some of your recruits and go through the city gathering up bacon grease and cooking and lamp oils…as much as you can. Bring it to the north rampart."

"I don't understand…bacon grease? Are we having a picnic?"

"The Turks are beginning to breach the walls there. I am planning on giving them a hot time."

The double walls of the fortress were crumbling under the Ottoman assault. On July 21 the Sultan began an all-out attack lasting all day and into the night. Turks rushed into the city. Hunyadi was ready with incendiaries and a wall of flame rose between the Turks and the Hungarian army. Hunyadi's troops rushed against the invading hoard and beat them back. Hand to hand fighting up and down the city streets gave the advance to the knights; Hunyadi's leadership rallied the defenders. The result was a massacre of the Ottoman forces inside the walls. Now outside the tide was also turning in favor of the defenders.

The Hungarian army rode forth, their horses wearing spiked armor. Turks unable to dodge the surging steeds were shredded like cabbage. Arrows flew in all directions, often arbitrary as to their targets. The Ottoman cannon were useless in the mixed multitude of battling soldiers. Horsemen used lances to skewer their opponents. Scimitars swept with deadly accuracy against the horses' loins, felling them. Arquebus muskets fired at close quarters with devastating effect. The Sultan, demoralized by his loses, called a retreat to the Ottoman camp. Hunyadi pulled his men back into the fortress and put them to barricading the breached walls.

The next day János and László Hunyadi and John of Capistrano stood on the high wall and looked down at the scene of death and destruction below. Carrion birds circled, waiting expectantly. Horses lay dead amongst dismembered men. Discarded swords were being picked up by both sides. Among the maimed and the bloody lay the

Perihelion

body of Titusz Dugovics who had struggled with an Ottoman standard-bearer on that very wall. Both had fallen to their deaths. Dugovics would one day be immortalized in a painting by Alexander von Wagner (some future historians would doubt Dugovics was a real person). Now the Turks were removing their dead and wounded. It looked as if they were ready to abandon the siege.

"Let us honor the bravery of the enemy," said János Hunyadi. "Tell the men not to harass nor to loot the enemy camps. We will bury our dead…let them take away theirs in peace."

Yet as they watched, a group of the peasants recruited by Capistrano ventured out into the killing field below, engaging some of the Turks. The unnecessary encounter escalated into a full-fledged battle. Capistrano, hurrying to the scene ordered the peasants back but the foray continued. He had little choice but to give the peasant army leadership and direction. Now the Hungarian troops were called into action. While Capistrano forced the Ottomans back across the Sava River, Hunyadi attacked and captured the enemy cannon positions. Sultan Mehmed II was wounded by an arrow and fell. Unconscious, he was carried away to one of the remaining ships. A panic broke out among the Turks. By evening they began their retreat to Constantinople.

The Ottoman advance toward Europe was stopped, at least for about the number of decades it would take for the comet to return. Turkish casualties numbered at least 50,000; the Hungarians lost only 10,000. A plague ran through the ranks of the peasant army still at Belgrade and János Hunyadi was infected. He died three weeks later on August 11. His younger son, Matthias I, became king of Hungary in 1458. Two months later, John Capistrano died. Pope Callixtus III ordered the church bells to be rung at noon throughout Europe. The practice still exists today. The Pope died two years later.

Jean Bréhal, a Dominican priest, became the Inquisitor-general of France in 1452, then in 1455 he again set out to review the trial of Joan of Arc's conviction. There began an extensive re-examination of witnesses both to the life and character of Joan and to the mechanics of the original trial. By late June of 1456, as the angelus rang, he was ready to announce his findings.

Jane Marie Pinzino in "The Condemnation and Rehabilitation Trials of Joan of Arc"[11] gives a detailed summary of the many interrogations that led to Bréhal's conclusions. Régine Pernoud, in *The Retrial of Joan of Arc*,[12] sites example testimony from the proceedings. Jules Quicherat's *Procès de Condamnation et de Réhabilitation de Jeanne d'Arc*[13] contains most of the Rehabilitation documents and is quoted in translation by many writers. We will draw on these sources.

The inquisition panel, including Jean Bréhal, Jean Juvenal des Ursins, archbishop of Rheims, Richard Olivier de Longueil, bishop of Coutances, and Guillaume Chartier, bishop of Paris looked into the original judges' impassioned partiality, the violence of Joan's imprisonment including improper behavior of her guards, the many irrelevant questions, threats, falsified articles, and the abjuration obtained by violence. The tribunal traveled to the sites where Joan had lived or visited.

In Lorraine the tribunal interviewed those who knew of Joan's upbringing and personal conduct. Of interest was the "Fairies' Tree" in Domrémy and its nearby spring. Legend suggested that the waters at this tree possessed healing powers. The judges at her trail alleged that Joan conjured evil spirits at this site. Contrary to this accusation, Joan's acquaintances told only that there was a picnic each spring in which all the village youth sang and danced at the tree.

Next, in Paris, nineteen individuals including several assessors from the heresy trial and several of the guards gave their testimonies. Now the injustice and prejudice of the trial began to come out. It was clear that the English had manipulated the French court for their own purposes, and out of fear and hatred for Joan the Maid. Then in Rouen the final nullification hearings took place.

Guillaume Manchon, the chief trial notary, told the inquisitors, "I was compelled to serve as notary in this matter, and I did so against my will, because I would not have dared to oppose an order given by the lords of the Royal Council. And the English conducted this trial, and by their expense. I believe however that the Bishop of Beauvais [the pro-English Pierre Cauchon] was not forced to prosecute Joan, nor was the Promoter [Jean d'Estivet]; on the contrary they did it voluntarily. Concerning the assessors and other advisors, I believe they would not have dared to put up any opposition, and there wasn't a single one who was not afraid."[14]

Jean Massieu, bailiff at the trial testified, "Indeed the Bishop [Cauchon] was staunchly supportive of the English faction, and many of the counselors [assessors] were in great fear. ...as I had often heard from LeMaitre himself, who told me: I see that unless one acts in this matter according to the wishes of the English, death is imminent."[15]

Friar Martin Ladvenu stated, "...one time during the trial, some were sent by order of the judges to advise Joan; but were driven away by the English, and threats made against them. ...I only know that Joan was in a secular prison [i.e., rather than a Church prison], in shackles and bound with chains, and no one could speak with her except by permission of the English, who guarded her day and night."[16]

The eyewitness testimonies of the nullification trial contradicted the accusations of the condemnation trial. Inquisitor Jean Bréhal pointed out the illegality of procedures including the lack of a defense counsel, the youth of the defendant, mortal hatred on the part of her judges, leading questions intended to entrap her, the secular rather than ecclesiastical prison, the location of the trial, omission of evidence favorable to her case, and omission of eyewitness testimonies.[17]

Inquisitor Bréhal drew up his final analysis in June 1456, which described Joan as a martyr and implicated the late Pierre Cauchon with heresy for having convicted an innocent woman in pursuit of a secular vendetta. In the Archbishop's palace in Rouen on 7 July 1456, Bréhal, the judges and commissioners for the case, the Archbishop of Rheims, the Bishop of Paris, and the Bishop of Coutances, Joan's aged mother Isabelle and her brothers Jean and Pierre, as well as spectators, and clergy including Martin Ladvenu, the Dominican friar who had received Joan of Arc's final confession before her death, and Guillaume Manchon, the chief notary during the original trial were gathered to hear the verdict. The Archbishop declared the case ended and the original verdict annulled. The Archbishop spoke:

"We state and pronounce, decree and declare the aforesaid trial and sentence being filled with fraud, false charges, injustice, contradiction, and manifest errors concerning both fact and law, together with the aforementioned abjuration, execution and all that resulted, to have been, to be, and will be null, without effect, void, and of no consequence.

"And notwithstanding, we hereby nullify, void, and annul them and entirely strip them of all effect, declaring that the aforesaid Joan and her family the plaintiffs did not contract or incur any mark or stain of disrepute as a result of the abovementioned matter; and that she is and will be freed and also completely exonerating her."[18]

A copy of the accusations made against Joan of Arc in 1431 was then ritually torn up.

In 1896 Mark Twain published his last, his favorite, and as he himself said, his best novel, *Personal Recollections of Joan of Arc*. Twain presented it as a translation by a fictional Jean Francois Alden of the memoirs of Joan of Arc's page Louis de Contes (a fictionalized version of the real person). It is a passionate and often emotional account of her life, trial, death, and retrial. Louis de Contes, or at least Twain's version of him writes that he was with her almost every minute. Twain has him give us this description of her last moments, a vivid portrait of "…that wonderful child, that sublime personality, that spirit which in one regard has had no peer and will have none…":

"Then the pitchy smoke, shot through with red flashes of flame, rolled up in a thick volume and hid her from sight; and from the heart of this darkness her voice rose strong and eloquent in prayer, and when by moments the wind shredded somewhat of the smoke aside, there were veiled glimpses of an upturned face and moving lips. At last a mercifully swift tide of flame burst upward, and none saw that face any more nor that form, and the voice was still."[19]

---

1   Pernoud, Régine, *The Retrial of Joan of Arc* (translated by J. M Cohen), Harcourt, Brace and Company, New York 1955.

2   Bartolomeo Sacchi, known as Platina (1421 – 1481), was a humanist writer and allegedly the author of the world's first cookbook. In his *The Lives of the Popes* (*Vitæ Pontificum* 1479) he wrote that Pope Callixtus III, in his papal bull of June 29, 1456, had called for public prayer for success in his crusade against the Turks and that the pontiff considered the appearance of a comet at that time to be an ill omen:

"A maned and fiery comet appearing for several days, while scientists were predicting a great plague, dearness of food, or some great disaster, Callistus decreed that supplicatory prayers be held for some days to avert the anger of God, so that, if any calamity threatened mankind, it might be entirely diverted against the Turks, the foes of the Christian name. He likewise ordered that the bells be rung at midday as a signal to all the faithful to move God with assiduous petitions and to assist with their prayers those engaged in constant warfare with the Turks."

The French mathematician and astronomer Pierre-Simon Laplace (1749 – 1827) who had made a study of comets, with Platina as his source for this absurd idea wrote in his *System of the World* (*Exposition du Système du Monde* 1796) that the pope had ordered the comet to be exorcised. This led to the false idea that Callixtus had in fact excommunicated the comet.

3   Pierre Miget, Prior of Longueville-le-Giffard in his deposition of 1456: "...and they decided to bring a judicial action against her which, in my view, the judges undertook under pressure and provocation from the English, since the English always detained her in their own custody and did not allow her to be held in ecclesiastic prisons."

——Quicherat, J., *Proces de condamnation et de rehabilitation de Jeanne d'Arc*, volume 3, p. 130. Paris, 1842, (quoted by Allen Williamson in "Joan of Arc's Trial - Motives & Conduct, Excerpts from the Testimony On This Subject At the Appeal" http://archive.joan-of-arc.org/joanofarc_Condemnation_Trial_Motives_Conduct.html).

4   "...her outfit was equipped with two layers of hosen securely fastened to the doublet, the inner layer being waist-high conjoined woolen hosen attached to the doublet by fully twenty cords, each cord tied into three eyelets apiece (two on the hosen and one on the doublet), for a total of forty attachment points on the inner layer of hosen. The second layer, which was made of rugged leather, seems to have been attached by yet another set of cords. Once this outfit was thus fastened together by dozens of cords connecting both layers to the doublet, it would be a substantial undertaking for someone to try to pull off these garments, especially if she was struggling."

——"Primary Sources and Context Concerning Joan of Arc's Male Clothing". Robert Wirth (editor), Virginia Frohlick (peer-review), Margaret Walsh (peer review), Allen Williamson (authorial contribution and translation). Historical Academy (Association) for Joan of Arc Studies. ISSN: 1557-0355 (electronic format).

5   Vlad III was from the House of Drăculeşti. His father was called Vlad Dracul which means Dragon in Romanian (in modern Romanian it means Devil). Vlad III adopted the appellation. Sources say he signed letters as "Dragulya" or "Drakulya" and later historians refer to him as Dracula, Dracuglia, or Drakula. Bram Stoker borrowed the name Dracula for his vampire, basing this partly on German stories about Vlad, some of which may have suggested that he drank the blood of his victims, although this is probably far from the truth. Stoker knew very little about Vlad and had never visited Romania or Transylvania. Although he was probably born in Transylvania, Vlad never lived there or built a castle there.

6   Laonikos Chalkokondyles: The Histories, Volume II, Books 6–10 (Translated by Anthony Kaldellis) (2014). Harvard University Press. ISBN 978-0-674-59919-2.

7   German and Russian stories published during Vlad III's lifetime painted him as an evil, demonic, insane, and sadistic man. Here a few examples:

Perihelion

Michael Beheim wrote a lengthy poem about Vlad's deeds. The poem, called "Von ainem wutrich der heis Trakle waida von der Walachei" ("Story of a Despot Called Dracula, Voievod of Wallachia"), was performed at the court of Frederick III, Holy Roman Emperor in Wiener Neustadt during the winter of 1463. According to one of Beheim's stories, Vlad had two monks impaled to assist them to go to heaven, also ordering the impalement of their donkey because it began braying after its masters' death.
——David B Dickens and Elizabeth Miller. "Michel Beheim, German Meistergesang, and Dracula" Journal of Dracula Studies.

"Turkish messengers came to [Vlad] to pay respects, but refused to take off their turbans, according to their ancient custom, whereupon he strengthened their custom by nailing their turbans to their heads with three spikes, so that they could not take them off."
——Antonio Bonfini: Historia Pannonica.

[Vlad] had a big copper cauldron built and put a lid made of wood with holes in it on top. He put the people in the cauldron and put their heads in the holes and fastened them there; then he filled it with water and set a fire under it and let the people cry their eyes out until they were boiled to death. And then he invented frightening, terrible, unheard of tortures. He ordered that women be impaled together with their suckling babies on the same stake. The babies fought for their lives at their mother's breasts until they died. Then he had the women's breasts cut off and put the babies inside headfirst; thus he had them impaled together.
— About a mischievous tyrant called Dracula vodă

The following is an account from the Greek historian Chalkondyles of what greeted the invaders:

"He [the Sultan] marched on for about five kilometers when he saw his men impaled; the Sultan's army came across a field with stakes, about three kilometers long and one kilometer wide. And there were large stakes on which they could see the impaled bodies of men, women, and children, about twenty thousand of them, as they said; quite a spectacle for the Turks and the Sultan himself! The Sultan, in wonder, kept saying that he could not conquer the country of a man who could do such terrible and unnatural things, and put his power and his subjects to such use. He also used to say that this man who did such things would be worthy of more. And the other Turks, seeing so many people impaled, were scared out of their wits. There were babies clinging to their mothers on the stakes, and birds had made nests in their breasts."

——Laonikos Chalkokondyles: The Histories, Volume II,

One of the German pamphlets (Nuremberg 1488) notes the following episodes:

"He had some of his people buried naked up to the navel and had them shot at. He also had some roasted and flayed.

"He captured the young Dan [of the rival Danesti clan] and had a grave dug for him and had a funeral service held according to Christian custom and beheaded him beside the grave.

"He had a large pot made and boards with holes fastened over it and had people's heads shoved through there and imprisoned them in this. And he had the pot filled with water and a big fire made under the pot and thus let the people cry out pitiably until they were boiled quite to death.

"He devised dreadful, frightful, unspeakable torments, such as impaling together mothers and children nursing at their breasts so that the children kicked convulsively at their mothers' breasts until dead. In like manner he cut open mothers' breasts and stuffed their children's heads through and thus impaled both.

"He had all kinds of people impaled sideways: Christians, Jews, heathens, so that they moved and twitched and whimpered in confusion a long time like frogs.

"About three hundred gypsies came into his country. Then he selected the best three of them and had them roasted; these the others had to eat."

——Miller, Elizabeth (2005). "Vlad The Impaler". Vlad the Impaler. n.p. Retrieved 16 February 2015.

8	Miller, Elizabeth (2005). "Vlad The Impaler".

9	Rigge, William F.. "An Historical Examination of the Connection of Calixtus III with Halley's Comet". Popular

Perihelion

Astronomy, Maria Mitchell Observatory, provided by the NASA Astrophysics Data System.

10   Saint Petca Parasceva was born to wealthy, noble, pious landowners. Petca started dressing poor people in her expensive clothes. Her parents objected, finding the girl's charity more than they could understand or support, and tried to get her to stop. To follow her calling, Petca left her parents, her wealth, and status, and ran away to Constantinople. She received visions of the Virgin Mary during her prayers. In one of the visions, she received the message that she should go to Jerusalem. After some time in the city, she joined a convent in the Jordanian desert. A few years later, she returned to Constantinople.

Legend says that many years later an old sinner was buried near her grave. Petca appeared in a dream to a local monk, showed him the place of her burial, and demanded, "Take that stinky corpse away from me. I am light and sun, and I cannot bear to have near me darkness and stench." The monk obtained some local help and began to dig at the place he had seen in his dream. When they found the remains of the Saint, they found her body incorrupt and emitting a spiritual fragrance. Each time her remains were transferred from place to place they had not deteriorated.

    ——Patron Saints Index. http://saints.sqpn.com/saintp2c.htm.

11   Pinzino, Jane Marie. "The Condemnation and Rehabilitation Trials of Joan of Arc". Southern Methodist University, Dallas, Texas. https://faculty.smu.edu/bwheeler/ijas/pinzino.html.

12   Pernoud, Régine, *The Retrial of Joan of Arc* (translated by J. M Cohen), Harcourt, Brace and Company, New York 1955.

13   Quicherat, Jules, ed.; *Procès de Condamnation et de Réhabilitation de Jeanne d'Arc, dite la Pucelle* (5 Volumes). Société de l'Histoire de France, 1841, 1844, 1845, 1847, 1849, Paris.

14   Pernoud's *The Retrial of Joan Arc*, p. 180.

15   Quicherat, Vol III, pp. 152 – 154.

16   Ibid., pp. 166 – 167

17   Pinzino, Jane Marie. "The Condemnation and Rehabilitation Trials of Joan of Arc".

18   DuParc, Pierre, ed.; *Procès en Nullité de la Condamnation de Jeanne d'Arc* (5 Volumes). vol II p. 610. Société de l'Histoire de France, 1977, 1979, 1983, 1986, 1988; Paris.

19   Mark Twain. *Personal Recollections of Joan of Arc, by the Sieur Louis de Conte.* Vol 2, p 94. Classic Literature Library, https://marktwain.classic-literature.co.uk/personal-recollections-of-joan-of-arc-vol-2/.

Miracle of the Flowers

I am wondering where I may gather some pretty, sweet flowers.
Whom shall I ask? Suppose that I ask the brilliant humming-bird,
the emerald trembler; suppose that I ask the yellow butterfly;
they will tell me...
——"Song at the Beginning" Nahuatl poem[1]

They dwell in the place of spring, in the place of spring,
here within the broad fields, and only for our sakes
does the turquoise water fall in broken drops
on the surface of the lake.

Where it gleams forth in fourfold rays, where the
fragrant yellow flowers bud, there live the Mexicans,
The youths.
——"A Christian Song" Nahuatl poem[2]

August 26, 1531. Tolpetlac, a small village near Tenochtitlan, the former capital of the Aztec Empire, known now as Mexico City, Mexico. A Mexica named Cuauhtlatoatzi, whose name in Nahuatl translates into English as Talking Eagle, has left his home to journey to the Franciscan mission station at Tlatelolco where he has become a neophyte. The padre at the mission, Padre Miguel Ángel Capilla, had given Cuauhtlatoatzi and his wife their Spanish names, Juan and María Lucía Diego. They had been among the first Indians, Chichimecas[3] as the Aztec's called them, to be baptized soon after the Spanish conquest of Tenochtitlan. María Lucía was gone two years now, a victim of the smallpox epidemic the Spanish had brought with them.

Juan Diego is concerned about the appearance in the sky of a bright star with a long shining tail. He is afraid it is Quetzalcoatl, the feathered serpent god of the Aztecs, who once set himself on fire and who, according to some, had returned in the form of the Spanish conquistador, Hernán Cortés. Quetzalcoatl invented the calendar and books and had brought maize to mankind. But he was also the symbol of death and resurrection. Too many signs of prophecy appeared in the heavens. Last spring the entire sky had darkened for many minutes[4] suggesting that Huitzilopochtli, the solar deity was angry. Juan Diego is seeking the guidance of the padres at the mission. If they do not help him understand the significance of this strange fiery dragon he will go directly to see Father Juan de Zumárraga, the Bishop in Mexico City.

Juan Diego remembers the city when it was Tenochtitlan. It was a beautiful city, built on Chinampas, man-made islands of heaped up mud on the great Lake Texcoco, islands of rich soil dredged from the lake and fertile enough to support the large population of the empire. A beautiful city in four urban sections surrounding the central square where the Templo Mayor, the Great Temple stood. This was a large, stepped pyramid with shrines to Tlaloc and Huitzilopochtli; it had been where the human sacrifices were held. Although Juan had never been inside the walls of the square he knew of the great ball court and the tzompantli, the skull rack displaying the severed heads of sacrificial victims whose bleeding bodies had been thrown down the steps of the Templo Mayor.

Until about ten years ago the ruler of the Aztec nation had been Moctezuma II Xocoyotzin, "He frowns like a lord." Spanish galleons had reached the shores of Mexico in 1517 and Moctezuma was aware of this. He was aware of the hostilities of the Spanish toward the Mexica peoples. When in 1519 Hernán Cortés docked in the harbor at San Juan de Ulua, Moctezuma sent envoys to greet him with gifts, hoping to placate him. But Cortés allied himself with enemies of the Aztec, the Tlaxcalteca, and instigated revolts against the monarch in many towns as he marched toward Tenochtitlan. He also burned his ships so that his soldiers could not mutiny and return to Spain.

Bernal Diaz del Castillo was one of the soldier/conquistadors who accompanied Cortés on his conquest of Mexico. In later life he wrote his memoirs[5] and these detailed annals are a main source for the history of the founding of Mexico City which we now relate. He tells of the indigenous peoples they met, traded with, sometimes fought and conquered, and sought to convert to Christianity:

"In dress and language this people differed entirely from the Mexicans, whom Motecusuma [sic] had sent to our camp. They had large holes bored in their under-lips, in which they wore pieces of blue speckled stone, or thin plates of gold; the holes in their ears were still larger in size, and adorned with similar ornaments."[6]

The Spaniards found that Moctezuma's tax-gatherers required the surrounding communities to provide human beings for sacrifices at the capitol, a circumstance that greatly angered the people of these settlements. Cortés ordered the Mexican tax-gatherers to be imprisoned. He fastened the prisoners to long poles, by collars which went round their necks, making movement quite difficult. One of them who made resistance, Diaz tells us, was "whipped into the bargain." Cortés forbade the villagers further obedience to Moctezuma, inciting a rebellion against the monarch.

In each town they went through the Spaniards burned the idols of the Nahuatls and erected large wooden crosses. Even in these small communities human sacrifice was practiced. Diaz tells of seeing piles of human skulls at one temple: "…there must have been more than 100,000; I repeat, more than 100,000. In like manner you saw the remaining human bones piled up in order in another corner of the square; these it would have been impossible to count. Besides these, there were human heads hanging suspended from beams on both sides."[7]

Conquest and submission of the population was not always easy. The Tlascallans attacked in force. Diaz describes the battle:

"They had broad swords, which are used with both hands, the edges of which are made of hard flint, and are sharper than our steel swords. They were also armed with shields, lances, and had feathers stuck in their hair. They defended themselves right valiantly with their swords and lances, wounding several of our horses. The blood of our men now also began to boil, who, in return, killed five of the Indians. At that moment a swarm of more than 3,000 Tlascallans rushed furiously from an ambush, pouring forth a shower of arrows upon our cavalry, who now immediately closed their ranks. At the same time we fired among them with our cannon, and so at last we obliged the enemy to give ground…"[8]

Cortés subdued the Tlascallans and enlisted them as allies as he continued to march toward Tenochtitlan. They arrived at the future Mexico City on November 8, 1519. After many negotiations with Moctezuma's officials (the Spaniards' requesting a meeting with the monarch, the Aztecs insisting they go away), and after much exchanging of gifts (the Aztecs showering the Spaniards with items of gold, and the Spaniards showering the Aztecs with glass beads), Moctezuma finally relented. Moctezuma met Cortés and his entourage on a narrow causeway leading towards the district of Cojohua.

Moctezuma was "sumptuously attired, had on a species of half boot, richly set with jewels, and whose soles were made of solid gold. The four grandees who supported him were also richly attired.... Besides these distinguished caziques, there were many other grandees around the monarch, some of whom held the canopy over his head, while others again occupied the road before him, and spread cotton cloths on the ground that his feet might not touch the bare earth. No one of his suite ever looked at him full in the face...."[9]

They were invited to stay with the king at the palace and given comfortable rooms. In the following days they attended many dinners with Moctezuma presiding, although he sat behind a wooden screen.[10] They were given tours of the central square including the Templo Mayor, the great pyramid, which Cortés climbed and witnessed the bloodied altar and learned of the nature of the human sacrifices.[11] More and more he became convinced he must convert these barbaric Indians to Christianity.

After a short time had elapsed, they became aware of a conspiracy by certain members of Moctezuma's court, including his nephews, to murder them in their rooms and then attack and eliminate the troops encamped outside the palace. This, Cortés believed, the Aztecs could easily accomplish due to their superior numbers, even considering the Spanish cannon and cavalry. They decided to take Moctezuma prisoner to assure their safety. They invited the monarch to their rooms and persuaded him, through threats of violence (and a smattering of reason) to stay there under their control. It was something less than being under house arrest as Moctezuma was allowed to visit his temple and his wives. It was seen by Moctezuma's followers as the king's betrayal, however.

During this time Moctezuma offered one of his daughters in marriage to Cortés and said that he should "quit Mexico, with the whole of his men, as all the caziques and papas were upon the point of rising up in arms to destroy us all, in compliance with the advice given them by their gods."[12] Cortés accepted the daughter but did not take the advice. From here on it gets a bit complicated.

Perihelion

One of the Spaniards came to Cortés very wounded. He had been to Tlacupa, a nearby town, to fetch some women belonging to Cortés' household and a daughter of Moctezuma, but had found the road filled with Aztec warriors. The women were taken and the man barely escaped with his life. Angered at this betrayal, Cortés dispatched one of his captains with 400 men armed with crossbows and muskets. About half-way down the causeway they were "met by a vast body of Mexicans, who, with those posted on the tops of the houses, attacked him so furiously that eight of his men were killed at the first onset, and most of them wounded."[13]

The men fought their way back to the Spanish quarters. The attackers had killed 23 of them and set fire to the quarters. Cortés decided to bring out his army in full force. The situation was clear: although Moctezuma had agreed to swear allegiance to the Spanish king, his nephews and other principals of the realm had not. His cousin, Cuitláhuac, was about to be crowned in Moctezuma's place. The attacks continued and retreat from the city seemed impossible:

"All the volleys from our heavy guns and muskets were to no purpose; it was in vain we rushed forward upon them, and killed from thirty to forty of their numbers at a time; their ranks still remained firmly closed, while their courage seemed to increase with every loss."[14]

During the following days the Spaniards built two movable wooden towers under each of which twenty-five men could stand and from which heavy guns could be fired. Thus armored, they pushed forward toward the temple, the great pyramid devoted to Huitzilopochtli. They killed many along the way yet their enemy persevered and shouted at them that they "were to be sacrificed to their gods, our hearts were to be torn from our bodies, the blood was to be drawn from our veins, and our arms and legs were to be eaten up at their festivals. The remaining parts of our bodies would be thrown to the tigers, lions and serpents, which they kept in cages; these had not been fed for these two days, in order that they might devour our flesh the more greedily."[15]

Then occurred what most historians, Diaz not included, called a massacre of the Aztecs at the temple.[16] Returning to their quarters, Cortés told Moctezuma to address the angry multitudes of his people from the top of the building, to order them to cease their hostilities and allow the Spaniards to leave the city unharmed. Reluctantly,

Moctezuma did so but his subjects replied that they had named a new king and would continue to wage war against the Spanish. Cortés' men had covered Moctezuma with their shields as the furious mob approached and stones began to be thrown. Then an arrow struck Moctezuma in the leg. He died soon after. By 1521, the Aztec nation no longer existed as such.

It is August 26, 1531. Juan Diego is headed for the Franciscan mission at Tlatelolco where he will ask Father Miguel Ángel Capilla about the vision he has had of Quetzalcoatl, the feathered serpent who is hanging in the western sky like a fiery dragon. Juan Diego has accepted Jesus Christ as his savior and taken him into his heart but…Juan Diego is also the Chichimeca called Cuauhtlatoatzi, and he has found it quite difficult to disbelieve in the old gods.

He still remembers that time when the Spaniards first came, how they destroyed the temple and went out into the land enslaving those who rebelled and branding them with their mark. Yet their religion was about peace…they did eat the flesh and drink the blood of their savior, but it was symbolic. No longer were there human sacrifices at the temple.

His path takes him past the hill of Tepeyacac. He is tempted to climb the rocky slope where he might view the whole of the valley. There, at the base of the basalt expanse, once sat the shrine to the goddess Tonantzin, but this has been destroyed by the Spanish. Tonantzin: Our Sacred Mother, Bringer of Maize, Mother Earth, also known as Quilaztli, and as Cihuacoatl the Serpent woman.[16] He remembers the idol to the goddess that once stood inside the humble shrine, her skirt of writhing snakes and her necklace of human hearts and skulls. And yet her countenance had a benevolence that seemed to shine by some inner light…she was a goddess of fertility and reproduction and the protector of all women. Juan remembers a song to Tonantzin/Quilaztli:

Quilaztli, plumed with eagle feathers, with the crest of eagles, painted with serpents' blood, comes with her hoe, beating her drum, from Colhuacan.

She alone, who is our flesh, goddess of the fields and shrubs, is strong to support us.

With the hoe, with the hoe, with hands full, with the hoe, with hands full, the goddess of the fields is strong to support us.

Perihelion

With a broom in her hands the goddess of the fields strongly supports us.

Our mother is as twelve eagles, goddess of drum-beating, filling the fields of tzioac and maguey like our lord Mixcoatl.

She is our mother, a goddess of war, our mother, a goddess of war, an example and a companion from the home of our ancestors (Colhuacan).

She comes forth, she appears when war is waged, she protects us in war that we shall not be destroyed, an example and companion from the home of our ancestors.

She comes adorned in the ancient manner with the eagle crest, in the ancient manner with the eagle crest.[17]

But she hadn't protected them when war was waged. And now the Spanish have destroyed her abode in these bleak hills. Juan pauses for a moment to consider this. He thinks he can hear a soft sighing—the lament of the goddess? Some have said as much. Perhaps it is only the wind pushing through the dried branches of the lone cedar tree that clings to the escarpment, twisted and bent with age. Twisted and bent like Father Capilla at the mission. Father Capilla who will ease his mind about the dragon in the sky above.

"It is but a comet," Father Miguel Ángel Capilla tells Juan Diego. "They are seen in some years. Not always do they announce events of great importance. This comet surely means nothing to us but to provide a dazzling spectacle for out amusement."

"But Father," insists Juan, "what of the Star of David? In the story you told me of the birth of Our Savior, there is a star that prophecies…"

"That was of Divine Origin. And I do not think it was a comet. You are learning your lessons well, though, my son. I am very pleased with your progress."

Father Capilla is seated in a hand-carved wooden chair, stiff-backed and not very comfortable. But it suits his mood which is always officious and formal. The adobe building that serves as a mission had been built several years ago by rural peoples taken as slaves by the conquering Spanish. People who might have been distant relatives of Juan Diego. Now a young girl enters the room carrying a tray.

Byron Grush

"Your coffee, Father," she says. There is a small clay pot, steaming with the fragrant aroma of freshly brewed coffee, and a single tin cup on the tray. Juan is not to be offered any libation today.

"Thank you, Rosita," says the Padre.

Rosita is Rosita Delgado (her given Spanish name). Her Nahuatl name was Acxoyatl, which means "wild laural." The girl looks a bit peaked Juan thinks. Other times he has seen her she has been perky, vibrant, presenting the promise of alluring womanhood. Juan should be ashamed to be imagining her as an adult; but he is not. She gives him a weak smile as she exits the room.

"Father," asks Juan, "the Holy Mother Mary...how is it that she was a virgin? Did she not have a husband?"

"It is told in the Bible that Joseph was an old man. Mary was given her birth of the Christ Child through an act of God. She herself was born free of sin; this is the Immaculate Conception."

Joseph was an old man, thinks Juan, like me. (Juan has turned 57 this year). Then he remembers a line from the song of Tonantzin/Quilaztli: she came "from the home of our ancestors, Colhuacan." Colhuacan means "the place of the old men." She was the mother of Mixcoatl, the Star God and she helped Quetzalcoatl create humans by grinding up bones and mixing them with his blood. Was she also a virgin, free of sin? He thinks he had better not quiz the Padre on this point.

For his own part, Father Capilla is not normally prone to reminiscing, but today, because of the acolyte's questions about the Virgin Mary, he sinks into reverie. Father Capilla came originally from the Cáceres province of the high plains of Extremadura near Madrid in Spain, the same region where Hernán Cortéz was born. There is a shrine there in which was placed a wooden statue, about two feet tall, that depicts the figure of the Virgin as a Black woman.

The story of the Black Madonna involves a humble shepherd to whom the Virgin Mary had appeared. The Lady told the shepherd to dig up a statue of her which had been buried. It was said that this statue was carved by Luke the Evangelist.[19] The simple wooden figure is now elaborately dressed in flowing golden robes and is housed in the Monastery of Santa María de Guadalupe. The image of the Virgin based on this statue is the same as the one carried by Cortéz to the New World. The conquistadors erected this image of

Perihelion

the Virgin on the top of the pyramid of Templo Mayor—it was later destroyed by Moctezuma.

Summer has passed, fall has passed, it is December 1531, the year of the comet. Juan Diego has learned that the servant girl, Rosita Delgado, has died of smallpox, the Spaniards' disease. He is still not over the death of his own wife, and now this. He leaves early in the morning for his usual walk to the mission. The dull orange glow of the rising sun brightens into a golden hue as he approaches the Tepeyácac hill. What happens next has been told again and again;[20] it is the stuff of legend, of inspiration, of hope. And of miracles.

From the top of the hill came the sweet sound of singing, like that of birds, but not like that of birds. Juan was familiar with the sound of the coyoltótl and the tzinizcan, and of gorriones, and of jilgueros. And it was said of the zenzontle that it could mimic the song of other birds. But this music was like nothing Juan had ever heard before. Something about it seemed to be calling him: "Juantzin, Juan Diegotzin," the birds called. As if in a dream, Juan climbed up the rocky slope.

When he neared the top of Tepeyácac hill he saw no birds, but a vision came to him of a lovely woman surrounded by an aura of light. It looked as if she were standing, not on a crag of ordinary grey stone, but on jewels whose inner glow was almost as radiant as the lady's vermilion tunic, her white mantilla, her mulberry-colored belt, her brooch of shining gold. The sparse vegetation all around her sparkled like gemstones; the prickly pears looked like giant emeralds; the scruffy junipers shone like turquoise. The lady beckoned.

Juan drew close. As first he was struck dumb by the glorious vision before him, Then he managed to say, "Tonantzin Coatlaxopeuh? (Lady who emerges from the region of light like the Eagle from fire?)"

The vision answered this saying, "Juanito, el más pequeño de mis hijos, ¿adónde vas? (Little Juan, the smallest of my sons, where are you going?)"

"My Lady, I go to seek guidance from the good padres at the mission. This is my daily ritual, my duty. Are you the Mother of Earth? Tonantzin?" Juan stammered.

"And if I say I am not she, who would you believe me to be, little son?"

"I know not. Please tell me."

[author's note: here we present the Lady's answer as it is told in the Nican mopohua ("Here it is told...") of Luis Lasso de la Vega.]

"Know and have understood, you the littlest of my sons, that I am the ever-Virgin Holy Mary, Mother of the true God by whom there is life; of the Creator from whom everything exists; Lord of heaven and earth. I intensely desire that you erect me here a temple, in order to show and give all of my love, compassion, aid and defense in it, for I am your pious Mother, to you, to all of you together the residents of this land and the rest of my devotees who call upon me and trust in me; to hear there their laments and to remedy all their miseries, sufferings and pains. And in order to realize what my clemency endeavors, go to the palace of the bishop of Mexico and you will tell him as I have sent you to show him what I much desire, that here on the plain he may build for me a temple. You will tell him exactly what you have seen and admired, and what you have heard. Be certain that I will thank you well and you will much deserve that I recompense the work and fatigue with which you will strive to attain what I entrust to you."[21]

Juan de Zumárraga is a Franciscan priest who is the first bishop of Mexico. His residence is in Mexico City, not far from the Tepeyácac hill. Juan Diego hurries there to do the Lady's bidding but is delayed at the gate by the Bishop's servants. When he finally gets to see the Bishop and tell his story, the Bishop does not believe him. "Go away and come back tomorrow," he is told.

Juan returns to the hill and again the Virgin Mary appears to him. He asks her to please find someone else for the task as he is obviously not worthy and not skilled in the art of persuasion. "I am a man of no importance," he tells her. But the Virgin instructs him to try again. She is not angry with him, but she is stern. He is being tested. He must obey no matter how inadequate he feels. It is like being thrown by a great wave in an ocean of doubt with only one rock with which to cling: Our Lady.

The next day he goes again to see the Bishop. "She is adamant that a temple be built so that those who ail may be relieved by her Grace," Juan tells Bishop Zumárraga. The Bishop shakes his head. He has heard of miracles, of people seeing the Virgin—that story of the shepherd of Guadalupe in Spain and others. But he is not convinced.

Perihelion

"Go you back to your Lady and say that you must have some sign by which I, the authority of the Church here in Mexico, will know it is she. Then I may build your temple," says the Bishop. After Juan leaves Bishop Zumárraga instructs his servants to follow Juan, to observe for themselves this so-called vision. This they do, but they lose sight of him and have nothing to report.

The next day Juan discovers that his uncle, Juan Bernardino, has been taken ill with the Spanish disease. He goes to tend to his uncle and does not return to the place of the Virgin. He worries now that he has greatly offended her. But on the following morning, a crisp, cold wintery morning, he passes the hill on his way to summon a priest to hear his uncle's last confession when the Virgin suddenly appears.

Juan explains that his uncle is at the point of death so he is going to the mission where he will call one of the priests to give confession. "Because in truth for this we were born, we have come to await the work of our death," he says. He assures her he will return to the task she has given him as soon as he can.

"Cuix amo nican nica nimonantzin? (Am I not here, I, who am your mother?)" she asks him. "You need not fear this illness or any other illness. You are in the hollow of my mantle, in the crossing of my arms. You need a sign? Go you to the top of this barren hill. You will find flowers there where none have ever bloomed before. Pick them and bring them to me."

Juan obeys. At the top of the hill he finds, remarkable in the coldness of the season and the forbidding terrain of rock and gravel where there should be nothing but thorns, flowers blooming of many varieties including some not native to this land. He picks the red blooms of roses such as those of Castile and brings them to the Virgin. Certainly this is a miracle...but will the Bishop believe it? The Lady handles the flowers then gives them back to Juan.

"Place them in your cuexantli," she tells him, "and take them to your Bishop as a sign of my presence."

He folds them into his cuexantli, the blanket-like cloak worn over his shoulder, also called a tilma. He returns to the Bishop's residence but is stopped once more at the gate. The servants see he is hiding something in his tilma: flowers! They try to grab them, but the blooms are now appearing to be something painted or woven on the tilma. Next comes the miracle.

Byron Grush

Juan is standing now before the Bishop. He tells him he has brought flowers, impossible to have been blooming this winter on the hill, as a sign from the Virgin. He opens his tilma. The flowers fall to the floor at the Bishop's feet. An image has appeared on the tilma where the flowers had been. It is the image of the Holy Mother, the Virgin Mary! The Bishop falls to his knees. The bishop, with tears, begs that she pardon him for not having fulfilled her will. He takes the tilma from Juan Diego's neck and takes to his private chapel.

The following day, Juan Diego shows the Bishop the site where the Lady has asked for her shrine to be built. He then goes to see his uncle who had been dying and finds the man to be fully cured. Juan Bernardino says that he had been healed and at that exact moment he had seen the Virgin just as she had appeared to Juan. She told him, he says, to appear before the Bishop and describe what he had seen, as well as his miraculous cure. He should also name her image, she told him, as the Perfect Virgin, Holy Mary of Guadalupe (Cenquizca Ichpochtzintli Santa María de Guadalupe).

Perihelion

from "Felicidad de México" (1666)

    A small chapel was erected at the foot of Tepeyácac hill and Bishop Zumárraga installed Juan Diego's tilma there for all to see and to worship. During the procession bringing the tilma to the chapel an Indian was struck by an arrow and appeared to have died, but miraculously, was brought back to life in front of the altar. This was the first of fourteen miracles[22] that would be associated with the image of the Virgin of Guadalupe. The image is now housed in the Basilica of Our Lady of Guadalupe built in 1709 near Tepeyácac hill in Mexico City. Philip Callahan gives us a description of the image:

Byron Grush

"The image features a full-length representation of a girl or young woman, delicate features, and straight, unbraided hair simply parted in the middle framing her face. The subject matter is in a standing posture showing in contemplative prayer with hands joined and little finger separated and head slightly inclined; she gazes with heavy-lidded eyes at a spot below and to her right, and to left in viewpoint of the observer. She is dressed from neck to feet in a pink robe and blue-green cerulean mantle, one side folded within the arms, emblazoned with eight-pointed stars with two black tassels tied at high waist, wearing a neck brooch featuring a colonial styled cross. The robe is spangled with a small gold quatrefoil motif ornamented with vines and flowers, its sleeves reaching to her wrists where the cuffs of a white undergarment appear. The subject stands on a crescent moon, allegedly colored silver in the past, now having turned dark. A feathered cherubic angel with outstretched arms carries the robe on her exposed feet which is uncolored. A sunburst of straight and wavy gold rays alternate while projecting behind the Virgin and are enclosed within a mandorla. Beyond the mandorla to the right and left is an unpainted expanse, white in color with a faint blue tinge."[23]

There are detractors to the story, of course. They point to what they call the silent time, the lack of records between the event in 1531 and the first published account in 1648. Is it possible that the published accounts were simply propaganda to assist the Spanish in converting the Indian population to Christianity? Why did the Virgin ask to be called "Perfect Virgin, Holy Mary of Guadalupe" when the region of Guadalupe was in Spain, not Mexico? Did Juan Diego report his vision to the Bishop not of the Madonna but of the goddess Tonantzin? In contemporary Nahuatl-speaking communities the Virgin in commonly called "Tonantzin." Her appearance is commemorated each year on December 12.

During the 1950s photographic examinations of the image seemed to show that within the eyes of the Virgin there appeared to be human figures. Philip Callahan:

"First, the same figure seems to be in both eyes. Second, in the right eye, which is more clearly rendered, there are two or possibly three instances of the human figure, in the locations, sizes and orientations one finds in the reflections on a human eye, known as Purkinje-Sanson images.

Perihelion

"The strength of these assertions, however, is limited by the resolution of the images. While the primary image of a bearded man's face is clearly recognizable in the right eye, it is less clear in the left eye, which is generally less detailed and may have been retouched. Also, the second and third Purkinje-Sanson images are not obvious human forms. The latter, in fact, is little more than a bright dot. While this evidence is consistent with the sizes of Purkinje-Sanson reflections, we are dealing with a scale that approaches the resolution of individual threads. ...These more extravagant claims are not substantiated by expert analyses, and belong in the realm of cloud-reading."[24]

Canonical coronation was granted for the Virgin of Guadalupe by Pope Leo XIII on October 12, 1895. Juan Diego, the first Catholic Saint from the Americas, was beatified in 1990 and canonized in 2002 by Pope John Paul II.

---

1   Brinton, Daniel Garrison, trans. *Ancient Nahuatl Poetry: Containing the Nahuatl Text of XXVII Ancient Mexican Poems.* D. G. Brinton, Philadelphia. 1887. P. 55.

2   Ibid., p. 87

3   Nahua peoples of Mexico referred to the nomadic tribes of the region as Chichimeca, a term picked up by the Spanish and often used to mean "barbarian". However, Michael E. Smith writes, "Chichimec...refers primarily to non-sedentary hunting populations living to the north of central Mexico, although it may also designate simple farming groups in the north. ...the term is extended to cover central Mexican immigrant populations whose ancestors had been either hunters or northern farmers..."

——Smith, Michael E. (1984). "The Aztlan Migrations of Nahuatl Chronicles: Myth or History?" (PDF online facsimile). Ethnohistory. Columbus, OH: American Society for Ethnohistory.

4   In 1531 there was a full solar eclipse over Mexico on March 28, at 3:06 pm. Halley's Comet achieved its perihelion on August 26.

5   Bernal Diaz objected to the academic accounts of the history in which he himself had taken place. As an eyewitness, he was, he said, better qualified to tell the truth of those events. His narrative, written in 1632, is particularly kind to Cortez and vilifies the Aztecs, but it is extremely detailed and lyrical in execution.

——Bernal Diaz del Castillo. *The Memoirs of the Conquistador Bernal Diaz del Castillo, Vol 1 (of 2) Written by Himself Containing a True and Full Account of the Discovery and Conquest of Mexico and New Spain.* Trans. John Ingram Lockhart. The Project Gutenberg EBook #32474, 2010.

6,7,8,9 Ibid.

10   "We were told that the flesh of young children, as a very dainty bit, was also set before him sometimes by way of a relish. Whether there was any truth in this we could not possibly discover; on account of the great variety of dishes, consisting in fowls, turkeys, pheasants, partridges, quails, tame and wild geese, venison, musk swine, pigeons, hares, rabbits, and of numerous other birds and beasts; besides which there were various other kinds of provisions, indeed it would have been no easy task to call them all over by name."

——Ibid.

11   "Respecting the abominable human sacrifices of these people, the following was communicated to us: The breast of the unhappy victim destined to be sacrificed was ripped open with a knife made of sharp flint; the throbbing heart was then torn out, and immediately offered to the idol-god in whose honour the sacrifice had been instituted. After this, the head, arms, and legs were cut off and eaten at their banquets, with the exception of the head, which was saved, and hung to a beam appropriated for that purpose. No other part of the body was eaten, but the remainder was thrown to the beasts which were kept in those abominable dens, in which there were also vipers and other poisonous serpents, and, among the latter in particular, a species at the end of whose tail there was a kind of rattle. This last-mentioned serpent, which is the most dangerous, was kept in a cabin of a diversified form, in which a quantity of feathers had

Perihelion

been strewed: here it laid its eggs, and it was fed with the flesh of dogs and of human beings who had been sacrificed."
——Ibid.

12,13,14,15 Ibid.

16   "As soon as day had fully broken forth, we commended ourselves to the Almighty, and sallied out with our war-towers. This time again we killed a great number of the enemy; but with all our fighting we could not force them to yield ground, and if they had fought courageously the two previous days, they stood the more firm this time, and fought desperately. We however determined, if it were even to cost us all our lives, to push forward to the great temple of Huitzilopochtli. For whenever our cavalry galloped in upon the enemy's ranks, our horses were assailed by so many arrows, stones and lances, that they were immediately covered with wounds; while their riders, however courageously they fought, could make but little impression upon the foe. If they pushed further on, the Mexicans either jumped into the canals or into the lake, where the cavalry could not follow them, and where a whole forest of lances stared them in the face: equally fruitless were all our attempts to set fire to their houses, or pull them down, as they stood, in the midst of the water, and were connected to each other by drawbridges only. If at times we did succeed in firing a house, it took a whole day in burning down, nor did the fire spread, from the buildings being at too great distance from each other, and their being surrounded by water, so that all our efforts that way completely failed.

The reader should have seen how we were covered with blood and wounds! Above forty of our men lay dead at our feet; but at last, with the aid of Providence, we succeeded in reaching the point where we had erected the image of the holy Virgin [the top of the pyramid…the Virgin's image had been removed by Moctezuma, however]. We now set fire to the Mexican idols, and part of the chapel was on this occasion burnt down, with Huitzilopochtli and Tetzcatlipuca. While we were occupied with this work, the battle on the platform continued without intermission; for here stood a number of priests, and more than three or four thousand of the principal Mexicans, who fell upon us with great fury, and even beat us back again down the steps of the temple."

——Ibid.

17   Cihuacoatl was the mythical mother of the human race. Her name, generally translated "serpent woman," should be rendered "woman of twins" or "bearing twins," as the myth related that such was her fertility that she always bore two children at one lying-in.... She was also known by the title Tonan or Tonantzin, "our mother" ...Still another of her appellations was Quilaztli....
——Various, *Rig Veda Americanus - Sacred Songs Of The Ancient Mexicans, With A Gloss In Nahuatl*. Project Gutenberg EBook #14993, 2005. (from Library of Aboriginal American Literature. No. VIII. Ed. D. G. Brinton. 1890).

An ancient Mexican story tells that before the Spaniards' arrival, a lament of a woman crying was heard in the lake of Texcoco saying: "My children, beloved children of Anahuac, your destruction is next." The priests thought it was the goddess Cihuacoatl who prophesied the destruction of the Anahuac. Shortly after the Mexica people's defeat, when the Spanish destroyed the great "Templo Mayor" and Tonantzin's temple in Mexico City and Tepeyac's hill, the lament of the goddess was also heard, crying for her dwelling which had been defiled by the invader. This story eventually gave way to the legend of "La Llorona."
——Tonantzin... the deity behind "Our Lady of Guadalupe" Yucatan Times on December 12, 2020.

18   Various, *Rig Veda Americanus - Sacred Songs Of The Ancient Mexicans, With A Gloss In Nahuatl*. Project Gutenberg EBook #14993, 2005. (from Library of Aboriginal American Literature. No. VIII. Ed. D. G. Brinton. 1890).

19   According to Richard Segerstrom, writing for the Catholic Exchange (catholicexchange.com/another-lady-of-guadalupe), the statue of Our Lady of Guadalupe was carved by Saint Luke the Evangelist, and given to Saint Leander, Bishop of Seville, by Pope Saint Gregory I in gratitude for converting the Visigothic kings, Saint Hermengild and Recared to Catholicism. In 714 the Moors invaded Spain, reaching Seville where the statue was held. To save the statue,

Perihelion

priests buried it in the hills near the Guadalupe River. Segerstrom relates the following legend:

"At the beginning of the fourteenth century, a shepherd named Gil Cordero began to report apparitions of Our Lady in his field near the present day city of Cáceres. Our Lady ordered Gil Cordero to enlist the help of priests to dig at the place where She had appeared to him. The priests soon unearthed the statue along with all of the documents and found Our Lady of Guadalupe to be in perfect condition."

20   There are four narratives of the story of Juan Diego and his vision of the Virgin Mary which are considered to be the prime sources. The earliest account was published in 1648 by Padre Miguel Sanchez (1606 – 1674) entitled *Imagen de la Virgen María, Madre de Dios de Guadalupe. Milagrosamente aparecida en la ciudad de México. Celebrada en su historia, con la profecía del capítulo doce del Apocalipsis* (*Image of the Virgin Mary, Mother of God of Guadalupe. Miraculously appeared in the city of Mexico*).

Luis Lasso de la Vega (1600 - 1660) who was then the chaplain of the shrine of Guadalupe published in 1649 his version of the story in the Nahuatl language, *Huei tlamahuizoltica Omonoxiti ilhuicac tlatoca ihwapilli Sancta María* (*The great occurrence in which appeared Our Lady the Queen of Heaven, Holy Mary*). It is usually known by the titles of two of its components, "Nican mopohua," which is the account of the apparitions, and the "Nican moctepana," which is the account of the later miracles.

In 1666 Luis Becerra Tanco (1603 - 1672) published his own version of the Guadalupe narrative, based on access to old manuscripts and then in 1688, the Jesuit priest Francisco de Florencia published a scholarly account of the Guadalupe story in his *La Estrella del Norte de México* (*The Star of the North of Mexico*), based on an early manuscript lent to him by the scholar Carlos de Sigüenza y Góngora (1645 - 1700).

For a definitive analysis of these sources see "Historiography of the Apparition of Guadalupe" by Daniel J. Castellano: https://www.arcaneknowledge.org/catholic/guadalupe.htm

21   Luis Lasso de la Vega, "Nican mopohua" from *The great occurrence in which appeared Our Lady the Queen of Heaven, Holy Mary*. English translation by the Indian scholar Antonio Valeriano. 1649.

22   The fourteen miracles:

An Indian killed by an arrow during the procession was miraculously restored to life.

In 1544, during a severe plague, the Franciscans in Tlatelolco led a procession to Tepeyácac. From that day onward, only two or three persons died each day, instead of a hundred.

Juan of Totoltépec, the Indian who discovered Our Lady of Los Remedios, fell ill and was brought to Tepeyácac, where he was cured.

A young relative of don Antonio Carbajal was dragged by his startled horse for half a league, but was miraculously spared any injury. He had invoked Our Lady of Guadalupe, whose shrine they had passed.

A large hanging lamp fell on a Spanish man who was praying at the shrine. The witnesses thought he died, but he was uninjured and the lamp was undamaged and still lit.

The vicar of the shrine, Juan Vázquez de Acuña, was about to say Mass, when all the candles went out. While he waited for someone to get a new fire, two beams of light appeared and lit the candles, to the marvel of those in attendance.

A spring appeared behind the shrine. Its water is clean but acidic, and countless cures have been attested by those who drank or bathed in it.

A Spanish lady who lived in Mexico City began to have swelling in her belly. After ten months of failed treatment, she was brought to the shrine of Guadalupe in the morning. After praying and drinking some water from the spring, she fell asleep. An Indian saw a snake come out from under the sleeping woman, and she awoke in fright.

Perihelion

They killed the snake, and her swelling went down. Four days later, she was able to walk back cured.

A noble Spaniard, a resident of Mexico City, had strong pains in his head and ears. He was brought to the shrine of Guadalupe, where he prayed to be healed and swore that, if cured, he would make an offering of a head of silver. He was cured shortly after his arrival, and he remained in her shrine for nine days.

A youth named Catalina had dropsy. The doctors said she could not get up, or she would die. She was carried to the shrine of Guadalupe. She prayed for her health; then two men came to take her out, and she used all her strength to go to the fount, and drink the water there. She was instantly cured as she drank.

A discalced Franciscan friar, named Pedro de Valderrama, had a pestiferous cancer in his toe, which needed to be amputated. They took him to the shrine of Our Lady of Guadalupe. In her presence, he untied the rag around his toe and prayed to be healed. He was instantly cured and walked back to Pachuca on foot.

A Spanish nobleman, don Luis de Castilla, had a badly swollen foot, which the doctors could not cure, and so he was sure to die. It is said that the above-mentioned friar told him of his cure by Our Lady of Guadalupe. The nobleman ordered silversmiths to make a foot of silver, the size of his foot, and he sent it to the shrine to be placed before her, entrusting her to heal him. When the messenger left to deliver the foot, the sick man was so afflicted that he wanted to die. Yet when he returned, he found the man well, having been cured.

A sacristan named Juan Pavón, who was in charge of the temple of Our Lady of Guadalupe, had a son with a large swelling in the neck. He was so gravely ill that he wanted to die and could not breathe. The sacristan took his son to the presence of Our Lady and anointed him with oil from the lamp that was burning. He was instantly healed.

Don Francisco Quetzalmamalitzin, of Teotihuacán, turned to Our Lady when his town was destroyed and left deserted, because they opposed being deprived of the Franciscan friars. The viceroy Luis de

Velasco wanted to replace the Franciscans with Augustinians, which the townspeople thought a great offense. Since he was sought everywhere, don Francisco went in secret to Azcapotzalco, to pray to Our Lady of Guadalupe to change the heart of the viceroy and nobles so that his people would be pardoned and could return to their homes, and again be ministered by the Franciscans. This indeed occurred: the people were pardoned, including don Francisco and his courtesans in hiding; the Franciscans were again sent there, and all could return to their homes without incident. This was in the year 1558. Don Francisco entrusted his soul to Our Lady of Guadalupe at the hour of his death, which was 2 March 1563.

——Castellano, Daniel J. "Historiography of the Apparition of Guadalupe."

23 Callahan Philip Serna, "The Tilma under Infrared Radiation." CARA Studies on Popular Devotion, vol. II: Guadalupanan Studies No. 3, pp. 6–16

24 Ibid.

Perihelion

The Gift of God

In 1606, King James I (king of England, Scotland, Ireland, and France) naming his "loving and well-disposed Subjects" degreed, "We would vouchsafe unto them our License, to make Habitation, Plantation, and to deduce a colony of sundry of our People into that part of America commonly called VIRGINIA,[1] and other parts and Territories in America, either appertaining unto us, or which are not now actually possessed by any Christian Prince or People...." He went on to establish two separate companies, "one consisting of certain Knights, Gentlemen, Merchants, and other Adventurers, of our City of London and elsewhere," and the other "consisting of sundry Knights, Gentlemen, Merchants, and other Adventurers, of our Cities of Bristol and Exeter, and of our Town of Plimouth."[2]

These two companies, in competition with each other, were the Virginia London Company and the Virginia Plymouth Company. The so named subjects in King James' charter were expected to finance the ventures, in which separate territories would be established with an overlapping buffer zone. The Plymouth Company was given territory between the 38th and 45th parallels, from Chesapeake Bay to the Canadian border. The London Company was granted the area between 34th and 41st parallels. The company creating the superior colony would then acquire the overlapping territory, or at least, that was the idea.

It had taken a while for the Crown to get around to agreeing to an expedition for the settlement of colonies in the new world. In 1602, Captain Gosnold followed in 1603 by Captain Martin Pringle, set out from Dartmouth and landed at about the 43rd latitude along the east coast of North America. Near Narragansett Bay they attempted a settlement but could not persevere. They managed, however, to name the Elizabeth Islands and Martha's Vineyard. The Spanish were settling in Florida and the French in Canada about this time.

Next in 1605, Captain Waymouth sailed from Plymouth in search of a North-west Passage. We learn from *A Briefe Narration of the Originall Undertakings of the Advancement of Plantations Into the Parts of America* (1658) that "...falling short of [h]is Course, hapned into a

Perihelion

River on the Coast of America, called Pemmaquid, from whence he brought five of the Natives, three of whose names were Manida, Skettwarroes [Skiddwares], and Tasquantum, whom I seized upon; they were all of one Nation."[3]

The native Americans created great interest in England. They related for the knights, gentlemen, merchants, and other adventurers "…what great rivers ran up into the land, what men of note were seated on them, what power they were of, how allied, what enemies they had and the like."[4] Another factor which may have caused the gentlemen and other adventurers to lobby the King for a charter was the notion that great quantities of gold could be found in this wilderness of abundance.

In 1606, the Plymouth Company sent the ship *Richard* captained by Henry Challons with two of Waymouth's natives, Maneddo and Assacomiot to use as interpreters. Venturing too close to the coast of Florida, it was captured by the Spanish. A second ship with another captured native, Dehanada, followed, but avoided the southern route. In command of this vessel were seasoned explorers Martin Pring and Thomas Hanham. Dehanaba directed them to the Pemmaquid River at the Sagadahoc Bay in what is now Maine. Instead of establishing a colony there, they returned to England with news of a most excellent site for a colony. Meanwhile, the London Company launched three ships, the *Discovery*, the *Susan Constant*, and the *Godspeed*. They would land in the Chesapeake Bay area and establish the first English colony in North America, Jamestown—but that's another story.

German mathematician, astronomer, and astrologer Johannes Kepler left his teaching position in Graz in 1600 to become the assistant of the astronomer Tycho Brahe in Prague. Tycho Brahe's observatory had just been finished at Benátky nad Jizerou. Kepler and Brahe argued, with Brahe refusing to share data from his observations with Kepler. Briefly returning to Graz, Kepler became embroiled in religious difficulties stemming from his refusal to convert to Catholicism. He was banished from Graz.

Reconciling, Tycho took Kepler on again but died suddenly in 1601. Kepler was named Brahe's successor as imperial mathematician. Now he began to complete Tycho Brahe's work, especially the study of the orbit of Mars around the Sun. By 1604 he began to realize that planetary orbits were not shaped like perfect circles but were ellipses. He deduced that the Sun was the source of some mysterious force that controlled the movements of the planets, that it was the locus of the ellipses. He published his *Astronomia nova*, the "new astronomy," in 1609 in which he described his first two laws of planetary motion: 1. The orbit of a planet about the sun is an ellipse with the sun at one focus, and 2. A line joining a planet and the Sun sweeps out equal areas in equal intervals of time. Other scientists of the time disagreed with Kepler's theories, notably, Galileo and René Descartes.

In 1607 there was a comet in the sky. It had not been recognized as the occasional visitor later to be named after astronomer Edmond Halley, but it was one and the same. Johannes Kepler began observing the comet, noticing the broad "tail" that seemed to emanate from it. Kepler thought it was moving in a straight line across the sky and noted that the tail always pointed away from the sun. He postulated that the sun was heating the comet up, causing it to shed its particles. Somehow, he failed to realize that the comet, like the planets, traced an elliptical orbit around the sun.

Early 1607. At Wellington House in Somerset County, England, Lord Chief Justice Sir John Popham sat across from Sir Ferdinando Gorges, the governor of the port of Plymouth, sipping brandy and chatting with the one-time naval commander and long-time friend. Popham had a storied history, having been an attorney, Speaker of the House of Commons, Attorney General and now Chief Justice. He had presided over the trials, and had sentenced to death among others, Mary Queen of Scots, the Earl of Essex, Sir Walter Raleigh, and most recently, Guy Fawkes, a key figure in the failed Gunpowder Plot of 1605. It was to Sir John that in that same year, Captain George Waymouth had brought two of his captured Native Americans.

Gorges was an enthusiastic promoter of various schemes to colonize North America for the benefit of the aristocracy. He had been instrumental in persuading King James to enact the Virginia Charter. As Popham was amenable to financing the Virginia Plymouth Company, Gorges was ready to suggest participants with whom he had relationships, i.e., cronies of the first order.

Joining the two icons of British wealth and influence was Sir John's nephew, George Popham. George was then acting as the chief

Perihelion

customs officer of the Bridgewater Port in Somerset. He was named in King James' First Charter of Virginia as one of the "humble suitors" for the King's license to establish a colony in the new world, a circumstance that certainly pleased the Lord Chief Justice. Now his uncle would bestow upon him the honor of leading that expedition.

"When Captain Waymouth returned he made a chart for sailing to the spot he selected on the coast of Virginia. You will find there on an island a wooden cross he erected so to claim the territory for the Crown," the Lord Chief Justice told his nephew.

"*I* will find?" asked George Popham, a little nervous as he usually was around his uncle. The man had always frightened him although this fear was totally unfounded. It stemmed from the judge's size which was considerable, and a scowl that seemed permanently printed upon his face. And perhaps from the judge's reputation as a "hanging judge."[4]

"We have chartered two new ships, the *Gift of God* and the *Mary and John*. Raleigh Gilbert will captain the *Mary and John* and you shall be captain of the *Gift of God*. We are sending the savage, Skiddwares, to lead you to the correct spot and to act as interpreter."

"This man speaks English?"

"He was versed in French when found. Apparently, the French, who are settling north of where you are going, in what they call New France, had contact with his people. He is picking up the King's English quite well now."

"Where will you find people to become colonists?" asked George, anticipating an answer he might regret.[5]

"We will find good men and true who believe in the project as we do. The best people."

George shook his head. "Men and women?"

"Just men for now. There is much work to do and undoubtedly many hardships…savages and the like. We should be ready by spring."

"The King," added Sir Ferdinando Gorges, "has provided in his charter that each of the two colonies may elect a council to govern them and…this is significant…oversee the exploration and the mining of rare minerals and metals, in other words, gold and silver, the fifth part, of course, going to the King. We may wish you to be president of the council of your colony and to that effect we are choosing carefully those more important members who will vote."

Byron Grush

"I believe I understand my roll," said George, "and be assured that I shall undertake to do my duty to King and country…and to the Plymouth company."

The port town of Falmouth was ideally situated at the mouth of the River Fal on the south coast of Cornwall, England, for the departure of ships headed across the Atlantic Ocean. George Popham expected some small display of excitement as the *Gift of God* readied for sail, but only a small gathering of sea gulls was present to see them off. On deck he met and shook hands with the ship's master and real captain of the vessel, John Elliot. As Popham had no experience in ocean travel, much less captaining a ship, this was the real gift from God.

Other gentleman adventurers who knew their way around a quarter deck included John Havercombe from Dorset, Peter Grisling from Plymouth who would be the master's mate, John Diamond from Stoke Gabriel who would be the quartermaster, as well as Timothy Savage and Launcelot Booker, both hailing from London, and a regular sailor from Limehouse, Stepney, John Fletcher. Most of the rest of the crew were, thought Popham, somewhat swarthy and unsavory looking; they exhibited the blank stares of the disenfranchised and the awkwardness of men not used to normal society. Where had his uncle found these men? He did not wish to speculate.

Next to the *Gift of God* in the harbor was her sister ship, the *Mary and John*. Raleigh Gilbert had arrived to greet his co-captain, Robert Davis. Unlike Popham, Gilbert had at least a small amount of salt water in his blood. His father, Sir Humphrey Gilbert, was a famous navigator who had perished when his ship sank during a violent storm in 1584. His uncle was none other than Sir Walter Raleigh. Traveling on the *Mary and John* would be the Reverend Richard Seymour, the grandson of Sir Edward Seymour the Duke of Somerset, who had been the brother of Jane Seymour, the third wife of Henry VIII.

Reverend Seymour said a blessing for the two ships then climbed the gang plank, the final addition to colonists who, between the two ships, numbered 120. The sails were set and the *Gift of God* made off on a northeasterly course followed by the *Mary and John*.[6] It was the first of June, 1607. Hailey's Comet was approaching its perihelion,

Perihelion

but it would be several months yet before Johannes Kepler would observe it.

Excerpts from "The Journal of George Popham"[7]

June the first. The ocean is exhilarating! Never have I experienced the lifting of spirit that these crisp breezes and peaking waves bring me. Sea birds have followed us for several leagues; perhaps they have a familiarity with ocean-going vessels that throw food scrapes overboard. Watching the sailors climb the rigging to drop the great expanse of canvas or to furl them back sets me to wondering at their skill and apparent disregard for danger. What is accomplished easily in good weather may yet prove hazardous in bad. We shall see.

June the fifth. The Indian, Skiddwares (I cannot bring myself to call him a "savage"), stood with me at the rail today, gazing longingly across the great expanse of the grey-green ocean. He wears the clothing of a well-bred Englishman now and speaks passable English although lapsing into French or his native tongue occasionally. Does he long for his homeland? It is written in those dark, pensive eyes and furled brow. I asked him about his people but he was silent and instead pointed out a porpoise bounding and leaping alongside of the ship.

June the twelfth. Lost sight of the *Mary and John*. We keep a westerly course with north by northwest corrections. Perhaps they have kept due west and a little south of us. We should reach the Azores within two weeks and will, with God's good graces, rendezvous with them there. We have seen only one other sail—a vessel out of Salcombe in Devon bound for Newfoundland. Captain Elliot knows the ship's master, a fellow named Sosser.

June twenty. A squall came up today. Now I'm getting my sea legs the hard way! Rain dashing across the deck in a fury. Crewmen climbing the sheets while the ship rocks in troughs of the angry ocean. We tacked through it without incident other than some seasickness among the landlubbers among us.

Twenty-fifth day of June. We came off the coast of Da Grasiosa, an island in the Azores. The helmsman turned south toward an island within sight which he called "Flowers," but it was not. Upon consulting the chart I corrected the course west again to reach desired island where there is a substantial port. Thus we were following the course set down by Captain Waymouth in his successful trip to Virginia two years ago.

Twenty-six day of June. Presently we came upon Das Flores, which means flowers in Portuguese, and anchored there to take on wood and water. This is a beautiful island created by volcanic activity many thousands of years ago and covered with richly verdant mountains and deep valleys in which one may find crystal clear lakes. The island gets its name from the thousands of brilliantly blossoming hydrangeas. We were met with some resistance from the locals. They resent the English because of the activities of privateers that use the islands as a refuge. They still remember the capture of the great Portuguese ship *Madres de Deus* by Sir Walter Raleigh in the last century—what long memories they have!

June 29. As we left Das Flores we sighted the *Mary and John* coming into port. They hailed us but as we were under way we did not reconnoiter.

Excerpts: the journal of J. Davies on the *Mary and John*[8]

The twenty-fifth day of June we fell with the Island of Garsera, one of the islands of the Azores. The 26th of June we had sight of Flowers and Corve, and the 27th, in the morning early, we were hard aboard Flowers, and stood in for to find good road for to anchor, whereby to take in wood and water.

The 29th of June being Monday, early in the morning those two sails we had seen the night before were near unto us, and being calm they sent their boats, being full of men, towards us, and after the order

of the sea they hailed us, demanding us of whence we were, the which we told them and found them to be Flemens and the state's ships. One of our company, named John Goyett, of Plymouth, knew the captain of one of the ships, for that he had been at sea with him. Having acquainted Captain Gilbert of this, and being all friends, he

Perihelion

desired the captain of the Dutch to come near and take a can of beer, the which he thankfully accepted, we still keeping ourselves in a readiness both of our small shot and great. The Dutch captain being come to our ship's side, Captain Gilbert desired him to come aboard him and entertained him in the best sort he could. This done, they to requite his kind entertainment desired him that he [Gilbert] would go aboard [the Dutch ship] with them, and upon their earnest entreaty he went with them, taking three or four gentlemen with them, but when they had him aboard of them they there kept him perforce, charging him that he was a pirate, and still threatening himself and his gentlemen with him to throw them all overboard, and to take our ship from us.

In this sort they kept them from ten of the clock morning until eight of the clock night, using some of his gentlemen in most vile manner, as setting some of them in the bilboes, buffeting of others, and other most vile and shameful abuses; but in the end having seen our commission, the which was proffered unto them at the first, but they refused to see it, and the greatest cause doubting of the Englishmen being of their own company who had promised Captain Gilbert that if they proffered to perform that which they still threatened him that then they all would rise with him, and either end their lives in his defense, or suppress the ship, the which the Dutch perceiving, presently set them at liberty, and sent them aboard unto us again, to our no small joy.

Captain Popham, all this time being in the wind of us, never would come round unto us, notwithstanding we making all the signs that possibly we might, by striking our topsail and hoisting it again three times, and making towai'ds him all that ever we possibly could, so here we lost company of him, being the 29th day of June, about eight of the clock at night, being six leagues from Flowers, west-north-west, we standing our course for Vyrgenia. From hence the wind being at south-west, we set our sails and stood by the wind, west north-west towards the land, always sounding for our better knowledge as we ran towards the mainland from the bank.

Both ships finally reached St. George's Island off the coast of Maine where Captain Waymouth had placed a large wooden cross to claim it for England. It was August 9, 1607. The *Mary and John* had overshot this goal and searched through a series of small islands until they found the *Gift of God* anchored near St. George's. Most of the company of both ships now embarked to stand before the cross as Reverend Seymour delivered a sermon. It was, perhaps, the first Thanksgiving. Only one Indian was present, however, that being Skiddwares.

As most of the colonists returned to their ships, the council that had been appointed by King James met for the first time. (Back in England, King James was, this year of the comet, coordinating the beginning work on a new translation of the bible. It would be published in 1611.) Besides Raleigh Gilbert and George Popham, the council included John Havercombe, Gawem Carey, John Elliot, Jim Davies, Edward Harlow, Peter Grisling, Ellis Best, and Reveremd Seymour. Ten against the wilderness. Now their task was to elect a president. The two Captains, Popham and Gilbert were considered the frontrunners. There was some grumbling about Popham's failure to come to the aid of the *Mary and John* in the Azores. Gilbert, however, put forth Popham's name as his choice to lead to colony. This came as a surprise to Havercombe, who was adamant about the incompetence of Popham. But the majority ruled, that majority having been counseled by "hanging" Judge Sir John Popham even before the voyage had begun. George Popham was now President of the colony that would be named the Popham Colony in honor of his uncle.

"What do we do now, Mister President," asked Ellis Best.

"We head up the river to look for a place to establish the colony, of course," he answered. "And I for one will be searching for fresh water...a stream or a lake...where I may take a bath. Then I shall sleep for several days."

Meanwhile, 750 miles to the south, the other chartered company called the London Virginia Company had landed three ships, the *Discovery*, the *Susan Constant*, and the *Godspeed*, on Cape Henry in April of this year. They had built a fort on the banks of the Powhatan River (which they renamed the James). The colony would be called Jamestown. During the voyage from England, somewhere in the Canary Islands, the captain in charge of the three ships, Captain Newport, had charged a certain Captain John Smith with mutiny and held him in chains awaiting execution. But upon their arrival at Cape

Perihelion

Henry they learned that by order of the King, Smith was to be one of the council, so he was released from his bondage.

Smith and Captain Newport explored the area around what is now called Chesapeake Bay and encountered the Native Americans who dwelled there. Interaction with these indigenous peoples by the settlers would become myth and legend (and a little history) that would fascinate into contemporary times. But who would tell the story from the Native American point of view? Smith, in a later narrative, describes a key figure in the legend:

Their chiefe ruler is called Powhatan, and taketh his name of his principall place or dwelling called Powhatan. But his proper name is Wahmfonacock. He is of peri'onage a tall well proportioned man, with a stern looke, his head somewhat gray, his beard so thinne, that its none at all, his age neare sixty; of a very able and hardy body to endure any labour.[9]

Smith and Newport were treated with courtesy and kindness by Powhatan on their first visit to his village. There was dancing and a feast of fish, bread, strawberries and mulberries, and the Englishmen gave the Indians beads, pins, needles, and looking glasses. Powhatan exchanged one of his warriors for one of the settlers to give Smith a guide.[10] Relations would not continue to be this cordial for long.

The Popham colonists had also encountered Indians; an expedition of the ship's boats going up the Pemmaquid River in search of a site suitable for building the colony had brought them to the village where Captain Waymouth had once taken captives. It was Skiddwares' village. The sandy beach soon filled with warriors carrying bows and arrows. The chief, a man named Nahanada, came forth and recognized Skiddwares immediately. Captain Popham then sent Skiddwares to talk with the chief, to assure him of their peaceful intent. Nahanada expressed to Skiddwares that the Englishmen should not land there. Skiddwares, returning to the colonists, expressed a desire to not be taken back to the *Gift of God*, but to be allowed to remain in his own village. This first encounter was not a successful one; thick with tensions and filled with ominous mutual distrust.

Skiddwares' and Nahanada's people were Algonquian speaking Penobscots, members of the Wabanaki "People of the Dawn." They had lived in the region for over 11,000 years. DNA evidence suggests they may have been visited by Celts sailing from Ireland and Vikings who came from Norway or Sweden to settle later in Greenland. In more recent times before the English came, they had traded with French explorers. Their approach to Europeans was at best cautionary.

Primarily a peaceful people, they had occasion to enter into conflict with another Native American people, the warlike Mi'kmag, also called the Tarrantines. This tribe was probably responsible for the rumor heard by Captain Gilbert of cannibals living in the area with sharpened teeth three inches long. In the years to come the Tarrantines would attack and nearly eliminate the Naumkeag people, a tribe "discovered" by Captain John Smith. Plague (diseases brought by the Europeans) would decimate the Naumkeag but spare the Tarrantines.

Excerpts: the journal of J. Davies on the *Mary and John*

Tuesday being the 11th of August, we returned and came to our ships where they still remained at anchor under the island we call St. Georges.

Wednesday being the 12th of August, we weighed our anchor, and set our sails to go for the river of Sagadehock. We kept our course from thence due west until twelve of the clock midnight of the same, then we struck our sails, and laid a hull until the morning, doubting for to overshoot it.

Thursday in the morning, break of the day, being the 13th August, the Island of Sutquin bore north of us, not past half a league from us. We set our sails and stood to the westward for to seek it two leagues further, and not finding the river of Sagadehock, we knew that we had overshot the place. About midnight there arose a great storm and tempest upon us, the which put us in great danger and hazard of casting away of our ship and our lives, by reason we were so near the shore. Here we plied it with our ship off and on, all the night, oftentimes espying many sunken rocks and breaches hard by us, enforcing us to put our ship about and stand from them bearing sail when it was more fitter to have taken it in, but that it stood upon our lives to do it, and our boat sunk at our stern, yet would we not cut her from us in hope of the appearing of the day. Thus we continued until the day came; then we perceived ourselves to be hard aboard the lee shore, and no way to escape it but by seeking the shore.

On August 16 the *Gift of God* arrived to help the stranded *Mary and John*. The next day they took the ship's boat up the Sagadehock River and found it to be "broad and of a good depth" where the two ships could now easily navigate. By August 18 they had found a site at the mouth of the river where they "made a choice for our plantation, and there we had a sermon delivered to us by our preacher."

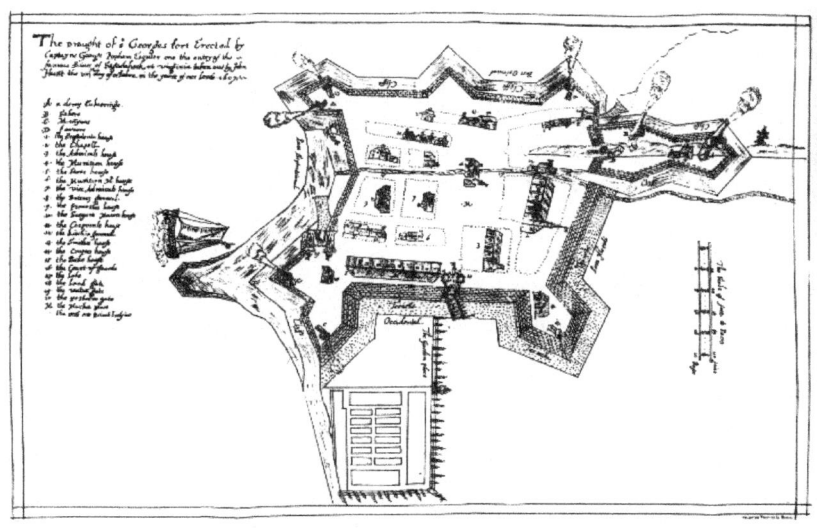

John hunt's map of the Popham Colony, 1607

Excerpts from "The Journal of George Popham"

Late October, 1607. I have not written for some time. Events have consumed me that I had not anticipated. Once we selected

Byron Grush

Sabino Point (as the Indians call it) for our site I put all hands to work building a fortification and some houses. Another group, under the direction of Master Digby the shipwright, undertook the building of a small bark which we shall use for exploration. She will be square rigged, take a small draft as the soundings in the rivers here require, and come in at perhaps 30 tones. The council has voted to christen her the *Virginia*, after out most beloved and dear departed Virgin Queen Elizabeth.

The fort is now completed and takes on a most impressive military aspect which should stand as an example for the world of the might of Britain and her intent to dominate in this New World. It is shaped with sharp angles at its corners, like a star. I find this to be significant as a new star in the heavens is just been seen. The navigators tell me it is of the type as is called a comet and will travel away after a time, but it is a most wonderous sight for us these days. The Indians have noted it and incorporate it into their myths, of which I will tell at a later time.

We have placed a garden on the side of the fort on a level terrace. This also is walled but outside of the main fortification. We have water on three sides and a series of rocky ledges on the fourth where any intruder would be highly visible. Canon are placed at all corners. In an unfortunate event we have had a fire which demolished the storehouse as the result of malfeasance by our Indians friends, which episode I will now tell.

Captain Gilbert and a few of his fellows took a shallop upriver to parlay with Skiddwares and Nahanada but found the camp empty and all their belongings gone. Continuing a league, they came to an island full with pine trees and oaks where some Indians were sighted, but they were of a band unknown to us. Here were many things growing such as sarsaparilla, hazel nuts and whorts in great abundance. On both sides of the river there is a great store of grapes growing which are good and sweet. So the men wished to stop and gather the fruit but approaching the island where they had sighted the Indians, there came to the shallop three canoes of them.

The Indians had some broken English and straight away the most prominent of them introduced himself as Sabenor adding he was Lord of the river of Sagadehock, and the Sagamo (which is the Indian word for Chief) of these parts. In the canoes they had tobacco and some skins of no value which they wished to trade, but Captain

Perihelion

Gilbert waved them away. One of the Indians had entered the shallop and seeing a man ready upon lighting his pipe and holding in one hand a fire brand for the purpose, the Indian grabed this from him. There was a supply of building materials near the stern of the boat and the Indian promptly threw the burning fire brand at this and then jumped off into the river. The men of course extinguished the flames which had not yet set fire to the boat, but the shock of it was troublesome.

Yet Captain Gilbert again spoke with the Sagamo, saying that not withstanding the action of this one "savage" that still they extended friendship to them. This was a grievous fault on the part of Captain Gilbert, for in the next week a party of Sabenor's warriors came by the fort, again with trade goods that were of little value to us save that by trading with the natives some good will might be achieved. What followed was the destruction of our storehouse and the contents within that were to see us into the harsh winter.

We learned on this occasion the fate of Skiddwarres' and Nahanada's people, the reason for their absence. It seemed that Sabenor's clan had attacked Nahanada's and that Sabenor's son had been killed. The resulting battle had driven away the Indians with whom we were so friendly and whose assistance in learning to live in this wilderness was so important to us. Captain Gilbert still sided with Sabenor and invited his warriors into the fort and took them to the storehouse to select from it what items of trade, as axes and other implements such that they desired. It may have been an accident as Gilbert maintains, but I wonder. When shouts came from the direction of the storehouse, I ran hurriedly to see flames leaping upwards. The Indians had disappeared. There was a quantity of gunpowder stored there which ignited. I wondered if the affair in the shallop had been a prelude to this destruction. There were those of us who wished to retaliate against the Indians but I would not allow it.

Now to the legends of Skiddwarres' people. Their main hero/deity is called Gluskabe. There are many legends of him saving the Penobscot people by fighting and defeating Aglebemu, the giant lake monster, or of riding Bootup the whale across the ocean. There are tales of the Giwakwa who are evil giants who eat men, of the Badogiak who cause thunder and lightning, and of the Manogemasak, a race of river elves. Although we have never seen giants or little people here abouts, these entities are very real to these people. Now the comet has come and an old tale of a man named Wa-Ba-Ba-Nal who climbed the Milky Way to the land of the Northern Lights has been altered to include a flaming serpent who nearly swallows him.[12] Of course he was saved from this fate by Gluskabe and together they slid back down the Milky Way to home.

In September, after the meeting with Sabenor, Captain Popham had sent the *Mary and John* under the captainship of Robert Davies back to England to inform the company of their safe arrival and the successful start of their plantation. Later, in December, the *Gift of God* also returned to England bringing home about 50 of the colonists, the reason for their return is not known. Popham sent along the map drawn by John Hunt and a letter written in Latin to King James describing, among other things, the Indians' tales of a great ocean of boiling hot water to the west, and of the cordial relationship the colonists had established with the indigenous population (although future critics would maintain the colonists treated the Indians rather harshly[13]).

Also in December, at the Jamestown settlement, Captain John Smith found himself in hot water. As he foraged along the Chickahominy River, a band of Native Americans led by Opechancanough captured him. He was taken to the Powhatan village at Werowocomoco where Chief Powhatan was informed of his capture. He was in danger of being executed. In his later writing (*True Travels* 1630) Smith told the story of being rescued by a young Indian girl named Pocahontas. Other of his writings give differing accounts which has led to skepticism concerning the story.

The schism between Popham and his followers and Gilbert and his followers widened. By January, the winter had become extraordinarily cold and snowy. That time has been called "The Little Ice Age" by modern-day climatologists as the severe weather and dropping temperatures hit Europe as well. On February 5 of 1608 George Popham died. Raleigh Gilbert became the new president of the colony, what was left of it. There is no record of how Popham died.

Supply ships arrived at the colony in May of 1608. They brought the news that Sir John Popham had died, their principal benefactor. There is very little record of the colony during the summer, how they fared or what their relationship with the Native Americans was like, but although there were few deaths, their numbers had lessened, and they must have been discouraged. The *Mary and John* returned in September bringing the news that Raleigh Gilbert's brother had died having made Raleigh the sole heir to his estate. Gilbert decided to go back. With no leadership to keep them there, all the remaining colonists now abandoned the fort and sailed home on the *Mary and John* and the *Virginia*, ending the Popham Colony's 14-month attempt. The failed colony was forgotten until the later part of the 19th century.

---

1   The entire eastern seaboard of North America from Main to the Carolinas was named Virginia, after the "Virgin Queen," Queen Elizabeth I.

2   "The First Charter of Virginia; April 10, 1606." *Hening's Statutes of Virginia*, I, 57-66. Source: *The Federal and State Constitutions Colonial Charters, and Other Organic Laws of the States, Territories, and Colonies Now or Heretofore Forming the United States of America*. Compiled and Edited Under the Act of Congress of June 30, 1906 by Francis Newton Thorpe. Washington, DC: Government Printing Office, 1909.

3   Sir Ferdinando Gorges. *A Briefe Narration of the Originall Undertakings of the Advancement of Plantations Into the Parts of America* (1658), chapter II, Papers of John Adams, volume 2, Adams Papers Digital Edition - Massachusetts Historical Society.

4   Most people found Sir John Popham a capable and trustworthy man, a respectable member of the British government—but not everyone thought as much. Lord Campbell in his *Lives of the Chief Justices*, did call him the "hanging judge." Campbell maintained that in his youth, "He frequently sallied forth at night from a hostel in Southwark, with a band of desperate characters, and, planting themselves in ambush on Shooter's Hill, or taking other positions favorable for attack and escape, they stopped travelers and took from them not only their money, but any valuable

commodities which they carried with them. The extraordinary and almost incredible circumstance is, that Popham is supposed to have continued in these courses after he had been called to the bar..."

———Campbell, John Campbell, Baron, 1779-1861, and James Cockcroft. *The Lives of the Chief Justices of England: From the Norman Conquest Till the Death of Lord Tenterden.* New and rev. ed. Northport, Long Island, N.Y.: E. Thompson co., 18941899. P. 210.

5   There was a conspiracy theory concerning the Popham Colony that surfaced around 1866 which was debated through various letters to the editor of the *Boston Daily Advertiser.* Pertinent to our story at this point was the theory put forth in an address given in 1865 at the annual Popham Celebration by Prof. James W. Patterson, of Dartmouth College and a notice published in the *Advertiser* in April 11, 1866 by a Mr. Poole assailing certain claims made by Patterson, to wit, that "a colony of convicted felons landed here in 1607." Some writers to the editor pointed to the fact that Lord Chief Justice Popham had a controlling interest in all the jails and penitentiaries and that he had "invented the plan of sending convicts to the plantations." Possibly there were, among the hale and hardy men chosen to construct the colony, some malefactors eager to erase their crimes (which were possibly political). But the law for the transportation of convicts was not enacted or enforced in England until 1619. Judge Popham died in 1607, only days after the *Gift of God* left port for the Americas. See:

———*The Popham Colony a discussion of its historical claims, with a bibliography of the subject*, by William Frederick Poole, Rev. Edward Ballard, and D.D. Frederick Kidder, with letters from the *Boston Daily Advertiser* and the *Portland Advertiser* (1866), published by J. K. Wiggin and Lunt, Boston, 1866. Gutenberg Project Ebook 42484, 2013.

6   There are conflicting accounts of the dates and places of the departure of the two ships. In an article examining papers found in the Public Record Office in London relating to a lawsuit against the *Gift of Go*d many years later ("NEW DOCUMENTS RELATING TO THE POPHAM EXPEDITION, 1607" -proceedings of the American Antiquarian Society), Charles Edward Banes states that according to the testimony of officers and seamen of the *Gift of God,* this vessel "sett saile from the Sound of Plimouth for Virginia about the 1st of May" while according to the Griffith MS the *Mary and John*

"departed from the Lyzard the firste daye of June Ano Domi 1607 beinge Mundaye about 6 of the Cloke in the afternoon." If they left one month apart, how is it that they arrived at the Azores on the same day? Other accounts have the *Mary and John* leaving from Lizard on the same day that the *Gift of God* left from Falmouth.

7   There is no "Journal of George Popham" as far as we know. Nor are there any logs or journals from the *Gift of God*. There are a few narrations by travelers on the *Mary and John* and some letters to Sir Ferdinando Gorges. I've tried to imagine a journal for Popham based on some of these sources which, however, often contradict each other. Principle among these are "The Relation of a Voyage unto New England, as found among the papers of Ferdinando Georges by William Griffin," reprinted by Rev. B. F. Decosta, Ed., as *A relation of a voyage to Sagadahoc : now first printed from the original manuscript in the Lambeth Palace Library*. John Wilson and Son, Cambridge 1880, and Strachey: *The Historie of Travaile unto Virginia Britannia*, edited by R. H. Major, Esq. Chapters VIII., IX., and X, Hakluyt Society London, 1849.

8   Decosta, ED, Griffin MS in *A relation of a voyage to Sagadahoc*. Decosta submits that the author of the narrative was James Davies, not Robert Davies as Strachey maintains in his *History*. Strachey calls him Captain Davies which probably refers to the captain of the *Mary and John* during its return trip to England from the Popham Colony.

9   John Smith. *The General Historie of Virginia, New England, and the Summer Isles*. printed by Edward Blackmore. London. 1624.

10   W. Gilmore Simms, Esq. *The Life of Captain John Smith of Virginia*. Vol. 2, Illustrated Library. Geo. F. Cooledhe and Brother Publishers, New York. 1846.

11   Another conspiracy theory from *The Popham Colony a discussion of its historical claims* concerns the *Virginia*, the first ship built in New England. One writer contradicts the "first ship" claim saying, "a vessel was built in the harbor of Port Royal (now Hilton Head) forty-four years before this, by Huguenot colonists." Well, there was a Spanish explorer, Francisco Cordillo, who reached the Port Royal Sound in South Carolina in 1521. But the French Huguenots settled

in South Carolina along the Santee River north of Charles Town in the late 1680s. The letter writer puts the construction of the vessel as beginning in December and claims there was not time to build a seaworthy vessel between then and Spring when the colonists were said to have departed for England in it. But James Davies states in his journal that they began work on the *Virginia* as soon as they disembarked at Sabino Point. Conspiracy theorists often begin from a false premise, hoping you won't notice. The same writer says the "pretty Pinnacle" was constructed from green pine in midwinter and could not be safe. He says there were "probably not ten carpenters in the whole company." And another writer claims that the *Virginia* never reached England...perhaps it was never built? The area around the colony was surrounded by old growth hardwood forests, not pine. No carpenters? Who built the fort and the houses (somewhere between 5 and 50 depending on who you believe)? Brain (Brain, Jeffrey P. *Fort St. George on the Kennebec*. Peabody Essex Museum, 2007) writes that "The rigging, the sails and iron were brought from England along with a Master Digby, shipwright. Wood for the ship was harvested and milled locally." The John Hunt map of Fort St. George shows the *Virginia* moored in the harbor. The *Virginia* sailed for England to return some of the colonists and then sailed back, landing at Jamestown to resupply the colonists there. During a third trip across the Atlantic she may have been lost when a severe storm came up. Currently at Bath, Maine, a project is underway to build a 51-foot replica of the *Virginia* based on plans found in the Spanish Royal Archives. For more information on the project, visit Maine's First Ship (http://www.mfship.org).

12   This embellishment to the tale of Wa-Ba-Ba-Nal apparently never survived to the present day through the usual verbal storytelling of the tribal elders. Certainly, the Native Americans saw Halley's Comet in 1607. What would they have thought about it?

13   In his letter to the editor, "The Last Popham Address," (Boston Daily Advertiser, April 11, 1866), Mr. William Frederick Poole, Librarian of the Boston Athenæum, refers to rumors of maltreatment of the Indians, possibly by the alleged convicts in the party:

Perihelion

"...a colony of convicted felons landed here in August, 1607, more than half of whom deserted the next December, and all abandoned the spot the following Spring, leaving with the neighboring Indians the memory of the most shocking barbarities committed upon them? (See Relations des Jésuites, 1858, tom. i. p. 36; Parkman's Pioneers of France, p. 266.) Was it because these sportive colonists enticed friendly Indians into this same Fort, under the pretense of trade; and, causing them to take the drag-ropes of a loaded cannon, fired off the piece when the Indians were in line, and blew them to atoms? (See Williamson's Hist. of Maine, vol. i. p. 201.)"

There is no documentation of such an event in literature contemporary with the time of the colony. From our history as a country inclined toward genocide it would not be surprising were it true or even simply exaggerated. It is also doubtful that convicted felons would wish to return to England where they would face prison or worse. Where there is a lack of historical documentation, theorists will fill in the gaps with whatever suits their opinions. I am not exempt from the practice, I confess.

Riding Over an Arm of the Sea on a Cow

Nec fas est proprius mortali attingere divos.
It is not lawful for mortals to approach divinity nearer than this.
——Edmond Halley[1]

Edmond Halley was born in Hagerston, Middlesex, England on 29 October 1656. He was the son of the Senior Edmond Halley, a prosperous salter and soap maker with properties in London that brought in substantial rents. (His father supported him but was murdered in 1684.)[2] He attended St. Paul's School and Oxford University, Queen's College. He left Oxford before graduating having developed a keen interest in astronomy, and with the approvable of his father and the assistance of King Charles II and the East India Company, traveled to St. Helena in the South Atlantic where he spent a year charting stars. Returning to England, Halley was granted an honorary degree for his work and made a Fellow of the Royal Society. His "Cataogue Stellarum Australium" was published in 1679. In it he dedicated a planisphere of the southern hemisphere stars to Charles II.

In 1675, Halley became the assistant of John Flamsteed who was first Astronomer Royal at Greenwich Observatory. Flamsteed and Halley would later have a stormy relationship, but at first it was cordial and mutually advantageous. Flamsteed was preparing a 3,000-star catalogue, "Catalogus Britannicus," and a star atlas called "Atlas Coelestis" which would triple the number of stars earlier chronicled by Tyco Brahe. In 1681 Flamsteed postulated that the recent observation of two comets was actually the discovery of the same comet first coming, then going. Halley's friend Sir Isaac Newton disagreed but later admitted that this was probably true. Halley may have been been privy to these observations, but Flamsteed kept secretive and somewhat incomplete records. Later, Halley made Flamsteed's notes available to Newton and together the two of them published a bootleg copy. Flamsteed, infuriated, obtained many of the copies and had them burned.

A trip to Danzig, Poland, brought Halley into contact with astronomer Johannes Hevelius, a developer of advanced telescopes. He had been sent by the Royal Society to settle a dispute between

Perihelion

Hevelius and Robert Hooke who claimed Hevelius' observations were not accurate. He sided with Hevelius against Hooke. 1680 saw him embarked on a Grand Tour of France and Italy. He visited the Paris observatory. In Calais he witnessed the comet of 1680. Now thoroughly engrossed in the science of astronomy he would return to England and begin a study of lunar orbits.

Islington, England, 1682. Halley married Mary Took, daughter of the auditor of the exchequer, on 20 April at St. James's Dukes Place, just a stone's throw from his father's residence on Winchester Street in London. Mary came from a notable family of lawyers and had inherited property.[3] They moved into a modest house in Islington not far from the King's Head Tavern on Upper street. Halley installed there his large, metal, telescopic-sighted sextant which had been constructed specially for his St Helena expedition. It had a five- and one-half-foot radius. He also had a twenty-four-foot-long telescope equipped with two micrometers for measuring arcs, and a two-foot diameter telescopic quadrant that he had used at Oxford.[4]

Edmund Halley sat at his desk in his study. In front of him, next to an ink bottle and quill pen, was an old college notebook he was using to make notes of his observations of the moon. On the cover was written "Edmund Halley his Booke and he douth often in it Looke." On the inside of the front cover was written, "August 16, primum visus ad initium Leonis," referring to his first observations of the comet that would someday be named after him. He turned to a fresh page and wrote "Saturday, August 26, 7h. 29'," and following this heading, jotted down in Latin the position of the comet with regard to Ursa Major.[5] There will be many entries in this notebook interspersed with old data on his geometric calculations of the parabola; some will be written in the margins, some written on top of the original notes. The last entry on the comet will be on September 9, 1682.

"Eddie," called Mary Halley, "dinner is ready."

Mary had overseen the preparation by their hired cook of a veal pie spiced with nutmeg, mace, and cloves. A generous mug of cider also awaited the astronomer. Halley kissed his new bride on the cheek upon entering the dining room. "Lovely," he said.

"Yes," answered Mary, "it looks to be a lovely spread set before us."

"No, I meant you."

The Halley's marriage had been arranged by their parents during Edmund Halley's European tour. An old friend of the family, just after the ceremony at St. James's, had commented, "Well, that will never last!" In fact, it would last for fifty-five years, up until the time of Mary's death—a devastating time for Edmund. They would have three children.

Some days later after a meeting of the Royal Society in September, Edmund Halley joined friends at Jonathan's Coffee House in Exchange Alley, just off Cornhill and Lombard Street in London (the future location of the London Stock Exchange). Coffee was now becoming almost as popular a drink as tea and the coffee house was an important venue for socialization and discussions of everything from gossip to politics to scientific scholarship, the latter of which was the catalyst for Halley's frequenting of Jonathan's. He had acquired a taste for mixing good conversation with the healing power of the strongly brewed drink from his college days at Oxford when he could get a cup for a penny at the Angel Coaching Inn and listen to the ideas of such luminaries as architect Christopher Wren.

Wren and Robert Hooke had joined Halley at Jonathan's for a discussion of a favorite topic, the elliptical orbit of planets. In his *Astronomia nova* of 1609, Johannes Kepler had proposed that planets moved in elliptical orbits; it was his first law of planetary motion. Could the inverse square law be used as a proof of this theory? The question was debated, the cups were filled and refilled, and the aroma of coffee spread throughout the common room, a foil against the cold rain that fell outside. There was one thing in which they were in agreement: they should get the opinion of Isaac Newton on the subject. (In 1684 just before the death of his father, Halley did go to visit Newton at Cambridge and encouraged, then helped him to publish the *Principia*.)[6] Suddenly, Halley changed the subject.

"Comets," he said in perhaps the briefest statement he had ever made.

"Comets? Oh yes," said Christopher Wren, "I have heard there is a new one…although, due to the awful quality of the air in this city, I have not seen it. Is it important?"

"Aristotle said that comets were nothing else than sublunary vapors or airy meteors and dismissed them as unimportant. But would one not think it worthwhile to observe, and to give an account

Perihelion

of the wandering and uncertain paths of vapors floating in the ether? I have been observing this new comet," Halley told them, "and I've noticed something quite interesting."

"Don't tell us you think the comet has an orbit," said Hooke.

"It is a parabola, or more probably an ellipse. I have calculated its orbit just as I did with the Kirch Comet of 1680. Then I used Flamsteed's data which may not have been accurate, but this time I made my own measurements."

"Just being parabolic does not mean it is in orbit around our solar system. Its path may just be being bent by the pull of the sun as it travels through the universe."

"Ah, but there is more. In the year 1456 a comet was seen passing retrograde between the Earth and the sun. And I have examined what data there is from that and two others, the 1531 and the 1607 comets. They are so similar to our current wanderer of the ether as to intriguingly suggest that they are one and the same. Dare I venture to foretell that it will return again in the year 1758?"[7]

He did and it did.

It may have been the dawning of the Age of Enlightenment, peopled by giants of advanced thinking and deeds like Edmund Halley, Christopher Wren, Isaac Newton, and Robert Hooke, but it was also the twilight of an era of superstition and intolerance that would not die easily. Some 160 miles south-west of London in the county of Devon was the peaceful hamlet of Bideford. This same year of the comet, 1682, the peace and tranquility of Bideford was shattered by accusations and retributions harking back to a darker time. It all began with a magpie flying through a window.

Where the Bristol Channel meets the Celtic Sea on the north coast of Devon County's peninsula, the sandy beaches of Bideford Bay are pierced by an estuary which feeds the rivers of Taw and of Torridge. Where the estuary begins to narrow into the Torridge the port town of Bideford occupies both the west and east banks. The name may have originated from "by the ford." Spanning the river is the Long Bridge, built of wood in 1286 and reconstructed from masonry in 1474. The bridge has 24 arches of different sizes, not for aesthetic purposes but due to the placement of random river stones that formed its base when it was built.

Byron Grush

Not far from where the bridge met the quay on the west bank on Honestone Street was the Pannier Market. Here were stalls offering everything from sea food to freshly butchered meat to Irish wool to tobacco from the American colonies in the New World. The market dated to 1272 and had been sponsored by then Lord of the Manor of Bideford, Sir Richard Grenville, and his cousin, Sir Walter Raleigh, both famous sea captains. Now, in 1682, the year of our comet, produce brought from farms in the countryside in woven baskets (panniers) slung over the sides of donkeys was being stacked on tables near wooden cages in which hens and partridges flapped worried wings and near racks of hanging carcasses of butchered pigs and sheep dripping blood.

On June 29, a Monday, Anne Wakely had made her selection of brown hens' eggs and a chicken, whose neck had been rung for her by the stall proprietor. She exited the market, pausing for a moment to glare at a man secured on a pillory at the adjacent town stocks. Head and hands protruding from the wooden frame, the unfortunate man reminded her of the livestock in their wooden crates back at the butcher shambles, the hapless pigs poking their snouts out between the slats. Wonder what his infraction was? Probably cursing…he looked the type. She would have spit at the man but her mouth was dry and she was in a hurry.

On Meddon Street she passed an almshouse, an infirmary where many of the plague victims of a few years ago had been housed, and turned up a narrow alley, so insignificant it had no official name (but was referred to by its inhabitants as "the dead end"). At a stoop leading up to the front entrance of a boarding house she sat down to rest. Looking up at the weathered clapboards on the old building she realized this was where her friend, Grace Thomas had her lodgings. Grace had been ailing as of late and Anne thought she might look in on her. Soon, but not today. Suddenly, there was a fluttering sound and a black and white shape, all wings and feathers, flew at the building and entered an open window above Anne's head. A magpie. The window was certainly that of Grace Thomas' meager rooms. The magpie…well, was that really what it was?

The next day, concerned about the magpie incident, Anne Wakely went to consult the old woman of Old Town who she knew only slightly and that by her reputation as a sort of seer. Her name was Temperance Lloyd. There were other rumors about Lloyd, that

Perihelion

she had once been tried for murder and accused of witchcraft but had been acquitted.[8] In spite of this disreputable history, Lloyd was often consulted by her neighbors about matters of seemingly supernatural import. Temperance Lloyd was a widow, which of course made her suspect of every dire possibility, especially of witchcraft.[9]

"Do you know of any bird as being black and white like a magpie that would come to flutter at a window?" Anne asked.

"A black bird?" answered Temperance. "Instead I think it is a bird as I know of which changes into a black man."

"Of what purpose? Is it then, a devil?"

"It is the Devil, indeed. And I have met him. He walks the streets in the form of a black man."

Anne and her husband, William, lived close to Thomas and Elizabeth Eastchurch. Thomas Eastchurch was a shopkeeper with a store fronting along the quay. Anne and Elizabeth gossiped often and the story of the magpie that changed into a black man was just too good for Anne not to relate to her friend. Elizabeth was a bit of a nonconformist and attended religious conventicles that were not exactly socially acceptable. She suggested to Anne that she go back to Temperance Lloyd and ask to see if she bore the Devil's mark. Why did she think, she asked Anne, that Grace Thomas had been ailing? That evening, she told her husband, Thomas, the story, possibly embellishing it somewhat.

On Saturday, July 1, 1682, Thomas Eastchurch made a complaint about Temperance Lloyd to the town constables. Forthwith Temperance was arrested and placed in the old chapel at the end of the bridge to await an appearance before the justices on the following Monday. According to Frank Gent, writing in *The Trial of the Bideford Witches*, "The two justices that year were the mayor, Thomas Gist, and one of the aldermen, John Davie. Also present was the town clerk, John Hill, who recorded all the statements that were made. On that Monday statements were made by Thomas and Elizabeth Eastchurch, Grace Thomas, who was Elizabeth's sister and the alleged victim, and by their neighbours Anne Wakely and Honor Hooper."[10]

This was not the only accusation of witchcraft that would be heard in Bideford that July. On the 16th, even as Temperance Lloyd was incarcerated in the Bideford jail, two things happened: Grace

Byron Grush

Thomas' pains miraculously subsided, but another woman, Grace Barnes, began to have a series of seizures that were so intense it took four men and women to hold her down. Among them were Grace's husband John, and her neighbor Agnes Whitefield.

Outside in the street at that moment were two women, Mary Trembles and Susan Edwards, who because of the food shortage that plagued the poor areas of the town, had been begging for food. They had happened to pass by the Barnes' house just at the time of the seizures. Agnes Whitefield heard something outside and went to the door. Opening it she saw Mary Trembles standing there holding a clay pot in her hands. There was some food in the pot which Mary accidentally dropped on the steps at Agnes Whitefield's feet. In her hysteria, from her bedchamber, Grace shouted out "That woman bewitched me!"

Exeter, Devon, England, July of 1682. Built into the northern corner of the old Roman city walls in Exeter was Exeter Castle which dated to 1068, built following Exeter's rebellion against William the Conqueror. In 1607, another of the years of Halley's Comet's perihelion, a courthouse, the High Gaol, was added within the castle walls. Temperance Lloyd was committed to Exeter Gaol on Saturday, 8 July 1682, and Susanna Edwards and Mary Trembles on Tuesday, 19 July, and there all three awaited their trial. The trial took place at Exeter Castle on Monday, 14 August 1682

The following narrative draws from a document (quoted heavily in many other sources concerning the three women) entitled, "A True and Impartial Relation of the Informations against Three Witches..."[11] which contains depositions made by the witnesses to the magistrates as well as statements by the defendants—and their last words.

Dorcas Coleman, the Wife of John Coleman, about the end of August 1680 was stricken with tormenting pains, pricking in her arms, stomach, and heart. She saw a Doctor Beare who examined her and told her, "It is beyond my skill to ease you of these pains for indeed, I believe you to be bewitched." John Coleman, her husband, told the inquisitors that his wife had been sick some months since, when his wife was sitting in a chair, the defendant, Susanna Edwards, came to see her. Dorcas tried to rise from the chair but was unable to do so. Then Dorcas slid from chair and lay on her back on the floor, unable to move. Just as soon as she had come, Susanna Edwards was gone.

Dorcas told the inquisitors that she later learned that Edwards was in the prison in Bideford. She went to visit her and asked her, had she, Susanna Edwards, bewitched her and done her bodily harm? Edwards replied that she had so done. She had, she said, bewitched her.

It was known that Susanna Edwards was an acquaintance both of Mary Trembles and Temperance Lloyd. The next witness gave a similar account of having been bewitched. Grace Thomas said that on about the 2d day of February 1680 she was taken with great pains in her head and all her limbs, which continued on until the first day of August and then began to abate, and she was then able to walk abroad to take the air. She was going up High Street when she met Temperance Lloyd coming from the other direction. Temperance fell to her knees and wept saying, "Mrs. Grace, I am glad to see you so strong again." Grace asked her why she wept for her. Temperance replied, "I weep for Joy to see you so well again." This implied the woman had some knowledge of Grace's condition—but there was no reason she should.

Grace told the inquisitors that she "that very night was taken very ill with sticking and pricking pains, as though pins and awls had been thrust into her body, from the crown of her head to the soles of her feet, and she lay as though it had been upon a rack." Her pains went on, getting worse and worse. Then, she said, upon the first day of this July, as soon as Temperance Lloyd was apprehended and put in the Prison of Bideford, she immediately felt her pricking and sticking pains to cease and abate. She believed, she said, that Temperance Lloyd had been the instrument of doing much hurt and harm unto her body.

Then this: Elizabeth Eastchurch said under oath that on July 2, Grace Thomas, then lodging in her house, complained of pains on her knee, and upon examining Grace's knee she saw "she had nine places in her knee which had been pricketh; and that every of the said pricks were as though it had been the prick of a thorn." Mrs. Eastchurch then went to Temperance Lloyd and demanded if she had any wax or clay in the form of a picture with which she had pricked and tormented Grace Thomas. "I have no such wax or clay, nor do I have a picture," answered Lloyd. But she confessed that she had a piece of leather which she had pricked nine times.

Anne Wakely, the Wife of William Wakely, then testified. She said that upon the second day of July she, "by order of the Mr. Mayor, did search the body of the said Temperance Lloyd, in the presence of Honor Hooper, and several other women." And she said that she "did find in her secret parts two teats hanging nigh together like unto a piece of flesh that a child had sucketh. And each of the said teats was about an inch in length."

Anne Wakely then demanded of Temperance whether she had been sucked at that place by the black man, by which she meant the Devil. Temperance did acknowledge, Wakley testified, that she had "been sucked there often times by the black man; and the last time that she was sucked by the black man was the Friday before she was searched, the 30th day of June." Wakley also told the story of seeing the magpie at Grace Thomas' window and that Lloyd had admitted the bird to be a shape taken at times by the black man.

Mr. Hann was a clergyman who officiated with his son in the parish church in 1681. He believed himself to have been bewitched by Temperance Lloyd. He visited the witches who were imprisoned in Exeter Gaol during the trial and also questioned them when they were brought to the gallows. He asked them, "Was not the devil there with Susan when I was once in the prison with you, and under her coats?" Came the answer, "He was there, but is now fled." They asserted that the devil came with them to the prison door and there left them.[12]

One of Susanna Edwards' visitors at the gaol was John Dunning of Torrington to whom she allegedly had given a full confession of her activities as a witch. Joan Jones claimed to have overheard the confession and then reported to the justices. During the judges questioning of Edwards, Anthony, Joan Jones's husband, who was present in the guildhall, remarked that Susanna Edwards "did nervously gripe and twinkle her hands upon her own body." He accused her, saying, "Thou devil, thou art now tormenting some person or other." She replied, "Well enough, I will fit thee!" Later, Jones cried out, "Wife, I am now bewitched by this devil!" and leapt like a madman, and fell shaking, quivering and foaming, and lay there for the space of half an hour like a dying or dead man.[13]

Perihelion

According to most of the witnesses the women were admitting to being witches. But it was just hearsay. Until…

"Temperance Lloyd, being brought before us by some constables of the said Burrough, upon the complaint of Thomas Eastchurch of Bideford, you are charged upon suspicion of having used some magical art, sorcery, or witchcraft upon the body of Grace Thomas, and to have had discourse or familiarity with the Devil in the shape of a black man. We ask you therefore, how long since you have had discourse or familiarity with the Devil in the likeness or shape of a black man?"

"I say," answered Temperance Lloyd, "that about the 30th day of September last past I met with the Devil in the shape or likeness of a black man, about the middle of the afternoon of that day, in a certain street in the Town of Bideford called Higher Gunstone Lane. And then and there he did tempt and solicit me to go with him to the house of Thomas Eastchurch to torment the body of the said Grace Thomas."

"And this you did, or did not do?"

"I at first did refuse to so do. But afterwards, by the temptation and persuasion of the Devil in the likeness of a black man I did go to the house of Thomas Eastchurch. Both of us went up into the chamber where Grace Thomas was, and there we found one Anne Wakely, rubbing and stroking one of her arms."

"And then what followed? Remember you have sworn an oath."

"I then and there pinched with the nails of my fingers Grace Thomas in her shoulders, arms, thighs and legs, and afterwards came down into the Street together where I did see something in the form or shape of a grey or braget cat. The cat went into Thomas Eastchurch's Shop." She continued:

"The last time I was at Mr. Eastchurch's house was Friday the 30th day of June last past. The Devil in the shape of the said black man was there. We went up again into the chamber and found Grace Thomas lying in her bed in a very sad condition. We did torment her again with the purpose to put her out of her life. The black man, the Devil, promised that no one should discover me."

Lloyd further confessed that the black man (or rather the Devil) did suck her teats which she now had in her secret parts, and that she did kneel down to him in the street, as she was returning to her own house, and after that they had tormented Grace Thomas in manner as mentioned.

"What is the stature of the black man? She was asked.

"The black man was," she said, "about the length of my arm, and his eyes were very big, and he leapt in the way before me, and afterwards did suck me again as I was lying down. And his sucking was with a great pain unto me, and afterwards he vanished clear away out of my sight."

The mayor and the justices then questioned her concerning other witcheries which she had practiced upon the bodies of several other persons within the town. She confessed that in the year of 1670 she was accused of practicing witchcraft upon the body of William Herbert and was tried and was acquitted. However, she said, she was indeed guilty as by the persuasion of the black man she did prick Herbert to death. And furthermore, in the year 1679 she was accused of doing bodily harm to Anne Fellow but as no proofs could be found, this charge was dropped. She had, she said, done some bodily hurt to the Anne Fellow, and that "thereupon the said Anne Fellow did shortly die and depart this life."[14]

Similar crimes were attributed to Mary Trembles: she cursed Grace Barnes after being refused food; she went invisibly into Grace's house; she had a teat for the devil to suck in her "privy parts" and she had carnal knowledge of the devil who, it was claimed, came to her in the form of a lion. Susanna Edwards was accused of bewitching Dorcas Coleman, also of being invisible, of attempting to murder Grace Barnes, of causing fits, of allowing the devil to suck her breasts and "secret parts" and of having carnal knowledge of the devil when he came to her in the form of a boy.[15]

Why had the women confessed? In Temperance Lloyd's case, she believed the so-called black man, or Devil, would protect her. Perhaps she convinced the others they would not, therefore, go to the gallows. The illnesses that afflicted the victims were not uncommon. Taking credit for them may have been an act of self-affirmation or to get attention. As to the pin pricks, who can say? But faced with the gallows, they recanted.

On the 25th of August 1682, Temperance Lloyd, Mary Trembles, and Susanna Edwards were taken by cart to the Gallows Cross in nearby Heavitree. It was the day before Edmund Halley made his first observational notes on his comet. The Reverend Hann was in attendance to hear the last words of the women.[16]

"Mary Trembles," Hann asked, "what have you to say as to the crime you are now to die for?

"I have spoke as much as I can speak already, and can speak no more."

"In what shape did the Devil come to you?"

"The Devil came to me once, I think, like a Lyon."

"Did he offer any violence to you?"

"No, not at all, but did frighten me, and did nothing to me. And I cried to God, and asked what he would have, and he vanished."

"Did he give thee any gift, or didst thou make him any promise?"

"No."

"Had he any of thy blood?"

"No."

"Did he come to make use of thy body in a carnal manner?"

"Never in my life."

"Have you a teat in your privy-parts?"

"None. The Grand Inquest said it was sworn to them."

"Thou speakest now as a dying woman, and as the Psalmist says, I will confess my iniquities and acknowledge all my sin. We find that Mary Magdalen had seven Devils, and she came to Christ and obtained mercy: And if thou break thy league with the Devil, and make a covenant with God, thou mayst also obtain mercy. If thou hast anything to speak, speak thy mind."

"I have spoke the very truth, and can speak no more."

Then Hann questioned Lloyd:

"Temperance Lloyd, have you made any contract with the Devil?"

"No."

"Did he ever take any of thy blood?"

"No."

"How did he appear to thee first, or where in the street? in what shape?"

"In a woeful shape."

"Had he ever any carnal knowledge of thee?"

"No, never."

"What did he do when he came to thee?"

"He caused me to go and do harm."

"And did you go?"

"I did hurt a Woman sore against my conscience: he carried me up to her door, which was open. The woman's name was Mrs. Grace Thomas."

"What caused you to do her harm? what malice had you against her? Did she do you any harm?"

"No, she never did me any harm, but the Devil beat me about the head grievously because I would not kill her. But I did bruise her after this fashion." (Lloyd here lay her two hands to her sides.)

"Did you bruise her till the blood came out of her mouth and nose?"

"No."

"How many did you destroy and hurt?"

"None but she.".

"Temperance, how did you come in to hurt Mrs. Grace Thomas? did you pass through the key-hole of the door, or was the door open?"

"The Devil did lead me upstairs, and the door was open, and this is all the hurt I did."

"How do you know it was the Devil?"

"I knew it by his eyes?"

"Had you no discourse or treaty with him?"

"No. He said I should go along with him to destroy a woman, and I told him I would not. He said he would make me, and then the Devil beat me about the head."

"Why had you not called upon God?"

"He would not let me do it."

"Did you never ride over an arm of the sea on a cow?"

"No, no, Master, 'twas she, Susan."

When Temperance said 'twas Susan, Susanna Edwards said she lied. "She was the cause of me being brought to die!" Susanna exclaimed. "When she was first brought to gaol, she said if that she was hanged, she would have me hanged too. She reported I should ride on a cow before her, which I never did."

"Susan, did you see the shape of a bullock? At the first time of your examination you said it was like a short black man, about the length of your arm," said Rev. Hann.

"He was black, Sir.".

"Are you willing to have any Prayers?"

Perihelion

Then Mr. Hann. prayed, and they sang part of the 40th Psalm, at the desire of Susanna Edwards. As she mounted the ladder, she said, "The Lord Jesus speed me. Though my sins be as red as scarlet, the Lord Jesus can make them as white as snow. The Lord help my soul." Then she was executed.

Mary Trembles said, "Lord Jesus receive my soul. Lord Jesus speed me." And then she was also executed.

Temperance Lloyd said, "Jesus Christ speed me well. Lord forgive all my sins. Lord Jesus Christ be merciful to my poor Soul."

Then the sheriff said, "You are looked on as the woman that has debauched the other two. Did you ever lie with Devils?"

"No."

"Have you anything to say to satisfy the world?"

"I forgive them," said Temperance Lloyd, "as I desire the Lord Jesus Christ will forgive me. The greatest thing I did was to Mrs. Grace Thomas, and I desire I may be sensible of it, and that the Lord Jesus Christ may forgive me. The Devil met me in the street and bid me kill her, and because I would not, he beat me about the head and back."

"Did the Devil never promise you anything?"

"No, never."

"Then you have served a very bad Master, who gave you nothing. Well, consider you are just departing this world. Do you believe there is a God?"

"Yes."

"Do you believe in Jesus Christ?"

"Yes, and I pray Jesus Christ to pardon all my sins."

And so was she was executed.

---

1   Last hexameter of the Latin verses, "In viri praestantissimi isaaci newtoni opus hocce mathematico-physicum saeculi gentisque nostrae decus egregium" by which Edmond Halley expressed his admiration of Isaac Newton's work. These were prefixed to Newton's *Principia*, for which Halley supervised the publication. Translation as given in Peter Gay, *The Enlightenment: Vol II, The Science of Freedom*. Alfred Knopf, New York. 1996. 131.

2	"In April 1684 Halley's father was found dead on the shore at Stroud in Kent, probably murdered, possibly on account of having been in the Tower as a yeoman warder the day the earl of Essex was found dead there in 1683 and knowing too much of the circumstances—so at least contemporary pamphlets asserted. He had made no will, and Halley became involved in chancery actions with his stepmother. These apparently never came to trial; the parties divided the elder Halley's personal estate of some £4000 about equally."

——Alan Cook. "Halley, Edmond (1656-1742), astronomer" Oxford University Press. 2004.

3	"Halley married Mary Tooke at St James. Duke Place, in 1682; her father, uncles and father's father were Inner Temple lawyers while her mother's father, Gilbert Kinder, was a mercer in the parish of St Helen's Bishopsgate. Kinders and Tookes are also to be found in the registers of St Peter le Poer....

The Tookes were a legal family, and like the Halleys were litigious. Shortly after her marriage Mary engaged in a Chancery action with her sisters to obtain payment of a legacy from an uncle (Charles) who was the executor of another uncle, Edward, who had died in 1668. She also inherited lands from her father Andrew Tooke, Hooke's successor as Gresham Professor of Geometry.... The Royal Society met in his rooms in Gresham College."

——Alan Cook. "Halley the Londoner." Notes and Records of the Royal Society of London 47, no. 2 (1993): 163-77.

4	David W. Hughes and Andrew Drummund. "Edmund Halley's Observations of Halley's Comet" Volume: 15 issue: 3, page(s): 189-197. Journal for the History of Astronomy, University of Sheffield. Science History Publications Ltd. 1984.

5	A. S. Eddington. "Halley's Observations on Halley's Comet, 1682." Nature, May 26, 1910 No. 2117, Vol. 83 --- 372-373. Nature Publishing Group. 1910.

6	Halley perceived that the central force of the solar system must decrease inversely as the square of the distance. In August 1684 he journeyed to Cambridge to consult Newton which resulted in the

Perihelion

publication of the *Philosophiæ Naturalis Principia Mathematica*, aka *Principia* (1687).

From I. Bernard Cohen, "An Interview with Einstein", in Anthony Philip French (ed.), *Einstein: A Centenary Volume* (1979), 41. Cited in Timothy Ferris, Coming of Age in the Milky Way (2003):

"In 1684 Dr Halley came to visit him at Cambridge, after they had been some time together, the Dr asked him what he thought the Curve would be that would be described by the Planets supposing the force of attraction towards the Sun to be reciprocal to the square of their distance from it. Sr Isaac replied immediately that it would be an Ellipsis, the Doctor struck with joy & amazement asked him how he knew it, why saith he I have calculated it, whereupon Dr Halley asked him for his calculation without any farther delay. Sr Isaac looked among his papers but could not find it, but he promised him to renew it, & then to send it him."

Quoted in Richard Westfall, Never at Rest: A Biography of Isaac Newton (1980), 403.:

"For some months the astronomer Halley and other friends of Newton had been discussing the problem in the following precise form: what is the path of a body attracted by a force directed toward a fixed point, the force varying in intensity as the inverse of the distance? Newton answered instantly, "An ellipse." "How do you know?" he was asked. "Why, I have calculated it." Thus originated the imperishable Principia, which Newton later wrote out for Halley. It contained a complete treatise on motion."

———Eric Temple Bell In The Handmaiden of the Sciences (1937), 37.

7   Edmund Halley published "Synopsis Astronomia Cometicae" (A Synopsis of the Astronomy of Comets) in 1705 describing in detail the parabolic orbits of 24 comets that had been observed between 1337 to 1698. He maintained that the comet sightings of 1531, 1607, and 1682 were of the same comet, orbiting our sun in 75- to-76-year intervals. He predicted it would return in 1758. When the comet did return in 1758 it became known as Halley's Comet.

8   "The earliest case of witchcraft in Bideford for which any record has survived occurred in 1658. Grace Ellyott was accused of witchcraft and sent by the justices to stand trial at the Exeter assizes. In the Bail Book it was recorded how she was dealt with: 'Josias Ellyott of Bideford, mercer, and Richard Wann of Great Torrington, tailor. That Grace Ellyott, wife of the aforesaid Josias Ellyott do appear next [assizes] and be of the good behaviour on suspicion of witchcraft. Appeared and discharged. Surety in twenty pounds apiece.'

One of the people accused of witchcraft at the Exeter assizes in 1671 was Temperance Lloyd of Bideford. This was her first appearance, accused of 'killing William Herbert by witchcraft' but on this occasion she was acquitted. On 15 May 1679 'Temperance Lloyd was accused for practising of witchcraft upon Anne Fellow the daughter of Edward Fellow, of Bideford gentleman (Gauger of Excise). Evidences against her were: Anne Fellow the mother, Mr Oliver Ball apothecary, Elizabeth Coleman, Dorcas Lidston and Elizabeth Davie. Upon the 17 May 1679 the said Temperance was searched by Sisly Galsworthy and others.' The papers were filed, but no further action appears to have been taken."

——Gent, Frank J. *The Trial of the Bideford Witches*. Published by Frank J. Gent, England (1982). Also available online as http://gent.org.uk/bidefordwitches/tbw.pdf. Gent here is quoting: C. L'E. Ewen *Witchcraft and Demonianism* (1933), and Sessions of the Peace Book for Bideford, 1659-1709 (DRO: 10640/S0 1).

9   Ibid.

10   Ibid.

11   Document title: "A True and impartial relation of the informations against three witches, viz., Temperance Lloyd, Mary Trembles, and Susanna Edwards, who were indicted, arraigned and convicted at the assizes holden for the county of Devon, at the castle of Exon, Aug. 14, 1682 with their several confessions, taken before Thomas Gist, Mayor, and John Davie, alderman, of Biddiford, in the said county, where they were inhabitants: as also, their speeches, confessions and behaviour at the time and place of execution on the twenty fifth of the said month."

Perihelion

——LONDON: Printed by Freeman Collins, and are to be Sold by T. Benskin, in St. Brides Church-yard, and C. Yeo Bookseller in Exon. 1682. [Public Domain].

12   Gent, Frank J. *The Trial of the Bideford Witches*. [Quoting from a pamphlet published around the time of the trial.]

13   Gent, Frank J. *The Trial of the Bideford Witches*.

14   "A True and impartial relation of the informations against three witches…"

15   Gent, Frank J. *The Trial of the Bideford Witches*.

16   "A True and impartial relation of the informations against three witches…"

A String of a Thousand Grains of Wampum

Lomewe, luwe na okwes xu laxakwihele xkwithakamika.
Long ago it was said that a fox will be loosened on the earth.

Ok nen luwe newa ahasak xu peyok.
Also it was said four crows will come.

Netami ahas kenthu li guttitehewagan wichi Kishelemukonk.
The first crow flew the way of harmony with Creator.

Nisheneit ahas kwechi pilito entalelemukonk, shek palsu ok ankela.
The second crow tried to clean the world, but he became sick and he died.

Nexeneit ahas weneyoo ankelek xansa ok koshiphuwe.
The third crow saw his dead brother and he hid.

Neweneit ahas kenthu li guttitehewagan lapi wichi Kishelemukonk.
The fourth crow flew the way of harmony again with Creator.

Kenahkihechik xu withatuwak xkwithakamika.
    Caretakers they will live together on the earth...
    ——"The Prophecy of the Fourth Crow" ancient Lepane story as told by Robert Red Hawk Ruth and Translated by Shelley DePaul.[26]

    In the Prohlis district of Dresden in Saxony, about 107 miles south of Berlin, Germany, on a cold Christmas evening in 1758, a farmer named Johann George Palitzsch looked through his telescope at a point just above the horizon. Palitzsch was an amateur astronomer, self-taught by secret study (as his stepfather had opposed his scholarly interests). He had inherited the farm and now he was able to assemble a library and construct a workshop complete with telescope of an eight-foot focal length, more than adequate for the task at hand. His wife of 11 years, Anna Regina, was calling him to come say goodnight to their daughter, but Johann could not take his eye away from the viewing optic.

Perihelion

A bright speck entered his field of view. A blueish fan of glowing ions trailed out from it: a comet! And not just any comet. The world had awaited the return of the comet predicted by Edmund Halley in 1705. French astronomer Charles Messier in Paris had expected to see it since spring but so far had it had alluded him. Now it was the sole discovery of Johann George Palitzsch, that was, if he could publish his findings.

Palitzsch went to the scholar Christian Gotthold Hoffmann. Together they published his observations in "Dreßdnische Gelehrten Advertisements," (The Russian Scholar Advertisements).[1] Word got around. The comet, its path now measured and calculated by world scientists, became Comet 1P/Halley, better known as Halley's Comet.

Self-taught, Palitzsch also studied agricultural botanics, using microscopes for biological studies. He helped to introduce the potato as a common food in Saxony. He introduced the lightning rod in Saxony. When he died in 1788, Palitzsch left behind a library of 3,518 books, some of which were handwritten copies he had made from scientific works which were too expensive for him to purchase. A crater and a valley on the Moon are named after him. The asteroid 11970 Palitzsch also is named after him.

On October 27, 1682, another year of our comet, William Penn founded the City of Philadelphia, Pennsylvania. That same year Penn met the indigenous population that lived in the Delaware Valley of eastern Pennsylvania and New Jersey. Among the many tribes sharing common languages and hunting grounds were a people called the Lenni Lenape. The name came from Lenni, which may mean "genuine, pure, real, original," and Lenape, meaning "real person" or "original person." The English settlers would refer to the Lenape as the "Delaware" and fail to recognize their many clans as distinct. By the time of their European "discovery" the Lenape were reduced by disease, famine, and war and had begun to consolidate their families into three main clans, each with 12 subclans. One of clans, perhaps the most important, was the Turtle, or Pùkuwànku clan.

Penn and the Quaker colonists initially signed a treaty with the Lenape. But after William Penn died in 1718, his heirs and others in power in the new colony abandoned many of his policies. They thought to sell the Lenape lands to new colonists and produced a deed, supposedly dating to 1680, which was anything but legitimate. The next few decades saw a "convoluted sequence of deception, fraud, and extortion orchestrated by the Pennsylvania government that is commonly known as the Walking Purchase."[2] The Lenape were methodically being forced from their homelands. In 1758, this year of our comet, a new treaty was signed, the Treaty of Easton,[3] which required the Lenape to move west, away from the Delaware Valley. At the final negotiations on the 26th of October, the Nations presented, as their proof of agreement, strings of a thousand grains of wampum.[4]

The principal chief of the Turtle clan was Netawatwees. His name translates as "skilled advisor," and the European settlers called him "Newcomer." (see footnote 19) Netawatwees was unhappy with the governors of the Nation. These chiefs had no power to convey lands to anyone yet they had accepted a small handful of gold pieces and had agreed to release deeds for all those lands where the people had lived since Nipahuma, the Grandmother Moon, and Muxumsa Pethakowe, Grandfather Thunder, had created the first humans.[5] Lands where their ancestors were buried and the hunting was good. A great many lands.[6] Yet they had received no guns, no ammunition, and even had to beg for wagons to convey the people west!

Netawatwees and members of his clan at the time of the treaty lived in a settlement at the mouth of Beaver Creek, a tributary of the Ohio River by present-day Pittsburgh. The Turtle clan would soon move to Ohio near what is now Cuyahoga Falls, south of present-day Cleveland. It would be a long journey, a trail of tears. The Lepanes were not nomads and only moved when their hunting grounds were depleted or their fields failed to produce. They were an agricultural people, planting mainly corn, beans, and squash. They planted the beans next to the corn so that the plants could use the corn stalks as climbing poles.

As the Europeans advanced across the Native Americans' territory, pushing them out, the Lenapes and other tribes reacted with violence, raiding and often taking women and children captive (see footnote 11, re: Penn's Creek Massacre). Often the white women would be taken as squaws and the children adopted and raised in the same villages. There is a story, related in a journal of explorer Christopher Gist,[7] of his meeting a white woman in 1751 (her story would go down in history as "The Legend of the White Woman")

Perihelion

named Mary Harris. Mary Harris had been captured at the age of ten during a French and Indian War raid on Deerfield, Massachusetts in 1704. When Gist met her, Harris had a husband named Eagle Feather who had taken another wife named Newcomer. At some point both Eagle Feather and Newcomer were killed, possibly by Harris, although there is only rumor to support that part of the story. The town of Newcomerstown, Ohio, may have gotten its name in this manner. A different version of the town's name origin points to the Indian settlement called Gekelukpechink, (meaning "still water"), founded by our Chief Netawatwees (aka Newcomer) at a much later time. But we are getting ahead of our story.

The French and Indian War took place within the years between 1754 and 1763. The French and the British were in contention over who "owned" the Upper Ohio Valley (it could not have been the indigenous peoples, now could it?). The British outnumbered the French who were centralized in New France, present day Canada. Indigenous peoples supplied the French with additional manpower. Most Native American tribes took sides in the conflict: Iroquois, Catawba, and Cherokee gave support to the British while the French enlisted the aid of the Wabanaki Confederacy, including Abenaki and Mi'kmaq, and the Algonquin, Ojibwa, Ottawa, Shawnee, Wyandot, and of course, the Lenape.

One turning point of the war came with a major disaster for the British: The Battle of the Monongahela on July 9, 1755. Major General Edward Braddock, British officer and commander-in-chief for the Thirteen Colonies, with a company of 1,200 crack British soldiers and a few colonists, rode to take Fort Duquesne at the confluence of the Allegheny and Monongahela Rivers. A young officer named George Washington warned Braddock that his European military tactics were impractical in the rough, heavily wooded terrain of Pennsylvania. Benjamin Franklin also told him that his plans were dangerous. In his autobiography Franklin wrote:

"But I ventur'd only to say to him, '...The only danger I apprehend of obstruction to your march is from ambuscades of Indians, who, by constant practice, are dexterous in laying and executing them; and the slender line, near four miles long, which your army must make, may expose it to be attack'd by surprise in its flanks, and to be cut like a thread into several pieces, which, from their distance, cannot come up in time to support each other.' He (Braddock) smil'd at my ignorance, and reply'd, 'These savages may, indeed, be a formidable enemy to your raw American militia, but upon the king's regular and disciplin'd troops, sir, it is impossible they should make any impression.' "[8]

General Braddock led his troops up a narrow road which had been laboriously hacked through the forest. They marched in single file, beating drums and carrying their banners high. The Indians fell on them from the woods, picking them off easily.[9] The General had ordered his men to form platoons to fire at the enemy, which was nearly impossible in the tight quarters of a path only a few feet wide. Braddock's horse was shot out from under him. He was fatally wounded and died a few days later. It was a crushing and embarrassing defeat for the British.

One side effect of this disaster, an effect pertinent to our story, was that the shock of this defeat prompted the building of a series of forts to protect the colonists from French and Indian attacks. Bordering the counties of Cumberland and Franklin in south-central Pennsylvania was the town of Shippensburg, first settled in 1730 by Scots-Irish immigrants. A dozen of these families built homes along Burd's Run, a tributary of Middle Spring Creek, near the town. Hearing of General Braddock's defeat, Pennsylvania Governor Robert H. Morris ordered construction of a fort at Shippensburg. It would come to be called Fort Morris.

The fort was a stockade of rough-hewn logs, star-shaped with four bastions and a single gate. There were guns on three of the bastions. Brigadier-General John Forbes visited the fort in 1758 (our year of the comet) and described it in a memorandum[10] as having nine huts or houses, a barracks, a magazine, and a storehouse adequate for 150 to 200 men. When hostilities from local Indians occurred, residents of Shippensburg would take shelter in the fort. In 1758, a number of families came to the fort bringing with them their cattle. Two of these families were the Campbells and the Stewarts who shared a house near Burd's Run.[11]

Mr. and Mrs. Stewart had four children, one an infant. The Campbells had three boys, Daniel, William, and Dougal who was named after his father, and a daughter, Mary. In the spring of 1758, Mary Campbell was seven years of age.[12] She had red hair, freckles, and dark eyes, all of which reflected her Scots-Irish heritage. She and

Perihelion

William were the closest together in age and played together whenever their mother was not putting them to chores or tutoring them in the alphabet and arithmetic. Sometimes father let them bring the cows in from the field along the creek's edge. But of late this was discouraged because of reports that Indian bands were abroad. The Campbells and the Stewarts made the decision, therefore, to move into the fort in nearby Shippensburg.

The town was growing rapidly. Its founder, Edward Shippen, had obtained the land patent from William Penn's heirs as part of the so-called Walking Purchase. The influx of colonists here had broken the earlier treaty with the Native Americans and left them angry and resentful. Yet with the fully garrisoned fort under the command of Colonel James Burd now at the center of town, an attack was unlikely. Off-duty, the soldiers frequented the nearby Widow Piper's Tavern so their presence in the town was obvious to any Indian who crept up at night to spy.

The Campbells and the Stewarts found conditions at the fort crowded and supplies short. The children could not run freely as they had on their own land. The cattle were corralled at the edge of the town along Middle Spring Creek and still needed tending, which meant venturing out of the fort for a short but possibly dangerous time. Tents had been set up within the stockade for the settlers, old army blankets serving as flooring.

In the tent on a day in mid-May, Dougal Campbell looked longingly at his wife, Margaret. His thoughts flew back to the homestead they had left in County Down in Ulster, not that many years ago. The Mountains of Mourne, the Donard Forest, The Glen River. The great expanses of land running down to the sea. But he also remembered the persecution of Scottish Protestants which had prompted the migration. Even upon their arrival in the colonies there had been prejudice from the German population in Lancaster County. Now the Indians threatened the peaceful existence they sought by moving westward. Persecution, prejudice, and hostility! A stubborn streak ran through the man, however. He would not be forced to cower in this fort which smelled of too many people, where the sun barely peeked over the walls.

"Margaret," he said, "I have heard that the soldiers think the savages have left. Colonel Burd sent a patrol to scout up and down Canncoquin Creek and found no sign of them."

"That is good, husband," said Margaret. "Will they stay away?"

"There is no way to know. The British are attempting to invade New France, so the focus of the war is to the north of us. The Indians hereabouts favor the French. Perhaps they will leave to fight against the British army."

"We came here to be part of the New World. And now forces of the Old World fight each other over the right to own the land that doesn't belong to them in first place, drawing us into the fight," said Margaret.

"There is much resentment here against the British who would have our wagons and horses, our tools and our food to transport their troops."

"Dougal, do you suppose we might be able to return to our home? If the Indians are truly gone…"

"My love, I was hoping you would come to that decision. I will talk to the Stewarts tomorrow."

May 21, 1758. Kau-ta-tin-Chunk Kittochtinny—this is the Native American name for the Blue Mountains on the north-western boundary of the Cumberland Valley. It translates as "Endless Mountain." South Mountain forms the other boundary of the valley. The long, high ridges of coarse gray slate and reddish sandstone are immense folds resembling those on an old man's forehead (when viewed from the perspective of the comet). The valley itself is partly wooded with crab apple, plum, evergreen and oak, dotted with springs and small creeks, softly rising hills and dales. It is crisscrossed by old Indian trails. Some of the timber has been cleared by Scots-Irish and German immigrants since the valley was purchased from the Indians in 1734.[13]

This spring the land is resplendent with hazel and buttercup and many other wildflowers. The settlers' cattle have returned to roam freely on the grassy plain and blackbirds follow their progress waiting for the rise of insects disturbed by the cows' hooves. There is a calmness and a bucolic ambience in this pastoral setting. Yet the war with the French and the restlessness of the indigenous peoples of the region are like a storm front just over the next ridge. Only last year there was a major Indian attack in the environs around Shippensburg.[14] There is a major army supply route passing through

Perihelion

Shippensburg and, of course, the fort, so maybe the danger is less than the settlers believe it to be. Maybe.

It is a pleasant day for children to be out and about. Fathers Dougal Campbell and Charles Stewart have taken the wagon into town to buy more feed. Mother Mary Jane Stewart has gone to a neighbor's house on the other side of Burd's Run and taken baby Evan along, leaving her other children at home. Margaret Campbell, with seven children now under her wing, is torn between giving in to the children's pleas to venture out of doors and her fears of Indian attack.

"Mother," pleads William Campbell, "may we go bring in the cows? We won't be out of sight of the cabin for long."

She considers this, knowing that the cattle must be brought in and put in the corral before long; they could be stolen by the Indians if they wander too far afield. William is a level-headed boy. And so, against her better judgement, she gives in.

"You may go," she says, "but take Samuel with you." Samuel Stewart is seven, the same age as Mary Campbell.

"I want to go too," says Mary.

"Alright, but hurry back, we have chores to do and lessons as well."

The cattle are of an ancient breed probably introduced to the New World by the Pilgrims in the last century. They are called Devon Milkers, from the North Devonshire region of England, and are intelligent animals, covered with a dark red coat and they sport long, thick, white horns. Their horns are tipped with black points. The cattle stand out in sharp contrast to the pale green grass of the meadow. The children spot them easily even though they have strayed considerably from the site of the cabin. The herd, four in number, is grazing close to the edge of the forest.

William has brought a length of rope to tie to Hilda, the lead cow; the others will follow her as William brings her back. He has to jump a little to loop the rope over one of her horns as she is taller than he. Hilda casts a long shadow on the grass where Mary and Samuel are playing ring-around-the rosy. The shadow has grown extra parts: tall, feathered parts. Three Lanape braves come from the woods and rush at the children. They are naked except for loin cloths. Their heads are shaved so that only a strip of hair remains forming a scalp lock standing up like the crest of some exotic bird. Into this are woven turkey feathers. Their faces, arms, and chests are painted with abstract designs resembling birds or animals. Two have quivers of arrows strapped to their backs and bows strung over their shoulders. The third is brandishing a tomahawk.

The children run. The brave with the tomahawk hurls it at Sammy. The child falls, not being cut by the wicked weapon, but cold-cocked. William pauses to help his friend—a mistake. Now all three children are captured, the Indians holding each of them in a menacing embrace. As they begin to drag them toward the forest, the Indians are arguing whether to take one or two of the cows.

"Nati wehshumwis (Fetch the cow)," one brave tells another.

"Atam tekening! (Let's go into the woods!)" he replies.

As they argue, another four more Lapane warriors emerge from the thickly wooded area. "Mesakwikaon! (Log house!)" one yells, pointing. They head for the cabin which they can see just over a low rise. In their enthusiasm for potential plunder they let out a series of yells the likes of which later writers of Wild West fiction would probably describe as "whoops." This is not a good tactic when attempting to surprise and the result is that Margaret Campbell, tending to the children, hears them.

"Children, quickly," she says, "gather your things and follow me. Hurry now!"

They are out the door and headed across Burd's Run toward town. By the time the Lapane get to the house they have disappeared into a low stand of brush. They stop here, cowering out of sight. The children begin to cry.

"Mother," Dougal asks, "what of Mary and William?"

Margaret Campbell does not answer, afraid of the worst.

Mary Jane Stewart returns from her visit to the Magaws further up the Burd's run where it joins Middle Spring Creek. Baby Evan is asleep in her arms; it has been a long day for him. As she approaches the cabin she senses that something is wrong. There are no sounds of children playing, no smells of food cooking, no cows in the corral. Cautiously, she opens the door. She is shocked to find the furniture broken and in disarray. Her mother's china that she brought from Ireland so carefully packed in excelsior also lies on the floor, broken into sharp shards. Curtains have been ripped down. There is no one in the cabin. She backs away from the door and stands breathing heavily, wondering what has happened. A Lapane warrior comes around the side of the cabin. He grabs her, his hand clasped over her mouth although there is no one to hear her screams. "Chitkwesi! (Be quiet!)" he tells her. "Wichei, xkwe. (Come with me, woman.)"

The Indians return to the edge of the forest, Margaret Stewart and Baby Evan in tow. The others are waiting, still arguing about the cow.

"Machitam awossachtenne, (Let's go home...over the mountain)" says the one with the tomahawk. Perhaps he is the leader, for they obey. They leave the cow; it will only slow them down. Certainly, the soldiers will soon follow. In the dense forest they can lose them.

[author's note: what follows is taken from an article in the *Summit County Beacon* by L.V. Bierce, written in 1851, almost one hundred years later. Bierce was an historian who wrote copiously about local events and people. His source would have to have filtered up through time from Mary or, more likely, Mrs. Stewart, from some contemporary interview which is now lost. Additional details of the capture were added by William Henry Perrin in his *History of Summit County*, but it appears his source was Bierce. The family tradition only tells that they were taken (year and location are different from these writers).][15]

They enter the forest, the long ridge of Blue Mountain looms ahead, gullies and streams, outcroppings of sandstone, but a road exists through this desolation, a road being built for war by the British: Forbe's Road. They can skirt this, staying deep in the trees and brush, out of sight and mind. They can forage, hunt, fish. But first comes a long expanse of poplar and pine, brambles covering the ancient paths of their ancestors.

It is a forced march for the children and the woman; they are unskilled in this type of trek. Mary sees demons grabbing out at her in every branch and limb that obstructs their passage. A thick carpet of dried pine needles is underfoot, hiding unknown terrors...dead things, Mary is certain. She stays close to William and lowers her head whenever an Indian glances back at her, as if in so doing she can hide her fear from him.

The Indians are being slowed down. Not only that, the infant is letting out screams punctuated by sobs when his breath gives out. The warrior with the tomahawk, let's call him Xinkmaxkw, which means "Big Bear," becomes so irritated by the baby's crying that he grabs Evan away from his mother. With a curse he swings the baby by its feet and smashes it against a tree trunk, splattering brains and blood onto the path. He tosses the child into the brush. "Atam! (let's go!)" he yells. Mary Jane Stewart is shocked into misbelief; this can't have happened! The other children cry out in terror. "Chitkwesi! (Shut up!)" says Big Bear. The warriors push the group of captives ahead.

They reach the foot of the first series of ridges as night falls. They make camp in a shallow depression surrounded by weathered rock and sparse bush. There is a fire, food in the form of dried jerky and a possum one of the Indians has killed using a dart from a blowgun. There is water from a nearby stream. The captives are unable to sleep. Mary curls up in Mary Jane Stewart's arms. "I am afraid," she says in a small voice that is mostly a sob. The boys now also come to cling to the woman. "I could kill him," Mary Jane says softly, referring to Big Bear.

The next morning they climb the low ridges and valleys that form the ripples of the Appalachian Basin. This is Tuscarora Mountain, a rich game area where they pause to hunt. They are unable to bring down a deer; perhaps the crying of the children has scared them away. Several rabbit and squirrel carcasses now hang from the belts of the warriors. It shall have to suffice. Samuel Stewart has been lagging, slowing their progress. His injury from the chase in the field near his home is the cause. Big Bear is furious but hides his anger from the woman who he knows will protect the boy and to whom he has taken a liking; she would make a good squaw, he thinks. He whispers something to one of the other braves, let's call him Mexkalaniyat, which means "Red-tailed hawk."

Mexkalaniyat, at Big Bear's prompting, leads Samuel by the hand off into the deep brush. There is nothing Mary Jane can do about this. When the Indian returns he is alone. Hanging from his belt is a scrap of curly hair. Seeing the horror on Mary Jane Stewart's face he says, "Conunmoch! (Otter!)," but of course she knows what it is. Her world is being destroyed one child at a time. Desperately she clings now to Mary and William.

After descending the last ridge they pass by the village of Burnt Cabins[16] and begin following the Forbes Road keeping just out of sight. Four days later they reach the Raystown Trading Post near the

Perihelion

outskirts of Fort Bedford, now under construction. They give this a wide berth as there are soldiers in the area who would consider them as hostiles. It will be another three weeks before they reach their destination.

Their trail takes them past the confluence of the Allegheny and Monongahela Rivers with the head waters of the Ohio River. Here the French-built Fort Duquesne has been taken by British General Edward Braddock and Major George Washington. Now General John Forbes is constructing a new fort to be named Fort Pitt. The settlement here will be named "Pittsborough".

There is a Senaca village here at "Forks of the Ohio" which is called Diondega. The Lapanes will call the "Forks of the Ohio" Menacht-sink which means "where there is a fence" (the fence being the fort). It takes the Lapane careful negotiations with the Senaca to obtain passage across the river by canoe. This they do under the very eyes of the British army who believe them to be allies—which they are not.

As the Ohio turns north past the future city of Pittsburgh it is fed by Beaver Creek, called by the Lapane, Amockwi-sipu or Amockwi-hanne.[17] Here chestnut, black walnut, hickory, and wild plum are in abundance. Geese patrol the banks where turtles bask in the warm sun. There are gently rolling hills of fertile soil; it had been an excellent location for a village. The village of the Lapane here is called Sawkunk or Sacunk, meaning "at the mouth of a stream."[18] It is here that the warriors bring their captives, the woman and the two children. It is here that the Chief of the Turtle Clan lives: Netawatwees.[19]

Netawatwees is very pleased with the two children, especially the fire-headed young girl. "Xkwechishtet (little girl)," he says, "keku hech kteluwensi? (what is your name?)." It will be years before Mary Campbell learns the language. Netawatwees realizes this. He decides he will adopt the girl and she will be brought up by one of his squaws. William is given to the household of Tamaqua, the brother of Lapane leader Shingas, who is called "Shingas the Terrible". Tamaqua is known to the whites as "the Beaver" or "King Beaver."

Mary Jane Stewart now stands before Netawatwees. What will happen to the woman? He considers. Perhaps he will let her choose between two of the warriors who have brought her here. Xinkmaxkw who bashed her baby's brains out, or Mexkalaniyat, who killed

Byron Grush

Samuel and scalped him. The alternative, remaining "unmarried" would not be allowed. Mary Jane does not yet realize she will have to make this choice.

In Summit County, Ohio, hundreds of feet above the Cuyahoga River Gorge, is a half-dome of sandstone and shale originally known as Old Maid's Kitchen. It is a natural rock formation created by the river thousands of years ago. Under the overhanging shelf of shale and eroded limestone, in the center at the back of the cave, is a bronze plaque. It reads:

In Memory of Mary Campbell

Who in 1759 at the age of twelve years was kidnapped from her home in Western Pennsylvania by Delaware Indians. In the same year these Indians were forced to migrate to this section where they erected their village at the big falls of the Cuyahoga. As a result Mary Campbell was the first white child on the Western Reserve and this tablet marks the cave where she and the Indian women temporarily lived. Later, in 1764, she was returned to her home.

Erected by the Mary Campbell Society Children of the American Revolution of Cuyahoga Falls, 1934.

There are some who say Mary Campbell never lived in this cave.[20] Although the date and age do not match most accounts, the DAR did extensive research before making the decision to erect this plaque. Here is what our sources say happened:

The Treaty of Easton was signed in October 1758 between the British colonial government of the Province of Pennsylvania and the Native American tribes in the Ohio Country. Native Americans agreed not to fight the British during the French and Indian War. The Forbes Expedition was sent to drive out the French from the contested Ohio Country. The French abandoned and burned Fort Duquesne. With the British now controlling the area around what they called Pittsborough, and therefore the Senaca and Lapane villages along the Ohio River, Netawatwees decided it was once again time to relocate.

The Turtle Clan migrated northwest into Ohio, arriving in three weeks at the falls of the Cuyahoga River near present-day Akron, Ohio. It was Autumn of the year 1758. There they found rushing

Perihelion

rapids and three perpendicular falls—one about twelve feet high, the second falling sixteen feet, and the lower, called "Big Falls," a drop of twenty-two feet. They called it the Crooked River—Cuyahoga. Netawatwees selected a spot above the Big Falls for his new camp. During construction of the camp the women were sheltered in a cave once carved out by the meandering river, and now identified as the Mary Campbell Cave.

By now Mary and Mary Jane had met and befriended the few other white captives of the Turtle Clan, all of them women or children. Regina Hartman and a friend named Susan, 13 and 6 respectively, had been taken from Berk's County in Pennsylvania by the Lapane. They would become good companions for Mary Campbell in the months and years to come. From a 1755 raid in the Tuscarora valley had come a Mrs. Gallway and her two children, and a Mrs. McClelland and her two children. Mrs. McClelland's husband David had been murdered during the raid.[21] The woman had become, if not fluent, at least serviceably adequate in the Unami language spoken by the Turtle Clan.

Mary Jane Stewart learned that she was not alone in being forced to choose a husband from the tribe. When Mary Jane, upon the day of her arrival at Beaver Creek had been shown the two Indians that had killed her children, she had screamed and thrown herself at them, fists pounding and nails scraping. Both men had backed away and refused to take her as their squaw. The issue had yet to be settled. There was a Dutch woman from one of the German settlements who had been given a choice between what Mary Jane later related was "the ugliest Indian I ever saw," and the adopted uncle of Mary Campbell. She chose the uncle.

Regina Hartman was unable to talk about the massacre in Berks County when she was taken. Mary learned from Regina's friend Susan, in bits and pieces over the years of their captivity, that the Hartmans had been at the grist mill when the Indians swooped down on them. Their father and a brother had been killed and scalped. Regina's sister, Barbara, had been taken at the time but was killed during the march, her battered body left along the trail.

By December, the Turtle Clan and their captives were settled in at the camp above the Big Falls. Halley's Comet could be seen in the sky. Perhaps, thought Netawatwees, it was one of the Pèthakhuweyok, the Thunder Beings that live in the sky and cause thunder and lightning. Or perhaps it was Mànàka'has, the Rainbow Crow who created fire.

As the years passed Netawatwee treated the white children well. Mary learned to hoe the corn fields using an implement made from the bones of a deer. The white women were taken as wives and learned the way of squaws: they ruled the clan when it came to issues of agriculture, family, and kinship. The only thing the men were good for was hunting, fishing, and war.

By 1763 the French and Indian War was all but over with the British successful in establishing dominion over the Ohio valley and the Great Lakes Region of what is now the United States. Not everyone was happy, however. There were still raids against the settlers by the tribes. This year the area around Shippensburg was attacked and many houses were burned.[22] There arose a new leader among the dissatisfied Native Americans: Obwandiya, also known as Pontiac.

Ottawas, Ojibwes, and Potawatomis from the Great Lakes region, Miamis, Weas, Kickapoos, Mascoutens, and Piankashaws from eastern Illinois, Lenape, Shawnees, Wyandots, Senaca, and Mingos from the Ohio valley banded together in a last attempt to drive the British from their ancestral lands. Pontiac led assaults on at least eight different British forts, including Fort Pitt. The British authorities sent Colonel Henry Bouquet to the rescue.

Bouquet was not a nice man. During the siege at Fort Pitt, along with General Jeffrey Amhers, he was responsible for instituting a new tactic: biological warfare. Two blankets and a handkerchief that had been exposed to smallpox were given to the Indians in a deliberate attempt to expose them. It was the beginning, but not the end, of a campaign of genocide that would be perpetrated upon the indigenous peoples by the white military. At the Battle of Bushy Run in August, Bouquet was successful in securing Fort Pitt.

Most of the conflicts were ending by mid-1764 although a few tribes ignored treaties. In October, Bouquet marched from Fort Pitt to the Muskingum River in the Ohio Country to engage the Indians of Ohio. He demanded the return of prisoners from the Lapane and Seneca tribes. Reluctantly, they agreed. Many of the captives, now assimilated into the Indian culture, were reluctant to leave. Regina Hartman was sent to Carlisle where parents were to claim their lost children. Regina's mother was unable to identify her own child in the line. Regina's mother then began to sing the old German hymn "Alone, Yet Not Alone."[23] Regina suddenly recognized her and ran to her, tears streaming down her face.

Mary Jane Stewart was among the captives "delivered to their friends" at Fort Pitt on November 29, 1764. Her name appears on a list of returned prisoners sent to General Gage from General Bouquet. On another list appears the name Mary Campbell, but the date is given as 10 May 1765.[24] The family tradition related by Eleanor Womer tells us that "Mary Campbell's brother Dougal Campbell went with Colonel Bouquet when he made the peace treaty with the Indians. He stepped on a log or something that raised him so he could see over the crowd and called 'Mary Campbell' and from his position saw a squaw clap her hand over a girl's mouth and that was how she was recovered. In telling it she said as she watched her brother before she knew who he was she thought him the most handsome man she ever saw."[25]

From "The Prophecy of the Fourth Crow":

Nisheneit ahas kwechi pilito entalelemukonk, shek palsu ok ankela.

The second crow tried to clean the world, but he became sick and he died.[26]

---

1   Hoffmann, Christian Gotthold (1759 January 20) "Nachricht von dem Kometen, welcher seit dem 25. December gesehen wird" (News of the comet, which has been seen since the 25th of December), Dreßdnischen Gelehrten Anzeigen, 2nd issue.

2   Harper, Steven Craig (2006). *Promised Land: Penn's Holy Experiment, the Walking Purchase, and the dispossession of Delawares, 1600–1763*. Bethlehem, PA.

3   The Easton Treaty was an agreement between the British and the Indigenous peoples of the Delaware Valley. Meetings lasting weeks involved British colonial officials and more than 500 chiefs, representing 15 Woodland Indigenous peoples, Mohawks, Oneydos, Onondagas, Cayugas, Senecas, Tuscaroras, Tuteloes, Nanticokes and

Conoys, Chugnuts, Delawares, Unamies, Mohickons, Minisinks, and Wapings. The British successfully neutralized the French-Indigenous alliance in the Ohio Valley during the Seven Years' War (1756–63) by guaranteeing the protection of Indigenous lands from Anglo-American colonists.

The "Friendly Association of Pennsylvania," a group of Quaker pacifists, pushed for the Easton Treaty to include a firm boundary set at the Allegheny Mountains, reserving the vast Ohio Valley for the Indians. However, the promises made at the Easton Treaty were soon forgotten, or simply ignored. Pennsylvanians continued to settle the Ohio Valley, and the British failed to stop them.

——Anthony J. Hall, Gretchen Albers. "Easton Treaty" article published online August 14, 2014, Canadian Encyclopedia. https://www.thecanadianencyclopedia.ca/en/article/easton-treaty.

4   Negotiations during treaty talks involved the exchange of wampum strings and beaded belts. Some excerpts from the minutes of those meetings:

With this String, I wipe the Sweat and Dust out of your Eyes, that you may see your Brethren's Faces, and look chearful. With this String, I take all Bitterness out of your Breast, as well as every Thing disagreeable that may have gathered there, in Order that you may speak perfectly free and open to us. With this String, I gather the Blood, and take it away from the Council Seats, that your Cloaths may not be stained, nor your Minds any ways disturbed.

Eighth Day of October, 1758.

A large white Belt, with the Figure of a Man at each End, and Streaks of Black, representing the Road from the Ohio to Philadelphia.

By this Belt, we heal your Wounds; we remove your Grief; we take the Hatchet out of your Heads; we make a deep Hole in the Earth, and bury the Hatchet so low, that no Body shall be able to dig it up again.

Perihelion

The 23d of October.

A string consisting of a Thousand Grains of Wampum.

With this String of Wampum, we condole with you for the Loss of your wise Men, and for the Warriors that have been killed in these troublesome Times, and likewise for your Women and Children, and we cover their Graves decently agreeable to the Custom of your Forefathers.

A String of a Thousand Grains of Wampum.

We disperse the dark Clouds that have hung over our Heads, during these Troubles, that we may see the Sun clear, and look on each other with the Chearfulness our Forefathers did.

26th of October, 1758

Some Wine and Punch was called for, and mutual Healths were drank, and the Conferences were concluded with great Satisfaction.

——The Minutes of a treaty held at Easton, in Pennsylvania, in October, 1758. By the lieutenant governor of Pennsylvania, and the governor of New-Jersey; with the chief sachems and warriors of the Mohawks, Oneydos, Onondagas, Cayugas, Senecas, Tuscaroras, Tuteloes, Nanticokes and Conoys, Chugnuts, Delawares, Unamies, Mohickons, Minisinks, and Wapings.

Woodbridge, in New-Jersey: Printed and Sold by James Parker, Printer to the Government of New-Jersey, 1758

5   "Now, Nipahuma, our Grandmother Moon, having been set in the night sky, her Spirit became lonely and so she asked the Creator for a companion. The Creator sent her a Spirit, Grandfather Thunder, Muxumsa Pethakowe, to keep her company. With him she conceived, and when she came to lend her powers of fertility to the Earth to help in the creation of life, she gave birth upon the Earth to twins - one a man, and the other a woman. Thus it was humankind was the last of beings created. Though they were different, man and

woman found a wholeness in union with each other. Only together were they complete and fulfilled, only together could they fulfill their purpose. The Creator gave man and woman a special gift, the power to dream. Nipahuma, our Mother who goes by night, the first mother, the mother of all mothers, nurtured her children, and when her purpose was complete she returned to the spirit world; but before she left she told first man and woman that she would never forget them. She continues to watch over us at night as the Moon. The children promised to remember Grandmother Moon whenever she appeared in the sky, giving her light to guide our paths."

——"Native Languages of the Americas: Lenape/Delaware Indian Legends and Stories." http://henryhahn.net/myths/

6   "Lands at Wioming, Shamokin and other Places on the Susquehannah River, all the Lands lying in New-Jersey, South of a Line from Paoqualin Mountains at Delaware River, to the falls of Alamatung, on the North Branch of Rariton River, thence down that River to Sandy-Hook and including all the remaining Lands in New-Jersey, beginning at Cushytunk, and down the Division Lines between New-Jersey and New-York, to the Mouth of Tappan Creek at Hudson's River, and down the same to Sandy-Hook, thence to the Mouth of Rariton, thence up that River to the Falls of Alamatung, thence on a strait Line to Paoqualin Mountains, where it joins on Delaware River, thence up the River Delaware to Cushytunk."

——The Minutes of a treaty held at Easton, in Pennsylvania, in October, 1758. Etc.

7   "January 15—Reaching the Whitewoman's Creek, about four miles west of the present town of Coshocton. [approximate location of present-day Newcomerstown] Mary Harris, the white woman, doubtless was the same person who was captured at the assault and burning of Deerfield, Massachusetts, by the French and Indians from Canada, February 39, 1704; this White Woman was taken away from New England, when she was not above ten Years old, by the French Indians; She is now upwards of fifty, and has an Indian Husband and several Children — Her name is Mary Harris..."

——Christopher Gist's Journal, Google Books.

Perihelion

8	Project Gutenberg's "Autobiography of Benjamin Franklin, by Benjamin Franklin." Ed. Frank Woodworth Pine. EBook #20203. 2006.

9	"Despite Washington's warnings, Braddock's troops marched in typical European fashion – long rows of men, drums beating and banners flying. For the French and Indians hiding in the woods and behind rocks, it was target practice. Whenever the English soldiers tried to break ranks and fight the same way as the enemy, the English officers beat their men back into their columns. The English, including Braddock, were slaughtered..."
——Ryan Moore. "Tactics during the Seven Years War" http://web.archive.org/web/20090103081542.

10	"...a regular square with 4 bastions and 1 gate in that curtain which faces due east towards the town. There are three swivel guns on
the salient angles of SE, SW, and NW bastions, but none on the NE. These guns are so fix'd in that they can't be pointed to any object, but in one horizontal line. Loopholes are in many places intirely wanting, and where they are, are badly and irregularly cut, being only about four feet from the ground on the outside, tho' more in some places on the inside. There are nine huts and houses within the fort sufficient for Barracks, magazine, and storehouse for about 150-200 men, a good draw-well, and an oven."
——memorandum written on August 13, 1758 by Brigadier-General John Forbes after visiting the fort. Quoted in "Shippensburg's Fort Morris," Shippensburg Digital History Museum, 2009. http://webspace.ship.edu/jqbao/ShipMuseum/page3/page44/page44.html.

11	There is no documentation that specifically places the Campbells and the Stewarts at Shippensburg in 1758. It is my assumption based on examining the possibilities that make sense in the various conflicting accounts. As is often in the case of history by hearsay, there are several versions of the story, different dates, places, and sometimes names. Family-told accounts seem to indicate Mary Campbell was abducted from either a house or a fort or outside the fort in a field where she was tending cows at Penn's Creek, which is given as being in Cumberland County, although it is actually in Snyder County. The confusion here may have arisen from the similar Indian raid and abduction(s) at Penn's Creek on October 16, 1755.

According to Wikipedia, "...a group of eight Lenape warriors attacked the settlement of Penn's Creek, killed 14 and took 11 captive. ...Twelve-year-old girls Marie Le Roy and Barbara Leininger were given as property to the Lenape warrior named Kalasquay." There are three young adult novels and a film based on their story.

—— en.wikipedia.org/wiki/Penn%27s_Creek_massacre

As related in Provincial Records, N. 340, reprinted in *History of the counties of Berks and Lebanon*:

"October 15, 1755, a party of Indians fell upon the inhabitants on Mahahany (or Penn's) creek, that runs into the river Susquehannah, about five miles lower than the Great Fork made by the juncture of the two main branches of the Susquehannah, killed and carried off about twenty-five persons, and burnt and destroyed their buildings and improvements, and the whole settlement was deserted."

Also in the *History of the counties of Berks and Lebanon* is:

"Under date of October 31, 1755, the Secretary, states: 'An Indian trader and two other men, in Tuscarora valley, were killed by Indians, and their houses, &c, burned; on which most of the settlers fled and abandoned their plantations.'

Nov. 2, 1755, the settlements in the Great Cove were attacked, their houses burned, six persons murdered, and seventeen carried off, and the whole settlement broken up and destroyed.

From the following extract, taken from the Pennsylvania Gazette, of Nov. 13, 1755, the names of the murdered and missing at Great Cove, may be seen—Elizabeth Gallway, Henry Gilson, Robert Peer, William Berryhill, and David McClelland were murdered. The missing are John Martin's wife and five children; William Gallway's wife and two children, and a young woman; Charles Stewart's wife and two children; David McClelland's wife and two children. William

Perihelion

Fleming and wife were taken prisoners. Fleming's son, and one Hicks, were killed and scalped."

——*History of the counties of Berks and Lebanon.* cdn.website-editor.net.

——*History of Bedford, Somerset, and Fulton Counties,* Pennsylvania. Chicago: Waterman, Watkins & Co., 1884. (in this nearly identical account it relates that "...a party of about one hundred Indians, Shawnees and Delaware, among them Shingas, the Delaware king, entered the Great cove and began murdering the defenseless inhabitants and destroying their property.")

[note: here the names Charles Stewart's wife and two children appear. Could this be our Mrs. Stewart?]

More circumstantial evidence: The Scotch-Irish immigration to Pennsylvania in the early 1700s met a snag as relations with the German population in Lancaster County and elsewhere were bitter and strained. Wayland Fuller Dunaway writes:

"The ill feeling between the two races [Germans and Scots-Irish] sometimes took the form of riots at elections and was a cause of concern to the provincial authorities. As a consequence, the Penns instructed their agents in 1743 to sell no lands to the Scotch-Irish throughout this region, but to make them generous offers of removal to the Cumberland Valley, farther to the westward. ...The first great settlement of the Scotch-Irish in Pennsylvania was in the Cumberland Valley, now comprising the counties of Cumberland and Franklin- one of the most beautiful and fertile sections of the commonwealth. ...While the Chambersburg settlement was being founded, a group of Scotch-Irish located on Middle Spring Creek, where in 1730 they began to occupy the land roundabout. They later laid out the town of Shippensburg, next to York the oldest town west of the Susquehanna River."

——Wayland Fuller Dunaway. *The Scotch-Irish of colonial Pennsylvania.* University of North Carolina Press, Chapel Hill. 1944.

The Summit County Beacon, in an article about the Mary Campbell story reported that the family "had a house on the bank Canncoquin Creek, in Cumberland County, Pennsylvania." Burd's

Byron Grush

Run is a tributary or a run-off of Canncoquin Creek via its branching with Middle Spring Creek near Shippensburg.

——Bierce, Lucius Verus. "Early Scenes in Ohio." Summit County Beacon, November 8, 1851, 1:7. University of Akron, L.V. Bierce Library.

12   Mary's age at the time of her capture has been a matter of debate. The date of the capture ranges from 1757 to 1759 and Mary's age is represented as seven, ten, or twelve depending on the source. The Mary Campbell Website analyses many accounts including the *Summit County Beacon* article cited above, an ad placed by Mary's father in *The Pennsylvania Gazette* of October 11, 1764, William Henry Perrin's *History of Summit County, with an outline sketch of Ohio* (Chicago, Baskin & Battey, 1881), Peter Peterson Cherry's *The Portage Path* (Akron, O., The Western Reserve Company, 1911), a report to the Cuyahoga Falls Chapter of D.A.R., June 1934 by Mrs. J. B. McPherson which examines many sources, and the family tradition accounts of daughter-in-law Mary Ann Enochs, daughter Merry Flanagan, a another relative Eleanor Womer, and the Willford History (Mary's married name). The consensus on age is that she was seven years old in 1758, the assumed date of the abduction.

——Mary Campbell Website https://web.archive.org/web/20080522014845/http://www.geocities.com/marycampbellwillford/index.htm.

13   The land was purchased from the Indians on October 25, 1736, and the Land Office was opened in January of 1737 for sale of land on the usual terms. The amount paid the Indians for the valley was "600 lbs. of lead, 500 lbs. of powder, 45 guns, 60 stout water match coats, 100 blankets, 100 duffle match coats, 200 yards of half thick, 100 shirts, 40 hats, 40 pairs of shoes and buckles, 40 pairs of stockings, 100 hatchets, 500 knives, 100 hougles, 60 kettles, 100 tobacco tongs, 100 scissors, 500 owl blades, 120 combs, 2,000 needles, 1,000 flints, 24 looking glasses, 2 lbs. of vermillion, 100 tin pots, 24 dozen of gartering, 25 gallons of rum, 200 lbs. of tobacco and 1,000 pipes."

——"History of the Messiah Evangelical United Brethren Church, 1866-1966, Shippensburg, Pennsylvania" by Rev. D. Homer

Perihelion

Kendall, Pastor. "Area History: Early History of Shippensburg: Cumberland/Franklin Counties, PA."

http://files.usgwarchives.net/pa/cumberland/history/local/messiah 01.txt.

14   "On July 18, 1757, six men were killed or taken away near Shippensburg, while reaping in John Cesney's field. The savages murdered John Kirkpatrick, Dennis Oneidan; captured John Cesney, three of his grandsons, and one of John Kirkpatrick's children. The day following, not far from Shippensburg, in Joseph Stevenson's harvest field, the savages butchered inhumanly Joseph Mitchell, James Mitchell, William Mitchell, John Finlay, Robert Stevenson, Andrew Enslow, John Wiley, Allen Henderson, and William Gibson, carrying off Jane McCammon, Mary Minor, Janet Harper, and a son of John Finlay. July 27, Mr. McKisson was wounded, and his son taken from the South mountain."
    —— *An Illustrated History Of The Commonwealth Of Pennsylvania*, By William H. Egle, Harrisburg, De Witt C. Goodrich & Co., 1876, Page 612 - 635.

[note: this detailed account does not mention the Campbells or the Stewarts, but the date matches that of some of the accounts. Was this the incident in which Mary Campbell was taken? There was a change in the calendar in the mid-eighteenth century. Wikipedia: "In England and Wales, Ireland, and the British colonies, the change to the start of the year and the changeover from the Julian calendar occurred in 1752 under the Calendar (New Style) Act 1750. In Scotland, the legal start of the year had already been moved to 1 January (in 1600), but Scotland otherwise continued to use the Julian calendar until 1752. …The European colonies of the Americas adopted the new style calendar when their mother countries did." Would this account for the discrepancy in the date?]

15   Bierce, Lucius Verus. "Early Scenes in Ohio" *Summit County Beacon*, November 8, 1851, 1:7. ABJ Microfilm Series. University of Akron, L.V. Bierce Library.

Byron Grush

Perrin, William Henry. *History of Summit County, with an outline sketch of Ohio.* Chicago, Baskin & Battey, 1881.

[note: Bierce is probably to be trusted as to his account of the Mary Campbell "legend" but it is curious that he does not mention it in his *Historical Reminiscences of Summit County* published three years later. He profiles Cuyahoga Falls, the site of one of Netawatwees' villages where Mary was held captive, and even mentions a cave or cavern which was so small one had to stoop to enter it (so probably not Mary's Cave). Nothing, however, about Mary Campbell or the Indian village.]

——Bierce, Lucius Verus. *Historical Reminiscences of Summit County.* United States: T. & H.G. Canfield, Publishers, 1854.

16   Burnt Cabins was originally a settlers' village of about 11 cabins at the foot of the Tuscalora Mountains where Native Americans occupied the area. In 1750, to appease the Indians and maintain peace in the region, the order to burn the squatters' cabins was given and carried out.

17   "History of Beaver County, Chapter 1" - PA-Rootswww.pa-roots.com.

18   "There was a settlement about three quarters of a mile or a mile, below the mouth of the Beaver, and there was a hamlet near its fording. Both are spoken of in the journal of Bouquet's march against the Ohio Indians in 1764, as elsewhere quoted, as follows:

'About a mile below its [the Beaver's] confluence with the Ohio stood formerly a large town on the steep bank, built by the French of square logs, with stone chimneys, for some of the Shawnese, Delawares and Mingoes, who abandoned it in the year 1758, when the French abandoned Fort Duquesne. Near the fording of Beaver creek also stood about seven houses, which were deserted and destroyed by the Indians after their defeat on Bushy run, when they forsook all the remaining settlements in this part of the country.'"

——"History of Beaver County, Chapter 1"

Perihelion

"The Indian settlement at the mouth of the Beaver (Sauconk, King Beaver's Town, Shingas' Town, etc.) extended to the bluff above the Ohio about a mile below the mouth of the Beaver at various times in the history of this settlement."
⸺C. Hale Sipe. *The Principal Indian Towns of Western Pennsylvania.* Journalsjournals.psu.edu.

19 "Netawatwees was probably born in the lower Delaware River Valley around 1686. He was part of the Unami-speaking Lenape, the southern part of this coastal people whose territory extended to the lower Hudson River, western Long Island, and Connecticut. When he was young, he moved west with his family and tribe to escape encroachment from European-American colonists. In July 1758, he was living in a Delaware Indian settlement at the mouth of Beaver Creek, a tributary of the Ohio River below Pittsburgh. Records identify him as 'ye great man of the Unami nation.'"
⸺"Netawatwees - Newcomer - Ohio History Central - A product of the Ohio Historical Society".
http://www.lenapelifeways.org/lenape1.htm.

20 "No evidence found to support Mary Campbell story in Gorge Metro Park. …The 107 artifacts found included several fragments of pipe and drainage tiles dating back to the late 1800s and early 1900s that reflected how the site was drained to make it easier to visit. … Other interesting finds included a bullet casing and the bottom of a Coca-Cola bottle printed with the words "Akron Ohio" that was only manufactured in Akron in 1928 and 1929. …Given the lack of evidence to support the Mary Campbell story, the park district is in a transition period and moving to referring to the feature only as Old Maid's Kitchen on signage, maps and its website."
⸺ Beacon Journal reporter Emily Mills.
https://www.beaconjournal.com/news/20200202/no-evidence-found-to-support-mary-campbell-story-in-gorge-metro-park.

[note: there is no evidence to prove she wasn't held here in the cave. Is this an example of revisionist history?]

21 "History of the counties of Berks and Lebanon" cdn.website-editor.net.

22   "But again in July 1763, there was a terrible invasion of the valley. The Indians swooped down again. The whole countryside west of Shippensburg became the prey of the fierce savages. They set fire to houses, barns, corn, and hay. People were massacred with great cruelty. The residents of Shippensburg took many fleeing people in and gave them protection. There were 1,384 people; 301 men, 345 women, 738 children. Every stable and hovel was crowded with miserable refugees. Even the streets were filled with people."

——"History of the Messiah Evangelical United Brethren Church, 1866-1966, Shippensburg, Pennsylvania" by Rev. D. Homer Kendall, Pastor. "Area History: Early History of Shippensburg: Cumberland/Franklin Counties, PA."

23   *History of Berks County, Pennsylvania.*
http://www.timevoyagers.com/bookstore/penna/berkshist.htm.

24   "As a condition of the peace with the Ohio Indians, Bouquet demanded the release of prisoners held by the Delawares and Shawnees. By the Articles of Agreement concluded in November 1764, 3 of the chieftans of these nations agreed to cease hostilities against all British subjects; to collect and deliver to Bouquet's forces, all English prisoners, deserters, Frenchmen, Negroes, and any other White people living among them...

The Shawnees were not as prompt in complying with the Articles of Agreement as the Delawares. However, they turned over 9 captives on January 5, 1765, and 44 additional captives on May 10, 1765."

——Swing, William S. Indian Captives Released by Cornel Bouquet. Clements Library, University of Michigan.
http://frenchandindianwarfoundation.org/wp-content/uploads/2016/02/bouquest-hostage-list.pdf.

25   Mary Campbell Website.

26   "We have chosen to tell the story of the Lenape in Pennsylvania through 'The Prophecy of the Fourth Crow,' an ancient story passed down among the Lenape for generations. This story relates the ways in which Lenape people have struggled to survive and to keep their community and culture intact. Chief Red Hawk summarizes the current interpretation of the Prophecy in the

Perihelion

following way: 'We now know that the First Crow was the Lenape before the coming of the Europeans. The Second Crow symbolized the death and destruction of our culture. The Third Crow was our people going underground and hiding. The Fourth Crow was the Lenape becoming caretakers again and working with everybody to restore this land.' "

——"The Prophecy of the Fourth Crow" ancient Lepane story as told by Robert Red Hawk Ruth and Translated by Shelley DePaul.

http://wakinguponturtleisland.blogspot.com/2011/02/neweneit-na-ahas.html

https://www.penn.museum/sites/fap/prophecy.shtml

Byron Grush

Return of the Wayfaring Stranger

On Friday, August 21, 1835, *The New York Sun* began to run a series of articles it claimed had originated in a supplement to the *Edinburgh Journal of Science* about a discovery, it said, made by the noted scientist and astronomer Sir John Herschel at his observatory at the Cape of Good Hope. Herschel was in fact at his Vatican Observatory there and was among the first to observe the return of Halley's Comet. He did not however report, as the *Sun* claimed, that he had discovered life on the moon.

The articles described Herschel's telescope as measuring 24 feet in diameter, an absurd size. It said that with this massive device he had seen basaltic rock covered with red flowers, lunar crystals, herds of bison-like creatures of a bluish hue, a spherical amphibious creature that rolled across a pebbled beach, bi-pedal beavers walking upright and living in huts, and inside of a circle of red hills he called the "Ruby Colosseum," human-like beings. These beings were described as covered with copper-colored hair and having membranous wings. In illustrations these creatures looked like giant devil bats. Herschel allegedly called these "Vespertillo-homos." There was an abandoned temple of polished sapphire with a yellow metal roof that resembled flames enveloping a large copper sphere.

Observations eventually ceased as Herschel had left his telescope open one day and the brilliant sun had set it on fire (according to the articles). It was an elaborate hoax, of course, but many people believed it. The *New York Herald* called it an ingenious hoax. However, Horace Greeley's *New Yorker* said, "The promulgations of these discoveries creates a new era in astronomy and science generally." Edgar Alan Poe claimed the story had been plagiarized from his own story "The Unparalleled Adventure of Hans Pfaall" published two months earlier, in which his protagonist traveled to the moon in a hot air balloon and lived there among the Lunarians.

Herschel was initially amused by the hoax but unhappy that it took publicity away from his actual work, tracking Halley's Comet. Besides Herschel, the comet was observed by Olmstead and Loomis at Yale College in Connecticut, by Struve at the Dorpat Observatory, by Cooper at Markree Observatory in Ireland, at observatories in Paris and Quebec. It would reach its perihelion in November, about the time Charles Darwin on the HMS Beagle was exploring the Galapagos Islands, Mark Twain was being born in Florida, and President Andrew Jackson was making his annual State of the Nation Speech before Congress.

Jackson had begun his year of the comet by nearly being assassinated. On January 30, he was leaving the Capital after the funeral of Representative Warren R. Davis of South Carolina when a man stepped out from behind a pillar. Richard Lawrence, an Englishman and unemployed house painter, had been waiting with two newly purchased handguns. He pointed one of the guns at Jackson's back and pulled the trigger. Nothing happened. He tried the second pistol but that too misfired. It was a damp day and moisture had interfered with the operation of the weapons. Jackson turned and struck Lawrence with his cane. The man went down but Jackson's aides hurried him away from the scene. Lawrence was restrained by two other men who had been present; one of them was Davy Crocket. The President was a man for his times, a white supremacist.[1]

In August, P. T. Barnum purchased a slave woman named Joice Heth from another promoter. He began to exhibit her claiming she was 160 years old and had been the wet nurse of George Washington. She was blind and partially paralyzed, and probably only around 80, but she could sing and tell stories about the boy she called "Little George." She was a sensation at Nibo's Garden in New York City, kickstarting Barnum's career as a showman. His first enterprise was called "Barnum's Grand Scientific Theater."

In the New England village of Worcester on a cool Autumn evening, Dotty Christopherson was in a tither. Her husband, Nickolas, was out in the street again while the supper she had slaved over was getting cold on the table. Nickolas had set up his telescope on a wooden tripod and had trampled her chrysanthemums to do it! It was a Newtonian refracting telescope with a silvered metal mirror inside a brass tube and had cost a pretty penny. Nickolas Christopherson was an amateur astronomer and often scanned the night sky when conditions were favorable to get aa glimpse of Mars or Venus or the Pleiades. But tonight he was focusing on a certain wayfaring stranger, a visitor who appeared only in 75 year intervals: Halley's Comet.

Perihelion

The children, Trudie and Ty were assembled watching father fiddling with the telescope. He had corralled them to supplement their education, and perhaps to show off his knowledge a bit. He would begin his inevitable lecture in a few minutes and then let each in turn look into the long brass tube for a better view of the comet. Up in the western sky the comet's tail was stretched horizontally southward, a streak of silver in a pool of blackness, dwarfing stars and planets and outshining those cosmic specks.

Trudie smoothed down her skirts which the night wind had blown into a tangle of cotton and brocade. "Father," she queried, "it looks so like it is on fire! What will happen if it falls to Earth?"

"Now Trudie," replied her father, "what does fire require? Remember we studied this from your science book."

"Well, fuel, like wood or something, and…oh, I know…oxygen!"

"And what is space composed of?"

"Um…nothing?"

"It is thought there is something called the ether, but that is conjecture. More likely space is just that…nothing. So how can a comet be on fire?"

"Oh," said the girl. "I guess it can't"

Trudie was ten, very interested in science and history and quite clever for a girl in an age when young women were required only to be pretty and anticipate a good marriage and the rearing of their own children. Ty, on the other hand, two years her senior, was interested, like most boys his age, in hunting and fishing and (to the displeasure of his mother) in wrestling. Sports would become his life's ambition in a few years when he was old enough to visit his brother in New York City. Brother Jessye was a cadet at West Point and had told Ty stories about a new sport they played there called baseball.

"Father," said Ty, "I'm getting hungry!"

The newly completed Boston and Worcester Railroad had opened for regular business in July. The company was still using Concord Stagecoaches mounted on flat cars to transport its passengers, but it was contracting with Davensport and Kimball of Boston to build passenger cars. Its locomotive, the steam driven Yankee[2], was the first such engine to be built in New England. Leaving the Boston station on Washington Street, a 170-foot trestle took the train over the Back Bay and through Newton, and Framingham to Worcester. It made three round trips every day.

It was October 21, 1835. Alicia Kelley had boarded the train in Worcester and had spent the duration of the 40-mile trip looking out the window at the landscape of virgin forests and lakes as it sped by. She wasn't being rude, it was just that the other six people in the coach were obviously businessmen, judging by their drab-colored frockcoats (decorated with oversized gilt buttons), their waistcoats of fine kerseymere, their square-cut shirts of linen (as delicate as lady's chemises and serving the same purpose for underwear), their high collars and thin cravats. Was that gentleman on the middle bench wearing a corset? Perhaps, men exhibited the same "hourglass" figure as women these days. Alicia had nothing in common with these fellow travelers and being the only woman in the coach she deemed it only proper to remain incognito.

Once she arrived in Boston and a porter loaded her valise into a waiting Hansom cab, she directed the driver to take her to the newly opened American House on Hanover Street. *Gleason's Pictorial* had called the hotel "one of the finest ornaments of the city, presenting a beautiful front of the Italian style." It had recommended American House for its splendid rooms, its "unique plan, combining the utmost convenience of arrangement with great elegance and thoroughness of finish, and the introduction of all the desired modern improvements." It was those modern improvements that Alicia was most interested in after having stayed in a lesser establishment with no modern plumbing on a previous visit to Boston.

As she entered the lobby, she encountered yet another flock of well-dressed businessmen, standing about, chomping on unlit cigars and giving her the eye. Apparently, this place attracted these chattering popinjays—had she made a mistake in coming to this hotel? Well, she was used to predatory glances from men; a young single woman traveling alone always elicited the veiled vulgarity of secret thought that nonetheless revealed itself in body language.

No matter. Soon she would be meeting her friend, Henrietta Sargent and Hen's sister, Catherine, at the Old Province Coffee House for a bite to eat and a catch-up on events. Later they would go to their meeting. The women were members of the Boston Female Anti-Slavery Society. It was an independent organization whose ultimate goal was the immediate emancipation of colored people

Perihelion

nation-wide. Slavery, they said, the law of men, was a direct violation of the law of God. Not to mention the Constitution.

The meeting was being hosted by William Lloyd Garrison at the offices of his anti-slavery publication, the *Liberator*. It was rumored that the famous British abolitionist George Thompson was to give a speech. Thompson was well-known in New England and raised the ire of many Northern whites who, although they did not live in slave states, felt their society was threatened by the very idea of abolition. They sometimes reacted violently. Thompson and the poet, John Greenleaf Whittier had recently been stoned by a mob in Concord, New Hampshire. Had Alicia been privy to the mumblings of the men she witnessed in the hotel lobby, she would have heard these respectable men discussing the appearance of George Thompson in opportunistic terms, terms dripping with venom.

Sally Freeman lived in a rented flat in a two-story walkup on Robertson Alley. She was recently widowed and was raising two children as a single mother, juggling her time between Sammy and Belinda and her part-time job at Jorgensen's Market. The twins went to the Abiel Smith School on Belknap Street next door to the African Meeting house. Abiel Smith had been a white philanthropist who had left a substantial gift in his will to the City of Boston, stipulating that it be used for the education of Black children. The new school building had been completed just this year and all Black children in Boston were assigned to it. Separate and equal. Maybe not so equal, but definitely separate.

Sally would have to take the omnibus to the meeting at the *Liberator*, way over to Cornhill Street. The building was near the Customs House where in the square, in 1770, colonists had formed a mob to harass British soldiers, throwing snowballs and sticks at them, resulting in the killing of several by the Redcoats in what was now called the Boston Massacre. Irony? The mob in that case was demonstrating for independence, for freedom, for the chance to form a more perfect union, where all men (and women) were created equal. In 1835 there were 147 race associated riots across the nation. Many of them took place in New York, Philadelphia, and especially in Boston.

When Sally arrived at the *Liberator*, she was directed to the adjoining meeting space called Stacy Hall. There were already about

Byron Grush

25 women in the hall including the Society's founder, Maria Weston Chapman. Eventually the women would number 40 in all. There was another crowd forming at the entrance, men clearly not members of the anti-slavery movement. They would eventually number over one thousand. They had taunted Sally as she pushed through their midst to join the other women, calling her a n____ and other vile aspersions. How had they learned about the meeting? What was their intention?

For the most part, the angry crowd was not composed of working class or itinerant people. These were not goons hired by the elite to do their dirty work for them. These *were* the elite. Politicians, businessmen, figures from high society, the wealthy and the want-to-be wealthy who had shown up, without much organization, but with a common purpose: to disrupt the proceedings. And they were after George Thompson. A foreigner, no less, who had arrived to inflame Southern Negroes to rise up against the government. They had been prompted by handbills run off by the editor of the *Boston Commercial Gazette* which offered $100 to the person or persons who laid "violent hands" on George Thompson so that he could be tarred and feathered forewith.

Thompson, however, had been forewarned and did not attend the meeting. William Garrison offered to speak in his place. President of the Society Mary S. Parker opened the meeting with a short prayer and a reading from the bible. "From 1 Thessalonians 5:8," she said, "But let us who are of the day be sober, putting on the breastplate of faith and love, and as a helmet the hope of salvation." But the crowd of angry men was getting loader and beginning to drown out the speaker.

"Someone should get the constables to come and disperse that unrulily crowd," Alicia Kelley said to Henrietta Sargent. "Call the mayor!"

"I think the mayor is heading up that group," replied Henrietta.

Boston's Mayor Theodore Lyman had been the keynote speaker at a meeting back in August. That one, held in Faneuil Hall to a record crowd of Bostonians had been attended by some of the very same people, the "Friends of the Union," that were assembled here today. That meeting had been an anti-abolitionist meeting, one in which men like the mayor called George Thompson and William Garrison dangerous men. Mayor Lyman was partly responsible for

Perihelion

the crowd, later described by the Boston Commercial Gazette as "an assemblage of fifteen hundred or two thousand highly respectable gentlemen." Respectable gentlemen who now shouted, "Down with the damned Abolitionists!" And, "The peace of the city is destroyed by them. Our Liberties must be preserved!" And also, "Lynch them! Lynch them! Lynch the rascals!"

The crowd was pressing against the flimsy partition that separated Stacy Hall from the rest of the building. They were close to breaking through it. They had effectively blocked the entrance so that the abolitionists could not now leave. Things were coming to a head and it appeared that violence was likely. Garrison was urged to leave and so he retreated to his office. The crowd, unable to apprehend Thompson, was willing to settle for Garrison. The tar pot awaited.

Mayor Lyman now arrived at the Liberator office accompanied by several constables. The crowd cheered him, but Lyman saw at once the danger that could erupt here and fling the city into chaos and upheaval. He knew he had to satisfy the mob but must avoid bloodshed at all costs. Someone was tearing down the sign advertising the meeting from the front of the building. Someone else yelled, "We want Garrison! Bring him out."

Lyman shood on a chair before the turbulent mob and told them to disperse. They did not move. "Alright," he said, "let me go talk to Garrison." Lyman entered the hall and first addressed the women.

"Go home, ladies, go home," he called out. "Ladies, do you wish to see a scene of bloodshed and confusion? If you do not, go home."

Mary Weston Chapman responded, "Mr. Lyman, your personal friends are the instigators of this mob."

"I know no personal friends, I am merely an official," he answered. "Indeed, ladies, you must retire. It is dangerous to remain."

Chapman retorted, "If this is the last bulwark of freedom, we may as well die here as anywhere."

"If you go now, I will protect you, but cannot unless you do."

Mary Parker now called for a vote to adjourn. "It is up to you," she said.

"We can reconvene at my house," said Chapman.

They voted to leave, but orderly, two by two, hand in hand. Alicia Kelly took Sally Freeman's hand. Many of the coupled abolitionists were composed of a white woman and a Black woman, which infuriated the crowd as they passed through them to gain the street.

Had it not been for the presence of the constables, there indeed might have been bloodshed.

Now the crowd gained access to Garrison's office but did not find him there. Lyman had anticipated this move and had urged Garrison to exit via a window into the back alley. He hid in a shop belonging to a carpenter, but the crowd found him, broke down the door, tied a rope around him, and began to drag him into the street. Some yelled for tar and feathers, some yelled for a lynching. At the last minute before an inevitable beating could take place, Lyman and his constables arrived, took Garrison into custody, and ushered him into City Hall. The mob surrounded the building. Eventually, the Suffolk County Sheriff showed up with 30 or 40 men and hauled Garrison to the safety of the county jail, charging him with disturbing the peace.[3]

Sally Freeman returned home safely and continued to attend meetings and to communicate with the other members during the following years of its active campaign against slavery. Alicia Kelly formed a chapter in Worcester and coordinated with the Boston group. The Boston Female Anti-Slavery Society continued their efforts with pamphlets and many fundraising fairs and joined with other groups in conventions and freedom suits against the Commonwealth of Massachusetts. They were involved in the Abolition Riot of 1836 which revolved around the arrest of fugitive slaves and which eventually led to the Liberty Act of 1843 prohibiting such arrests. The Society dissolved in 1840.

At West Point, Cadet Jessye Christopherson's thoughts went back to his family in Worcester, his brother Ty, sister Trudie, mother and father and, especially, his mother's apple pie. It was mid - November, and if he were lucky, he might score a pass to return home for Thanksgiving. This was the coldest November he could remember. The temperature at night dropped into the double digits below zero! The Hudson river was frozen, which was good for skating if you could stand the artic-like cold, and if you had leisure time and a girlfriend. Which he did not.

Down south in Florida the freeze was the worst in history. It was devastating the citrus industry, killing fruit trees which would never grow again. Even there a river, the St. Johns, had frozen so much that people could walk across it. Something Floridians had never

Perihelion

before experienced. In New York State cold winters were common, but this one, Jessye thought, was ridiculously frigid. He pulled the wool blanket up to his chin; the barracks were drafty enough in normal weather to be chilly and tonight he was shivering.

The call to arms came around 10 PM. Was it one of those hazing routines perpetrated by the upper classmen, he wondered? He soon learned that a work force was being assembled to lend aid to the struggling New York City Volunteer Fire Department which was fighting a raging fire in the financial district. There was much grumbling among the cadets—this was curtailed by sharp orders from the officer on duty. The cadets assembled in short order.

It was the night of November 16, 1835. Since the opening of the Erie Canal, New York City was fast becoming the financial and cultural center of the country, even vying with London, Paris, and Berlin for international importance. It was a city of contrasts; elegant buildings of various architectural styles lined streets that were filled with mud and horse manure. The brownstones of the wealthy stood next to the wood-framed tenements of the poor. Uptown there were still farms and small villages, streams and forests. Downtown, in the financial district, few people lived. This year, this November, that was a blessing.

In a five-story warehouse at 25 Merchant Street near the intersection of Hanover Square and Wall Street, a gas pipe burst. Fumes reached a nearby coal-burning stove and a blaze started. A nightwatchman patrolling nearby on Pearl Street smelled the smoke and ran to give the alarm. James Gulik, the chief engineer for the volunteer firefighters was alerted and a call went out to all available fire companies. These men were weary and somewhat disorganized. Two nights ago, they had been called to extinguish two large fires and now the cisterns that had held the sparse supply of the city's water were empty, as exhausted as the men. Nonetheless, they rose to the occasion and did what they could.

They were faced with an inferno whipped up by a fierce gale blowing from the northeast and spreading the fire from building to building as it rushed toward the East River. There was no water to pump onto the flames. Frantically, the firefighters chopped holes in the ice of the frozen East River and dropped hoses into it. The temperature hovered at 17 degrees below zero. Water that ran through the fire hoses quickly froze. Even when they stomped on the hoses with their heavy boots to release what water they could, this spilled out onto the pavement and refroze. It looked as if the entire city would soon turn into a smoldering ash heap.

When Jessye Christopherson arrived with the other cadets from West Point it was just after midnight. An extraordinary and horrific sight greeted them; it was staggering. Flames hundreds of feet high dominated the skyline. The glow was seen as far away as Philadelphia. The heat was so intense it was like standing next to a blast furnace…no, inside of a blast furnace. Copper sheeting on the roofs of buildings was melting and dripping down into the street. Ships on the East river were aflame. Barrels of turpentine sitting on the docks exploded and torrents of fire splashed into the river turning it into a burning red maelstrom. The Stock Exchange was burning, churches were burning, warehouses filled with fabrics of silk and satin and dangerous chemicals and booze were burning. The Merchant's Exchange building caught fire.

Someone yelled, "The statue…rescue the statue!" Inside the rotunda of the Merchant's Exchange stood a marble statue of Alexander Hamilton created by sculptor Robert Ball Hughes. It was a mostly symbolic icon of the elegance and pride of the commercial life of the city, albeit a token of its decadence. It seemed, however, worth saving. Jessye and some of his mates rushed into the smoke-filled building and began to wrestle with the figure of Hamilton, inching it ever so slowly toward the outside. There was a crash as a cupola that topped the roof of the rotunda fell. The would-be rescuers fled, escaping just as the roof caved in, crushing the statue into fragments.

Now there was something more sensible to do. The cadets joined with some sailors from the Merchant Marine to control the crowd that had begun to form along Broad street. The curious, the seekers of thrills, the accidental onlookers, all clustered and craning necks to watch the astounding destruction of their city, not realizing or perhaps not concerned with their own peril, presented a formable challenge for the cadets. Jessye pushed back at the crowd, admonishing them to disperse. Most moved away. One young man stood his ground.

"Please, Sir," said Jessye, "you must leave this spot for your own safety."

Perihelion

"I observe all things be they darkness or light," he replied. "Don't concern yourself with my safety. I am part of the world and the world will succor me...or it will not."

"Who are you?" asked Jessye, feeling dazzled by this man's cool manner and obvious self-confidence, incongruous as he stood gaping into the gates of Hell.

"My name is Walter Whitman. I have come to the city as a journeyman and I work setting type for a printer. But I am leaving soon to become a teacher, and I would experience as much life as I may so that, if I become a good teacher, those who are my students may someday reject my lessons in favor of their own experiences."

Jessye walked away feeling confused and helpless in the face of the impenetrable logic of this wayfaring stranger, this future poet. Now there came shouts for more help from a detachment of U.S. Marines who had been on the scene since the middle of the night. They had been ordered to cross the East River to procure barrels of gunpowder from the Navy Yards. Earlier, the firefighters had attempted to blow up some of the buildings in the path of the fire using what gunpowder they could find but it had proved inadequate.

The Marines had wrapped the barrels in blankets so that windborn embers would not ignite the gunpowder prematurely. They had brought the barrels to the west edge of the fiery onslaught. Jessye and the cadets helped place these at the base of yet unburned buildings. Charges were set and the powder blew the buildings into a wall of rubble which the inferno could not cross. It reached the river to the east and could go no further. After it had raged for fifteen hours, the Great New York Fire burned itself out.

Every building south of Wall Street and east of Broad Street, an area of 17 blocks, had been destroyed or reduced to smoldering rubble: 674 buildings in total. The cost, $20 million, put nearly all of the city's fire insurance companies out of busines. Luckily, only two people lost their lives. The city would rebuild, a new fire department would be organized, a better water supply would be created, and life would go on. Some lessons were learned. But the underlying cause of tragedy is often a defect in the very soul of humankind. Thoughtless greed? Denial of misfortune? Avoidance of accountability? Walt Whitman later wrote:

Byron Grush

[It] seems perpetually goading me—the soul—If all seems right—it is not right—then corruption—then putridity—then mean maggots grow among men—they are born out of the too richly manured earth—[5]

1	President Andrew Jackson signed The Indian Removal Act in May of 1839 which authorized him to negotiate with Native American tribes living in southern States to move to Federal land. These tribes were told they could either move, trading their ancestral lands for questionable living conditions in the New West, or lose their sovereignty. In 1835, the Florida Seminole refused to leave, leading to the Second Seminole War. Cherokee, Creek, Seminole, Chickasaw, and Choctaw nations were forcibly relocated to Indian Territory during the years between 1830 and 1850 in what became known as The Trail of Tears. Thousands died during the move. It began on Jackson's watch.

2	The "Yankee" steam locomotive, built by R. M. Bouton's Mill Dam Foundry in Boston, was a 2-2-0 or Planet type engine with a wheel arrangement of two leading wheels on one axle, two powered driving wheels on one axle, and no trailing wheels. Concord Stagecoaches mounted on flatcars were the first passenger cars used by the B and W Railroad. Melody Groves, in *Butterfield's Byway: America's First Overland Mail Route Across the West* describes the Concord: "There are three bench seats accommodating up to nine people though models to seat six and twelve passengers were available. The benches at the front and back of the body have limited headroom. Passengers on the center bench are given no backrest but steady themselves with a broad leather harness suspended across the coach by straps from the roof."

3	Some details and dialog used were found in "The Garrison Mob of 1835, Boston." By Patrick Brown on historicaldigression.com, and from Kelsey Gustin's blog post "the-boston-mob-of-1835".

4	In 1835, Walt Whitman did work in Manhattan as a composer and a journeyman printer, and later in Brooklyn for a printer named Erastus Worthington. In the following year he became a teacher on

Perihelion

Long Island and then in Norwick. It is unknown if he was in New York City during the Great Fire. Did he see Halley's comet? It is interesting to speculate. In 1865, Whitman wrote "When Lilacs Last in the Dooryard Bloom'd," a discourse on the death of Abraham Lincoln. In it he uses a "droop'd star" as a metaphor for the loss of the President:

1
When lilacs last in the dooryard bloom'd,
And the great star early droop'd in the western sky in the night,
I mourn'd, and yet shall mourn with ever-returning spring.

Ever-returning spring, trinity sure to me you bring,
Lilac blooming perennial and drooping star in the west,
And thought of him I love.

2
O powerful western fallen star!
O shades of night—O moody, tearful night!
O great star disappear'd—O the black murk that hides the star!
O cruel hands that hold me powerless—O helpless soul of me!
O harsh surrounding cloud that will not free my soul.

In 1865, Wilhelm Tempel discovered the comet 55P/Tempel–Tuttle. This comet is responsible for the Leonids Meteor Shower which has a has a cyclonic peak about every 33 years. Was Whitman aware of this comet?

5   The Oscar Lion Papers, 1914–1955, New York Public Library, New York, N.Y.

Byron Grush

Fire and Ice

Three new stars were discovered this year. Two of these, Nova Sagittarii No, 2 *and* Mova Arae *were found by Mrs. Fleming on plates taken at Arequipa during the early part of the year. ...The third new star,* Nova Lacertae *was discovered by the Rev. T. E. Espin, of Walsingham, England a few days before the end of the year.*

The periodic comets due to return in 1910 were Tempel II, D'Arrest's, Swift's (1895 II). Brooks's (1889 V), and Faye's. *The discovery of Halley's Comet, which was due to pass through perihelion this year, was noticed in the Year Book for 1909. Of the above comets all but* Tempel's *and* Swift's *were reported.*

——*The New International Yearbook, A Compendium of the world's Progress for the Year 1910,* ed., Frank Moore Colby, M.A., Dodd, Mead and Company, New York, 1911.

Samuel Clements, better known as Mark Twain, said in 1909, "I came in with Halley's Comet in 1835. It is coming again next year, and I expect to go out with it. It will be the greatest disappointment of my life if I don't go out with Halley's Comet. The Almighty has said, no doubt: 'Now here are these two unaccountable freaks; they came in together, they must go out together'." He was not disappointed. Twain died on April 21, 1910, two days after the comet's perihelion, its closest approach to Earth. In 1907, Mark Twain wrote a short story for Harper's Magazine called "Captain Stormfield's Visit to Heaven" in which the main character rides a comet toward heaven but arrives at the wrong gate. It was his last published work.

In 1906, four years before Halley's return and the predicted passing of the Earth through the tail of the comet, the British author H. G. Welles published another of his science fiction novels called *In the Days of the Comet*. Unlike predictions of "the end of all life on Earth" from other writers (see footnote 1) Welles had a different take on the result. The comet sucks the Earth's nitrogen from the air (he calls it "the old azote") and changes the atmosphere into a "respirable gas...helping and sustaining its action, a bath of strength and healing..." and a change comes over everyone resulting in beauty and happiness and "peace on earth and god will to all men." The book's narrative of polyamorous love caused a bit of a scandal.

As one era transitions into the next, the world often witnesses the demise of those of greatness who influenced their own time and set the standards for the next. In 1910, among other notables, death claimed the Prime Minister of Egypt Boutros Ghali, American abolitionist Lucy Stanton, Anglo-Irish writer and suffragist Anne Isabella Robertson, King Edward VII of the United Kingdom, William Sydney Porter better known as O. Henry, Florence Nightingale, William James, Henri Rousseau, Marie Pasteur, Winslow Homer, American abolitionist and poet Julia Ward Howe, and Leo Tolstoy.

It was the beginning of the second decade of the new century. It was a bridge between the corruption which Twain called "the Gilded Age" and the new Progressive Era of reform. It was the age of a new intellectualism that saw the likes of Egon Schiele, Vasily Kandisky, Arnold Schoenberg, and Gabrielle Chanel. It was the beginning of a decade of innovation spearheaded by Henry Ford, the Wright Brothers, Thomas Edison, and Nikola Tesla. But it was not all reform. Howard Taft had succeeded Theodore Roosevelt as President. The Vatican introduced a compulsory oath against Modernism. The Mexican Revolution caused racial conflict across the border into Texas (as we will see). There were new stars in the sky. There was fire and ice on the Earth.

The telephone which the Ridleys had rented from AT&T was made of a synthetic plastic called Bakelite. It was black and had a cloth-covered cord that tended to coil up in a tangle. Only about 8 percent of households in America had a telephone in 1910, so Fred Ridley was justly proud of his. Trouble was, there were not many of his friends he could call. When it started to ring, Fred almost jumped. He picked up the receiver.

"Hello?" he said.

"Fred, this is Harvey Greenwood. I'm over at O'Malley's Tavern. Some of the boys are hootin' it up and we're missin' you."

Fred took a moment to consider this, then: "Aw, Harv, I'm a homebody tonight. Betsy is over to Doris Haverman's for a hen party. Something about votes for women. Can you beat that?

Perihelion

Anyhoo, I'm stuck with the kid. He wants to me to help him work on his model ship. Petey's got a real talent for stuff like that."

"Okay, okay. You ain't missin' all that much, I guess. There's talk about the comet that's pretty scary if you believe in stuff like that."

"Stuff like what," asked Fred.

"They say the Earth is going to pass right through the tail of Halley's Comet. Some French egghead[1] says the tail is full of poison gas. It's gonna snuff out all life on Earth!"

"Kook."

"I dounno, they's plenty people takin' it serious. Jay Jorgensen's old lady bought a comet umbrella."

"A what?"

"It's supposed to keep the comet dust off you. Special fabric."

"Kooks!"

"Ya, I guess. Well, I'll tip one for you."

"And have one of them pickled eggs O'Malley keeps in that big jar on the bar for me too."

"Ya. Bye."

"Bye."

It wasn't just any ship model that Petey Ridley was building. It was a model, not exactly to scale but as close as the picture he had found in the encyclopedia at the school library would allow, of Henry Hudson's famous ship, the *Halve Maen*. Hudson, an Englishman working for the Dutch East India Company, had sailed the 85-foot, square-rigged, three-masted ship, also known as the *Half Moon*, into an obscure river on the Atlantic coast of America in September of 1609, just two years after a sighting of Halley's Comet by Johannes Kepler. The river is now named after him; the harbor he found is now called New York City.

Petey was studying the rigging in the drawing of the ship which he had copied from the encyclopedia. He was waiting for the glue to dry on the mast he had just set and for his father to come to help with the construction. Ship building, on this scale, was challenging but it had piqued his interest in naval design. Perhaps one day he could find a profession that would bring him close to these vessels that sailed the seven seas. Perhaps he would join the Navy.

Now, Petey Ridley felt lucky not to have a job. In these days many 15-year-olds like himself—and younger—did work in textile mills, coal mines, and glass factories, often under hazardous conditions and for very little pay. It was estimated that by 1910 over 2 million children worked in these circumstances to help support their families. Reforms were underway, but it would be years before congress would act to establish Child Labor Laws. It was the same all over the world.

In Belfast, Northern Ireland, children were employed in the linen mills and at the shipyard. Health and safety were secondary to profit. The training of the young people that worked at the yards was left up to the adult workers who sometimes slacked off this responsibility or simply said, "Just watch me." Petey Ridley might have been very interested in watching the big ships coming into being at the Harland and Wolff shipyard at East Belfast. But he might have been horrified at the working conditions.

Samuel Scott was 15, the same age as Petey Ridley. He worked as a catch-boy with a riveting team in Belfast on the ship designated as SS 401. A catch-boy was one who waited while a bellows-boy heated an iron rivet over a bucket of red-hot coals. Once the rivet was so hot it began to glow, the bellows-boy picked it up with tongs and hurled it through the air at the catch-boy who caught it with his own set of tongs. He would then place the rivet in a hole in a steel plate and a holder-on would strike it with a sledgehammer, then hold it in place until another worker flattened it from the other side. SS 401 would require over 3 million rivets. It was a very large ship.

In the early morning of April 20, in this year of the Comet Halley's perihelion and its first sighting this spring, Sammy left his home at 70 Templemore Street in the Ballymacarret area of Belfast and walked through the narrow streets to the yard. The sun was trying to burn through the heavy fog that seemed perpetually to hang over the harbor. At the work site he received his assignment from Artie Frost, the shipyard's foreman. He picked up a set of tongs and began climbing up a gantry 228 feet in height.

He waved hello the fitter Bobby Knight. "How's your mother, Sammy?" Knight called back. "She's grand, thanks," Sammy answered. Half up the ladder he saw Alfie Cunningham, another of the fitters on the crew. "Hallo, Mr. Cunningham," Sammy yelled to the man. "Hallo, my good fella. How's she cuttin'?" "Manky an' Knackered, Mr. Cunningham. Manky an' Knackered." "Say, call me Alfie, will ya, boyo? Crack on now." These were the top men on the

Perihelion

shipyard crew. They would be going with the ship to do maintenance on its maiden voyage across the Atlantic to New York City.

Sammy started work catching rivets and being careful never to drop one as this could get him fired. About mid-afternoon as Sammy was standing on a ladder, a piece of timber fell and struck him, knocking him off. He fell to the ground hundreds of feet below. As he lay there bleeding with a concussion, the timber fell on him, completing its murderous work. Samuel Scott became the first death that would be associated with SS 401, later to be launched as the *HMS Titanic*. Frost, Knight and Cunningham as well as six others from the building crew went down with the ship when it hit an iceberg two years later. Ice.

Fire. Nine days after the tragic death of Samuel Scott in Belfast, a fire broke out in the Blackfeet National Forest in Northwest Montana. The Missoula Press reported that Forest Rangers were optimistic about the agency's ability to cope with the blaze. However, they were understaffed and underfunded, and now they would be overworked.[2] Small fires were popping up all over the northwest, in Montana, the Idaho panhandle, Western Washington State, and in Oregon. In Spokane, at O'Malley's Tavern, there was much speculation about the fires. This time, Fred Ridley was present, munching on a pickled egg at the bar.

"It's a big 'un," said Tony Atchison. "Ya can smell the smoke all the way to here. Hurts my eyes"

"It's the comet, alright," said Harvey Greenwood, raising a mug of frothy beer as if in a salute. "Comet caused those fires."

"Aw, how can that be?" objected Fred.

"It's a big ball of fire, ain't it?" said Harvey. "You see how big it was in the sky last night?"

"Harv," answered Fred, "I don't think you're right on that. I read somewhere that comets is composed of ice and dust and so forth."

"Ice? That's crazy."

"There's fires all a time in those forests," said Tony. "They'll get it under control. Nothing to worry about."

"I'll drink to that," said Harvey.

A comet had been blamed for horrific fires once before: in 1832 when Comet Biela appeared for its periodic visit, it was noted that the comet had split into two pieces—debris may have fallen to Earth as our planet passed through the debris field of the comet some years later. There were some that said the two major fire storms occurring on October 8, 1871[3] were the fault of Comet Biela. One great fire devastated an area of 10 by 40 miles around Peshtigo, Wisconsin, killing over 1,200 people, another simultaneously laid waste to the City of Chicago.

> *And what would happen to the land,*
> *And how would look the sea,*
> *If in the bearded devil's path*
> *Our earth should chance to be?*
> *Full hot and high the sea would boil,*
> *Full red the forests gleam;*
> *Methought I saw and heard it all*
> *In a dyspeptic dream!*
> ——from "The Comet," Oliver Wendell Homes, 1832

Fred Ridley was mostly right about Halley's Comet being dust and ice. Halley's nucleus is shaped like a peanut shell about 9 miles in length, 5 miles in diameter, and it consists of a so-called "dirty snowball," a cluster of particles in the nucleus which may be frozen gases and space dust. As it nears the sun some of the gases, like carbon dioxide and carbon monoxide as well as frozen water, begin to melt. The tail of the comet, which appears brilliant through a telescope, is just the emissions, the coma, of the silicate particles and gases caught by the solar wind, the radiance of the sun.

In 1910, Halley's tail stretched for millions of miles. The tail always points away from the sun and in this year, Earth passed right through it. Halley's debris field causes meteor showers called the Eta Aquariids in late May and the Orionid every October. Like the debris from Comet Biela which fell as meteors to Earth, bits and pieces of Halley could have ended up in the forests of Idaho. It is unlikely that Halley meteors would have been hot enough to ignite the forest. Or would they?

It was hot and dry that summer in the northwest. Petey Ridley did not get to go to summer camp because of the fires that flared up here and there and everywhere. April showers, common in the Idaho panhandle, failed to materialize. On May 19 the Earth passed through the tail of Halley's Comet. The small fires that were springing up in

Perihelion

Montana and Idaho persisted through July. Nothing that could be called a conflagration, unless you considered them as part of one enormous raging disaster (the word disaster, from the Latin, means "bad star").

People volunteered to fight the fire and come to Northern Idaho where the epicenter of the big blaze seemed to be. Large fires broke out on Pine Creek, Graham Creek, and along the North Fork of the St. Joe River. People came from Missoula, Montana, and Spokane, Washington in the thousands. One such volunteer was young Petey Ridley. He would earn a wage of 25 cents per hour.

By August 8 President William Howard Taft finally agreed to send Federal troops to aid the Rangers and the volunteers. Two companies of Black troops from the 25th Infantry arrived on August 15. Along with these reinforcements, rangers from the U.S. Forest Service's newly organized Coeur d'Alene station found themselves in the middle of a battle for the future life of the forest.

In a memoir about the Great Idaho Fire, or the "Big Blow-Up," as it came to be called, staff correspondent of the *Spokesman-Review* Dave Bond wrote that this was "the year the mountains roared." On the morning of August 20, 1910, the wind picked up. The fires in and around St. Joe had been thought to have been under control and many of the fire fighters had been dismissed. But the wind reached near hurricane proportions and fanned the fading embers into torches and flung them into fresh timber. Flames leaped hundreds of feet into the smoke-filled sky. The call went out to evacuate.

Petey Ridley had joined a group of men working along on the west fork of Placer Creek about three miles from Wallace, Idaho. It was an area where deposits of quartz had attracted miners in the previous century. There were several mines having small cabins, but the fire fighters did not make use of these for shelter, instead they camped in the open, away from the fire lines. When Petey arrived, there were about 45 men and two horses patrolling a line that was threatened by the nearby firestorm.

The man in charge was U.S. Forest Ranger Edward Crockett Pulaski. Ed Pulaski had been a miner, had worked on a railroad and on a ranch before becoming a Ranger. He claimed to be a descendant of Casimir Pulaski, a Polish military commander who has been called "the father of the American cavalry." Like his forebearer, Pulaski was well suited to lead, to keep his head "when all about you are losing theirs and blaming it on you" as Rudyard Kipling said in his poem, "If".

Pulaski had just returned to the camp from Wallace where he had been getting food and supplies. Smoke filled the air and cinders rained down constantly. Pieces of burning tree bark had blown in and small fires had ignited. He worried that the town would burn to the ground, yet Wallace might be a refuge for his crew, should they need to find shelter.

High wind and intense heat from the fire worked in tandem, sending up a shower of fire brands and thick smoke. Trees were so dried out they cracked from the heat and fell providing fodder for the inferno. There was confusion in the camp. It looked like retreat from the camp was blocked by a backfire. Pulaski gathered the men together.

"Boys," he said, "it's no use, we've got to dig out of here, we got to try to make Wallace, that's our only chance."

Wallace was seven miles away. As they marched toward town, they found yet another wall of flame blocking their way. Some of the men were beginning to panic. Petey Ridley ran up to Pulaski shouting, "Mr. Pulaski, come quick. There's a man down!" S. W. Stockman had fallen from exhaustion. Petey helped the Ranger hoist the semi-conscious man up unto his horse. As they backtracked, looking for a clear path between to the two fire lines, they found another fallen man. This one had burned to death and resembled a burnt log more than a human being.

Now Pulaski said, "Boys, there is just one chance left for us. Maybe we can get into the War Eagle Tunnel."

Pulaski had prospected throughout the area in the past and knew of the mine tunnel. The length of this particular adit was over 1,300 feet. It could be the protection they desperately needed. His words seemed to reassure the men and although tired and stressed, they dutifully followed the Ranger. It was late afternoon as they walked along the creek bed, heading for the tunnel which was still over a mile away. The fire crowned around them and cut across their path. Now the men began to panic. They were not going to be able to reach the War Eagle Tunnel.

"There's two other tunnels, fellows. We'll get to one or the other of them instead," Pulaski said.

Perihelion

Petey knew three of the men who had come from his hometown of Spokane, Washington: Ben Smith, John Jackson and Joe Miller. Staying close to these men gave the boy some degree of confidence although he would have been surprised to learn that his presence was giving them a purpose beyond saving their own lives. They adopted the boy as their personal responsibility and shared water with him from their canteens. Water that was about to become a precious commodity.

The first tunnel they found proved to be too short to accommodate all the men. Still they squeezed into it, all but two or three who voiced their intention to try to get to Wallace even though the fire, a fierce barricade of incineration, was now on all sides. Pulaski told them to wait while he searched for another tunnel he was sure was not far away. Inside the small tunnel, Petey asked John Jackson, "Are we going to die?" Jackson had no answer for the frightened boy.

Pulaski returned, having found the location of a larger tunnel. He formed the men into a line, single file, and together they rushed through burning underbrush, dodging falling trees that were aflame. The smoke became a nearly impenetrable wall, the heat a suffocating nightmare. At one point a large bear crossed their path fleeing for its own life. There were now 42 men following the Ranger, most of them panicking, some of them reluctant to enter the tunnel once they arrived at its opening.

Pulaski ordered the men to enter the tunnel and lie down, wetting jackets and blankets with water from their canteens to cover their faces. One man tried to bolt. Pulaski drew his revolver and forced the man back into the tunnel. "The first man who tries to leave this tunnel I will shoot," he told them. He brought the two horses into the tunnel; they were as fearful as the men. Outside, balls of fire flew through the air propelled by the tornado of the firestorm. The tunnel mouth was enveloped in flames; the mine timbers began to burn. The tunnel was filling with smoke. Pulaski hung blankets over the entrance and stood there, batting at the smoldering timbers.

They would be imprisoned in the tunnel for five hours. One man prayed while next to him another man was weeping. Several of them were unconscious. A horse collapsed and died. The other horse staggered and soon, suffering from smoke inhalation, also fell dead. Someone yelled out, "I can't take it anymore! I'm getting out of here," Pulaski said, "Oh no you're not. It's certain death out there." The man calmed down but cursed the Ranger under his breath.

Joe Miller, one of the men from Spokane, was lying next to a young man, a boy not much older than Petey Ridley. The boy was writhing with convulsions. Miller told him to press his face down into the mud to escape the smoke. Suddenly the boy rolled over onto Miller and grabbed him around the throat, choking him. Miller tried in vain to free himself and was saved from strangulation only when the boy died and his fingers relaxed.

As Pulaski batted at the flames at the tunnel mouth an ember struck him in the face. One of his eyes was injured and he was blinded for the duration of his ordeal. Eventually he collapsed from the smoke. Meanwhile, back in Wallace, the sun disappeared behind a haze of thick smoke and raining cinders. Buildings caught from fire brands blowing in the wind. The newspaper office burned and the brewery went up in flames exploding barrels of beer. Mayor Hanson finally declared that evacuation was imperative.

When Pulaski awoke he heard someone say, "Come on, boys, the boss is dead. Let's run." "Like hell I am," Pulaski yelled. But looking outside, he could see that the fire had subsided enough that escape was now possible. Five men had died inside the tunnel, the rest had nearly expired from lack of oxygen. John Jackson emerged in a crawl and headed for the creek bed. Others followed, the forest still burning around them. One by one the survivors followed the creek bed back to Wallace.

Pulaski, although never rewarded for his bravery, was heralded as a hero of the fire. He would write his memoirs and newspapers would publish several firsthand accounts of the other survivors. Petey returned to Spokane, his own story to tell. The men received their back pay of four dollars per day

During the five horrific days of the Big Blow-up, a total of 1,736 fires burned more than 3 million acres destroying an estimated 7.5 billion board feet of timber. 85 people were killed. A number of small towns were completely destroyed; one-third of Wallace was burned. The disaster eventually led to reforms in the way forest fires were fought. But the year of fire and ice was not over yet.

Some say the world will end in fire,
Some say in ice.

Perihelion

From what I've tasted of desire
I hold with those who favor fire.
But if it had to perish twice,
I think I know enough of hate
To say that for destruction ice
Is also great
And would suffice.

——Robert Frost

Rocksprings, in Edwards County, Texas, was a small town near the border with Mexico in what was called the "Brown Belt." In November of 1910, across the border in the Mexican States of Coahuila and Chihuahua, a revolution was percolating. Francisco Madero was about to dispose President Porfirio Diaz and Pancho Villa was about to become a folk hero.

Many Mexican Nationals were immigrating, sometimes illegally, to the United States to escape the turmoil. Race relations between Texans and these Mexicans was already strained. Rocksprings was to become a catalyst for violent reprisals against the immigrants, actions called La Matanza—"The Slaughter." The worst attacks and lynchings by white Texans would be perpetrated by vigilantes and the Texas Rangers (local Mexican ethics called the Texas Rangers "los diablos Tejanos"—the Texan devils), but ordinary white folks had their days of infamy as well.

Antonio Rodriquez was a migrant worker from Guadalajara, Mexico who had come to Rocksprings looking for work. He was 20 years old. On November 2 he arrived at the Henderson ranch and knocked at the door. Mrs. Lemuel Henderson[4] answered the door. Rodriquez asked for food and Mrs. Henderson, Rodriguez later said, talked mean to him. The men of the ranch were away on roundup, so Mrs. Henderson was alone. Rodriguez shot and killed the woman, perhaps from anger and frustration or in reaction to the way Mexicans were treated by white Texans. The details of the killing are unknown as there was no trial. Even the suspect's identity is unclear.[5]

The next day, a posse apprehended Rodriquez at a neighboring ranch where he was again asking for food. He was brought to the Rocksprings jail and locked in a cell. He confessed to killing Mrs. Henderson. Word got around town. A suitable tree was found and a pyre was constructed from scrap lumber. An angry mob stormed the jail, overpowered the deputy, and pulled Rodriguez from his cell. He was tied securely to the tree and a torch was applied to the kindling. In moments, flames leaped up engulfing the poor man.

If there had been anti-American sentiment in Mexico before, it was now as incendiary as this incident. It was reported in the press internationally. The Mexico City daily, *El Diario del Hogar*, characterized the people of the United States as "giants of the dollar, pygmies of culture and barbarous whites of the north." Mexican Ambassador to the United States, Francisco León de la Barra, demanded reparations from the United States Department of State. Border towns saw mobs attacking American businesses. The American flag was the next thing to go up in flames. In retaliation for Mexico's demand for reparations, a rumor was started that Antonio Rodriguez had actually been born in New Mexico—fake news?

Burn Woman's Slayer at Stake.

Petey Ridley had returned home safely after his ordeal in Idaho. He was now a celebrity with many a tale to tell. When the United States of America joined the conflict known then as the Great War, Petey enlisted, not in the Navy, but in the Army. When General John Joseph "Black Jack" Pershing launched the Meuse-Argonne

Perihelion

Offensive in late September of 1918, Petey was part of the 93rd Division and fought shoulder to shoulder with the Buffalo soldiers of the 92nd. Arriving home after the Armistice, he caught a bad case of the flu. He died on February 20, 1919.

---

1   French astronomer Nicholas Camille Flammariion did indeed warn that the comet could "impregnate the atmosphere and snuff out all life on Earth." He pointed out that a spectral analysis of the comet indicated the presence of a toxic gas called cyanogen. He had published a great many volumes on astronomy, some considered classics. But he was also influenced by Spiritualism and became obsessed with the afterlife. Some of his writings are considered science fiction. Among them are *La pluralité des mondes habités* (The Plurality of Inhabited Worlds) 1862, *Lumen*, a series of dialogues between a man and a disembodied spirit 1872, *La Fin du Monde* (The End of the World) 1893, and *La planète Mars et ses conditions d'habitabilité* (The planet Mars and its conditions of habitability) 1892.

"This end of the world will occur without noise, without revolution, without cataclysm. Just as a tree loses leaves in the autumn wind, so the earth will see in succession the falling and perishing of all its children, and in this eternal winter, which will envelop it from then on, she can no longer hope for either a new sun or a new spring.... The universe is so immense that it appears immutable, and that the duration of a planet such as that of the earth is only a chapter, less than that, a phrase, less still, only a word of the universe's history."

———Camille Flammarion, *La Fin du Monde* (The End of the World).

In 1839, Edgar Allen Poe published a short story in Burton;s Gentlemen's Magazine called "The Conversation of Eiros and Charmion" in which the end of the world is caused by a comet which steals all the nitrogen from the air. The remaining oxygen catches fire, incinerating the Earth.

2   In an article about the Great Idaho Fire of 1910, U.S. Forest Service Ranger James G. Bradley wrote:

"Led by Senator Woldon B. Hayburn of Idaho, a radical anti-conservation coalition in Congress had for years been strangling the

Forest Service financially. Western congressmen were strongly opposed to Theodore Roosevelt's establishment between 1901 and 1909 of 148,000,000 acres of national forests; they resented the arbitrary removal of such huge portions of their states from development. They felt that the resources of the West belonged expressly to the people of the West to develop and profit from.

The ultimate goal of these anti-conservationists had been the destruction of the Forest Service. Hayburn and his colleagues hoped to return all national forest lands to relaxed control for private citizens to exploit freely. As a step toward this goal, in March 1910, only a few months before the fire, they managed to slice the annual Forest Service appropriation to one-half the sum allocated the previous year."

3   For a fictionalized account of the Peshtigo Fire of 1871 see my short story, "The Fire Next Time," in the anthology, *Romeo's Revenge and other Wisconsin Stories*.

4   She is called Lemuel Henderson in an article in the *New York Times of* November 11, 1910, but Effie Greer Anderson by Francisco A. Rosales in her book, *Chicano!: The History of the Mexican American Civil Rights Movement*.

5   From the *Sacramento Union*, Volume 120, Number 130, 30 December 1910:

TEXANS DID NOT LYNCH MEXICAN
Antonio Rodriguez, Supposed to Be Dead, Alive at Home.

GUADALAJARA, Mexico, Dec. 29. Antonio Rodriguez, supposed to have been burned at the stake at Rock Springs, Tex. is in Guadalajara, hale and hearty. Dispatches from Rock Springs at the time of the lynching made reasonably certain the identity of the man as a resident of this city, and as an aftermath to the killing, anti-American demonstrations in Mexico were started. Rodriguez was arrested here several days ago on suspicion that he was an agent of the revolutionary leader Madero. His identity was established today and he was released. ROCK SPRINGS, Tex. Dec. 29. The man lynched here on November 5 for the murder of a cattleman's wife,

Perihelion

was known as Antonio Rodriguez and It was said he came to the United States from Guadalajara, Mexico. An effort will be made to establish the identity of the man killed.

The Astronomer's Lament

Autumn was measuring the landscape for splendor. The dark chartreuse of fern and moss, the shamrock-hued, the viridian, the verdigris of shadowed foliage—these were giving way to pale gray and soft brown, to sage and khaki, to deep champagne-yellow and tumble weed tan, to faded cornsilk and bisque. But the deadened and the dulled were but a harbinger of a bursting. Leaves still affixed tinged toward lemon meringue, mustard, and saffron; then deep umber and sienna; then bittersweet and cinnamon. Certain trees, those of age and stature, shouted out in cinnabar and oxblood, vermillion and rust. An intricate pallet for the eyes of woodland creatures, and perhaps, a few human souls venturing abroad. After all, this was Wisconsin. Wisconsin of the colors. Wisconsin of the glacier-formed hills and kettles. Wisconsin of the lakes.

The crystal waters of Geneva Lake tossed a tapestry of fallen leaves in eddies; lapped the shoreline rolling with rounded pebbles (taking back just a little here or there); saw the wooden piers pulled and piled early—some. Tips of willow branches gently kissed it; long-necked geese and wood ducks congregated on it; boats the size of yachts paraded around it. Its colors were sapphire and pewter blue in calm, deep ultramarine in shadow, periwinkle to light turquoise in sun, but tipped with quicksilver in wind. Water determined to remain pristine regardless of human traffic. Water so pure it was once harvested in winter to supply the City of Chicago with fresh blocks of ice.

Sixty feet deep, seven and one-half miles in length, shaped a bit like some prehistoric fish when seen from above (as the comet flies), it has a periphery of shoreline on which a public path is laid out where Potawatomi once walked; now this passes the great mansions of Wrigley, Schwinn, Wacker, Swift, Allerton, Montgomery Ward, Pinkerton, Sears, and others, some only peopled with the ghosts of wealth, power, and fashion, some with the nouveau riche. The lake walk is unobstructed for twenty-three miles.

I had promised the retired astronomer Frederick Valarian to contact him when, in my journey through history, expounding upon events during the years of Halley's Comet's perihelions, I reached

Perihelion

1986. So I suggested we take a stroll along the lake, not proposing a twenty-some mile hike, just an afternoon of walking and watching the last of the sail boats and the first of the migrating Canadian geese. We met on the campus of George Williams College and embarked in a clockwise direction.

When we reached Conference Point on the west peninsula of Williams Bay we found a bench and sat. Looking out across the water we could see a gaggle of geese, a whole community doing a water dance: males in the lead, females next, followed by scores of goslings, endlessly circumnavigating the bay in a great ellipse. Someone was tossing a ball into the water for a dog to fetch. The dog, a great lunking retriever of some sort suddenly spied the geese and took off swimming after them. As he neared the group the largest male began honking and flapping his wings against the water creating such a commotion that the dog immediately headed toward him. The goose led the aggressor away from the rest of the brood, skillfully tiring him out; the canine, outsmarted, retreated to shore. Still the geese circled.

"Like the orbit of a comet," I said. "Endlessly moving from one side of their universe to the other."

"What did you learn, researching those years of the comet's return?" Valarian asked.

"Well," I said, "there were a lot of battles, some fires, a volcano or two, earthquakes, tsunamis, plagues…"

"You attribute those things to the comet's influence? That is not very scientific. Those things happen whether or not there are comets in the vicinity."

"Yes, but it makes a better story if the comet is one of the actors. After all, Halley's Comet had a rock group named after it." (Here Professor Valarian grimaced.) I continued, "William Shakespeare said, 'there are more things in heaven and Earth than are dreamt of in your philosophy,' by which I think he meant science. And he said, 'when beggars die there are no comets seen; The heavens themselves blaze forth the death of princes.' "

"And he also said, 'the fault, dear Brutus, is not in our stars, but in ourselves.' So, you do think the approach of a comet has meaning beyond its celestial presence? Meaning interpreted by humankind as causal?"

"Symbolic, therefore casual, perhaps," I said. "Myths and legends attribute cause and effect to gods and goddesses who are usually personified as heavenly bodies. For example, Menippe and Metioche, the daughters of Orion, were blamed for a plague and ordered to be sacrificed. They stabbed themselves to death, but Hades and Persephone pitied them and changed them into comets. There is a Japanese legend where the divine parents stir the milky ocean with a jeweled spear and form a whirlpool in space where worlds then appear. A jeweled spear.[1] And astrologers think the position of comets within planetary houses have an influence. The comet's color may predict a disaster. Tyco Brahe and Johannes Kepler both cast horoscopes that included a comet's position."

"But their discoveries advanced the cause of science, not of superstition. I hold with science."

"I only mean to suggest that mythology was an attempt to explain physical and emotional phenomena…just as modern science does. Admittedly, if one believes the Earth is flat…"

"It can only lead to trouble. So when the Greeks saw comets as bad omens…"

"They acted in such a way that caused the disaster they predicted to actually happen. Effect becomes cause. Or should I say affect with an 'a'?"

"I think your idea stems from a faulty premise…a selective assumption. You don't take into account all of the times comets appeared when nothing of consequence happened, or the events like earthquakes and so forth that occurred when no comet was present. It might be interesting to conduct a statistical analysis of this."[2]

"What we have here is just a difference of the views between a scientist and an artist. The former thinks nothing exists that cannot be explained while the latter believes there are things which exist which can never be known or understood."

"Hmm."

I said, "There is a poem by Robert Frost that talks about stars as blind entities, things that are 'invisible at dawn.' By which I think he means they are at times unknowable. It is called 'Stars.' I've written it down and brought it with me."

I reached into my pocket and extracted a piece of paper folded twice into a neat rectangle. I unfolded this and read:

Perihelion

How countlessly they congregate
O'er our tumultuous snow,
Which flows in shapes as tall as trees
When wintry winds do blow!—

As if with keenness for our fate,
Out faltering few steps on
To white rest, and a place of rest
Invisible at dawn,—

And yet with neither love nor hate,
Those stars like some snow-white
Minerva's snow-white marble eyes
Without the gift of sight.

"I think," said Valarian, "Frost is saying the stars themselves have no real influence over the fate of humankind. 'With neither love nor hate...without the gift of sight.' Minerva was the Roman goddess of wisdom and medicine."

"And poetry and the arts..."

"And war."

"But I would like to ask you now," I said, "to tell me your story of seeing the comet in 1986. You were reluctant before. I don't mean to pry..."

"There was great anticipation and much preparation for the comet's return in 1986," Valarian said. "Now we had technology like never before. This was a star (although it is not a star) which would not be invisible at dawn! As early as 1982 it was seen through the 200-inch telescope on Mount Palomar in California. It was still many millions of miles away. Plans were made to make fly-by measurements from spacecraft. The European Space Agency's Giotto had excellent photographic equipment. The Japanese had two spacecraft, the Sakigake and the Suisei. The Russians had the Vega. And we, of course, were sending up the Challenger space shuttle."

"No, I won't try to say that Halley had anything to do with the Challenger disaster," I said. "This time I will side with Shakespeare and his comment to Brutus. The fault *was* in ourselves with that one. Say…you weren't involved with Challenger, were you?"

I had already researched the Challenger Disaster. I knew that several factors had caused the breakup of the ship and the subsequent deaths of the crew. It was a study in bad design, incompetence, noncommunication, and possibly, willful disregard for the known hazards of the launch. It began with a piece of rubber called an O-ring that measured 0.280 inches in thickness and several feet in length.

There were two solid fuel rocket boosters on the spacecraft. O-rings were used to seal joints to prevent gases from escaping. The O-rings had a long history of partial failures, but NASA did not consider them a mission risk. In 1984, for instance, the launch of Discovery resulted in a hot gas "blow-by" past the primary O-ring. Since the amount of blow-by was relatively small and had not affected a secondary O-ring, it was considered to be an acceptable risk. In 1985, seven of the nine shuttle launches using boosters displayed O-ring erosion or hot gas blow-by. On the launch of April 1985, the primary O-ring had been eroded and failed to seal; hot gases had eroded the secondary O-ring. But so far, nothing had blown up.

The challenger launch had been scheduled for January 22, then was delayed until the 25th, then moved to January 28. Now it sat on the launching pad waiting for an accumulation of ice to melt. Overnight temperatures had reached 18°F; it was now around 30°F, below the "red-line" temperature of 39°F, the assumed limit of safety. The Shuttle was never certified to operate in temperatures that low.

The engineers from Morton-Thiokol, the contractor responsible for the construction and maintenance of the shuttle's solid rocket boosters, and the engineers at the Marshall Space Flight Center had expressed concerns to NASA on several occasions. The evening before the launch, in a conference call, they recommended postponement. NASA staff opposed a delay. There was a second conference call at which the engineers were excluded. Thiokol management reversed their decision. Had there been pressure to go ahead with a risky mission?

Perihelion

President Ronald Reagan was scheduled to give his 1986 State of the Union Address on the evening of January 28. He was planning to mention the Challenger mission. There had already been two delays. It is possible he may have pressured NASA to proceed with the launch. This mission was unique in that for the first time, there was a civilian passenger on the shuttle: Christa McAuliffe, part of the Teacher in Space Project. Ironically, there was very little media coverage. Only CNN carried the launch live. Because of the Teacher in Space Project, NASA arranged for live television feeds to public schools. Many school children watched the launch—more about that later.

I had just asked Professor Valarian if he had been associated in any way with the Challenger launch. I waited for his answer, uncomfortable with having asked. But he had not wanted to talk about 1986 and I just could not leave without hearing his story. That it was something deeply personal I had no doubt.

"I really have no right to ask you," I said, "but I'm an incurable romantic and I'll just imagine something tragic like…"

"Like I might have warned them there would be a disaster but wanted the data on the comet so badly I held my tongue? No, I am not an engineer. I know nothing about rockets or O-rings. I would not have been in the loop. I did consult on what kind of observations we might expect. There were plans to use Challenger to deploy Spartan 203 to record UV spectra from Halley's coma and tail, but the satellite, of course, was lost with the shuttle. Halley's closest position to Earth was in November of 1985. It would be behind the sun most of the time. We were expecting to use the Columbia shuttle launch in March to send up Astro-1[3] which was an array of three ultraviolet telescopes with an automated pointing system the crew could utilize. But after Challenger, there was a three-year hiatus with nothing being launched. The package didn't get deployed until 1990."

"The Challenger," I said, "was one of those events you never forget." I was trying to egg him on…get him to open up. "We oldsters remember exactly where we were when we heard Kennedy was shot or Martin Luther King, or of the Kent state shootings. Most people can tell you where they were when the airplanes hit the Twin Towers…many watched it live on TV."

Byron Grush

"My niece...her name was Katherine...Kathy...saw it over NASA-TV at her school. It traumatized her. She was about ten, I think. Very much interested in space exploration. She idolized Christa McAuliffe. The whole school room was so excited to watch the liftoff. Then the plume of smoke and..."

Excerpts from the Report of the Presidential Commission on the Space Shuttle Challenger Accident:[5]

Just after liftoff at .678 seconds into the flight, photographic data show a strong puff of gray smoke was spurting from the vicinity of the aft field joint on the right Solid Rocket Booster.

The vaporized material streaming from the joint indicated there was not complete sealing action within the joint

Eight more distinctive puffs of increasingly blacker smoke were recorded between .836 and 2.500 seconds. The smoke appeared to puff upwards from the joint.

The last smoke was seen above the field joint at 2.733 seconds. The black color and dense composition of the smoke puffs suggest that the grease, joint insulation and rubber O-rings in the joint seal were being burned and eroded by the hot propellant gases.

At approximately 37 seconds, Challenger encountered the first of several high-altitude wind shear conditions, which lasted until about 64 seconds.

Main engines had been throttled up to 104 percent thrust and the Solid Rocket Boosters were increasing their thrust when the first flickering flame appeared on the right Solid Rocket Booster in the area of the aft field joint.

It grew into a continuous, well-defined plume at 59.262 seconds.

As the flame plume increased in size, it was deflected rearward by the aerodynamic slipstream and circumferentially by the protruding structure of the upper ring attaching the booster to the External Tank. These deflections directed the flame plume onto the surface of the External Tank.

Within 45 milliseconds of the breach of the External Tank, a bright sustained glow developed on the black-tiled underside of the Challenger between it and the External Tank.

At about 72.20 seconds the lower strut linking the Solid Rocket Booster and the External Tank was severed or pulled away from the

Perihelion

weakened hydrogen tank permitting the right Solid Rocket Booster to rotate around the upper attachment strut.

At 73.124 seconds, a circumferential white vapor pattern was observed blooming from the side of the External Tank bottom dome. This was the beginning of the structural failure of the hydrogen tank that culminated in the entire aft dome dropping away.

At this point in its trajectory, while traveling at a Mach number of 1.92 at an altitude of 46,000 feet, the Challenger was totally enveloped in the explosive burn.

The Orbiter, under severe aerodynamic loads, broke into several large sections which emerged from the fireball.

The consensus of the Commission and participating investigative agencies is that the loss of the Space Shuttle Challenger was caused by a failure in the joint between the two lower segments of the right Solid Rocket Motor. The specific failure was the destruction of the seals that are intended to prevent hot gases from leaking through the joint during the propellant burn of the rocket motor.

The Orbiter did not actually explode but broke apart. The two SRBs were remotely destroyed by the Range Safety Officer which was standard procedure. The crew cabin was flung from the breakup at a height of 65,000 feet. There had never been a strategy for escape upon liftoff as it was assumed this possibility would not occur, nor would there be a practical way of ejecting the cabin. The cabin probably did not lose pressurization, and the crew may have been alive and conscious during the freefall to the ocean below. None of the seven survived the impact: Francis Scobee, Michael Smith, Ellison Onizuka, Judith Resnik, Ronald McNair, Gregory Jarvis, and Christa McAuliffe went to a watery grave; their remains were recovered in early March after over a month in salt water. The next day the Japanese space probe Suisei flew by 1P/Halley to take measurements. One week later, the space probe Giotto came within 370 miles of Halley and recorded the first closeup photos of the comet.

Professor Valarian had been saying, "The whole school room was so excited to watch the liftoff. Then the plume of smoke and..."

"You said your niece Katherine *was*," I said. "Something happened to her as a result of her trauma?"

"Most girls her age would have had pictures pasted up in their rooms of, say, Bon Jovi or Madonna, but Kathy had pictures and articles about Christa on her walls. I often brought her to the observatory and let her look through the big telescope. She fantasized about traveling to the moon. She said, before the accident, that she was going to an astronaut someday."

"And after the accident?"

"I got the distinct impression she was avoiding me. She refused invitations to the observatory after that. Her parents told me that she was having bad dreams...mostly about her house burning down or about being abandoned in a big city...that sort of thing. I wanted to get her into some kind of program of treatment. There was a study made of trauma-specific fear in children and adolescents who experienced the Challenger disaster on television or at the Cape Canaveral viewing site.[5] Many of the symptoms similar to PTSD were found. Common was the avoidance of people who reminded them of disaster and the mundane fear of being alone."

"That seems pretty usual. Did they track the children later, to see if the fears diminished over time?"

"Most did. Often the children found ways of dealing with the trauma...drawing pictures, writing in journals, posttraumatic play. One child reported that she and her friends played a game where they were in a space shuttle and it explodes. It is winter and very cold, but they live. She said it was as if Christa lived and that made them happy.[6] Kathy was beginning to come out of it by spring. Finally, in March, she agreed to accompany me to Yerkes to look through the big telescope."

"I think I know what happened. She saw Halley's Comet and that pushed her back into her PTSD. It was like seeing a burning spacecraft."

"Well, no. We would have had difficulty seeing the comet anyway, but I purposely pointed the telescope away from its position. I wanted to avoid that very real possibility. The γ-Normid meteor shower was active, but it was below the horizon so we focused on the dwarf planet 136108 Haumea near the Constellation Coma Berenices in the Virgo cluster. She seemed to be renewing her interest in space."

"So what happened?"

Perihelion

"I warned her parents...her mother is my daughter...not to let her watch the news on television. There were reports of the breakout that year of Mad Cow disease in England and it was starting to appear in the U.S. so I worried that kind of catastrophic event would be bad for her recovery. But they were watching a documentary one night on the Loch Ness Monster. Some tour boat captain had snapped a picture of Nessy, although that later proved to be a hoax. It was interrupted by a news flash."

Professor Valarian paused in his story and gazed out across the lake. The mail boat was just coming around the bend. They were still delivering mail to people's piers, the ones that hadn't been taken in, with the postman jumping off and back on as the boat churned its way past the docks. A nice tradition and one that attracted tourists to Lake Geneva. After it passed. Valarian said just one word:

"Chernobyl."

Chernobyl. Another classic case of bad design and incompetent maintenance. On Saturday, 26 April 1986, near the city of Pripyat in the north of the Ukraine, nuclear power plant reactor number 4 was being tested for safety by a new, inexperienced crew who had just come on the job. The idea was to simulate an electrical power outage and to find a way to maintain the circulation of cooling water until the power returned. It was the fourth such test, the others having been unsuccessful in developing a procedure. When a reactor shutdown was triggered, instability and design flaws in the reactor's construction caused an uncontrolled nuclear chain reaction.

Boom. The explosion sent steam from the superheated cooling water into the air. A fire leaped from the reactor core. Radioactive contamination was spread across the USSR and western Europe, affecting Sweden and Finland and devastating nearby Belarus. The explosion killed two of the operating staff and sent 134 people to the hospital with radiation poisoning. 28 of these died within days. Radiation-induced cancer deaths followed. The release of airborne radiation was contained by May 4 and eventually the plant was covered with concrete. The meltdown was still thought to be unstable, however. In the decades to follow there would be an estimated 6,000 to 9,000 deaths world-wide related to the contamination.

"Just what your niece didn't need to hear about," I said.

"Let's walk some more," Valarian said.

We wandered back toward George Williams College on the lake path. Willow trees dipped their branches in the water. A gentle surge of boat wakes lapped at the low bank. We were almost to the lake front at Fontana where I was going to suggest we grab a burger at Chuck's Place when we turned off the path and entered a small park at the end of Kinzie street. Another bench, a well-deserved reprieve. On a tall pole was a white-washed purple martin house, a kind of bird condominium, but I did not see any birds.

"Kathy had a pen pal," said Valarian. "A Swedish girl named Hanne Lindström who lived in Norrköping, a city southwest of Stockholm. Across the Baltic Sea from Lithuania and Latvia and in the upwind drift from Chernobyl. As far as I know, Hanne and her family were not affected by the contamination.[7] But Kathy fixated on that possibility. She began to withdraw again. She stopped writing to Hanne, afraid she would get no answer. Dreams returned in which she was trapped under water in the Challenger cabin, running out of air. Finally her parents took her to see a child psychologist. By the fall she seemed improved and she returned to school.

"But she was fading…slowly consumed by melancholy so debilitating it was like trying to find her way in a dark room. Her teachers sent home worried notes. Finally they just sent her home; a bad influence on the classmates, a frustration to tutorial status quo. She…what did the poet say? Not with a bang but a whimper? She languished, almost catatonic, noncommunicative, fearful-eyed. It was her new identity. It was the aphelion of her existence."

"Life can be a chess game," I said. "Sometimes you get an en passant, but eventually there's a checkmate." I immediately regretted uttering such a cornball hyperbole."

"In 1988 she committed suicide. Not dramatically. She just wandered away during a bitterly cold winter storm. She was found the next morning frozen on a park bench, dressed in flimsy pajamas, clutching a favorite stuffed animal."

"That doesn't sound like suicide…not intentional, but accidental. There was no note?"

"No note. No endgame. No checkmate. Just a resignation."

"I'm sorry."

Perihelion

A breeze rustled the oak leaves on a tree that overhung our bench. A few rust-colored leaves fell at our feet. A purple martin suddenly appeared and examined the birdhouse but apparently deemed it inadequate and few away.

"You know," Valarian said, "1P/Halley isn't going to return until 2061."

"Well," I said, "I guess I'll have to wait until then to finish the book."

---

1   "In the beginning the universe was immersed in a beaten and shapeless kind of matter (chaos), sunk in silence. Later there were sounds indicating the movement of particles. With this movement, the light and the lightest particles rose but the particles were not as fast as the light and could not go higher. Thus, the light was at the top of the Universe, and below it, the particles formed first the clouds and then Heaven, which was to be called Takamagahara (High Plain of Heaven). The rest of the particles that had not risen formed a huge mass, dense

and dark, to be called Earth....

When heaven and earth came into existence, three gods collectively known as the Kotoamatsukami (Distinguished Heavenly Kami) appeared, who were then followed by seven generations of deities. The seventh and final generation of kami, a male-female pair known as Izanagi-no-Mikoto and Izanami-no-Mikoto are ordered to solidify and shape the earth, which was then like floating oil on the primeval ocean. The couple, using a spear, churn the ocean, thus forming the island of Onogoro....

Hereupon all the Heavenly Deities commanded the two Deities His Augustness the Male-Who-Invites and Her Augustness the Female-Who-Invites, ordering them to 'make, consolidate, and give birth to this drifting land.' Granting to them a heavenly jeweled spear, they [thus] deigned to charge them. So the two Deities, standing upon the Floating Bridge of Heaven, pushed down the jeweled spear and stirred with it, whereupon, when they had stiffed the brine till it went curdle-curdle, and drew [the spear] up, the brine that dripped down from the end of the spear was piled up and became an island. This is the Island of Onogoro [Japan]."

——*Kojiki* ("Records of Ancient Matters" or "An Account of Ancient Matters"), "The Kamitsumaki or first volume: The Beginning of Heaven and Earth." translated by Basil Hall Chamberlain. 1919.

https://www.sacred-texts.com/shi/kj/index.htm.

2   Occasions of other comets and events like wars:

On June 29, 1861, Comet C/1861, called The Great Comet of 1861, was visible to the naked eye for around 260 days. An image of Abraham Lincoln circulated entitled, "the star of the North or the Comet of 1861?" Private Charles F. Johnson of the 9th New York Volunteer Infantry wrote in his journal:

"I watched the comet, wondering if that mysterious little visitor was not perhaps at the same time watched by eyes that would beam gladly into mine; and I composed quite a number of beginnings of addresses to the curious thing, or whatever it may be. But the comet is now tired of his visit to these regions of space, or disgusted it may be with the appearance of things on this side of our planet, for he is now leaving in seemingly greater haste than he came, with his tail between his legs, for the unknown regions out yonder. Well, good-by and fare thee well, Stranger. And I fervently hope that thou mayst see the face of the Earth beaming with smiles where now her frowns are lowering, on thy next visit, if that should be while this little world is still in existence."

The "Mexican War comet" aka DiVico's comet (1846 iv), was first discovered by Professor W. C. Bond, of the Harvard University Observatory. Cambridge, Massachusetts, on February 28. just before the outbreak of the Mexican War. It has an orbit, like Halley's, of about 75 years.

From mid-January to February 1941, Comet De Kock-Parashevopoulos and its faint 20-degree long tail was in the sky. This comet was seen with naked eyes and was mainly a Southern Hemisphere comet. The United States entered World War II in December.

Perihelion

Although no comets were seen during World War I, there was a spectacular one in 1811. The Great Comet of 1811, formally designated C/1811 F1, was visible to the naked eye for around 260 days, the longest recorded period of visibility until the appearance of Comet Hale–Bopp in 1997.

——various, Wikipedia.

3   "Recovery after Challenger" In: *Space Shuttle Columbia. Springer*. Praxis Books in Space Exploration. Praxis. https://doi.org/10.1007/978-0-387-73972-4_3. 2005.

4   "Report of the Presidential Commission on the Space Shuttle Challenger Accident," U.S. Government Printing Office: 1986 0 -157-336. https://er.jsc.nasa.gov/seh/explode.html.

5   "Children's Symptoms in the Wake of Challenger: A Field Study of Distant-Traumatic Effects and an Outline of Related Conditions" Lenore C. Terr, M.D., Daniel A. Bloch, Ph.D., Beat A. Michel, M.D., Hong Shi, M.S., John A. Reinhardt, Ph.D., and SuzAnne Metayer. Published Online: 1 Oct 1999.
https://doi.org/10.1176/ajp.156.10.1536.

6   Ibid.

7   "Sweden received about 5 % of the total release of 137Cs from the Chernobyl nuclear power plant accident in 1986. The distribution of the fallout mainly affected northern Sweden, where some parts of the population could have received an estimated annual effective dose of 1–2 mSv per year.
  …the present study, although using both high quality cancer registry data and high-resolution exposure maps of 137Cs deposition, cannot distinguish the effect of ionizing radiation on cancer incidence in Sweden after the Chernobyl nuclear power plant accident—if there is any—from the natural variation in cancer incidence or influence from other possible risk factors."
  ——Hassan Alinaghizadeh, Martin Tondel, and Robert Walinder. "Cancer incidence in northern Sweden before and after the Chernobyl nuclear power plant accident."

Byron Grush

https://www.ncbi.nlm.nih.gov/pmc/articles/PMC4102770/.

The Fifth Horseman

Then the third angel sounded his trumpet, and a great star burning like a torch fell from heaven and landed on a third of the rivers and on the springs of water. The name of the star is Wormwood. A third of the waters turned bitter like wormwood oil, and many people died from the bitter waters. Then the fourth angel sounded his trumpet, and a third of the sun and moon and stars were struck. A third of the stars were darkened, a third of the day was without light, and a third of the night as well. (Rev 8:10–12)

…and there was a great earthquake; and the sun became black as sackcloth made of hair, and the whole moon became like blood; and the stars of the sky fell to the earth. The sky was split apart, every mountain and island were moved out of their places. (Rev 6:12-14)

Pittsburgh, Pennsylvania, April 10, 2048.

Zeke Demeter, 26, slight of build, sloppy dresser, prone to reverie, closet intellectual, apt to get lost in big cities—is in fact lost. The coffee shop (called Gateway Roasters after a famous café in Thailand which closed years ago during the Covid-35 pandemic) was supposed to be right around the next corner. He is already running late and Kat (his pet name for Kateri Awani, a beautiful Native American woman he has just met) will think he has stood her up.

Kateri is nursing a chai latte and looking through backward stick-on lettering on the window which says "WE ARE OPEN" at the traffic on the boulevard consisting mostly of mopeds and bicycles. She is wondering if she has made a mistake in encouraging this new young man who seems awkward—but charming in an intriguing way. They work in the same building, the Matthias Industries building on Forbes Avenue, she on the 34th floor, he on the 20th. Both of them are computer programmers—but these days, everyone is a computer programmer.

Zeke enters at last. "Whee!" he says as he sits at her table. "Didn't think I'd ever find this place. Couldn't we of met closer to work?"

"I'd forgotten," Kateri says, changing the subject, "how really, really red your hair was."

"Scotch ancestors on my mother side of the family."
"Mohawk on mine. You going to order something?"
"Hmm, could we go for a walk? I noticed the riverfront is near here."
"four blocks away, but...oh, you got lost, didn't you?"

* * *

Events Leading up to the Second American Civil War (Excerpts from *History of Earth, Book 14: 21st Century*)
Miguel S. Valentino, Department of History
Bezos University, Arsia Mons, Tharsis, Mars.
Googlemars Ebook #72890, 66 New Era.

In November of 2022 CE (38 BNE) at Mar-a-Lago ("between sea and lake") at Palm Beach, Florida, former president Donald J. Trump was found dead, mysteriously poisoned. Suspicions pointed to actions by Russian agents (Obrien, 43 NE, p. 120) eliminating their former operative whose usefulness was now over. Trump, under indictment for a series of crimes ranging from tax evasion to inciting insurrection and treason against the United States, was nonetheless still a popular figure among the most extreme right wing of the Republican Party and the various conspiracy theory groups and white supremacist organizations that had aided or participated in the Insurrection Riot ("The Storm I") of January 6, 2021 (see Martina, 40 NE, pp. 56-60). These groups blamed Trump's assassination on what they called the "Deep State" and a new figurehead was sought to take Trump's place.

Obrien suggests that the loss of Trump as a leader removed the rallying point (known as "the Big Lie") that Trump had the election stolen from him by the liberal government that succeeded him. Since they could no longer claim that Trump was still president, it weakened the rationale for the armed attack on the Capital to "stop the steal." What had been a loose association of distinct groups with somewhat different objectives and logically about to splinter and fade away, instead would solidify into a well-organized quasi-political faction under the immerging leadership of a charismatic and inspirational figure in the person of Xander Manly.

Manly brought together all the aspects of white supremacy, anti-Semitism, anti-government militia, neo-Nazism. neo-Confederate,

Perihelion

anti-LGBT, Christian identity hate groups, the KKK, anti-immigrant, misogynistic supremacy, anti-Muslim, conspiracy theory groups, and just about every anti-group you could think of, far beyond what the Trumpers could even imagine. A third party was formed similar to the Knights of the Golden Circle and the Lost Cause movements occurring shortly after the first American Civil War in the 19th century, and it was called the Dixie First Party. The DFP placed Xander Manly's name on ballots for the presidential election of 2024 in all but four states: California, New York, New Mexico, and Oregon.

Manly finished third, getting only 18 percent of the popular vote (the electoral college had been disbanded by this time). The new president was the former vice president, Kamala Harris, a woman of color, which further infuriated the losers. On Inauguration Day in 2025 Storm II marked the beginning of the Second American Civil War with a siege on the nation's capital and on several state capitals.

* * *

Zeke and Kateri are walking along the riverfront. It is a nice balmy day in April, the promise of spring comes in the breeze from the fragrances of flowering trees planted along the embankment. Zeke is trying to think of something to say that is not 1) work related, 2) inane small talk, or 3) politics. As he struggles, debating between sports (girls don't like sports, do they?), and food (Zeke is actually a decent cook, having lived alone for most of his adult life), a man comes rushing at them from the direction in which they are walking. He is waving his hands wildly. He is ranting:

"The holy Lord shall go forth in wrath, and upon them all shall great punishment from heaven be inflicted!"

Zeke stops in his tracks, places himself between the man and Kateri. "Oh, for God's sakes," he says.

Now the man is steps away. More exclamations in a high-pitched voice:

"Then shall the roots of iniquity be cut off, sinners will perish by the sword, and blasphemers will be annihilated everywhere. The moon shall change its laws, and not be seen at its proper period. But in those days shall heaven be seen. Every place of strength shall be surrendered with its inhabitants—with fire shall it be burnt."

Byron Grush

Once he sees the young couple is not drawn into his harangue, the man turns and walks away. Zeke utters a sign of relief. "I hate it when crazies confront you on the street. Seems like it is happening more and more these days," he says.

"You know, Zeke, sometimes the crazy ones have an intuition that we ignore. In the old days, my people would listen to one such as that man because they thought the crazy ones had visions and spoke truth."

"You think the world is going end?"

She is silent. She knows something he does not know. But she does not know him. Not well enough to relate what she has overheard. She is not sure what she has heard may mean. She needs more information. And she needs more confidence in Zeke. "No, of course not," she answers. "Look, there are some ducks in river. Let's watch."

It is still a nice balmy day in April. The promise of spring is displayed in the troop of ducklings following their mother, patrolling the shore of the riverfront of the busy city as if humans didn't exist, as if the flotilla of plastic spoons and paper cups didn't share their domain, as if the air, perfumed by magnolia blossoms wasn't thick with poisoned soot underneath. Life goes on for the most part.

* * *

Project Gutenberg Earth Archive
Ebook #4763900, retrieved 8/44 NE
(terms of the Project Gutenberg License given below)

ASTEROID STRIKES NEAR MOONBASE
By Henry Watson, Washington Post
Artemis Base, Shackleton Crater, Moon, August 6, 2033.

Since the landing of the Artemis 13 Mission here last June there have been concerns about the increase in meteor showers and the potential of the impact of space debris upon surface aspects of the base. The interconnected domed structures have been designed to withstand up to 500 meter per second (1,120 mph) impacts of small particles—emphasis on the term "small"—and it is true that living quarters for the crew and civilian visitors such as myself and other

Perihelion

members of the press are underground in the lava tubes, however, reports of damage to the colony being constructed by SpaceX on the other side of the crater came as a red flag warning that something out there in the cosmos might be aiming for us.

The astronomy team headed by Professor Arthur Bennington got to work using the radio telescope and on June 21st discovered the approach of a NEA (Near Earth Asteroid). Bennington told me off the record (now a moot point) that the NEA was probably a PHA—the acronym, for those of us science neophytes means Potentially Hazardous Asteroid. A PHA is one whose Minimum Orbit Intersection Distance (MOID) with the Earth is 0.05 AU or less (an AU, astrological unit, is the distance the Earth is from the Sun). This whole alphabet soup of jargon meant that the asteroid had a possibility of hitting the Earth.

It didn't. It hit the moon instead. Astronomers on Earth had the best view of the impact. The flash would have been visible through even the smallest of telescopes, provided one knew where to look. Lucky for us it missed us by 1,200 km. Our crater is literally a crater within a crater, the "mother crater" being the South Pole-Aitken basin, the largest and probably the oldest impact crater on the moon. The basin stretches across nearly a quarter of the moon and is more than 8 km (5 miles) deep. It missed us by about 700 miles—but that was too close for comfort.

It is estimated the asteroid was about 45 kg (100 lbs.) in mass and roughly 30 to 60 centimeters (1 foot to 2 feet) across. It hit the moon's surface at 38,000 miles per hour. The crater it made is about 10 to 15 meters (33 to 50 feet) in diameter. That may not seem like much of a hole but consider the moon stuff it launched into the very thin atmosphere here and where that stuff eventually landed. The far western dome has major damage from debris; the connecting tunnel has some minor damage. There were no injuries other than psychological ones. SpaceX escaped anything major and it is doubtful that the Chinese project (only just begun) has been impacted.

* * *

Summer in the city. All is well with our young couple. Zeke and Kateri are picnicking at Point State Park, a verdant triangle of grass and pathways at the apex of the city where three rivers converge. They can stroll over to the site of Fort Pitt (you can still see the outlines of the old fort) which had been constructed next to a French fort, Fort Duquesne, captured by the British in 1758 (another year of Halley's Comet's return). History. This had been a major victory for the British during the French and Indian Wars—Zeke wonders, but doesn't ask, if Kateri's ancestors fought in those wars. The park, at least, has survived the rapid growth of the city, once an industrial and steel producing center, now the new mecca of technology since rising sea waters inundated Seattle and much of the West Coast.

They get as close to the point as they can to spread a cloth for their picnic. Here they can see the Allegheny and Monongahela Rivers coming together to form the Ohio. They have brought a bag of bread crusts to feed the ducks and snow geese that parade the waterfront. They open the basket and bring out sandwiches wrapped in paper: corned beef on rye for Zeke, avocado and bean sprouts for Kateri (she is a vegetarian).

"You seem pensive today," Zeke says. He would very much like to broach the subject of co-habitation with her, but her mood…

"Just thinking. Work stuff." She decides she should tell Zeke why she is distracted. And so, "You know my firm has undertaken a lot of projects in artificial intelligence, don't you?"

"I often think my own boss is actually a piece of artificial ignorance. Sorry, go on."

"I'm on a project for some new corporation…they haven't told me the name of it, which I find strange…and the work is supposed to be top secret. It isn't government, however."

"Well, that's not unusual. Businesses like to protect their interests. Probably going to launch some new product. Programming though…"

"Exactly. What it is…I'm not supposed to tell you this…is a sort of lottery program. Only, the algorithms involved are pervasive in researching the backgrounds and activities and even the health history of potential lottery winners."

"What do they win?"

"I don't know. But why would they need so much information? And it isn't geared to select just one winner or even a few runners up. And, isn't it illegal to hack into all those third party data bases?"

"Hacking is certainly illegal, but not rare. Most sources share information and make a lot of money doing it."

"This isn't just sharing."

Perihelion

"Hmm. Well, since you told me your workplace concerns, I'll tell you mine," Zeke says, pausing to take a bite from his corned beef.

"You've got a little mustard...there," Kateri wipes his chin playfully with a just licked finger.

"My current project also involves artificial intelligence. My team is creating a guidance system for a space vehicle. It also is not government. And I don't know the name of the client either. What is interesting is that the spaceship, which I believe is what this is, appears to be huge. There is environmental sensing and control within the program on a scale that suggests a large crew...maybe many passengers. And we are under pressure to complete the program in a hurry, which is always not a good idea!"

"What do you think...moon colony?"

"Have you ever heard of Mars One?"

"No, what is that?"

"Was. In the early 2010s there was a private consortium, Dutch, I think, that proposed to colonize Mars. They went bankrupt, but they had elaborate plans and really, all they lacked were the resources to pull it off. There was enormous interest."

"You know what? It could be that your unknown client and my unknown client are the same unknown client!"

"Kat," Zeke says, "would you like to move in with me?"

* * *

Googlemars Ebook Preview
The End of Days Diary
a collection of rare documents with commentary
by Yishma'el Debbora
self-published, 42 NE.

Transcript of a fragment of a news posting found saved on a digital device belonging to an unknown blogger. The device was retrieved from a ruined building in the East Cincinnati area. The date stamp on the file is 7/13/2036 5:05 PM. The newscaster has been identified as Josefina Coghlan. Ms. Coghlan died 2/20/2042 CE according to Andersson's Biographical Dictionary, Vol I, Earth (20 NE).

...in other news, SpaceX announced this week that they are suspending tourist excursions to the moon until further notice. Rumors have been circulating among investment circles that SpaceX is negotiating the sale of their moon base to a consortium which wants the property as a staging area for building an interplanetary vehicle. The unknown consortium, sources say, has already launched a manned Mars mission and will be constructing a future colony there. The United Nations, we should point out, has put forth a declaration making private exploitation of Mars a violation of international law. This is expected to be vetoed by Russia.

When we come back, an update on climate change, a new vaccine pending approval, and an interview with presidential hopeful Alyssa D'Ambrosio.

[Here a commercial for the electric Buick Mini started to play and the blogger apparently paused recording until the news post came back.]

...approval will no doubt be rushed through. The first pandemic of this century, the Covid-19 virus, began to mutate before vaccines could be administered to achieve herd immunity, killing one million people in this country alone, six million worldwide. A repeat of deaths of this magnitude from the Covid-35 virus would be unconscionable. Luckily, we have an administration that does not deny science, as was the case with the first pandemic. Gunner?

[the screen switches to a head and shoulders shot of a middle-aged man standing on a street corner, a contact mic pinned to his shirt.]

Josefina: What do you hear from the conference on climate?

Gunner: Thanks, Josefina. Yes, I'm here at the new United Nations Building in Hoboken. Ironic, isn't it, that the old building is uninhabitable, having been inundated by rising ocean tides and surges of up to 9 feet. You would think the talks would be productive given the obvious evidence of climate change. But...

Josefina: But the fossil fuel industry is still strong in emerging nations even though the U.S. has transitioned to clean energy.

Gunner: That's right, Josefina, their argument is that global warming, which they claimed for years was a hoax, has not resulted in the projected six to eight degrees of temperature rise. However, the Global temperature is, according to a majority of scientists, increasing

Perihelion

by 0.2 degrees Celsius, that's 0.36 degrees Fahrenheit, every ten years. They ignore or misrepresent the facts and claim that short term economic growth in third world countries is important for the world economy…more important than saving the polar regions from melting, preventing forest fires caused by drought, avoiding severe weather such as the increase in hurricane activity that we've seen recently, or abating the rapid extinction of animal life that these conditions bring about.

Josefina: Well, let's hope they can come to an agreement for action. Thanks, Gunner. That was good reporting. And now, a short break and when we come back, I'll ask Alyssa D'Ambrosio how, if she is elected, she will deal with the stalemate in congress.

You have come to the end of the preview.

* * *

Albuquerque, New Mexico, June 15, 2052

Kateri Awani and Zeke Demeter are standing on the platform of the top terminal of the Sandia Peak Tramway (the world's longest passenger tramway) waiting for the return of the gondola. At 10,378 feet the air is thin and the view is dizzying. Kateri has enjoyed the trip up the mountain, a vertical rise of 3,819 feet at a speed of 12 miles per hour for the 2.7-mile length of the tramway; Zeke has not. Kateri pointed out Steller Jays and Canyon Wrens flitting between cedars on the jagged granite crags and the ruins of a single-engine aircraft that crashed into the side of the mountain over a century ago. Zeke just held his breath, tried hard not to close his eyes, or to be sick from the gentle swinging of the gondola.

"I just want to get back to the motel," Zeke tells Kateri.

They are staying, at the expense of Persistent Visions, Inc., the company Kateri works for, at the El Vado Motel, an historic, adobe-style motor inn on Central Avenue (formerly Route 66, the Mother Road). The company is also paying for their dinner tonight at the Range Café in nearby Bernalillo. It is a bit of a drive, Kateri's boss, Yusuf Chobin had told her, but it was a famous landmark with good food and a place where you were apt to see someone famous eating and enjoying the funky atmosphere. Persistent Visions has a shuttle to take them and the other 25 people in the group on a pleasant drive through the Rio Grande Bosque area and through part of the Sandia Pueblo. Today is for sightseeing; tomorrow is for personal interviews—the last phase of the Footsteps to Mars Project selection process.

"I still don't understand how you and I got chosen for this project," Zeke tells Kateri once they are back from the mountain called Sandia—"Watermelon" in Spanish for the pinkish color it turns at sunset.

"You don't remember the lottery project I worked on? There were all sorts of backdoors to the programming. Yusuf, I mean Mr. Chobin, had us make the algorithm give preference to a certain data base in which the social security numbers were listed of people who were heavy contributors or had other influential qualities. I stuck our socials into it."

"You little devil! Are you sure you want to do this? Go to Mars, I mean?"

"It's the chance of a lifetime," she answers. It was, although she did not know this at the time, the chance *for* a lifetime.

At the Range Café the tables are filed with candidates for Footsteps to Mars. Kateri and Zeke are at a table with Kat's boss, Yusuf, and two others. The waitress tells them there are two choices tonight: Chicken Mole or Chile Rellenos. Zeke chooses the chicken, Kateri, a vegetarian, goes for the Chile Rellenos. "Red or Green?" the waitress asks. "Christmas," Kateri answers.

"How'd you know to say that?" Zeke wants to know.

"I read a lot. Besides, it's something every tourist to New Mexico is told when they get their passport."

"Uh, Kat…I think New Mexico is a state."

"I'm just pulling your leg."

After the meal and a dessert of sopapillas with honey, a man stands and taps on his water glass for attention.

"Welcome to all of you," he says. "My name is Moyses Wojciech. You can call me Moses if you like as I will be leading this phase of your exodus." He pauses but there is no laughter. He continues:

"This group is one of six now meeting in this country and three more in France, Germany, and Italy. We have brought you to New Mexico because it is the closest place we have found to conditions on Mars. At least there is breathable atmosphere here. You will be

Perihelion

having two weeks of intensive...shall we say, orientation? You will be subjected to medical, physical, and psychological tests. You will learn to handle space suits and to operate microwave communication devices.

"I can tell you that...and this is not common knowledge...we have established a substantial footprint on the surface of Mars already. Much of the material you will need has been sent ahead, prefab housing units, greenhouses already stocked with plantings, and so forth. Once your training here is complete you will go to our launch facility (I can't reveal where this is at this time) and in groups of twelve you will be shuttled up to our base on the moon. For you history buffs, the base is the old SpaceX moon retreat, once a tourist destination. No water park though." Another pause, again no laughter. Wojciech continues:

"We have spent years and a virtual fortune constructing our Mars ship on the surface of the moon. The reason for this is to avoid the enormous energy needed to escape from Earth's gravity for a space vehicle of this size. It is big, big enough to carry hundreds of passengers as well as cargo. I like to call it The Mother Ship, but that term was discarded in favor of '*Enterprise*.' I did not get the reference, but apparently it has something to do with a science fiction video from the last century."

Zeke looks at Kateri with a grin; he does get the reference. But Kat is bent towards Yusuf and the man is whispering something to her. A pang of jealousy strikes him but he shrugs it off. Nothing to be worried about, after all, he is her boss isn't he?

"Now a few facts about Mars. Mars has a surface area about one third of Earth's, about the amount of the dry land on Earth. Mars has half the radius of Earth. A day on Mars lasts 24 hours and 40 minutes. The gravity of Mars is 38% that of Earth so you won't need to go on a diet."

[No laughter, but a few chuckles.]

"Water on Mars is scarce. It is much colder than Earth, temperatures between −125 and 23 °F. Dust storms are common. The thin atmosphere does not filter out ultraviolet sunlight. There is no magnetosphere which would prevent cosmic rays from reaching the surface. Atmospheric pressure and these other factors will require pressure suits on the surface. But not to worry...the habitats we are constructing will have complex life-support systems including water processing and sterile environments. And now if there are any questions…"

Someone asks, "How long is the trip to Mars? Will we be in frozen suspension?"

"No, cryonics is not a possibility. No human has ever been frozen and brought back to life. That's just science fiction. Now in the past, a trip to Mars required approximately nine months in space. The *Enterprise* uses a VSIM propulsion system, a Variable Specific Impulse Magnetoplasma Rocket, and travel time will be more in the range of forty days. Now, the atmosphere is too thin for aerobraking and landing a large spaceship. Our plan is to land on Mars' moon Diemos, which has an orbit of about 30 hours. From there we will shuttle down to the habitat at Hellas Planitia. The *Enteprise* has been designed to be modular. It can be disassembled into ten smaller shuttle vehicles. Sort of like wheels within wheels, if you don't mind the Biblical reference."

And when I looked, behold the four wheels by the cherubim, one wheel by one cherub, and another wheel by another cherub and the appearance of the wheels was as the color of a beryl stone. And as for their appearances, the four had one likeness, as if a wheel had been in the midst of a wheel.
—— Book of Ezekiel 10:9-10.

Back at the El Vado Motel in Albuquerque, Zeke asks Kateri what Yusuf Chobin was whispering to her. He feels self-conscious doing this, he ought to trust her by now, but…you never know.

"He asked me to come to his cabin for a nightcap," she tells him, not at all self-consciously.

"You said no, of course."

"I don't see the harm. He *is* my boss, you know."

"He *was* your boss. We are all Martians now. But if you really want to, go ahead. I won't mind. I've got my Ebook reader with me and I'm in the middle of a good story about time travelers."

"I won't be too late. I love you. Don't worry."

And she has gone out the door singing to herself an old spiritual: "'Zekiel saw de wheel, way up in the middle of the air…"

* * *

Perihelion

Googlemars Ebook #897865
The Life of Professor Elmer E. Gregory
Andersson's Biographical Dictionary, Vol I, Earth (20 NE)
Copyright 20, 46 NE. All rights Reserved.

Elmer Edmund Gregory III (67 BNE – 23 BNE) was an Earth astrophysicist noted for the discovery of the shift in the orbit of comet 1P/Halley. Gregory was born in 1993 CE in Peoria, Illinois. His father, Elmer II, ran a hardware store there and purchased an inexpensive telescope from the Sears and Roebuck catalog as a gift for his son's nineth birthday. After graduating from high school, Elmer worked at the local grain elevator to earn enough money to purchase a 5-inch refracting telescope and a basic astronomy book and taught himself observational astronomy.

Elmer attended Valparaiso University on a scholarship and studied electrical engineering, but his passion was focused on astronomy. In his spare time he began tracking asteroids, comets, and other near-earth objects. On the basis of his amateur work he was accepted to the doctorate program in astronomy at the University of Chicago. In a few years he obtained employment at NRAO, the National Radio Astronomy Observatory, also known as the Very Large Array, in New Mexico.

In 2033 CE (27 BNE) he observed the approach of a small asteroid that collided with the moon but was unable to warn the Artemis base before it hit nearby. In 2036 CE (24 BNE) he was studying data sent back from the European Space Agency's ARIEL, (Atmospheric Remote-sensing Infrared Exoplanet Large-survey space telescope) and comparing it to observations of the same interstellar areas returned by NASA's James Webb Space Telescope.

Of particular interest for Professor Gregory was the tracking of comet 1P/Halley coming out of its aphelion, its farthest distance from the Sun. He calculated a change in the comet's orbit and further calculated that at its perihelion, its closest point near the Sun, it would pass within the MOID (Minimal Orbital Intersection Distance to Earth, about .05 AU or less). He noted the potential for Halley to strike the Earth.

Only a few of his colleagues at NRAO knew of his discovery. His superiors forbade a public announcement, citing the near panic of 1910 when Earth passed through Halley's tail. Gregory was determined to publish his findings anyway. The following year he raised funds from several corporations for whom he had done freelance work in his college days. This enabled him to attend the International Astronautical Congress sponsored by Groupement Astronautique Français in Paris. He was prepared to present a paper there with the mundane (and disguised) title of "Distant Events and Objects in the Universe, a New Study."

Sadly for science, on the day he was to present, Elmer Gregory stepped from his hotel on the Rue Saint-Honoré and was struck and killed by a hit-and-run driver. The briefcase in which he had carried his papers was mysteriously lost. In later days, once the facts of the discovery of the comet's diversion from its expected path were known, conspiracy theories emerged that Gregory had been murdered to prevent him from divulging information useful to certain parties if keep secret. No evidence of a conspiracy was ever substantiated, and the theory has been debunked.

When Elmer Gregory's widow, Emma, died in 2054 CE (6 BNE), her son and daughter, Randy and Eva, were cleaning out the Gregory residence in Socorro, New Mexico, and found the original notes for the paper. These were later correlated, edited, and published in the *Bulletin of the American Astronomical Society* and *The Astronomy and Astrophysics Review* in 2059. By this time, however, the dangerously close approach of Halley's Comet expected for 2061 CE (1 NE) was common knowledge.

References:
200 Years of Excellence. Peoria, Illinois Bicentennial Book. 2025.
Bulletin of the American Astronomical Society. (BAAS; Bull. Am. Astron. Soc.)
"Conspiracy Theories Update." FactCheck.org. The Annenberg Public Policy Center. Internet Archive, Wayback Machine.
Illinois Blue Book 2037–2038. "Biographical Sketch of Elmer E. Gregory."
L'Opinion. Bey Medias Presse and Internet.
"Notable alumni". University of Chicago. Internet Archive, Wayback Machine.
The Astronomy and Astrophysics Review. Springer-Verlag GmbH Germany.

Perihelion

* * *

June 8, 2054, Jornada del Muerto Volcano, New Mexico

The Jornada del Muerto basin is a 100 mile stretch of arid desert and shrubland in south-central New Mexico between the Oscura Mountains and San Andres Mountains on the east, and the Fra Cristóbal Range and Caballo Mountains on the west. It runs north and south along the course of the Rio Grande but is separated from that great river by the mountains to the west. To the east is the White Sands Missile Range and Trinity Site where the first atom bomb was tested. It is dry and difficult to access. The Spanish name translates as "Single Day's Journey of the Dead Man," probably after a German man who died there while fleeing the Inquisition in the 17th century. An early trail led through the Jornado del Muerto linking New Spain (Mexico) with the settled regions north, called Nuevo México Province. This was part of the Camino Real de Tierra Adentro, a dreaded journey with no water, no shade, and no people.

Near the top of the basin is a malpaís lava field, about 10 by 15 miles in size, created by a shield volcano that erupted 760,000 years ago. The volcano is silent now, except for some unusual human activity. The cinder cone rises to a flat mount about 150 feet high and one mile across. Here, under the supervision of whiptail lizards and sleepy bats living in the lava tubes, the superstructure of a launch platform has been erected. Standing against the vertical steel service structure and connected to an astronaut walkway is a SpaceX Starship, a Falcon Heavy rocket powered by multiple Merlin engines which use liquid oxygen as rocket propellant. The rocket exhaust will be directed down a main lava tube, no doubt French-frying numerous bats. The payload is a lunar landing capsule which can hold ten human souls,

Command center is a long RV parked a good distance away from the cinder cone. Coming up the dirt road is a bus carrying the successful candidates from the Footstep to Mars project. Among these adventurous persons are Kateri Awani and her former boss, Yusuf Chobin. But where is Zeke Demeter?

Two years ago in Albuquerque the candidates had their final interviews before the selection process came to a close and the training began. Zeke happened to see Yusuf talking to Moyses

Wojciech just before he entered the motel room for his interview. He thought nothing of it at the time. He had been asleep the night before when Kat had returned to their room after having what she called a "nightcap" with Yusuf. He didn't know how late she had stayed. Nor did he think anything of this either. But...

"Mr. Demeter," said Wojciech, "you were born in Texas?"

"In San Antonio, but my parents moved to Pennsylvania when I was two years old."

"That was the year Texas seceded from the union along with Mississippi, Alabama, South Carolina, Georgia, what was left of Louisiana after the rising gulf waters swallowed New Orleans, and what was left of Florida. The New Confederate States of America. The Insurrectionists. But you returned to Texas in 2036."

"It was a family vacation. I was twelve. We still had relatives in San Antonio. And not all of Texas seceded. A swatch stretching from El Paso to San Antonio and Austin joined the state of New Mexico."

"Nonetheless, your relatives were Texans and may have been compliance in the revolt." (Here Zeke shakes his head vehemently.) "I'm sorry Mr. Demeter," Wojciech continues, "but your association with Insurrectionists, even innocent as it may have been, disqualifies you for the Footsteps to Mars project. You are instructed not to reveal anything you have learned here. Remember, you signed a waiver."

The gangway pulls away from the Starship. Billows of white smoke and vapor momentarily hide the blinding flare from the solid booster rockets. The spacecraft lifts, seemingly in slow motion. Then it shoots up into the sky, a needle-like form flashing in the sun. Kateri is on her way to the moon base. Her new life is beginning.

* * *

The Earth Panic of 2060 CE
(Excerpts from *History of Earth, Book 14: 21st Century*)
Miguel S. Valentino, Department of History
Bezos University, Arsia Mons, Tharsis, Mars.
Googlemars Ebook #72890, 66 New Era.

Perihelion

It was in 2056 CE (4 BNE), the same year that the first colonists touched down on Mars, that the general population of the world learned of a potential collision with Halley's Comet. The previously lost notes of astrophysicist Elmer Edmund Gregory were published in the *Bulletin of the American Astronomical Society* and in a similar German journal and at first were generally ignored, discounted, or simply not known. But soon popular media of the time picked up on the theory proposed by Gregory that 1P/Halley had good chance of coming within a hair's breath of our "big blue marble" and could possibly collide with it.

FactCheck.com was queried about the possibility of planet-comet collisions occurring and possibly destroying the Earth and gave its opinion. For an example it cited Comet Shoemaker–Levy 9, a comet that broke apart and collided with Jupiter in July 1994. Comet Shoemaker–Levy 9 had passed within Jupiter's Roche limit (the distance from a planet in which gravitational forces affect other objects in space), and Jupiter's gravity pulled it apart into fragments. The fragments entered Jupiter's southern hemisphere at speeds of 35 miles per second resulting in fireballs with plumes reaching a height of nearly 2,000 miles above the surface.

The giant planet of Jupiter is composed mostly of gases, therefore it swallowed up the fragments of the comet. Still, spots appeared on the planet indicating areas of impact. Had it been a planet with a rocky surface, no doubt impact craters would have been formed. FactCheck.com also pointed out that Shoemaker-Levy 9 may have had a nucleus of about 3 miles across and the fragments were considerably smaller. 1P/Halley measures 9 miles by 5 miles. So yes, said FactCheck.com, a comet could hit our planet and yes, damage to the Earth would be considerable.

Conspiracy web sites screamed, "Fake news!" They maintained that liberals had fostered the rumor to keep the population fearful and to distract them from upcoming elections. Less extreme detractors said that the comet would probably burn up as it entered Earth's atmosphere and do little if any damage. Religious organizations suggested that 1) it was the will of God to reap vengeance upon humankind for its wickedness or 2) God would surely turn the comet aside, sparing the righteous. Other theories included rescue via space aliens in UFOs, the Rapture, the Apocalypse, and Ragnarök or Twilight of the Gods.

Byron Grush

Yishma'el Debbora, author of *The End of Days Diary* (42 NE) includes a fragmented article from the *New York Times* in the year 2056 CE which details, as an example of the possibilities of mass extinction, The Cretaceous–Paleogene extinction event of 66 million years ago. A 6 to 9 mile wide asteroid or comet crashed to Earth at Chicxulub on Mexico's Yucatán Peninsula creating the giant Chicxulub crater, and releasing energy equal to 100 teratonnes of TNT (that's a lot). The result was a mass extinction of three-quarters of the plant and animal life on Earth. The initial shock wave, the subsequent fire storms, the encompassing dust cloud that circled the Earth and blotted out the Sun for decades, the acidification of the oceans, and the re-entry of ejecta into Earth's atmosphere causing intense pulses of infrared radiation, ended much of life on Earth, some immediately, the rest over a period of years. Could Halley's Comet cause a similar extinction, the *Times* asked?

A positive result of the concern about the comet was that various corporate entities and governments stepped up their Mars colonization programs. Space craft took off from all over the globe in the next years before the appointed time of Halley's perihelion. Google and Amazon joined together to upload copies of every bit of Earth data available onto solid state memory devices that were sent with the last of the ships. Had the Gregory notes not been lost for two decades perhaps more Earthlings might have made it to Mars. We will never know for sure.

The panic began in 2060 with confirmation by scientists that Earth was indeed in Halley's direct path. Space ports with ships still on their pads were stormed. Several politicians were kidnapped, and their dismembered bodies later found. In large urban centers "end of the world" venues sprang up with behavior of the most decadent and Bacchanalian sort. More than one religious cult committed mass suicide. The most bizarre reaction was from the stoic Zeno Society who purchased a mountain resort in Telluride, Colorado, and offered lodging (for a hearty fee) for those wishing a "best view" of the Apocalypse.

* * *

Then the kings of the earth and the great men and the commanders and the rich and the strong and every slave and free man hid themselves in the caves and

Perihelion

among the rocks of the mountains; and they said to the mountains and to the rocks, "Fall on us and hide us from the presence of Him who sits on the throne, and from the wrath of the Lamb; for the great day of their wrath has come, and who is able to stand?" (Rev 6:15-17)

They shall transgress, and think themselves gods; while evil shall be multiplied among them. And punishment shall come upon them, so that all of them shall be destroyed. (Enoch 79:9-10)

45. Brothers shall fight | and fell each other,
And sisters' sons | shall kinship stain;
Hard is it on earth, | with mighty whoredom;
Axe-time, sword-time, | shields are sundered,
Wind-time, wolf-time, | ere the world falls;
Nor ever shall men | each other spare. ...

57. The sun turns black, | earth sinks in the sea,
The hot stars down | from heaven are whirled;
Fierce grows the steam | and the life-feeding flame,
Till fire leaps high | about heaven itself. ...

66. From below the dragon | dark comes forth,
Nithhogg flying | from Nithafjoll;
The bodies of men on | his wings he bears,
The serpent bright: | but now must I sink.
———"Völuspá, The Wise-Woman's Prophecy"
[Ragnarök, Norse legend]
The Poetic Edda, Vol. I, Lays of the Gods.
Trans. by Henry Adams Bellows,
[1936], at sacred-texts.com.

San Antonio, (formerly Texas) New Mexico, May 10, 2061. Zeke Demeter has come to be with his uncle Clinton, his aunt Page, and their grown children Mort and Cassie, his only living relatives. When he arrives he finds them gone, a note addressed to him stuck in the door jam: "At cabin," it reads. Of course. Uncle Clint has a cabin on Medina Lake just west of San Antonio. Cabin? Some would call it a lake house or a retreat. Not your basic fishing cabin but lakefront property complete with pier and an outdoor hot tub. Uncle Clint socked it away during his working years and bought the place a few years back.

Zeke has been on an eye-opening road trip, driving from Pittsburgh to San Antonio over the last several days. After Albuquerque, the rejection by Footsteps to Mars and by Kateri, he had returned home, rejected, dejected, disillusioned, and dismayed. It is one thing to be jilted, yet another to be left by the woman you thought you might love for, not only another man, but another whole planet! True, he had told her she should go…the chance of a lifetime, wasn't it? He hadn't figured out the deception then: that Footsteps to Mars had kept the facts about Halley's Comet's return from them, and that Moses had been lied to about him by Yusuf.

Pittsburgh had become a madhouse once the truth was known. Roaming gangs broke into stores and looted. Fires burned everywhere. The police were nowhere to be seen; some were complicit. His company closed down, the building he lived in now had no electricity, no water, no janitor, no landlord. Zeke did something he never imagined himself capable of—he stole a car. He found it on a used car lot. Looters had broken into the office looking for money. Keys were hanging on a wall rack. It was easy. He took an older model Tesla that looked roadworthy.

He did not know where he wanted to go, just that he had to get away from the insanity of the city. Then he remembered his uncle. The navigation system told him San Antonio was 1,498 miles by the most direct route, a trip of 22 hours. But that took him through Louisville, Kentucky, Nashville and Memphis, Tennessee, then through Arkansas and Texas, all part of the Confederate States of America. He would be stopped at the border and he had no passport. Instead, he would go through Indiana and Illinois to Saint Louis, then follow old Route 66 to Tulsa, drive out the panhandle to New Mexico, then south to El Paso. 1,884 miles, 29 hours. Interstate until he got to the Oklahoma panhandle.

The Tesla did have solar panels and a range of over 750 miles on batteries, but he would still have to seek out charging stations along the route—worrisome in rural areas. Just how much did he want to see his uncle, anyway? He had rarely seen his father's brother and his family over the years. He did not remember much about his cousins, only that the boy liked sports (Zeke could care less) and the girl

Perihelion

snubbed him (she wasn't pretty anyhow). But family was family and Zeke was lonely. And he did not want to die alone.

Indianapolis, Springfield, and Saint Louis were exactly as he expected: like Pittsburgh, the cities were on fire. At Joplin, Missouri, he made the mistake of stopping at a stop light; an angry group of teenagers attacked the Tesla with bricks, cracking a window. Crowds of rioters would chase his car in large cities. He had had to detour around Tulsa and ended camping along the Arkansas River where it broadened into Keystone Lake. Here the Tesla died. The solar panels had given out and there were no charging stations to be found. He shouldered his backpack and walked. There were mobile home parks along the river and these were deserted except for feral dogs which barked viciously at him. Dodging a pack of dogs brought him to an old camp site. It was there he made a great find: an antique vehicle rusting away and nearly obscured by brambles and weeds. It was a very old Ford pickup truck, pre-electric—a gas-guzzler. Would it run?

Zeke knew nothing about motors except for what he had read in stories, novels about the early 21st century. He opened the hood and inspected the motor as if that were obligatory, a rite of passage into the past. It looked all right but did it have gas? He remembered something about starting a car without a key by "jumping" it...crossing the ignition wires. He reached under the dash and found some wires hanging there. After several attempts, red to green, green to blue, white to white, he found the right combination and with a grinding noise the motor sprang to life! He would be on the road again until he ran out of gas.

Far into the panhandle he passed farms deep in dust and decay. At one of these, next to a rusting tractor, he found an upright tank filled with gasoline. He scrounged some cans from a fallen down shed and filled these and packed them onto the bed of the pickup. He drove now into the setting sun, through the dismal and deserted sliver of Oklahoma that pointed at New Mexico. The brilliance of that sun, a rojo ojo (red eye) hypnotized him.

His route took him through Springer, Wagon Mound, Watrous, Las Vegas, Vaughn, small towns that seemed untouched by time or by the impending apocalypse. He left behind him a trail of dust and smoke and a jetsam of rusty metal. At Alamogordo he was able to purchase gasoline from a service station that still operated, still sold petrol, and whose proprietor was ignorant of or oblivious to the coming of world's end.

He had reached his uncle's house in six days. He had seen desolation, destruction, and disregard. He had been threatened by mobs, chased by dogs, and had slept in his car off the road. He had nursed the pickup over a lonely highway to Reuter's Cove on Medina Lake. He knocked. There was no answer.

Meanwhile on Mars, Kateri feels remorse at not having stayed on Earth with Zeke. Not that she wants to die, she hadn't known at the time of her leaving Earth of that inevitability, but she had been seduced by the romance of an adventure into space to a new world. And the romance of a new and interesting man. A man she now knows had withheld information about the comet and who had caused Zeke's rejection from the project. She wonders if she had made the correct choice. Would it have been better to die by fire with the one you...loved?

The colony has evolved from a situation of day-by-day survival to one of a new order of monotonous obedience to rules-that-save-lives. Posters on the walls of the habitats shout in brightly colored illustrations and large letters: WEAR YOUR RADIATION BADGE; PRESSURE SUITS REQUIRED IN WALKWAYS BETWEEN HABITATS; CONSERVE DRINKING WATER; REPORT FEELINGS OF DEPRESSION; BUDDY SYSTEM SAVES LIVES, also a poster of astronaut "Buzz" Aldrin with a caption of his famous quotation, "Forget the moon, let's head for Mars," and a smaller poster giving the title of the movie of the week: *Gone with the Wind*.

It had been predicted that the single most dangerous threat to the survival of the colony would be psychological and social: isolation from Earth and loved ones, living with strangers in cramped quarters, fear of suffocation or starvation, too much or not enough sexual activity. Contact with Earth through microwave transmissions was possible but not encouraged. This was the New Experiment, the New Empire. Forget Earth, celebrate Mars.

Real dangers existed in the deluge of cosmic radiation, the severe temperatures, and the lack of sunlight due to perpetual dust storms. Then there was the influx of other colonies. In the panic resulting from Halley's Comet every government or private concern capable of

Perihelion

launching spacecraft had done so, aiming at the Red Planet with or without having thought things through. Some had been planning for decades to visit Mars. Most had thought in terms of exploration and return. Now there would be no return.

Willy Ley proposed exploration of Mars in *The Conquest of Space* in 1949. Wernher Von Braun outlined how this could be achieved in *Das Marsprojekt* in 1952, published in English as *The Mars Project* in 1962. A crewed Mars expedition was studied and seriously proposed in the Soviet Union as early as 1956. NASA, of course, had planned a Mars project off and on since its inception in 1958. In 1991, the International Space University in Toulouse, France conceived of a nuclear-powered vessel with artificial gravity sending a crew to Mars. Ideas, ideas, ideas.

The European Space Agency, Mars Society Germany, the China National Space Administration, the Indian Space Research Organization, the Japan Aerospace Exploration Agency (JAXA), all had been aiming at mid-twenty-first century manned Mars missions. Non-government entities including Mars One, Inspiration Mars Foundation, Lockheed Martin's Mars Base Camp, and SpaceX Starship had similar ambitions. Probes had been launched. Robots had been landed. Funding had been sought. Now prefabricated habitats were sprouting all over the Martian landscape. What they had not given any thought to was the transportation, along with humans, of tiny bacteria and viruses. No plagues had broken out...so far.

Kateri is standing in line waiting to use the Mars to Earth radio telephone to try to call Zeke. Is he still at his apartment in Pittsburgh? She hopes so. While she waits she thinks about the thousands and thousands of people, Hispanics, Blacks, Asian Americans. Muslims, and especially her people, Native Americans, who hadn't made the cut for Footsteps to Mars or any of the other concerns that had established colonies here. It was not fair, and it was typically American. As she stands anticipating a wait of perhaps one or two hours judging by the throng of people ahead of her, a woman comes out to address the crowd:

"I'm very sorry," the woman says, "but there will be no more communications with Earth at this time."

"What do you mean?" someone says. "Why?"

Byron Grush

"Mars to Earth com line is down. We have been unable to raise anyone on the side facing us...the western hemisphere. In other words, the Americas."

* * *

The Comet Arrives; The Extinction Begins
(Excerpts from *History of Earth, Book 14: 21st Century*)
Miguel S. Valentino, Department of History
Bezos University, Arsia Mons, Tharsis, Mars.
Googlemars Ebook #72890, 66 New Era.

Halley's Comet had an estimated diameter of around 7 miles and traveled at speeds of 156,000 miles per hour. Normally, if one can say anything about a comet is normal, it would spend its perihelion somewhere between the orbits of Venus and Mercury. On May 10th, 2061 CE (1 NE) it approached Earth's Roche limit within which gravitational forces were able to act upon it. Some large chunks of the comet broke away and went into a temporary orbit. Slowly these entered the atmosphere as their orbits degraded. The inertia of the comet had sent these particles down like flaming meteors and where they hit they opened craters, started forest fires, and shattered buildings.

When it passed through the magnetosphere it picked up charged particles from the Van Allen Radiation Belts. Next it encountered the intersecting orbits of Earth's artificial satellites, nearly 20,000 in all. As it passed it knocked many of these down, hurling them into the atmosphere where most burned before hitting the surface of the Earth. Many found their way to terra firma, adding to the deluge of fire and causing extreme havoc when they hit cities. But the worst was yet to come.

As the comet plunged through the upper atmosphere, pushing air ahead, it left a hollow tube behind it which acted like a huge gun barrel, spitting up fragments of debris in an explosion of fire. Observers saw this phenomenon as a gigantic plume of flame rising back into the upper atmosphere. 1P/Halley struck Earth at a sharp angle with a force of about 100 million megatons resulting in a fireball that spread for nearly 150 miles, making a crater 55 miles in

Perihelion

diameter, and causing an earthquake of the magnitude of 10 on the Richter scale.

Ground zero was Wichita, Kansas, practically the center of the United States of America. The fireball swallowed what was left of Wichita and the surrounding countryside. Intense heat spread in a circle encompassing half of Kansas, Nebraska, Utah, and Colorado, starting forest fires and incinerating towns. Shock waves from the initial impact spread out even further, knocking over steel buildings as far away as Illinois, Mississippi, Texas, Northern Mexico, Nevada, Idaho, Montana, Southern Canada, and Minnesota. Trees were knocked over, people found their clothing set on fire.

The plume of fire, still hanging in the atmosphere, expanded at its top purging debris up into the stratosphere. Particles of various sizes began to fall back to Earth, spreading destruction across the northern and southern hemispheres. The raining inferno fell on Europe, Asia, South America, Africa, Russia, and China. A sizable chunk fell on London, obliterating the city. Australia and New Zealand were spared—for the time being. Reentry of the particles caused infrared radiation that burnt to a crisp any small animals or other organisms exposed to it.

A dust cloud formed over the impact crater and expanded, rising into the upper atmosphere. So much dust had been created that the sun was blotted out as effectively as if night had fallen. A deep gloom hung over Earth, a perpetual twilight that refused to dissipate. The sun disappeared for over a year after the impact. Plants died. Temperatures dropped drastically. The oceans absorbed acid rain from nitrogen oxides and sulfur dioxides formed from the comet dust. Microorganisms died. Aquatic fish and mammals dependent on the microorganisms died. The food chain essentially disappeared.

There was talk on Mars of launching a rescue mission to the dying Earth. It was decided, however, that the resources required for such an undertaking would adversely affect Martians whose own survival could be tenuous at times. The number of humans and animals which could be rescued would be minimal; it was the law of diminishing returns for human life. Predictions for planet Earth at the time of this writing are dire. An extinction similar to that which happened to the dinosaurs is thought to be underway and irreversible.

Byron Grush

* * *

Reuter's Cove on Medina Lake, near San Antonio

May 10, 2061. Zeke is knocking on the door of his uncle's cabin but there is no answer. That's funny, their cars are here, parked neatly in a row like sentinels to keep out the riffraff. The speed boat is up on a lift at the end of the pier, so they are not out on the lake. Zeke walks around to the back of the house. Screen porch, door open, no one in sight. He enters and calls out, "Uncle Clint?" Still no answer. Huh. He decides to wait. Maybe they are off on a walk. He sits on a rattan chair on the porch and puts his feet up on the coffee table before him.

On the table is a file folder open to a page that catches his eye. He bends to read. It is some kind of a dispatch or notice from the local State Police. It is a warning about the approach of the comet. Well, everyone knows about that. But this is a little different than your average public service announcement. It is addressed personally to Clinton Demeter and signed by Sheriff Wayne Harris. The last paragraph is shocking:

"Clint," it reads, "our information is that Halley's Comet will strike Earth on Tuesday, May 10th. As that is in just one week I strongly suggest that you finish stocking that old bomb shelter of yours with plenty of water and canned food. This is going to be a real catastrophe!"

Bomb shelter? Oh yes, he remembers now. The house on the lake that Uncle Clint bought had been built back in the 1950s. The original owner had put in a bomb shelter, believing in the possibility of nuclear war with the Russians. It was in pretty bad shape and his uncle rarely went into it. He joked about converting it into a wine cellar. Let's see, where was that thing? Up the hill in a little thicket of Live Oak trees. One other thing, what's the date today? Zeke looks at his phone—it is May 10th.

Zeke finds the shelter, just a rusty iron door obscured by grass and weeds in the little woods at the top of the hill. He pounds on the door with his foot, hardly thinking anyone could be down there. But a peephole opens in the door and voice says, "Go away!" He protests, yelling through the peephole that it is he, Zeke Demeter. The door opens. "Get the hell in here," Uncle Clint says. Just as Zeke

Perihelion

enters the bomb shelter, pulling the door closed behind himself, the sky lights up with a brightness that blinds.

The Lamb of God opens the seals on the scroll in God's right hand.
The first horseman rides out on a white horse, carrying a bow, and wearing a crown, and his name is Pestilence.
The second horseman rides out on a red horse, and carries a sword, and he is called the creator of War.
The third horseman rides out on a black horse, and his name in Famine.
The fourth horseman rides out on a pale green horse. His name is Death.
Then a Fifth horseman appears. He rides upon a comet, and his name is Extinction.

Aftermath

A few of the years of the comet we have skipped deserve an honorable mention. In the year 240 BCE, a comet was observed and recorded by Chinese astronomers; apparently the first written record of Halley's Comet:

"During this year (i.e. 240 BC), a broom star first appeared at the E direction; it was then seen at the N direction. In the month May 24 to Jun 23 it was seen at the W direction... The broom star was again seen at the W direction for 16 days." (Shih-chi, Annals).

"During this year a broom star was seen at the N direction and then at the W direction. During the summer the Empress Dowager died." (Shihchi, Chronological Tables).[1]

This was the year that Rome took control of Sicily and stationed a legion there. *Achilles*, the first tragedy by Livius Andronicus, was first produced. And the mathematician Eratosthenes estimated the Earth's circumference to be 252,000 stadia, a figure very close to modern measurements. No volcanos or firestorms, however.

Concerning the return of the comet in 87 BCE, F. R. Stephenson quotes the Chinese record: "In autumn during the month Aug 10 to Sep 8 a star emerged at the E," but says "As Kiang pointed out, if this star indeed refers to Halley's comet then either the month or the direction must be in error. Halley's comet should have been visible in the E for much of July - up to about Jul 25".[2] And he refers to the record of the comet for this year on Babylonian tablets: "the comet was seen 'day beyond day' for a month."[3]

Of interest in this year is the issuance of coinage depicting Tigranes the Great, King of Armenia (140 – 55 BC), who is depicted on the coins wearing a tiara decorated with a sun or star symbol between two eagles. According to V. G. Gurzadyan and R. Vardanyan, "On a rare series of tetradrachms and drachms and on more numerous copper coins depicting the goddesses Tyche and Nike, with a cypress tree, palm branch and tripod on their reverse, Tigranes's tiara is decorated with a single star, which has one of the righthand-side rays elongated and curved, which can be interpreted as

Perihelion

a comet."[4] Tigranes expanded the Armenian kingdom beyond its traditional borders and was called the "King of kings.".

In 1901 an ancient device was retrieved from a shipwreck off the coast of Crete. This item, the Antikythera mechanism, is currently dated to 100 BCE, plus or minus 30 years, placing its manufacture possibly in 87 BCE, the year of our comet. Only one third of the Antikythera Mechanism was recovered, but it is marveled as the earliest known "computer," an astronomical implement with set of scientific dials or scales, probably used to calculate and display information about the stars and the planets. By 2016, scientists investigating the relic using an X-ray scanner were able to document 3,500 characters of text embedded onto the device. The researchers are building a reconstruction of the full device based on what they have learned from the embedded text. While the device had a definite astronomical purpose, scientists now believe the machine may also have been used to predict the future.[5] Did it track comets?

Halley returned in 141 CE and was recorded in Chinese chronicles and in the Tamil work Purananuru. The Lycia earthquake occurred in that period (AD 141 to 142) with a magnitude of at least 7, possibly greater. It triggered a severe tsunami. NOAA, the National Centers for Environmental Information, describes the effect of the earthquake and tsunami on the region of the Roman provinces of Lycia and Caria and the islands of Rhodes, Kos, Simi and Serifos:

"This earthquake affected a large area in southwest Turkey and the Dodecanese Islands. Damage extended from the island of Cos and Rhodes to the Gulf of Antalya and to Cine in the north, an area of radius 90 km. ...The town of Rhodes was destroyed by an earthquake, and its ruins were washed away by the wave that rushed in so quickly that the citizens suffering the earthquake had no time to find their relatives; the sea water penetrated deep into dry land for several miles. The towns on the islands of Kos, Symi, Serifos suffered from the earthquake and tsunami."[6]

Now we come to Halley's Comet of 374 AD. In this year we meet Spearthrower Owl. In Teotihuacan and in the Maya cities of Tikal, Uaxactun, Yaxchilan, and Toniná are found logographs or glyphs depicting an owl and spear-thrower. Archeologists believe the glyphs represent a ruler of Teotihuacan at the start of the height of its influence across Mesoamerica in the 4th and 5th century, hence they call him Spearthrower Owl or "Atlatl Cauac". The Tikal Marcador, probably a ballcourt marker, and The Hombre de Tikal, a sculpture of a seated man with a large round belly, are classical Mayan sculptures with glyphic cartouches and deeply incised texts.[7] The Tikall Marcador text describes the arrival of the Spearthrower Owl to Tikal during a time of political transition. The Spearthrower Owl is believed to have been from Teotihuacan and was key in introducing Teotihuacano customs to the rest of Mesoamerica.[8] Inscriptions on the Tikal Marcador indicate that Spearthrower Owl ascended to the throne on a date equivalent to May 4, 374.[9] The first sighting of Halley's Comet in 374 AD was on May 4, and its perihelion is calculated to have been on February 16, according to Yeomans and Kiang (1981).[10]

There are more years and other comets, but for now, as the sun sets behind the cottonwood trees, let us bid farewell to the comet known as 1P/Halley. Until we meet again. One last word on the subject of astronomers. Having finished the book, I sought out my new friend Frederick Valarian, formerly of Yerkes Observatory. I was happy to learn that like myself, Frederick had received his Covid-19 vaccinations. I gave him a draft of the manuscript, hoping he would read it for technical errors. We decided, as it was becoming a tradition, to have lunch and chew (excuse the expression) the fat.

We met this time at the Mars Restaurant on nearby Lake Como. It was still too cool to sit out on the deck overlooking the lake, so we opted for the bar. I was happy to see that all the tables had been pulled apart at least six feet and that the waitresses were wearing masks. I thought, given the final chapter of the book, that eating at a restaurant named "Mars" was appropriate. Plus they had great cheeseburgers.

"You know, of course," said Valarian, "that Halley's Comet's closest approach to Earth was still over 3 million miles away."

Perihelion

"Hmm," I said. "837 CE. Egypt attacked Naples. What about 1910 when we passed through the tail of the comet?"

"Phillies beat the Cubs in the World Series that year. Must have been the fault of the comet."

The waitress arrived to take our orders. We ordered some deep-fried cheese curds as an appetizer and cheeseburgers with fries. I asked for a Spotted Cow, a local farmer's ale, and my companion decided on diet coke.

"Never imbibe before five o'clock," he said. "Actually...I don't imbibe at all. Alcoholic. But sober since 2008. It's been harder since I retired, but I'm surviving."

"I did not know that about you," I said, realizing I shouldn't feel sorry for the man...he was surviving. I couldn't help feeling empathy for him, however. There for the grace of God and so forth. Would there be a story to accompany this admission? It would not be proper to probe. But...

The cheese curds arrived with some blue cheese dipping sauce. Apparently, Wisconsin is one of the few places on earth where cheese curds are appreciated. The waitress looked a bit teary-eyed. I would never have said anything but Valarian said, "Anything the matter, sweetheart? Nothing we said, I hope."

"The waitress, her name, according to the embroidered tag on her uniform was Bev, answered, "You see that couple seated over by the window?"

"The loud talkers?" Valarian said.

"Yes. Well, that man came in without a mask. I told him he couldn't enter without one. Although he could remove it once seated. He told me it was his right not to mask up and he would tell the manager how rude I was!"

"Don't worry, said Valarian. "The owners here are nice people. I've known them for years. They will be on your side. Now, could I have some water?"

"I hate it," I said once Bev had left us, "when people make waitresses cry. Sometimes I think there are two kinds of people in this world, separated by DNA. Some meanspirited, self-absorbed, ignorant, arrogant, and cruel, while the rest of us..."

"Are Democrats. And I don't think that political parties created what are probably neanderthal descendants."

"True. Just look at the histories I've penned. The elite keep themselves in power through murder, suppression of the masses, propaganda (read, religion), and the perpetration of war."

"To your book," said Valarian, changing the subject, "I doubt that the colonization of Mars could take place as swiftly as you have it do."

"Oh, I think we would already be there except for NASA's troubles with funding and the bureaucracy within and without."

"Bureaucracy. Yes." [a pause] "So, you haven't asked about my alcoholism. I don't mind talking about it."

"Okay. I did wonder…"

"There was no single thing that started me drinking. No great tragedy, although the loss of my niece was terrible. No, it was gradual. It marched in lockstep with my career in teaching. You see, before I worked at Yerkes as a researcher, I was a college professor. At a prominent state-supported university which shall be nameless." [Valarian did name it, but I defer to privacy, notwithstanding the possibility of lawsuits.]

Valarian continued: "Higher education, now that's an oxymoron if there ever was one! I remember when I was first hired I was taken aside by the department chairman and told, 'Now don't spend you time worrying about teaching; your role here is to obtain tenure.' Talk about your self-serving society. The place was never about education. The keynote was 'the survival of the unfittest'. I came to view the other faculty members as the walking dead."

"Surely there were some dedicated individuals there."

"Of course. In the minority. And women on the faculty. But it was a good-old-boys club. Women were treated as second class citizens. I took early retirement as soon as I could and came to Yerkes where research was its own reward. And I got sober."

Our burgers arrived. The catsup bottle that had sat on the table was, of course, down to its last squirt. Bev brought us a new one. The fries were particularly good and the cheeseburgers almost rivaled some still lingering in my memory: the green-chile cheeseburgers at the Sonic drive-in in Santa Fe or at the fabulous Bob Cat Bite just outside of the City Different where one stood in line outside waiting for a table. Funny which foods one remembers and misses the most from a treasured era of one's existence: posole with red chile and sopapillas with honey at Tomasita's, tapas at El Farol, breakfast

Perihelion

burritos at Tia Sofia's, Frito pies at the Tesuque Village Market, Margarita's at Maria's, Tres Leches at the Plaza Restaurant. But I'm waxing nostalgic.

After lunch we said goodbye for a time. Valarian asked what my next book would be. I had no idea. It had occurred to me that a sequel might be in order, one in which my character Zeke emerges from the bomb shelter to a world of nuclear winter. Could I write about something that dark and depressing?

1	F. Richard Stephenson and Kevin K. C. Yau. "Far Eastern Observations of Halley's Comet: 240 B C to A D 1378" Journal of the British Interplanetary Society, Vol. 38, pp. 195-216, 1985. University of Durham, Durham, England.

2	Ibid.

3	Stephenson, F. Richard; Yau, Kevin K. C.; Hunger, Hermann (1985). "Records of Halley's Comet on Babylonian tablets". Nature. 314 (6012): 587–592.

4	V G Gurzadyan, R Vardanyan. "Halley's comet of 87 BC on the coins of Armenian king Tigranes?" Astronomy & Geophysics, Volume 45, Issue 4, August 2004, Page 4.6.
https://doi.org/10.1046/j.1468-4004.2003.45406.x

5	George Dvorsky. "New Model of Ancient Astronomical Device Reveals a 'Creation of Genius' "
https://gizmodo.com/new-model-of-ancient-astronomical-device-reveals-a-cre-1846465341?fbclid=IwAR1i7yqPgsShBzMgkxLqbYHL1B8TWLOeUSfCalb2CKXjWTFHP9a9eT_TBn0

6	NOAA, the National Centers for Environmental Information.
https://www.ngdc.noaa.gov/nndc/struts/results?eq_0=5883&t=101650&s=18&d=99,91,95,93&nd=display

7   O'Neil, Megan. (2009). O'Neil, Megan E. "Ancient Maya Sculptures of Tikal, Seen and Unseen" Res 55/56. Spring/Autumn 2009. Res: Anthropology and Aesthetics. 55. 119-134. 10.1086/RESvn1ms25608839.

8   Faith, Allison G.. "The Spearthrower Owl of Teotihuacan". HistoricalMX. https://historicalmx.org/items/show/76.

9   "People/Spearthrower Owl". https://peoplepill.com/people/spearthrower-owl.

10   Yau, Kevin Kam Ching (1988) "An investigation of some contemporary problems in astronomy and astrophysics by way of early astronomical records", Durham theses, Durham University. Durham E-Theses Online: http://etheses.dur.ac.uk/6331/.

Also:
      "Around the time of this extremely close approach to the Earth, Halley's comet would be almost in opposition to the Sun. It must have been a spectacular sight, but the brief records which have come down to us do not convey this impression in any way.
      'On Mar 4 there was a star emerging (po) at Nu (LM 11). It passed Ti (LM 3), K'ang (LM 2), Chueh (LM 1), Chen (LM 28), I (LM 27) and Chang (LM 26). On Apr 2 a broom star was seen at Ti (LM 3). On Nov 19 a star emerged (po) at T'ien-shih.' (Chin-shu, Astronomical Treatise).'
      'On Mar 4 there was a star emerging (po) at Nu (LM 10) and Hsu (LM 11)... On Apr 2 a broom star was seen at Ti (LM 3)... On Nov 19 there was a star emerging (po) at T'ien-shih.' (Chinshu Annals).' "
      ——F. Richard Stephenson and Kevin K. C. Yau. "Far Eastern Observations of Halley's Comet: 240 B C to A D 1378". Journal of the British Interplanetary Society, Vol. 38, pp. 195-216, 1985. University of Durham, Durham, England.

Perihelion

About the Author

Byron Grush was born and raised in Naperville, Illinois, just southwest of Chicago. He is a third generation native of that town. Grush studied art and design at the University of Illinois and filmmaking at the School of the Art Institute of Chicago. At the Art Institute he was a student of Gregory Markopoulos, one of the originators of the New America Cinema movement in the 1960s.

Grush then taught at The School of the Art Institute of Chicago, creating a course in film animation in the mid-seventies. He later became an Associate Professor at the College of Art at Northern Illinois University in Dekalb, Illinois, where he taught in the Electronic Media area. He is the author of a book on hand-drawn animation techniques entitled *The Shoestring Animator*. Becoming interested in genealogy, he wrote a trilogy of historical novels based upon what he had learned about his early ancestors.

He and his wife moved to New Mexico in the late 1990s, and opened an art gallery called Muse Image which featured Outsider and Visionary Art in Santa Fe. They returned to the Midwest to retire in the small town of Delavan, Wisconsin, a place that reminds them of their roots. Grush's films are in the collection of the Chicago Film Archives. Grush writes, paints and studies Tai Chi.

Other fiction by Byron Grush
All The Way By Water
Once Upon a Gold Rush
Road of Stars
Dance Beneath A Diamond Sky
Violet at The Breakers: a novella
The New Unwritten Law: a novella
The Scrapple Eater: a novella
1954 or Just press the I Believe Button
Luncheon at the Dead Rat
The Death of Time
Time Travelers Abroad

Short Story Collections by Byron Grush
Romeo's Revenge and Other Wisconsin Stories
The Cabinet of Curiosities of Barnaby Cannon and Other Stories

Nonfiction by Byron Grush
The Shoestring Animator

Made in the USA
Columbia, SC
10 April 2021